FALLOW GROUND

MICHAEL JAMES McFARLAND

BLOOD BOUND BOOKS

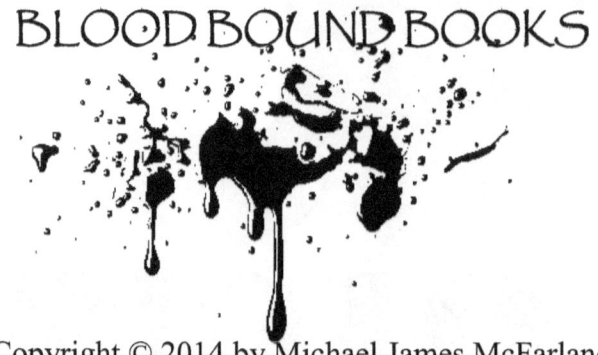

Copyright © 2014 by Michael James McFarland
All rights reserved

ISBN 978-1-940250-08-3

Artwork by Andrej Bartulovic

Printed in the United States of America

First Edition

Visit us on the web at:
www.bloodboundbooks.net

Also from Blood Bound Books:

400 Days of Oppression by Wrath James White

Habeas Corpse by Nikki Hopeman

Loveless by Dev Jarrett

The Sinner by K. Trap Jones

The Return by David A. Riley

Knuckle Supper by Drew Stepek

Sons of the Pope by Daniel O'Connor

Dolls by KJ Moore

At the End of All Things by Stony Graves

The Black Land by MJ Wesolowski

Mother's Boys by Daniel I. Russell

For Lillian McFarland, who only got to see one of my stories published, and the Henning Family, whose grounds I've been treading upon...

PROLOGUE:

Tearing Down The Barn

The barn was over half a century old and, since the death of her husband, Margaret Chambers had never found the time or the inclination to do much in the way of upkeep. There was little cause to do so, she reasoned, since the only livestock they kept these days were a dozen or so chickens (housed in their own smaller coop) and Dusty, a two-year-old palomino who looked positively lost in the two-story eyesore. It was big, drafty, unused for the most part, and, now that a dozen hard winters had taken their toll on it since Henry died, more of a hazard than an asset.

So in the spring of 1981, Margaret made the decision to have it torn down before it fell down of its own accord and killed someone. That, of course, meant building a smaller stable for Dusty. She spent several hours consulting the family finances, found the project feasible, and construction of the new stable began on May 3. Three weeks later, it was completed; Dusty took up immediate residence, and demolition of the old barn commenced.

The felling and uprooting of the barn turned up two interesting finds, and the workers, dirty with straw dust and sweat, knocked on the screen door to tell Margaret about the first.

A small pile of bones had been uncovered in hole along the back wall. They had belonged to rodents for the most part—mice, moles, and at least one small rabbit. The strange part was that they were all collected together, upwards of a dozen of them, in a grubby length of matted burlap, as if someone had been eating them. Out of sheer puzzlement, Margaret notified the sheriff. A deputy was dispatched, and the bones were bundled away to Colfax, where small, gnawing teeth marks were indeed detected.

The second discovery, made on the heels of the first, was even more disturbing.

Below the surface of the rough wooden floor, dug down into the soil itself, was a small, hidden space roughly the size of a dog kennel. In it lay the remnants of two woolen blankets, some old food wrappers, fossilized bits of human excrement, a gray tennis ball, and, lastly, a worm-eaten baby doll.

Something terrible, it seemed, was calling out of the past.

The sheriff returned, in person this time, and a real investigation was soon underway.

For Sheriff Jacob Garrett, it was as if old ghosts were calling him back.

On the drive out, he found his palms sweating queasily against the tacky grip of the steering wheel, his stomach complaining as if he had swallowed a bucket's worth of hot sand. Frowning, he dug in his pocket for the roll of antacid tablets he kept for just such afternoons—thankfully rare—and was still chewing on one when the Chambers mailbox came into view around a wide bend along Highway 195.

"Taylor" it used to read, painted in leaning black brushstrokes against the rusted gray of rounded sheet metal. But the box was a new one, stylishly square in shape and expensive looking. White on the bottom and light blue on the top. More fit for a place in town, he thought as he signaled right and turned into the driveway. Out this far, mailboxes were often fine targets for the passing sportsman and, as such, were generally bought as cheaply as possible.

Margaret Chambers—still a fair-looking woman, he observed, eyes safely hidden beneath the mirrored lenses of his sunglasses—stepped off the porch to meet him as he slowed to a halt behind a motley assortment of vehicles. Between the demolition crew and the sheriff's department, the barn was drawing quite a crowd.

He nodded as he climbed out of the cruiser. "Mrs. Chambers." Jake Garrett had weighed a trim 195 pounds during his glory days as a high-school football star. These days, the scales tipped around 225, though he had not let the extra weight settle around his gut as most men did; rather, it spread out and enveloped him like winter fat on a hibernating bear. He was fifty-eight years old and single.

She returned a troubled portion of his smile as her dark-brown hair caught the easterly breeze. "Good afternoon, Sheriff. I'm sorry to be such a trouble to you lately."

"Not at all," he assured her, looking across the drive to where a group of men lingered between piles of scrap wood. "We like to keep informed about this sort of thing."

"I believe your man is over at the far end of the barn," she said, pointing. "Careful on the way out; there's broken lumber and rusty nails all over the place. I wouldn't want to have to call an ambulance out here too."

Garrett chuckled and thanked her for the warning, adding that he would like to speak with her after he had had a chance to look around.

"All right," Margaret said, nodding. "I've got some work to finish up inside. Just knock on the side door when you're ready."

They parted, and Garrett threaded his way through the maze of parked cars. "Far end of the barn," he muttered wryly to himself, coming into the clear. There was very little to be recognized as a barn at this point; it was more like the ground had been scalped, and the missing patch was surrounded by rubble. Deputy Troy Stebbins, shuffling about one of the piles, raised a hand as he caught sight of Garrett.

The sheriff waved back. "I see you," he growled to himself, stepping around a dry pile of horse droppings.

The demolition crew, five men he knew from town, watched his approach with interest.

"Howdy, Jake," said Phil McCormick with a nod, a heavyset man roughly Garrett's own age and, by all appearances, the senior member of the crew.

"Phil," Garrett replied. It was not surprising that McCormick had found a measure of aptitude in such a profession; he was, after all, a man who liked to work with his hands. Garrett had arrested him four years back on a charge of assault and battery. The plaintiff had been his 105-pound wife, Penny. After dropping the charges, she had divorced him and moved somewhere down south. Oregon or California. McCormick had a great deal more gray in his face and hair these days, Garrett noted with some satisfaction. Perhaps his conscience kept him up at night.

He looked around at the rest of the group, finding eyes that dropped as his combed past. Two other men, Billy Carr and Bobby DeMint, had also spent time in his cells. The construction trade (or at least the demolition sect), seemed rife with bullies and roadhouse drunks: edgy, haunted-looking men with bodies either too large or too invulnerable to keep under check. They were exactly the kind of men he didn't needed hanging around while he attempted to conduct a proper investigation.

He turned back to McCormick. "You the foreman out here, Phil?"

McCormick straightened, glanced round the circle of his comrades and cleared his throat. "I guess I am."

"Tell you what: I'm gonna have to seal off this area as a crime scene, so I don't suppose Mrs. Chambers is going to need you for a day or two." He looked up. "If your supervisor has a problem with that, have him give me a call. Otherwise, I'll let Mrs. Chambers know when we're finished, and she can call you back. That all right?"

"Uh, yeah. Sure Jake." McCormick sighed. "No problem."

Garrett glanced at the group expectantly, but they seemed reluctant to tear themselves away. The shallow hole in the ground, brimming with ghosts, was drawing them in. Garrett could feel it too.

He clapped his hands together to break the spell. "All right, boys. That's about all." He dug in his pocket and found his car keys, which he tossed to his motionless deputy. "Troy, do me a favor, would you? Move my car to one side for me. I'm afraid I might be blocking somebody."

Stebbins fumbled with the ring, juggling it from hand to hand. "Sure, Jake." He regained his composure. "Come on, fellas," he said in an amiable tone. "You heard the sheriff. Let's give him some room."

Reluctantly, they turned and drifted down through the wreckage.

The cache beneath the floorboards was exactly what Garrett had envisioned on the drive out: a rough and sheltered hole gouged out of the earth where, presumably, the Taylor twins had huddled and scratched like animals in the unbearable heat of 1959 until they finally expired of thirst, exposure, or madness. As he paced slowly around the edges, examining it from every angle, he knew—without bodies, without bones—that this was the place that had eluded him all those years ago. Here was where those poor children had met their end.

He scowled. They had probably lain here throughout the preliminary search, when there was no cause to believe they were anything other than lost. Later, of course, and likely under darkness, they would have had to have been moved since nothing in that god-awful August heat would have kept long without raising an unbearable stench. Garrett had always suspected they were hidden away in the dry cellar underneath the farmhouse itself but could never come up with just cause for a warrant.

He recalled thinking they had searched *everywhere*, but of course that was under the assumption that the twins had wandered off, that Pru and Jonathan Taylor had *wanted* them found. Looking at the floor now, it was hard to imagine how they had missed it, though in all likelihood it had been covered by something at the time. He remembered that the barn had been full of hay, which had played hell with his sinuses when they stirred it up. That could have been why.

He heard footsteps picking their way through the debris and looked up from his reverie. It was Stebbins. Over his shoulder, Garrett saw the demolition crew leaving, a line of cars and pickup trucks breaking eastward from the head of the Chambers' driveway.

Stebbins held out the ring of keys and Garrett returned them to his pocket.

They stared down at the hole together, eyes drawn again and again to the baby doll's worm-eaten face, still smiling, half in shadow and half in light.

"Hell of a thing to find, huh, Jake?" Stebbins said at last, when it seemed the sound of the breeze whistling through his ears might drive him mad. A waxy candy-bar wrapper, brittle with age, fluttered and lifted lightly against the side of the pit, trapped but eager to be free.

"Hell of a thing..." Garrett echoed thoughtfully. He looked down the road; the cars and trucks were now gone beyond the bend. Gone to spread the word far and wide.

"You got a roll of barricade tape in your trunk?" Garrett said, his eyes now sharp upon his deputy.

"Yes, sir," Stebbins replied, doffing his hat to get at an itch along the back of his scalp.

The sheriff nodded. "I'm going down to the house to send for a field team. See if you can scare some stakes out of these scrap piles and string a wide barricade around the hole."

"All right." Stebbins put his hat back on.

"Other than that, make sure no one else comes tramping around here. I guess Mrs. Chambers is going to want to know what's going on."

The deputy hesitated before starting out. "Jake? What *is* going on? What's all this mean?"

Garrett turned and offered a humorless smile. "It means I was right—for whatever that's worth. Something that happened out here in the summer of '59." He shook his head. "Might as well be ancient history now."

And with that, he hitched up his belt and strode back down to the house.

Garrett rapped on the screen door and waited patiently on the welcome mat for Margaret to answer. He could smell something baking inside: something sweet yet tart, like wild huckleberries stuffed into a pie. It gave him a craving for strong coffee laced with cream, hot out of the percolator.

He tapped the dirt off his shoes and wondered how much he ought to tell her, mentally weighing what she needed to know and what she had a right to know. Dick Callen over at Palouse Realty sure as hell had not seen fit to mention it, not with the place standing empty so long and him with a solid nibble on the line. It would probably be best, he decided, to play it by ear: get a feel for how much she *wanted* to know before he led her down that particular path.

Margaret Chambers emerged as a pale shadow from the shade of the interior hall. Sunlight striking the screen rendered her wan and indistinct until she reached out and opened the door.

"Sheriff Garrett," she said, untying a white apron from around her waist. "Come in. I've got some fresh coffee if you'd like a cup."

"Thank you, Mrs. Chambers. I'd love some." He wiped his feet again and, removing his hat, stepped inside. "Would you mind if I used your telephone? I'm going to have to call in a few more men to give that hole a good look-over."

"Oh?" she replied, sounding somewhat surprised at the fuss her barn was attracting. "Well, no, not at all. There's one you can use in the kitchen. Right this way."

Garrett followed her through a short hallway, lined with framed photographs and swatches of needlepoint, into the kitchen.

"Right there, at the end of the counter," she said, pointing. She veered toward the coffee pot.

"Thank you."

"Do you take sugar or cream?" she asked, pouring out two cups.

"Just a dash of cream would be fine," Garrett answered as he punched in the number.

Margaret set the steaming cup on the counter beside him, at which Garrett smiled and nodded his thanks, and settled into a tentative seat at the informal table.

The sheriff concluded his brief conversation and replaced the receiver. He tried on a smile, but this time it was a poor fit, and he could tell it was making Margret nervous. He picked up his cup, blew into it, and sipped the cool layer off the top.

"Good and strong," he said, pleased, and walked slowly across the room. "I'm afraid you're going to have more company than you'll know what to do with this afternoon," he told her apologetically. "Not much we can do about that. I expect they'll be out of your hair by nightfall, though. Barring any surprises, you can call your crew back in a day or two to finish what they started." He glanced out the window. "I imagine that son of yours is itching to look through what's left of your barn. You'll want to keep him away from it for the time being. Your daughter, too."

"All right," she said, fidgeting and rotating her coffee cup on the table as if she was nervous. There was a second's hesitation, enough to take a breath, and Garrett, sensing what was coming, beat her to the punch.

"I imagine you've got some questions."

She laughed. "Yes…one or two."

He nodded soberly, then, for lack of a starting point, asked: "Did you ever hear of the family that lived here before you? Name of Taylor?"

PART ONE

Whitman County: 1954

1

What begins in madness and desperation must eventually end that way.

It began as a blossom of hope, in the sparsely populated farmland of eastern Washington...

2

If there was one thing that Prudence Taylor wanted more than anything else in the world, it was a child. A boy or girl to raise as she and her husband Jonathan saw fit, to dress and feed and play with while Jonathan worked the land he had inherited from his father. "That," she often told her husband as they lay in bed, "is the one thing to make our happiness complete."

Jonathan Taylor, who also looked forward to starting a family—preferably starting with a son—did his best to initiate such a blessed event, but for some reason his seed never took, and after two long years of failure, he found himself powerless to keep his wife from slipping into the gray waters of depression.

They tried adoption, certainly the most reasonable alternative, but the wait, especially for infants, stretched far beyond what they'd expected. Not many were put up for adoption each year, and those that were—colored babies or half-feral castoffs—were not at all what the Taylors had in mind.

After months of searching, Pru began to despair that she would go to her grave barren and childless, though at the time she had barely touched her thirties.

When it became apparent that they would not be able to adopt in the near future, Jonathan—unable to bear his wife's day-by-day deterioration—began to investigate other, less legal means of procuring a child. As a result, one fateful summer night, long after Pru had gone to bed—her depressive mood kept her in bed a great deal then—Jonathan received an unexpected (though not entirely unwelcome) visitor knocking at the front door.

"Mr. Taylor? *Jonathan* Taylor?" the stranger asked, standing on the doorstep, his eyes nervous and dark, like those of a rat: flickering everywhere, never settling.

"Yes," Jonathan said with a frown, ready to reach for the shotgun. The man looked like an outcast, a misfit begging for a handout in his weathered overcoat. "What do you want? How do you know my name?"

"I, I hear you're looking for something…you and your wife?" the derelict half whispered, his eyes moving left and right. "I wonder if I might come inside and discuss it with you?"

"You're a salesman then?" Jonathan said warily. "An odd time to be knocking on people's doors, wouldn't you say?"

"Please, Mr. Taylor. I'm not a salesman, though I've come to make you an offer." He put on a greasy smile and pressed closer. "I don't like to mention what it might be, not here on your doorstep, but I assure you it's something special, something very dear."

Jonathan's eyes narrowed in suspicion. "Dear things usually come dearly, and I don't have much money." His voice became low and brusque. "I think you'd better speak your mind, straight out, before I take a mind to turn you *off* my doorstep."

The man peered nervously about the wooden step, as if it were a stage floating upon the moonless night, lit for all to see; an amphitheater designed to throw his voice back to the highway. "Well," he said, darting out his tongue like a lizard, wetting his cracked lips, "I'd just as soon not go into the details out here, Mr. Taylor, but— " Again he glanced about. "I hear you're looking for a child to take in?"

This last part was pitched so softly that Jonathan wasn't sure that he had heard the man correctly.

"What did you say?" he whispered, his eyes growing wide.

"A child, Mr. Taylor," the stranger said. "A *baby*." He pronounced it slowly—*bay-bee*—as if it were some exotic treasure. A rare artifact hammered out of gold.

Now it was Jonathan's turn to sift the darkness. Except for the stars, the night seemed impossibly close; so much so that he imagined, just for a moment, that it had thickened around the dusty stoop to listen.

"Maybe you'd better come inside, Mister... ah...?"

"Smith will do very nicely, Mr. Taylor. And you're right: this would be better discussed in private." He wiped his dirt-speckled shoes on the mat and stepped inside, where Jonathan was able to get a better look at him. He was a thin man, wiry looking, with a long jaw and blond hair cropped close to his skull. His hair was going gray in uneven patches, as if from illness, and there was a small scar, badly healed, caught in the laugh lines of his left eye.

Taylor led him inside to the living room and motioned for him to take a seat before the hearth, where a fire was contentedly burning. He held up a cautionary finger to his guest and slipped out of the room and down the hall, where he peeked in on his wife. He found Prudence sleeping soundly; their conversation would not disturb her.

He joined Smith at the fireside, holding out little hope that this shabby-looking man could grant any kind of answer to their prayers. That the offer would be costly and underhanded he had no doubt, and a mixture of anger and apprehension struck him at the realization that his careful inquiries had been spread around like so much manure.

"How did you know we'd been looking for a baby?" Jonathan asked bluntly, not a man to wrap his feelings in cool pleasantries.

Smith smiled, slowly unbuttoning his overcoat. "I'm sure you can appreciate the need for absolute discretion in matters such as this, Mr. Taylor. I can assure you it is a practice I make a strict habit to follow."

Jonathan chewed silently on this assertion, staring contemplatively at his guest, then shifting his gaze to the fire. "If it's money you're after, you should know that I don't have enough. In fact, we're barely getting by as it is."

"I'm already aware of that," Smith conceded, grinning, his hands folded neatly in his lap. "I'm not in the business of *selling* children."

"Would you mind telling me then," Jonathan growled, "just what you *are* in the business of?" He was quickly losing patience with the man, who seemed to speak only in half-smiles and circles, as if at the center of his dance there was something too horrible or depraved to throw a light on all at once. It was a thing to be slowly warmed up to in degrees, and that had Jonathan worried. The price, once he got around to dragging it out, was apt to be very high. Very high indeed.

"I've come to ask you for a small service," Smith said. He bent his wrist and looked at the small crescents of black dirt caked under his fingernails. "Necessarily, it comes with a small amount of risk."

Jonathan Taylor laughed out loud, momentarily forgetful of his sleeping wife. "Who do you want me to kill?"

Smith maintained his patient smile. When Jonathan's laughter subsided, Smith continued. "As you've no doubt surmised, Mr. Taylor, I am not a native of this country." He crossed his legs at the knee, as if settling in for a long night. "I'm originally from London, but my travels have taken me to all parts of the world, often to places so distant and desolate they don't have names, much less places on a map. Along the way, I've made my share of acquaintances and adversaries; needless to say, I hope by the time I leave here tonight I may count you solidly amongst the former."

He paused, as if waiting for Jonathan to concede.

"For reasons I'd rather not go into, I would like to have a package shipped to me from England. It would be a large crate, you see, and would need to be claimed at the freight depot in Spokane. I am not a legal citizen of this country, Mr. Taylor, nor am I residing here legally, so it would be impossible for me to attach my current name or address to the package. Likewise, I would be unable to pick it up once it arrived." He looked into Jonathan's steady gaze, and the firelight caused his eyes to flicker. "I know that you have an open-bed truck and a barn to store such a crate in... I simply want to list *you* as the recipient and then have you pick it up for me at the depot and keep it here in your barn for a short while. No questions asked."

Jonathan stroked his chin thoughtfully. He didn't trust the stranger. The price was too easy. Smith could pay anyone to pick up a package for far less than it would take to deliver a baby. And even if he agreed, how could he be certain that a miscreant who crept to doorstep in the dead of night would keep his word?

"What's in the crate?" he asked.

Smith smiled and shook his head. The scar beside his eye winked in the low light.

No. Taylor didn't trust the man, but in the end he agreed to the deal just the same. Smith nodded and rose to take his leave, as if he had seen the answer long before he had even approached the Taylors' door.

3

Jonathan told Prudence of the deal he had made with the mysterious Mr. Smith over breakfast the following morning. Surprisingly, she voiced no worries or complaints over any part of it; in fact, she adopted the somewhat singular view that the whole sordid affair was somehow divinely sent. No doubt she held Smith to be a *slightly* lesser man than Christ himself based on Jonathan's description of him. She had not seen the man's eyes, the way they constantly shifted back and forth as if he feared something might come charging out of the shadows to gobble him up. And as cool and secretive as Smith was about conducting the business at hand, there had been an edgy desperation in his mannerisms, a haunted weariness sunken into his features. Perhaps that was the reason a child came so cheaply: his judgment was compromised by something breathing hot down his neck. Obviously, he wanted the contents of the crate very badly.

Over the following week, a nagging anxiety lingered around the edges of Jonathan's workday routine, a presentiment that he would bitterly regret this decision, but he had given his word and there was nothing else to be done but wait.

Once the crate arrived, Smith would contact him.

Almost five weeks after the visit, a smudged letter arrived for Jonathan in the mail, his name and address carefully penciled in small block letters. It bore no return address.

A premonitory chill moved through Jonathan's spine as he held it up to the light, regarding the envelope and its contents as if it had come from the Devil himself.

The details of the exchange were simple. Included with the brief letter was a claim ticket; Jonathan needed only to present it to the freight dispatcher at the railway depot and the package would be turned over to him. Their arrangement—crate for child—would be conducted at one o'clock Monday morning, which gave Jonathan four days to get into Spokane, an easy thirty-five miles north. After the exchange, neither party would attempt to contact the other again, for any reason whatsoever.

As he ate his lunch that fine, sunny afternoon, Jonathan ruminated over the generous leeway of his timetable. If he left straightaway, he would be back by late afternoon and therefore have two days and three nights alone with the crate before Smith came to fetch it. Certainly time enough to have a quick look inside and shut it back up again.

It wouldn't hurt, he thought, wiping mayonnaise from his lip, to have something to bargain with, just in case the stranger tried to pull a fast one.

He put his plate in the sink, gave his wife a tender kiss good-bye, and within an hour had the International Harvester pickup gassed and counting off the miles to Spokane.

4

The clock tower above the depot read 2:50 as Jonathan walked across the lot to the freight bay. Though the open warehouse was shady, it was uncomfortably warm. Overhead fans made a half-hearted attempt to stir the air about, but there was nothing cool to add to the mixture, and as he stood before the chaos that was the dispatcher's desk, he felt perspiration gathering on his neck and down the furrow of his spine. His underarms were steadily widening circles, and his face, reflected in a small mirror behind the desk, was a pale and apprehensive knot.

He waited silently as the dispatcher ran the tip of his pencil down a stack of inventory sheets attached to a battered clipboard.

"Here we are," said the man, looking up. "Looks like we got it for you in Bay Two. That's right down this way." He rose and pointed down a long, concrete throughway skirting the side of his office. "Hang a hard right at the soda machine there and I'll have a clerk meet you at the desk."

Jonathan folded the claim check Smith had given him into a tidy square and tucked it back inside his wallet.

"If you need any help with it, just ask one of the boys. They'll be more'n happy to wheel it out to your truck."

Jonathan nodded, setting off down the walkway.

Bay Two was a bustle of orchestrated activity. Forklifts moved in and out of a port door that opened onto a loading platform, carrying wooden crates and sealed boxes into the shadowy warren of the holding and inspection area. Amidst the commotion, Jonathan spied a tiny office to the right of the bay door and carefully made his way toward it. Outside, he could see the open boxcars marked with the Great Northern mountain goat.

He reached the office and found the receiving clerk behind a desk strewn with invoices, claim checks and inventory forms. The man was gesturing wildly into a telephone receiver. Jonathan rapped on the door to get his attention. The clerk glanced up and waved Jonathan in.

"Like I told your boy this morning: you bring me in a check or a paid receipt and it's yours. Otherwise, I need confirmation from the sending party before I can turn it over to you! No, no, we've gone through this song and dance before. Yeah? Well, that's fine, you do that, Bub!" He slammed the receiver down hard enough to ring the bell, then swung his chair around to face Jonathan. "What can I do for you?"

"You have a package for me," Jonathan stated, handing the man the claim check from his wallet.

The clerk unfolded the pale-yellow receipt and squinted at it. "Three-seven-zero-five-eight-one from London..." he mumbled, reaching for a large, loose-leaf binder. He shuffled through the pages for a moment and lit upon something. "Oh, yeah, we've got it. And there's a problem with it, too. A dark stain at one of the corners, like something broke inside and started leaking out. Smells something awful, too. Invoice lists the contents as 'Botanical Specimens.'" He looked up at Jonathan. "I don't know what you're expecting, mister, but we can open it up right here and see if anything's damaged; that way you can file a claim if you need to. Course, aside from the stain, the crate itself looks pretty solid, so if it's a question of improper packing, there's nothing we can do about that, claim or no claim. We just ship 'em, you know. We don't pack 'em. That's out of our hands, and it says so on the receipt." He waved the yellow ticket briefly in the air.

"No need to do that," Jonathan said, shaking his head. "I'm sure it's nothing serious." He swallowed nervously, unprepared for this. "If you could get a man to load it onto the back of my truck, I won't take up any more of your time."

"Gladly," the clerk said, relieved. He waved to someone over Taylor's shoulder and a young man popped his head into the office. "Terry, kindly take this gentleman's box out to his truck. Number 370581. Just follow your nose."

"Gotcha, Mr. Kane." The young man turned to Jonathan. "I'll have it for you on the south side of the dock if you'll bring your truck around."

Kane smoothed the invoice over a bare spot on his desk. "Just sign here, Mr. Taylor, and it's all yours."

The wooden crate, looming out of the freight depot on the front of Terry's forklift, was much larger than Jonathan expected. It was long and rectangular in shape, as if it might contain a full-sized refrigerator or the golden sarcophagus of some long-dead king. Terry set it deftly into the scratched bed of his pickup, leaving less than an inch to spare on either side. As the stench wafted forward, Jonathan frowned.

"Don't smell too pleasant, does it?" the good-natured operator hollered from the seat of his lift.

This was something of an understatement. *Lord o' mercy*, Jonathan thought, wearing a pinched expression. *Am I going to have to live with that for three days?*

"Sure am glad you're takin' it away," said Terry. "I swear, I go home and smell that thing in my sleep!" He laughed, sliding the forks from beneath the pallet and letting the full weight of the box settle onto the back axle with a creaky sigh. "There you go, mister. She's all yours now."

Jonathan thanked him and held out a dollar bill.

Terry shook his head reluctantly. "Thanks all the same, but if Mr. Kane saw me take a tip, he'd have my ass in a sling." He shrugged. "I'm happy just to get rid of the damn thing, y'know?" Despite the heat, a visible shiver went through him. "Kind of gives me the willies."

Jonathan nodded and put the bill back in his wallet.

Terry waved as he turned the lift around. A moment later, the shadows inside the building swallowed him up.

Jonathan regarded the stenciled sides of the box for a long moment.

London, England.

When he looked up again, he noticed several faces paused in their work and watching him. Satisfying their curiosity, he supposed, somewhat uncomfortably.

What have I gotten myself into?

He slammed the tailgate into place and turned to haul his burden away.

5

Prudence Taylor did not so much as bat an eye or twitch her nose at the smell emanating from the crate, nor did she seem at all curious about what might be inside. She simply told her husband to be sure it was locked up tight so nothing could happen to it. Nothing would be left to chance, nothing that might come between her and the baby Smith had promised.

Jonathan nodded and she gave him a kiss and a smile, declaring that she was going to fix him a fried-chicken dinner that he would remember for years to come. With that, she bobbed off toward the house, leaving him staring after her.

Jonathan grinned to himself. Perhaps this was going to work out after all; whatever trials might await them in the coming days, it was well worth it to have his wife back.

He turned back to the truck, its old motor tired and ticking from the long haul. His eyes were immediately drawn to the stain along the bottom of the crate, and his reflective smile was slowly replaced by an expression of troubled thoughtfulness.

The way the back end of the truck was sagging, he guessed the box must have weighed upwards of four hundred pounds. He would have to use the winch on the front of the tractor and some good strong planks to get it down. It was going to take a lot work and careful planning, but he did not dare go to any of his neighbors for help; crates of that size—smelly or not—invited curiosity, and what could he tell them?

It's a surprise. Wasn't that the unvarnished truth? *Something for Pru.* Also true, in a roundabout sort of way.

No. This was his burden; his to put down and his to hold on to.

He looked at his barn with a critical eye.

There were plenty of gaps and knotholes along the barn's outer walls, but nothing so bad that someone could walk a refrigerator through it, and he had a good padlock he could use to hang through the latch on the doors. The crate would be plenty safe there through the weekend.

He took off his shirt and laid it over the hood of the truck. He tossed his wristwatch onto the front seat for safekeeping. It was nearly six o'clock.

Time was wasting. Daylight too.

Two hours later the job was done. The crate lay on its side in a back area of the barn where Jonathan kept the pesticides and fertilizers. The corner already stank of noxious chemicals, he had reasoned, so the smell of the crate could do no worse.

He hooked a padlock between the large doors just as the sun touched the surrounding hills.

Prudence had a late dinner waiting for him when he went inside. As good as her word, the meal looked fit for a king: fried chicken, mashed potatoes, buttermilk biscuits and thick country gravy. He put it away like a man half starved.

It was good to see her smiling at the table again, chattering and making a fuss over him as she had once done, before they had tried to have a baby of their own.

He went to bed that night early and tired. He dreamt that something horrible awoke within the crate. It got out, slouched into the house, ate food from the refrigerator, and watched them sleep.

6

"All went as planned," Smith murmured wearily, dropping into a chair at a back table. "I watched him put it in his barn."

The man across the table, Daniel Shires, was edgy and dark, with olive skin that seemed to glow like tallow under candlelight. His eyes, by contrast, were blue, and these incongruent features seemed to hint at illegitimacy, of a childhood spent in side alleys and questionable haunts. "Good," Shires said with a nod. His accent was more pronounced than usual, which meant that the half-empty pitcher in front of him wasn't his first of the evening. He raised his glass and took a long swallow. "Let's get you a glass and you can help yourself," he said, gesturing the waitress over.

They were seated in a dark corner of The Plowman's Bar & Grill, a low-rent watering hole on the edge of Colfax, in the gray area where State Highway 195 became Main Street or vice versa. The mood in the place was typical Friday, a busy night for The Plowman. Country music—slow and mournful at this hour—blared from an abused jukebox, mixing agreeably with the shouts and laughter of late-night conversation. Young men in flannel shirts, tanned and muscular from the fields, swilled dollar pitchers of Olympia or Rainier as they leaned on pool cues and pinball machines. No one took much notice of Smith and Shires.

Smith poured himself a glass from the pitcher and chuckled softly. "I knew that he was our man. As soon as I mentioned the word 'baby,' I could see it in his eyes."

Shires frowned across the table at him.

Smith's smile faded, his eyes darting nervously about the smoky room. "It's all right. Nobody heard."

"A bloody good thing," Shires said in a hard, cold whisper. "Must I continually remind you, should this sordid business ever come to light, that your neck is just as snugly in the noose as mine?" He peered cautiously over the rim of his glass. "We shan't discuss it here any further."

"As you like," Smith said with a dismissive shrug. He watched Shires pluck a cigarette from a near-empty pack. There was no ignoring the way it shook between his long fingers, or the way he had to steady his hand to light it. The work was taking its toll on him—or rather, the *waiting*. He noticed the way Shires's eyes never left the door for long, as though he were expecting someone.

God forbid.

The feeling was contagious.

7

Daniel Shires knew how to breathe life back into the dead—a kind of life, anyway.

He worked with a reanimating agent stumbled upon by accident while conducting experiments in brain death in his native England. For years he'd been working under the tutelage of a brilliant mentor by the name of John Dunhill, and, the truth be known, the formula was more Dunhill's work than Shires, but that hardly mattered anymore. What mattered was that it worked, and in the years since, Shires had improved upon the original formula, making it stronger, more stable.

Still, the dead were never pleased about returning to life, and the longevity of the agent varied from subject to subject. Some lasted on the table for weeks—perfectly lucid in their madness—while others never came close to what might be deemed consciousness.

Their first success had taken place three years ago. Dunhill had caught a spider beneath the lab table and killed it in a jar of chloroform. He had been careless, foregoing the proper precautions in his eager rush to examine the specimen, and when it came back from the dead, it bit him. The spider had not been of a poisonous variety, yet Dunhill spent a week in bed with a high fever and the shakes while the bite grew dark and irritated. He screamed that it itched like barbs of fine glass under his skin.

Somehow the spider had been changed in the process, though whether that was due to the reanimating agent or something beyond the condition of death was never certain.

After five months of experimentation on insects and animals, they attempted the inevitable culmination of their research. Obtaining a suitable body had been costly, though fairly simple; there were always those fringe elements willing to do the work for a price. The results were mixed; while the dead man registered vital signs for nearly twenty minutes before slipping back behind the veil, there was never a glimmer of consciousness beneath his bruised eyelids. Dunhill cursed and administered a larger dose of the agent. The vitals returned and faded once again. Shires watched in horror as his mentor beat and mutilated the lifeless body in anger and frustration and then stormed out into the night, leaving the bloody mess still strapped to the gurney.

The experiments continued in the weeks that followed, as Dunhill frantically sought ever -fresher subjects to prod and practice upon. The result, however, was always the same: failure. Death had given them nothing but a succession of animated corpses, none of whom retained anything more than a tenuous residue of grunts and moans within their rotting heads. They gave up no secrets, or else there were no secrets to give. Dunhill considered this possibility: that death was simply an end, a complete cessation of the senses and withering of the soul. But in the end he couldn't accept that.

Something was missing from the formula, something elusive yet elemental.

He decided to give the matter further thought before they resumed their experiments. As it was, they were moving down a dead-end street.

Soon thereafter, they began a spiraling journey into the occult, delving into ancient and foreboding texts, searching for new and vital ingredients to add to the mix.

8

The crate sat in Jonathan Taylor's barn for almost forty-two hours before he made up his mind to open it.

Until then, his uneasy conscience had kept him from the task. The package was, after all, someone else's property. He couldn't afford to endanger the deal simply because it rubbed his curiosity the wrong way, and to cause Prudence to backslide into that dark room inside herself would be unforgivable.

Still, the damned thing was in his barn, and Smith had exacted no promises other than to have the box ready by Monday and, once the deal was done, to never contact him again.

In the end, however, two straight nights of foreboding dreams—unsettling visions that seemed to seep from the barn like ground mist—finally got the better of him. He made up his mind to pry it open, but carefully, in such a way that no one would be the wiser.

"Guess I'll do a little cleaning in the barn today," he announced, rising from the breakfast table. "With that damned crate, the place is getting so cluttered even I can't stand it!"

"All right, hon," Pru replied from the sink, her hands in hot, sudsy water. "While you're at it, make sure all those chemicals and fertilizers are locked up. And get rid of the old ones you've just let sit." She turned and offered him a wistful smile. "We've got to start thinking about things like that. It won't do to have them lying about where kids are bound to play."

"Uh-huh." He cleared his throat noisily. "I'll be in for lunch 'round noon."

"I'll call you."

Jonathan stepped out into the early-morning sunshine. He breathed deeply and felt his heartbeat strengthen. *A fine day*, he thought, surveying a nearly cloudless sky. *Nothing wrong at all on a day like this.*

He lowered his gaze to the barn.

The big double doors were propped open, resting on two dusty cinderblocks (he'd been out before breakfast, nervously checking on the crate), but the interior remained staunchly gloomy, as if the daylight couldn't touch it. His own footprints wandered inside and back out, like a ghost that had come in the night or a piece of a dream he couldn't quite recall. He tried to picture the crate resting inside, but the image that came instead was of a polished casket on two old sawhorses, glowing in the predawn twilight. It sent a shiver down his spine.

"Foolishness," he muttered and walked under the barn's cool overhang. Immediately the smell of the crate was upon him. The odor of hay and astringent chemicals permeated every pore of the old wooden structure, but the crate was even stronger. Its smell seemed to cling to the very shadows.

He lingered at the threshold, gathering his resolve, drawing the full miasma of the crate into his nostrils as he stepped inside.

Christ Almighty!

He paused for a moment or two, coughing, spitting, and swearing into the woodpile, waiting for his senses to dull themselves to the air inside, and then moved slowly toward the back of the barn. A bare light bulb hung on a cord above his work bench. He gave its beaded chain a yank. It was bright—one hundred watts—flooding the corner with enough light to work by.

"Okay," he exhaled, eying the long package with a mild foreboding.

He crouched and ran his fingers along the edge of the box, feeling for a niche from which to start. Bright, gray nail heads winked at him every six inches or so, and, by their diameter, he guessed they would be about three inches long.

A well-built crate, Jonathan thought, nodding. Whoever shipped it didn't want to chance it coming open along the way.

He stood and sighed. It would not be easy to get it open without leaving a mark, but if he started at a bottom corner (where one might expect some wear and tear to occur) and took his time, he reasoned it could be done.

He moved to the work bench and gathered the tools he'd need: a hammer, a pry bar, a strong putty knife, and a paint-stained coffee can to keep track of the nails.

He took up the putty knife and wiggled it patiently into the shadow of the bottom seam. He knew he was apt to ruin the tool in the process, but it was important not to damage the soft pine of the box. And what the hell—he could always buy himself a new putty knife.

He worked in the shadowy corner for a half hour before getting the needed space for the flattened end of the pry bar. He rose, spat into his hands, and wedged the bar into place. The wood screamed as the nails began to pull free.

Forty galvanized nails held the side of the crate in place, and by midmorning Jonathan had slowly and painstakingly removed every one. He rolled the last of them against his gritty palm (making sure it was straight enough to hammer) before dropping it into the coffee can.

Shafts of dusty sunlight knifed through the cracks and knotholes in the walls, and a light perspiration gathered on his skin, smudging the dirt already there. He closed his eyes and rubbed the tired lids, trying to soothe away the dull headache caused by the chemicals and the strain of concentration in the unevenly lit room. His back ached from stooping, and when he rose, his kneecaps cracked like dry sticks of maple.

By slow degrees, the stench leaching out of the crate had worsened; days later, he would find its bite so deep in his clothes that there was nothing to be done to save them short of exorcism, so they found the trash barrel instead.

Moving as a man in no particular hurry, he set his tools aside and turned back to look at the crate in the dusty light. Again he was reminded of a casket, a long box riding home on a mystery train.

Well, there it is. You've done all the work, now get on with it. Have a look.

With a feeling of detachment, a sense that he was dreaming, Jonathan's callused hands gripped the lid by its edges and lifted it away. The movement caused a fine layer of sawdust to take flight and dance, agitated, through a slanted beam of sunlight.

"Mother of mercy!" he said, gagging and taking a stumbling step back. He threw the heavy fabric of his sleeve over his nose and mouth to filter the full potency of the smell, which seemed to rise out in visible waves.

Yellowed newsprint blossomed from the crate with an audible sigh. Jonathan stepped hesitantly forward and tugged a leaf free, and a page from the *London Times* unfolded before him, over two years old. Caught in its brittle creases were flecks of what looked like dried soil or humus, bits of brownish grit that littered his workboots like grains of sand.

He let the page drop and pulled out another. Gradually, a shape emerged—dark and obscure—wrapped in layers of thick plastic tarpaulin.

No one needed to tell Jonathan what it was; he already knew.

It was a man, almost mummified, withered like an old banana in the dry summer heat.

29

9

Three weeks earlier, the sense of security Daniel Shires felt living in eastern Washington, on the outskirts of Colfax, eroded abruptly under his feet. This occurred during a chance meeting with a sheriff's deputy along State Route 272, also known as the Old Palouse Highway. The road, a warped and oft-patched twister of blacktop, rose up from the Colfax gulch and past the town cemetery, where Shires was spotted just outside the tall, wrought-iron gates.

The deputy had been cruising along the barren highway in the early-morning darkness—nothing but farm lights set back from the road and cool stars overhead—when a pair of headlights materialized out of nowhere. As the car passed, the young deputy—scowling into his rearview mirror—executed a quick U-turn and activated his overhead lights.

Shires pulled to a stop on the weedy shoulder and rolled down his window. Cautiously scanning the vehicle's interior with his flashlight, the deputy asked him what he had been doing.

"Ah, well..." He smiled sheepishly. "This is rather embarrassing, officer, but I had to urinate."

"May I see your driver's license, sir?" the deputy said, shining the light in Shires's face.

"Certainly." He opened his wallet, slipped out his U.K. license along with his U.S. permit, and gave them to the deputy.

The deputy frowned, as if he'd just been passed a handful of Monopoly money. He turned his light on the license.

"You're not a citizen of this country?"

"No, officer. I'm a resident of the United Kingdom, on temporary sabbatical."

The deputy nodded, told him to remain in the car, and walked slowly back to his cruiser. Shires watched him in the rearview mirror as he spoke into his two-way radio, listened, and then spoke again. His palms began to sweat on the steering wheel. Finally the deputy returned.

"Mr. Shires?" he began. "I'm just going to issue you a warning this time. We have a law about urinating in public here. You'd be best advised to hold it until you get to a filling station or home. The next time this happens you *will* be given a citation. Do you understand?"

Shires said that he did and thanked the deputy for his leniency. As he drove slowly away, he watched the cruiser turn around on the highway. It progressed down the road, turned inside the cemetery gates, and switched on a side-mounted searchlight.

Bloody hell.

He pressed down on the gas pedal and sped away as quickly as he could without drawing more attention to himself. When he got home, he packed up his laboratory equipment and moved it into the attic. As for the body in the trunk of his car, he wrapped it in tarpaulin and buried it over the rise behind his house.

Then he sat back nervously and waited for the police to come.

It took two days, but they finally did.

"Are you Daniel Shires?" the older of the two deputies inquired from the shade of the front porch. It was four o'clock in the afternoon.

Shires stared through the rusted screen. He had gone through this confrontation a hundred times in the last day and a half, turning and examining it from every angle, but when he saw them standing there, solid and undeniable in the light of day, he still felt off balance and unprepared.

"Yes, that's right," he replied.

"I'm Deputy Bolton of the County Sheriff's Department. This is Deputy McIntyre." The younger man, blond and as stout as a beer keg, nodded and rubbed the brim of his hat. "We'd like to ask you a few questions if you don't mind."

"Yes, of course." Shires cleared his throat and stepped back from the doorway. "Won't you please come in?"

The men removed their hats and entered, seating themselves upon the worn sofa at Shires's request.

"Could I get you something? Coffee or tea perhaps?" Being an Englishman, Shires couldn't seem to stop selling Americans on the idea of tea; to his horror, it leapt from his mouth at every opportunity, as if he were lining up commissions.

"No thank you, Mr. Shires. We're both just fine," Bolton said, not looking up as he smoothed a sheet of folded paper against his knee. "We don't want to take up too much of your time."

"All right." Shires's face slipped a bit, as if he would have been grateful for the distraction. Tense, he paced to the hearth and back, then forced himself to sit down in a worn recliner, folding his hands stiffly on his lap as if in a natural repose. "How can I be of service to you gentlemen?"

"I have a report here," Bolton said, indicating to the sheet, "that you were stopped night before last at 2:18 a.m. along State Route 272, less than a quarter mile from the cemetery gates." He looked up expectantly.

"That's correct," Shires said with a nod, trying for an expression of puzzlement.

"The reason we're here," Bolton said, adjusting himself on the sofa, "is that we've had a bit of vandalism out there. Some graves were disturbed."

"My God, that's dreadful!" Shires gasped, properly shocked. "Do you have any idea who it might have been?"

"No definite leads at this time," Bolton replied. "The disturbances are very minor in appearance and the graves themselves fairly new. For all we know, it may have happened several days ago. Possibly within the last two weeks."

"I see." Shires exhaled, settling back thoughtfully into his chair.

Bolton produced a pencil and tablet and resumed the interrogation. "What we'd like to know is if you happened to see or hear anything that night. Voices or noises coming from the cemetery, a vehicle prowling around inside, anything at all out of the ordinary?" The deputy had his pencil poised above the tablet, ready to jot down any words that would come.

Shires paused and gazed out the window, considering. "No... nothing like you suggest. At least nothing near the cemetery. I *do* recall, at some point, several cars speeding along the roadway. I remember because I thought they were going to run me down. Three or four of them, I should think, all clumped together. I had the impression they were filled with teenagers, hot-rodders, from the noise they made."

Bolton nodded, his pencil briefly scratching. "Did you get a look at any of them?"

"Oh, good God, no!" Shires said with a stray wave of his hand. "They were all headlights and exhaust!"

"And they were moving east, *away* from town?" McIntyre said, the first words he'd spoken since appearing on the doorstep.

"Yes, that's right."

There was a long pause while Bolton summarized his thoughts on paper, closing that particular alley. When his pencil stopped, his eyes were gazing at Shires. "Incidentally, how did you happen to be there at that time of night?" the deputy asked in a tone that suggested nothing more than idle curiosity. Something in his eyes, however, set off a warning bell in Shires's head. Whatever else they might profess, *this* was what they had come to ask, and he felt himself tighten up accordingly.

Careful, don't give them a reason to search the house, the car...

"I was returning from Potlatch. You see, I'm considering buying a house in the area, and when I can spare the time, I'll have a look at the properties for sale."

"A little late to be looking at houses, wasn't it?" Bolton said carefully. "This time of year it gets dark around eight."

Shires twitched in his chair. They were watching him very closely now.

He took a breath to compose himself. "Well yes, but... to tell you the truth, I had a couple drinks passing through Palouse, and I thought I'd better sober up a bit before driving home. I'm afraid I fell asleep in the parking lot... sitting in my car." He grinned sheepishly at the tops of his shoes, embarrassed, apparently nothing more to say on the subject.

The two deputies stared blankly at him, neither saying a word nor betraying the slightest hint what they were thinking. Two expert poker faces. A nervous smile appeared and disappeared on Shires's face; perspiration, prickly and irritating, broke suddenly on his back.

Bolton scratched his cheek. "Would there be someone at the bar who could corroborate your story? The bartender or one of the waitresses?"

Christ, I should have anticipated this!

Shires swallowed, stalling for time to think, pretending to give the question some thought as he wracked his brain for a plausible reason why neither would be likely to recall him. "Yes, I suppose so," he allowed, albeit hesitantly. "The place was fairly busy though... quite a lot of people in for dinner and drinks."

"Probably not a lot of guys with English accents," McIntyre said with a grin.

Shires conceded the point with a smile while Bolton took it all down on his pad. He finished writing and studied the notes he'd collected so far, not entirely satisfied, Shires inferred from the frown beneath his moustache.

"One more thing, Mr. Shires, if you don't mind my asking. Our report indicates that you stopped to urinate. That was less than a mile from the cemetery, which would put you less than five miles from here. Why didn't you just wait until you got home?"

Shires laughed, and to his surprise it came out sounding genuine. "Officer, you've driven that road, I assume?"

Bolton nodded, smiling, as if the two of them were sharing a joke.

"Full of dips and curves, potholes. Like driving over a washboard in places. What you might call a real kidney puncher. I'd been holding my bladder for better than ten minutes by that point, and, well... no one expects to see anyone drive past at two o'clock in the morning, much less a policeman."

Bolton closed his tablet; it disappeared inside his pocket. "I guess you're right about that," he said with chuckle.

Both men rose and took their leave, fitting their hats to their heads as they ambled casually down the steps. Shires exhaled loudly as they drove away. He couldn't kid himself that he'd pulled it off. They were still suspicious; certainly they would be keeping a much closer eye on him.

That meant changes.

10

The full moon drew near its apex in the dark sky above Colfax.

Smith and Shires wrestled the body down the narrow stairwell into the cellar and placed it in the center of the concrete floor. To counteract the awful stench, a brazier of incense burned in one corner while both men wore handkerchiefs over their faces, smeared with a strong menthol rub. Even so, it was bad enough to make one's eyes water.

Beneath the stark, uncompromising light of a hundred-watt bulb, the corpse grinned up at them, its eyes milky and shriveled, lips peeled back from graying teeth like blackened petals. Dark streaks of mildew colored its burial suit, and the white shirtfront was stained with blossoms the color of faded tea.

Because it was so badly decomposed, a circle was drawn in chalk around its splayed limbs, with hash marks set down about the perimeter to mark the points of the compass. While Shires made brief notations in a journal, Smith pulled the dead man's shoes together at the southern point, leaving smudges of greasy dampness on the concrete. Spider-like, he scuttled over the body and tipped the head up straight north.

"Go on, don't wait for me!" he hissed, casting a harried glance over his shoulder.

"The stones," Shires said, closing the journal and scowling against the harsh lamplight. "Don't forget to place the stones!"

"Yes, I know!" Smith replied, raising his voice as he thrust a trembling hand into his pocket. He extracted two rounded stones seemingly welded together. With great effort, he succeeded in breaking their magnetic attraction and placed one in each of the dead man's palms, spread east and west.

"Get out of the circle!" Shires said with an impatient wave of his hand, and Smith jumped free, breathless and perspiring. He looked at his watch, satisfied that they were on time, that the stars had not yet passed their ideal positions. On a table beside him, all was ready: atop a clean white towel lay a syringe filled with fifty cubic centimeters of the reanimating agent, thick and colorless; a large ampoule from which more could be drawn if needed; an ancient text bound in human skin and procured at great cost in a strange, shifting town on the border of the Rub' al Khali desert; and, just in case things went badly, a fully loaded .357 revolver.

He handed the pen and journal to Smith.

A simple injection of the agent was all that was required to bring a specimen back to life, though this met with varying degrees of success. The circle, the stones, and the incantations within the book were necessary (as Shires had learned from delving into the occult with John Dunhill) to bring back something that made sense, rather than an empty consciousness flailing its arms and legs, clawing its eyes and gnashing its teeth in mad disbelief. What the ceremony amounted to, in layman's terms, was a calling back of the soul to the form it had abandoned in the process of dying.

This had been why the London experiments had reached such a desultory and unsatisfying end. He and Dunhill had been reviving empty vessels: pure flesh and bone without the slightest residue of persona or intellect remaining.

That had been corrected… though again, with varying degrees of success.

Oftentimes the return to flesh was too much for their minds, and Shires was forced to dispatch them back to the ether with a well-placed bullet. Once, in a rage of screaming insanity, a test subject managed to dislocate Shires's shoulder and wreck the entire lab in less than two minutes before crushing his skull between his own two hands. Some of them were like that, unable to handle the strains of transmogrification.

With the dark apprehension that always came before a resurrection, Shires took up the book of incantations, opened it to a well-marked page, and took a breath. Forefinger pressed to the tallowy parchment, he began to chant the difficult, primordial syllables, uncertain even now as to their meaning.

A cold undercurrent settled over the basement upon completion of the first invocation. The incense, rising in smooth ribbons from the brass tray, manifested this in broken eddies. Both men peered about the shadowed room, their eyes uneasy over the folds of their scented handkerchiefs, their frowns hidden though apparent.

Shires set the book reverently aside, as if it were a tablet of brittle clay, and picked up the syringe. Taking care not to touch the chalked circle, he knelt and lifted the dead man's head, pushing it forward until its frail chin was resting against the moldering remains of its chest. He slipped the long hollow-bore needle below the base of the skull and injected the sluggish fluid into the tissue of the brain stem.

He lowered the head and glanced at his wristwatch. "Twelve o-four," he said. "Fifty cc's of reagent administered directly into the medulla oblongata." Standing against the raw concrete wall, Smith scribbled these notes into the journal and nodded.

Shires backed slowly away from the corpse, his heart beating rapidly. A smile, not quite sane, surfaced nervously in the naked light. From here on, anything might happen, and the thrill of secret knowledge—as powerful and addicting as any drug—charged him. With difficulty and force of will, he took up the book again and lowered his eyes to the pinched lines of text.

There were several verses yet to be spoken before the ritual was complete, but it seemed to both Smith and Shires that the tides were already at work. Something unseen but swirling about the dingy basement was forming a tenuous connection between this world and the next, a communion of tortured souls on the cusp of a starless abyss.

It was too early, yet it was happening.

"What *is* this?" Smith gasped, shrinking against the wall. His eyes looked very round in the shadowed light, his mouth a grim hook against the curve of his jaw. "Daniel, what's happening?"

The corpse's lips parted with a sigh, and a low moan issued from somewhere deep inside its rotted guts, rising like a gas from the floor of the cellar. Its eyelids fluttered and peeled back, revealing clouded pupils, eyes shriveled within their bruised sockets.

Shires shook his head, frowning. It was much too soon for a subject to show such potent signs of reinvigoration, especially one in such an advanced state of decay. Something, he feared, was very wrong here. A scream, shrill and inhuman, cut neatly through the chill air, and the book tumbled numbly from his hands, fluttering like a stunned bat to his feet, pages splayed against the rough concrete.

Shires picked up the revolver and, with a trembling hand, brought it to bear on the writhing corpse, hesitant to shoot until he absolutely had to. *Here*, he thought, *is something unexpected, unprecedented.* Damned if he was going to gun it down before he had a chance to see where it was leading. His partner, however, was blocked from the stairs and unarmed, his agitation and uncertainty growing as the violence of the spasms increased. Smith screamed at Shires to shoot it; for the love of God, *shoot it!*

The corpse twisted on its side, its neck extending and bulging with the strain as it attempted to right itself. Its brittle legs curled to support its weight as its blackened nails scratched at the concrete. It looked up at Shires, threads of black ichor depending from its nose and mouth, and instantly read the intention behind the muzzle of the revolver. The cellar rang with the raw bellow of its rage.

Shires knew that he must squeeze the trigger, but his hand refused to obey. It dipped and wavered, and in the breadth of a heartbeat he convinced himself that there was still time, that a secret was unfolding. If he only possessed the nerve and self-control to see it through, to stay his hand until—

The corpse leapt at him.

The last thing Shires remembered was firing an ineffectual round through one of the overhead joists as the thing propelled him into the foundation wall.

Consciousness was snuffed from him as easily as a flame from atop a candle.

When he came to, Shires found himself alone on the cold cellar floor, his head pulsing sharply as the light from the overhead bulb slashed his eyes. He tried to sit up, and a wave of nausea overtook him. Possibly he lost consciousness again. When his vision cleared, he tried to lift his head. Raw, white agony sprang from a bundle of nerves in the back of his skull. He felt as if he were pitching forward while the entire cellar turned lazy somersaults through the night. He held desperately to consciousness.

He was at the bottom of the stairs. The door above him was ajar, and a thin wedge of light splashed down the top risers, falling in a rough fan across the wall. His vision blurred and the door split in two.

Dazed, disoriented, he wondered if he'd fallen, so he sent out tentative feelers for broken bones. Then he remembered.

My God! The experiment!

He called out for Smith, but his voice sounded listless and unreal, as though part of his tongue were paralyzed. He tried again and heard what sounded like the soft scuff of a shoe against concrete.

In his mind's eye, he imagined the corpse in the cellar with him, its lurid face watching him from the shadows. He rolled over, getting his arms and legs beneath him, searching the floor for the lost revolver. The throb of his head pressed against his sinuses, causing the floor to tip beneath him.

Concussion, he thought and paused, lowering his center of gravity until it passed.

He crawled toward the bottom step and again thought he heard something shuffle against the far wall. It was a cautious sound, stealthy, and when he paused to listen it stopped too, as if listening back.

Shires's heart began to beat faster. A lopsided realization was taking shape in the depths of his mind, still unclear but menacing, as if the last seconds of his life were slipping through his fingers.

There came the slam of a door against a distant jamb and he looked up the stairs. Hurried footsteps, muffled yet perfectly traceable, wound from the living room through the kitchen, coming to a halt at the rear utility room. The door above his head creaked, and a silhouette appeared, swearing in an agitated whisper.

"Christ, Daniel!" Smith's said. "Thank God you're alive!"

Hurrying down the risers, his partner crouched beside him. A light shone in Shires's face, sharp and blinding.

"How do you feel?" Smith said, checking him over for blood or broken bones.

"Dizzy," Shires replied, touching a hand to his forehead. The room was still shifting lazily beneath him, tipping back and forth like a plate on the end of a stick. "And there's a hell of a knot rising on the back of my head. Bastard must have given me a concussion when he knocked me back."

Shires suddenly grabbed Smith by the sleeve and pulled him close. Beads of perspiration strained on his forehead, glowing like fever blisters in the reflected light. His eyes sifted the darkness back and forth. *"Where is it?"* he whispered, certain he could hear it moving again, edging closer.

With a deep exhalation, Smith sank to the floor, resigned to some unhappy fate.

"Gone. I lost him over the rise behind the house."

"Gone?" Shires said, feeling a dread he had never known steal coldly under his skin. "Did, did you say *gone?"*

Smith nodded glumly. His voice had a raggedness to it, a singed quality, as if it had been burned in the chase. "I ran out and checked the road, but there was nothing—it was empty. Then I heard a scuffling out behind the house. By the time I got there and caught sight of him, he was halfway up the hill, moving over those loose rocks and scrub like a goddamn coyote. He looked like he was down on all fours near that outcropping—must have cut his hands all to hell. Anyway, I took a few shots at him as he went over the top." Smith reached behind his back and produced the revolver, still smelling of black powder and cordite. Setting the flashlight on the floor, he removed the cylinder and ejected six spent casings. They hit the concrete with a hollow, agitated jangle, as if mindful they had been wasted on the cool night air. "The moon's fairly bright, but it was a thousand to one. I don't think I even nicked him."

As the simple tale of their subject's escape unfolded, Shires felt a tension creep through him. His forearms ached as his fists worried themselves into bony knots.

"By the time I climbed to the top of the hill, he was gone," Smith concluded, doing nothing more than stating the obvious. "The moon went behind a cloud and"—he shrugged—"well, he was gone."

Smith set the gun aside and looked around the cellar. Had it not been so barren to begin with, it would have been a shambles; as it was, it looked as if a powerful wind had blown down the stairs, overturning the table. Broken glass, the shattered remains of the ampoule, winked amid an oily stain on the concrete, and, nearby, the hypodermic syringe stared back accusingly with its long, steely eye. The book of incantations lay facedown where Shires had dropped it. Deeper in the shadows lay the creased and dog-eared cover of his journal.

"Look at *that*," Smith said, nodding at the chalked circle. It had been smudged in several places where the dead man had struggled to his feet.

The chalk had somehow turned a rusty color, looking for all the world like dried blood.

At its center, floating like dead moons at the moment of collision, were the two magnetic stones, having found one another again.

11

Three days came and went.

Neither Smith nor Shires heard a word of their escaped subject. Their activities were once again put on hold as they nervously awaited the worst, keeping an eye to the door and an ear to the wall for any hint of disaster. Each morning Shires combed the local newspaper for possible clues: pieces of murder or mayhem their man might leave like breadcrumbs for him to follow. But so far he was keeping underground.

Perhaps he felt more comfortable there.

Shires and Smith tiptoed through their days as if a massive weight were dangling over their heads, threatening to drop. Sometimes they could feel the black dread of its shadow over their lives; at other times it seemed almost invisible, as if the danger were fading. At night their dreams screamed in the high, bold print of newspaper headlines.

Six days.

Shires remained at a loss to understand what had triggered such a rapid and dramatic resurrection. He had composed several sketchy theories, but without a body they were little more than blind stabs in the dark, nothing he could dissect or ultimately prove. It was as if the man's consciousness, or soul, had never left his decaying body, remaining just below the parched epidermis, coiled and ready to leap. A prisoner in his own grave. And that was the crux of the thing. They had not called it back from the veil of death with their petty magnets and incantations; it was already *there*.

But how? Why? What condition or circumstance set it apart from every other withered corpse he had practiced upon? What difference?

Shires began to suspect the answer might lie not in death but within the tangible confines of the man's life, and for that, he needed information of a much more personal nature, more than a name or dates off a sunken headstone. Seeking this information would surely raise eyebrows and suspicions around town; after all, what business could two strangers, little more than idle drifters, possibly have in the life and habits of a dead local man?

The waiting was becoming intolerable.

Then there was the crate. With one dead man missing, run off into the night, it had shown up at the worst possible time.

12

Jonathan Taylor regarded the crate at the back of his barn. Now that he'd seen its contents, he kept imagining those dry, leathery eyes snapping open beneath the layers of heavy plastic, the darkened face coming to life within its pinewood box.

A chill passed through him, and he shook his head to compose himself.

He had thought that opening the crate would satisfy his curiosity toward his late-night visitor and the business he was involved in, maybe give him an ace to play in case the deal went sour. Instead it only muddied the waters.

What did Smith intend to do with it? Bury it? Cut it apart?

Something worse?

Jonathan scowled at the musty shadows. There was something both dangerous and highly illicit about the crate, nailed up without identification or refrigeration. And all the way from England, too.

What if it carried some sort of disease? Having torn the lid off and stared it in the face, Jonathan felt a little uneasy at the thought of that possibility. He found himself touching his forehead at odd moments, wondering if the slick sheen of perspiration there marked the advent of a fever.

And what about the footprints he'd seen that morning in the dirt? A shuffling loop across the driveway and back, meandering, almost drunken.

He didn't know. The only answer that came to mind was that someone—possibly Smith—was checking up on him, seeing that he was keeping his end of the bargain.

As these thoughts intruded and lingered, mostly in the middle of the night or at lonely times during the day, Jonathan began to have second thoughts about his decision. Was a child worth such involvement, such risk?

No doubt Pru would think so, but, then again, her conscience was clear. Certainly a child was worth everything he had to give and more.

He found himself wishing for a glimpse into the future, just far enough to see whether or not he was doing the right thing; whether he was buying his way into paradise… or someplace else.

Every night the crate sat in his barn, Jonathan Taylor dreamt of being watched while he slept.

13

Prudence Taylor went to bed early Sunday night—the eve of the trade—very much to Jonathan's surprise. "What?" he asked as she kissed him softly on the mouth and said goodnight. "Don't you want to wait up until the baby arrives?"

She shook her head. No. She simply wanted him to wake her when the evening's business was done and the child was theirs. "Bring me my baby when it's over," she said, retreating into the bedroom.

Left alone, Jonathan felt anger welling slowly inside of him. She was protecting herself, he thought, just as she'd been doing all along. Never asking about the bargain he had agreed to, or where the child was coming from, or who the men he was dealing with were. Nothing of the kind.

He frowned. She wanted to step in when it was over, when there was nothing left to do but love and care for the child, no feelings of guilt or a nagging conscience to keep her up nights. She was putting all that squarely on *his* shoulders.

Jonathan put down his book, stretched, and checked the clock over the mantel. Five minutes after midnight. Less than an hour to go.

He rose and walked to the window. He pushed the drapes aside and peered at the darkened highway. It was as empty as usual for an early Monday morning.

Good. It can stay that way.

He let the heavy fabric drop and went to the kitchen to rummage through the cupboards. He wasn't hungry, just restless; his hands were beginning to itch. He walked back to the living room, opened the curtains all the way, and sat down to wait.

The faint splash of headlights washed the far wall at 12:30, and he stood in time to see a freight truck go barreling by. He watched its tail lights until they sank beneath the horizon and the night grew still again. He returned to the chair and picked up his book. The best he could manage was to reread the blurb on the back cover. He put it back down and waited in the dark, listening to the house creak and settle around him as the clock ticked off the slow minutes.

His mind grew barren, as smooth as a stone in the midst of a river, nothing quite catching hold. Thoughts came and went as rushing currents, touching him briefly and then slipping away. He had trouble envisioning the approaching meeting, as if it were something conceived within a dream. Nothing but passing dust and fancies.

The clock chimed softly—one o'clock—and he shook himself from a light doze.

Several minutes passed, and another pair of headlights appeared: dimmer, as if dirt encrusted, and more furtive. They slowed at the entrance to his drive, hesitated, then winked out like candles. Jonathan's heart began to race as he listened to tires moving up the drive. He stared out the window and saw the silhouette of a small moving van approach the house.

It was happening. It really was.

He put on a light jacked, took the propane lantern from where he left it on the kitchen table, and went out to meet them.

"You're late," Jonathan said as Smith met him on the lawn. Over Smith's shoulder, he saw a shadow shift within the cab of the van. *The mother?* Jonathan wondered, though there was no sound of a baby crying. He decided that it must be sleeping or feeding.

Smith shrugged nonchalantly. "It couldn't be helped," he said with a crooked smile. "The children needed some attention before we took to the road. I didn't think you'd mind."

Jonathan's mouth fell slightly ajar. "*Children?*" His eyes looked warily toward the van. It seemed to glow in the slanted moonlight.

"Very good," Smith laughed softly. "You're a perceptive man, Mr. Taylor. I wasn't able to come up with a newborn, I'm sorry to say. But to make amends, I've brought you a set of twins: a brother and sister, just past their fifth birthdays. Two for the price of one. Your lucky day if you want the both of them...provided you've got the parcel?"

"I've got it," Jonathan said numbly, still in shock. *Twins!* "It's in the barn." He nodded vaguely toward the dark structure beyond the van.

Smith nodded. "May I see it?"

"It's yours. I don't see why not."

They crossed the wide dirt turnabout and stepped through the narrow space between the barn doors. Jonathan struck a match against an upright and lit the propane lantern, adjusting the clear, white light to where they could both see the crate through the heavy shadows.

"I won't be sad to see it go," he told Smith, laying a hand on the rough pine box. A greasy dampness seemed to be leaching through the wood. Jonathan took his hand away and wiped it on his pantleg. "The smell alone is enough to give nightmares."

Smith was looking over the jumble of rusting implements and moldering seed bags, sniffing distastefully at the older, more stubborn odor of chicken feathers and petrified feces, long gone to dust and trampled into the dirt floor. The faint spice of alcohol rode his breath, and, despite his glibness, Jonathan realized the man was desperately frightened. It gave him the boldness to ask: "What if I opened it up? Took a look inside?"

Smith's nervous smile glinted in the half light as the shadows within the barn lay over his narrow shoulders like a cape. "I doubt very much you fully comprehended what you were looking at."

"I said: *what if*," Jonathan said with a frown, conjuring up a halfhearted indignation. "You talk like I already have."

"Of course you have," Smith said impatiently, as if anxious to be away.

The two men looked at one another for a long moment.

"Well, at any rate, there it is," Jonathan said. "Safe and sound."

Smith stepped forward and put his hand on the crate, as if it represented the end of a very long road. "You must have gone to a great deal of trouble to get it in here."

Jonathan agreed, tugging on the dim, overhead light. "It will be just as hard to get out."

Smith began to unbutton his coat. "Then I suggest we get started."

The work went much quicker with two. Jonathan could sit atop the tractor and control the winch while Smith helped guide the crate along its path and through the doorway. No one took any notice of them from the highway (or, if they did, not enough to stop or slow down), and within forty-five minutes the task was done.

The whole time that they worked, Jonathan felt the uncomfortable presence of the undefined silhouette within the cab. The weight of its gaze was an altogether unsettling sensation, an itch down the length of his spine that smoldered slowly. Even as they wrestled the box into the back of the van, he couldn't make out much more than a shadow through the connecting window. It was watching their progress, though; of that he was certain.

"Now to fulfill my part of the bargain."

Smith rubbed his hands briskly after the ramp was pushed inside and the roll-down gate securely latched. "Wait here, please," he told Jonathan and disappeared around the passenger's side of the van. The door opened, and a short conversation ensued between Smith and his companion, too low for Jonathan to hear. The second voice belonged to a man, however, not a mother. It was accented and rough.

Two blanket-wrapped figures slipped free, and Smith herded them along to the back of the van. With a smile, he offered them to Jonathan. "Here you are, Mr. Taylor." He nudged the children forward, and they shuffled the last few steps on their own. In the strong moonlight, Jonathan looked down at their upturned faces. They gazed back at him with eyes that reflected the countless stars overhead like polished obsidian.

"One bit of advice, if you don't mind..." Smith added, drifting anxiously around to the driver's side. "You've got a nice little farmhouse here...no trouble at all to sell. I'd do just that, Mr. Taylor. Take your family someplace else and settle down. The further the better. People around here know your troubles too well. You understand?" He glanced sideways at the lamp-lit cracks in the barn. "The mother and father of those two darlings will never bother you, but I can't make the same guarantee for anyone else. Some people can't help but stick their noses into the affairs of others, and that's all I've got to say on the subject. As for the rest...well, I never saw you, and you never saw me."

He tipped a smile, climbed into the cab, and drove slowly away with the crate. It was the last Jonathan ever saw of him.

He looked down at the twins—*his* now—and tried on a welcoming smile. It felt false, uncertain, and he wiped it away before the cracks began to show. They watched him with the same stony silence, so smooth and unbreakable it unnerved him.

"Come on, you two. Let's get you inside." He held out his long arms to help them up the porch stairs. He needed to see them by a warmer light, something other than the moon and stars.

And Pru, no doubt, would be waiting.

14

Twenty-three hours after the early-morning trade at the Taylor farm, the looming weight that Shires and Smith had feared finally dropped.

It happened in the graveyard, where it had begun.

15

Monday nights were quiet around Colfax.

Wednesday nights were when the week's trouble generally took root, when the powers of chaos and misfortune gathered and drew their plans for the coming weekend: all the shootings and stabbings, the drownings, the abductions, the senseless accidents and bar fights—and who would win the lottery. With respect to the modern work week, Wednesday was hump day, and that, for some, was cause enough to celebrate. But things usually stayed under control until around eleven p.m. on Saturdays.

Saturdays were by far the worst nights for policemen.

But Mondays were quiet.

Officer Robert Powell sometimes wondered why they even bothered to send out radio cars to cover the early-morning hours, and two of them at that. The town seemed completely asleep, if not dead. Oh, occasionally there was some excitement, but it was usually nothing more vigorous than chasing a group of kids out of Schmuck Park or knocking on someone's door at midnight to tell them their yapping mutt was keeping the neighbors awake. Domestic squabbles didn't kick into gear until Friday or Saturday, and honest-to-God murders were relatively few and far between in a town the size of Colfax.

Occasionally you got a curve ball. Four or five months back, for instance.

During the early part of spring, Lloyd Davidson, a local insurance salesman with a history of depression and alcohol abuse, had committed suicide, and Powell had been the first officer to arrive on the scene. Divorced for less than a year and denied visitation rights to his two young sons, Lloyd had made a barely coherent telephone call to his ex-wife's apartment just after three o'clock in the morning. She in turn (after a half hour's indecision) notified the police, informing the desk sergeant of her former husband's turbulent bouts of despair and past attempts (*flirtations*, she had called them) at self-destruction.

Powell had reached the modest (and, of late, ill-tended) frame house on Jerome Street within five minutes of the call. The town had been empty at that hour, and he'd pushed the speedometer up to sixty at one point, flashing his blue and white bubbletops in and out of narrow streets and alleyways. He'd knocked twice on the door, calling Davidson's name loud enough to be heard within. Then, finding it unlocked, he proceeded inside.

The kitchen was awash in old food boxes, liquor bottles and dirty dishes. It had an unpleasant smell—sour and shut in, as if the man never opened a window or door except to go out. A television ran snow and static to a room full of attentive chairs, and in the back hallway, a glass frame of family snapshots was cracked and hung badly askew.

Davidson himself was on the bedroom floor, slumped over a pile of stale, gray bedsheets. He seemed in the grip of an unshakable sleep. Powell knelt and felt the man's neck for a pulse. The flesh was sticky, still slightly warm, and after he took his hand away, Powell wiped it on the slate blue of his trouser leg. He began CPR on the man (an exercise in futility that would give him nightmares for years to come), but ten minutes later, after the doctor arrived, Davidson was pronounced dead. The autopsy showed the cause to be an overdose of tranquilizers combined with alcohol. Davidson had been drinking one-hundred-proof vodka mixed with a splash of orange juice: as dull and unimaginative as the rest of his life.

Officer Powell flipped a cigarette butt out his car window, watching the sparks swirl on the roadway in his rearview mirror, and then swung his vehicle onto the old Palouse highway, heading east. He still recalled the sensation of a low, blue current twisting through his body as he stood over Davidson's corpse, though, all in all, it had been nothing spectacular, and afterward the nights would quickly return to the grind of well-worn routine.

Which was how he felt tonight: ground down and weary. The old highway was part of his normal route, a narrow loop he checked two or three times a shift (depending largely on his mood or the day of the week). Sunday through Wednesday he generally made the circuit twice, at midnight and at 3:30. This would be his last check of the night, including a spotlight prowl through the cemetery at the top of the hill.

The night sky was calm and exceptionally clear, allowing the light of the stars and the waning moon to shine down bright and unobstructed, casting shadows over the rolling, hoarfrost-covered hills of the countryside. It was the perfect backdrop for a nightmare and, turning onto cemetery loop a mile out of town, that's exactly what he found in the sharpened beams of his headlights.

What the hell?

At first, it looked as if someone—some crazy farmer, perhaps—had taken an auger to the turf. Here and there were piles of fresh, black earth, pushed up from the ground in neat, rounded cones. Scowling, Powell put a foot to the brake and skidded to a halt on the loose gravel. He switched on his mounted spotlight and scanned it slowly over the marbled grounds. The yellow beam sliced through the darkened landscape, dissecting stands of spruce, alder, and ghostly-white birch as it moved up and down the rounded hillside.

A decomposing smile caught his eye as the light tripped over the grisly remains of a head perched atop one of the mounds.

Oh Jesus!

The spotlight wavered in his hands.

As a boy, not more than ten years old, Robert—then Robbie—had dug a hole in the back corner of his yard, in a little dirt area between the cedar fence and a dusty juniper bush. About two feet down, he had been delighted to strike something that looked amazingly like a treasure chest. It was a box of sorts, about three feet by two with a rounded lid, just the right detail to suggest a pirate's secret booty. Robbie had worked diligently for a half hour to clear its hinged lid, and when it finally opened, it did so begrudgingly, like a yellowed tooth rotting in the soil. The word "Red" was carved beneath the latch in large, uneven letters, and Robbie figured that must be the dead pirate's name, sort of like Redbeard but without the beard. He pushed back the lid and the grin on his face immediately dissolved into a rictus of horror and disgust. The chest contained the remains of a large and snarling dog, lovingly buried by the house's previous owners, and the smell that came rolling up to his face was the worst thing he'd ever experienced in his ten long years. Worse even than the sight of the dog.

The still air that hung over the Colfax Cemetery held that same corrupt odor, not as concentrated as that long-ago memory but nevertheless the same. Powell gagged and felt his lunch, eaten a scant twenty minutes ago, come helplessly up his esophagus, triggered by simple association with that childhood event. He had just enough time to lean out the window before he lost it. Vomit burned between his teeth and fell in heavy clots down the side of the car.

The fit passed quickly, and spitting the sour taste out of his mouth, Powell righted himself in the saddle. He looked around surreptitiously, wondering if anyone had seen him in his moment of weakness.

It didn't seem likely.

Marshaling his strength, Powell climbed out of the car. An owl hooted a warning from a nearby tree as white headstones floated eerily in the moonlight. Pale flecks of exposed bone winked within the scattered piles of earth. Disinterred corpses had been flung aside or left half buried; the rounded dome of a skull lay beside an arm or a leg bone as the hollow grin of a ribcage sat nearby. And over it all, the choking smell of decay drifted over the landscape like a deadly gas.

"Christ alive," he moaned, stunned at the extent of the vandalism. It hit him like a well-placed kick to the testicles; all the blood drained from his vitals, leaving him with a sickening ache that had no specific location.

A ragged snarl tore across the hilltop, and he almost screamed. It sounded like an animal, panting and growling behind a low rise to his right, though there was just enough frustration and humanity in its timbre for Powell to picture Lon Chaney Jr. in full fangs and yak hair. The stubble along the back of his neck pricked against the starched blue of his shirt collar, and he glanced uneasily at the moon, thinking of wolfsbane and gypsy curses. For a paralyzing moment, he felt ten years old again and wished for six silver bullets to replace the lead in his service revolver. Suddenly conscious of his conspicuous position, he leaned through the window of the patrol car—careful not to rub against the trail of bile still making its way down the side—and flipped off the headlights and side-mounted spotlight.

The night fell like a blanket, softly covering him.

Over the gentle hillock, he made out a scratching that reminded him of storekeepers sprinkling rock salt on their icy sidewalks, digging it out of old coffee cans a handful at a time. He unsnapped his gun from its holster and pulled it free, pointing the barrel at the crown of the hill. A vague shadow, throwing flecks of fine-spun silver, appeared between two crooked obelisks, and he jerked his gun in its direction.

At this point he had seen enough to warrant backup. Not taking his eyes from the frantic rain of soil the shadow was unearthing, he crept back to the car and slid behind the wheel. Hand trembling, he reached down for the radio handset. He spoke quietly into the microphone, as if it were made of glass and might shatter. The reply from the station—Tom Huber's voice—came wrapped in static, too loud for Powell to bear. He scrambled for the volume control and twisted it down to the hiss of a distant stream.

"That you, Powell? I can barely read you," Huber said.

"Yeah, it's me. Listen, Tom, I'm up here at the cemetery off the old back highway. Someone's done a job on the place but *good*. There's at least half a dozen graves dug up and thrown all over the place. Dirt, old clothes, pieces of bodies... Christ Almighty!" A hungry rasp of breath rose over the hill, and Powell twitched. The eye of his gun, caught staring at the nearby grass, rose to attention. "The freak that did it is still here, not fifty yards from me.

I'm gonna need some backup, two men at least, but you'd better send me all you can spare. This guy sounds like he's foaming at the goddamn mouth!"

There was a long pause, almost as if the station house had fallen away, ceased to exist, and then the sergeant's voice returned, calm and unflappable behind the weight of his desk. "Roger that, Powell. Immediate assistance needed at the old highway cemetery." The radio sputtered. "I've got Thorenson five minutes away and proceeding in your direction. I'll wake up the chief and get back to you, so stay close, copy?"

"Yeah, I fucking copy that," Powell hissed, his palm sweating against the casing of the handset. He realized that he was squeezing it like an underripe orange. "Just hurry it up, will you?"

"Roger, Car Six. Over and out."

Powell set the mic back in its cradle. He looked at the shotgun seated in its mount and, setting the revolver within reach on the seat, broke it free. Holstering the handgun, he closed the driver's door, slid across the front seat, and crawled out the passenger's side, putting the car solidly between himself and the subject. Damned if he was going to be trapped inside the car if the lunatic decided to charge him. He straightened, put the butt of the shotgun to his shoulder, and propped his elbow on the roof of the car, ready to fire.

He kept his vigil in silence, watching for movement. The shadow was gone, but whatever it belonged to was still there. He could hear it panting, straining with sod and marble and God knew what else.

16

The return call came before Thorenson.

"I talked to the chief," Huber said. "He's on his way out with Parrish. Should be there in ten or fifteen minutes. Is Thorenson with you?"

"No." Powell glanced behind him to make certain. "Not yet."

"He should be any minute. I told him to approach without lights, so you might not see him until he's right on top of you. Chief says don't try anything until you've got backup, and then be damned careful. Approach with *extreme* caution."

"Fucking-A," Powell murmured by way of sign-off and tossed the handset back into the seat. Over the savage grunts and moans, he could hear the approach of a car on the highway. It slowed at the gates and turned onto gravel. Less than a minute later, Car Three pulled up quietly to his rear bumper. Paul Thorenson crept out and joined him, gun in hand.

"*Where?*" the tall, blond man whispered.

Powell pointed to the rise. "I don't think he knows we're here. *Listen.*"

Thorenson cocked his head, listening for movement beneath the soil. It came suddenly, strengthening as a palpable desperation set in. Soft wood cracked and splintered, and a piece of debris arced from behind the mound.

Thorenson leveled his head and frowned. "What the hell is he doing?" Without the aid of headlamps or a spotlight, the newly exhumed dead were merely lumps and disorderly scatterings of black in the pale moonglow, their grisly horror all but hidden from sight.

"Digging up your goddamn folks is what he's doing!" Powell whispered. "Maybe a few aunts and uncles too! *Jesus*, Paul, can't you *smell* it?"

"How bad is it?" Thorenson asked.

"*Bad*," Powell answered, a dry and humorless laugh bubbling up. "*Real* bad."

Thorenson swallowed, suddenly grateful for the darkness.

"Chief said to wait for you, and then move in with *extreme* caution."

"Goddamn right we will," Thorenson said, swinging the cylinder from his gun to see that he had six live rounds.

"He and Parrish are on their way, so let's save our asses a shredding and do this by the numbers; I guess Sarge got them out of bed." Powell put the shotgun back in its car mount and pulled his service revolver.

"Lucky Sarge."

A dry scratching noise rose over the hill, and they turned their heads, watching for movement.

"I think I had a dream like this once," Thorenson said, glancing up at the moon.

"Yeah? How'd it come out?" Powell asked.

The taller officer opened his mouth to answer, then apparently thought better of it.

"That bad, huh?"

Thorenson shrugged. "Who remembers their dreams anyway," he muttered, eyes lost in silhouette. He cleared his throat quietly. "So how do you want to go about this?"

Powell studied the terrain. "I figure our best approach is to split up and move in from both sides, at about eight o'clock and four o'clock so we don't get in each other's line of fire." He used his free hand on the roof of the car to describe the maneuver, circling left and then right around an imaginary mound. "That way we're separated and can catch him in a crossfire in case he tries anything cute."

Thorenson nodded. "Sounds good to me. I'll go left and wait for you to call him out."

"All right. I'll give you a minute or two to get into position."

The chromium scent of adrenaline drifted between them, and the two officers regarded one another carefully, as if measuring their own reflections.

Powell pulled his flashlight from his belt but kept it turned off. "Ready?"

"As I'll ever be."

They moved silently between the cars and across the narrow lane, cakewalking over the crunch of gravel. As they entered the lawn, the nearby owl hooted once and then took flight, sailing across the constellations without a sound.

17

Robert Powell moved slowly, using the light of the moon to pick his way over the shags of loose turf and flung debris. The damage up close was surreal; it was like treading through an old battleground, one where the combatants, men and women alike, met the enemy in their finest suits and silken gowns and were left to rot in the trenches.

He saw a dead man gazing at the spreading boughs of a cypress, his hair a silvery halo, his eyes white jelly. Farther on, a delicate hand lay nestled in a black spray of earth like a crouching spider, its tiny bones splintered and dry. Slabs of white marble and granite leaned on crooked shadows, uprooted by the winds of a passing tempest, one unencumbered by notions of reverence or respect.

He looked to his left and saw that Thorenson was getting ahead of him, slicing through the insanity without feeling its cold and crying touch.

Powell lifted his gaze from the raw earth and decay, hurrying now to get into position.

18

A stirring in the night whispered far below the threshold of reason, and Powell blanched at the scene unfolding in front of him. His skin shriveled as if he'd been in the bath too long, and he wound down in his tracks like a rusty toy. He wanted to scream, to shout a warning to Thorenson, but the best he could manage was a thick whimper in the back of his throat, slippery and useless.

The moon is a liar, a voice said inside his head, coming out of the gray folds like a snatch of dialogue from an old movie, half-remembered. *It lies not only in what it reveals, but also in what it* chooses *to reveal...*

Here was a perfect example. It poured down brightly over his shoulder as he watched the man grunt and toss clumps of sod out of a ransacked grave, and for a moment, just the briefest instant, Powell glimpsed the man's face and imagined it was someone—now dead—whom he had once known.

"No," he said aloud, shaking his head. This was just a man, and a pretty sick one at that. The initial shock ebbed, and his sense of duty returned. He recalled the gun and the flashlight in his hands and Thorenson creeping around the other side of the rise, waiting for him to make their presence known.

He edged closer, crouching as he tucked the flashlight back onto his belt loop. The moon was more than bright enough to proceed, and he guessed he would need both hands to hold his revolver steady. Thorenson must be in position by now, he decided, though for a moment he'd lapsed into the wreckage of a dream, where time had no measure or meaning.

He flattened himself against the cold belly of the earth and held his pistol out in front of him, dancing the notched sight along the lip of the grave. His heart beat heavily against the cool grass, and he forced himself to take deep, measured breaths:

One...two...three...

"*You there!*" his voice boomed out, surprisingly strong. "In the hole! This is the police! You are surrounded! Climb out of there with your hands in plain sight!"

A head rose out of the ragged hole and turned in Powell's direction, catching the full light of the moon. Over a distance of twenty-five yards, their eyes locked.

Sweet God... No!

Powell's body jerked as simple recognition ripped through him like a saw blade. With it came relief.

Sleep.

He *was* dreaming after all.

Since finding Lloyd Davidson lying dead in his stagnant bedroom, Powell had dreams of finding him again and again: stuffed under his car in the garage, rotting like damp insulation between the walls. Once, he'd even watched as Davidson's now-familiar remains had swollen from the size of a pin dot against a clear, blue sky and landed with a jolting *thrrrump!* in his wife's vegetable garden. That he should now be ravaging the town cemetery came as no real surprise, given the context of a dream.

It seemed that a link had been established between the two of them: that of corpse and finder. Being first on the scene to the small, white house on Jerome Street, he'd unwittingly broken some invisible but sticky seal across the threshold, inheriting a piece of Davidson's spirit in the bargain. As a result, Davidson's ghost found ways to haunt his dreams. Unlike in previous appearances, however, in which Lloyd was content to play a simple corpse (looking bruised and slightly rueful in the part), he had now assumed a more active and threatening role, one that demanded direct action from Powell.

Raging and snarling, his brain broiling under the heat of some strange fever, Davidson scrambled from the hole. He made a direct charge for Powell—arms outstretched, fingers curled into blackened hooks, eyes shining with a brilliant lunacy.

A shot rang out and Davidson stumbled, taking only a second or two to regain his stride. Powell glimpsed Thorenson crouched beneath a glowing white cherub with his service pistol raised in the cup of his hands. Thorenson shouted something at Davidson—loud, meaningless words that bounced off his hide like boiled peas. Then his weapon flashed, and another dull shot thundered through the cemetery.

Davidson howled, and Powell felt a warm mist—splatter from the bullet's impact—drift over his face and hands. It was at that moment that he began to register some alarm; a small sliver of his mind conceded the possibility that this *wasn't* a dream.

Too late. He fired his revolver but missed, and the monster knocked it easily from his hand. Something in his shoulder snapped, and he fell to the ground with Davidson. The two of them rolled over a loose pile of dirt. The gritty taste of the soil splashed into his face, wedging itself between his teeth and blackening his tongue.

The moon shone in Powell's eyes as he gagged helplessly under Lloyd Davidson's weight. He turned his head to spit and saw Thorenson advancing. The deputy's face was a smooth, black vacancy beneath the boxed corners of his cap, his blond hair now a wispy and magnificent gray.

Pressure and pain raked Powell's midsection, followed by a warm, floating sensation. It came two more times, quickly.

Thorenson screamed and fired his revolver point blank. Four loud reports and then the static click of the hammer falling on empty brass. Davidson's weight fell heavily, gasping as it hit the ground.

In Powell's dream, the night sky faded. Unlike Davidson, however, he never rose again.

19

"My head's a little fuzzy," admitted Sheriff Lonny Cornell, Jake Garrett's predecessor, tapping the bottom of his

Styrofoam coffee cup against the desk. "Would you mind walking that last bit by me again?"

He was seated in the office of the county coroner, Shiro Yahoto, and something about the room's acoustics was playing hell with him; it was either that or the way Yahoto kept talking down along his striped tie into the desk drawer, as if he were afraid his words might bounce out of the room and catch the wrong set of ears. Coroner, after all, was an elected position, and what he was suggesting sure wouldn't win him many votes come November. A nervous smile, absolutely humorless, twitched at the corner of Yahoto's thin lips; quite obviously, he was just as uncomfortable with the validity of his last statement.

"I don't know what to make of it myself," the coroner said, distractedly picking a piece of lint off the cuff of his shirt. His eyes returned to Cornell. "But these *do* appear to be the facts. Tissue samples do not lie."

"I understand that, Shiro," Cornell said, readjusting himself in the hardwood chair, not understanding at all. "But what you're saying, well...it doesn't wash. Surely you can see that?" He scowled, settling back. "One of your boys must've gotten his slides fouled up. Discombobulated. And, not to tell you how to do your job, but maybe you'd better run those tests again."

Yahoto folded his small, neat hands together atop the open file and listened to the sheriff's sensible recommendations. "I ran them myself," Yahoto said calmly, when the sheriff had had his say.

All in all, Cornell felt he was demonstrating remarkable tolerance and restraint. One of his deputies was dead, slashed open down the middle, and all Yahoto could tell him was that the man who purportedly did it was five months dead.

"Three full series. I was here until 2:30 this morning." The coroner looked pale, exhausted. "I'm sorry, Lonny, they all said the same thing. But if you find it difficult to accept my conclusions, you're welcome to have the tests repeated elsewhere."

Cornell dismissed the idea with an impatient grunt. He tapped his cup on the desktop again, looked at it as if he had no idea how it had come to be in his hand, and pitched it into the wastebasket. The chair creaked under his weight, and he sighed. "This case is so buggy it belongs on *The Late Late Show*. I've got one man dead, another in shock—so rattled by what he saw that he can barely remember his own name—mass vandalism at the cemetery, and a coroner who tells me straight-faced that my prime suspect is five months dead—a man who just happens, incidentally, to be the agent who signed my life insurance papers! Jesus Christ almighty God." Cornell pulled a roll of wintergreen mints from his pocket, unwrapped two and crunched them down with a bitter grimace. "Never in my thirty-eight years of law enforcement have I seen anything to equal *this* crap-happy mess."

Yahoto nodded once. "Yes, I know the feeling."

Cornell gazed at Yahoto with a flat, appraising stare, and then his eyes softened. "Doesn't look like you've had much sleep, Shiro. I'm sorry I had to drop this thing in your lap."

The coroner gave a small shrug. "You've considered the possibility that the one responsible for this is still at large?" he said hesitantly.

Cornell frowned. "Correct me if I'm wrong, but wasn't the point of these last twenty minutes to impress upon me the fact that he is, beyond all doubt, *dead*? I didn't nod off somewhere, did I?"

Yahoto shook his head as if to jumble that theory. He shuffled through the file to a copy of Thorenson's incident report and held it up to Cornell as evidence. "At least half a dozen graves unearthed, it says here. Surely Lloyd Davidson's is one of them. You said yourself your officer is in a deep state of shock, that he can barely recall his own name. How can you give his statement such credence? It was dark, and from what I understand the bodies were scattered all about the area?"

The sheriff smiled. "You can't keep good news down," he said wearily.

The coroner stared, puzzled. "I don't understand. Is it something else? Something not in the report?"

Cornell rubbed his long jaw, irritated by the prickly feel of the whiskers that had gone neglected for two days. Too many duties, too much excitement. He regarded Yahoto across the desk.

"No, we checked Lloyd's plot. It was more or less intact, though that got me to thinking about this bit of trouble we had out there a while back...some of the graves disturbed, though nothing like we had night before last." He leaned back. "This was relatively minor stuff. Dirt in the grass, the sod not packed down like it should have been... things you'd only notice in the daylight, and then only if you were real familiar with the grounds on a day-to-day basis. Anyway, like I said, I got curious and looked back into it. Guess what I found? Very interesting..."

Yahoto leaned forward. "This 'trouble' that you had before: one of the graves was Davidson's?" he said.

"Oh yeah." Cornell nodded. "Absolutely correct."

Both men fell into silence, contemplating the significance of this strange fact. The picture it suggested was inconclusive. The coroner inquired if the casket itself had also been disturbed.

"We never checked," the sheriff said, his voice becoming heavy and gray, his eyes gazing down at the floor, fixing and unfocusing the swirling patterns in the linoleum tile. "At the time, it seemed unlikely, though right now I wish to God we had." He blinked. "Interment had been recent—just two or three weeks—and the weather had been fair."

"What you are saying is, at the time, you didn't know whether or not the grave had actually been disturbed?"

Cornell looked up, his eyes sharp once again. "No. We decided to wait and see if anything more definite came of it before pushing the paperwork for an exhumation."

Yahoto nodded. "It appears that something has."

20

"I've been giving our Mr. Davidson some serious thought," Shires said to Smith, studying the woodgrain of the stocky table between them. He glanced up, his eyes bleary and tired. They were at the Ploughman, and word of the upheaval at the cemetery had spread quickly throughout town, though it was not common knowledge that the only suspect in the case was a dead man. Smith and Shires, however, had gathered what info they could and made certain inferences based on what they already knew.

"There's a very old theory—actually, it's more along the lines of superstition, common, to one degree or another, to Christian cultures all over Europe—that under certain conditions, the immortal soul of an individual can become lodged or trapped within the body after death. Vampirism, of course, was an offshoot based on such a belief. The body was given to rise after nightfall to seek human blood as sustenance, and so various precautions, such as a stake through the heart or the severing of the head, were taken to ensure that this unhappy event didn't come to pass. Similarly, the bodies of suicides were interred at crossroads, so if the body tried to rise—claw its way out of the ground after death—it wouldn't know which road to take and in theory became paralyzed with indecision. The Church has always taken a dim view of suicide, and the sin—seen as the refusal of God's most precious gift, *life*—

is considered unpardonable, the absolute *worst* a man could do. Do you follow?"

Smith nodded, though he was impatient to know the relevance of this history lesson.

"Very well. Now assume for a moment that the belief has some credence, a small kernel of essential truth embedded at its core, and apply it to our unfortunate Mr. Davidson, whom we now know to be a suicide. Does it shed any light on his startling and sudden reaction to the serum?"

Smith kept quiet for the moment, staring into the depths of his glass, sullenly unconvinced.

"Consider it! What if he's been there all along?" Shires said, expounding along a fragile line. "Five months underground, trapped inside his coffin, with only the worms and his own decomposing body for company, all conceptions of sanity erased by the constant and unrelenting horror of feeling oneself turn slowly to dust. Then along we come, digging him up in the dead of night and shooting him full of reagent." Uttering a sudden, frightening laugh, Shires fell against his seatback and hugged himself about the middle, trying desperately to keep his mirth inside. His glass, his first of the evening, sat untouched on the table.

Smith winced and shifted uncomfortably in his chair, squirming against the sound of his partner's laughter, the *madness* in it. He felt it lurking in himself as well, just below the surface, building a slow and steady pressure. He was afraid because, over the last few weeks, he could feel patches of himself wearing ragged and thin under the various uncertainties: the grisly experimentations, the shaky deal with Taylor, the days of waiting for Davidson to resurface, and now, in Shires's cellar, an unsettling crate waiting to be opened.

He looked at Shires and experienced a momentary urge to strangle him where he sat, to burn his house and all its contents to the ground and put an end to the madness, once and for all.

But would it end?

The thing in the crate, he knew, was not altogether dead. The thing that had once been John Dunhill, Shires's associate from London.

Shires once confided to Smith—when he was very drunk—that Dunhill had been injecting himself with the reanimating agent during his last weeks of life. Now Smith suspected that Shires was doing the same, riding it like a wave he'd become helpless to resist.

So if he killed Shires now, would he *stay* dead?

The laughter across the table ebbed, and Shires leaned forward to finger his beaded glass. He took a long, almost desperate quaff and wiped the thin foam from his lips with his trembling hand.

Smith sighed; his head tipped forward, fingers tangled in his thick brown hair. He shook his head, tired of such riddles. "I simply don't understand what he thought he was *doing* up there."

Shires smirked. "I can only hazard a guess."

Smith looked up, raising a weary eyebrow.

"Trying to find his way back."

Smith felt a chill along his spine.

"That hole I pulled him out of," Shires elaborated. "He knew he belonged there, not up here with us."

21

Four days after they were torn from the soil, the mortal remains of eight Colfax Cemetery residents, including those of Lloyd Davidson, were quietly laid to rest. They were reboxed and planted without ceremony, though several witnesses, most of them friends or relatives, came and watched in knots of tearful silence. Others were simply curious or bored, dry eyed and unconnected. This latter group unfailingly caught Sheriff Cornell's sharp attention as he drifted back and forth over the grounds. He had made it a point to be in attendance (unobtrusive in a neat charcoal suit and somber tie) from dawn's quiet groundbreaking to the afternoon's last tired tramping of sod. He watched the groups and the gates for one face in particular, but it never showed. Gloomily, he thought of having to return the following day (along with the majority of the force) for Rob Powell's funeral.

The case was eating into him. One of his men was dead, and the traces of decayed flesh in his wounds were utterly unacceptable. His men wanted answers, viable leads to focus their vengeance upon. What was he to tell them?

Daniel Shires.

The name flitted from stone to stone as he walked back to his car. He was the man who, despite his vigilance, hadn't appeared this day. It wouldn't hurt to put a deputy on his tail for a week or so, enough to dig up just cause for a search warrant. He had a suspicion, an intuition, the man would turn up dirty somehow.

In the meantime, he'd contacted his counterparts in the surrounding counties, asking for information on crimes of a similar nature. The inquiry had already paid off. Across the Idaho state line, Marty Kenover, sheriff of Latah County, shared a recent and unsolved case in the tiny town of Kendrick. A groundskeeper had reported an obvious disturbance, and a pair of six-year-old twins—brother and sister, recently interred—were found missing from their small caskets. They had drowned only five weeks earlier, swept away as they were wading in an irrigation spillway. The temperature that day had been in the triple digits, and over six hundred thousand cubic feet of swift, brown water had been released from the swollen reservoir.

Cornell slid behind the wheel of his car and started the engine. As he drove away, he thought of the enigmatic

Daniel Shires, the Englishman with the drinking problem and a penchant for relieving himself near quiet country cemeteries. A stranger in town, shadowy, without any visible means of support. Cornell held the memory of his face close to his heart, like a favorite son.

For the first time in four days, he had a course of action along which to proceed, and though it was slim, precarious, anything was better than nothing, or the impossible.

22

Smith began to dream of the dead, of the moon shining down upon acre after acre of open graves, each one known to him, each a private hell he'd created in a search that never ended. His fingernails were cracked and encrusted with a foul-smelling clay; he found tangles of whispery grass caught in his cuffs and pockets; tiny corpses fell out of the cupboards and closets in his dark apartment; and once, in an ill-tempered drawer where he kept the mismatched silver, a single shrunken eye, as hard as a dried pea, rolled in gentle circles around the hollow of a large serving spoon.

Then there was the crate.

Within Shires's cursed cellar, the crate he'd helped pull out of Jonathan Taylor's barn had grown to monstrous proportions. At times, unaccountably alone, he could hear it moving through the floorboards: scraping harshly over the concrete, knocking against the foot of the stairs with an impatient shudder.

At these times he would awake with a lurch, struggling to right himself against the damp tangle of bedsheets, with an unspoken scream, salty and bitter, on his lips.

And he knew the day was coming when Shires would want his help in opening it.

23

There was a rust-colored stain pooling on the white plaster over Smith's bed. It had long been dry, of course, but at times—when the evening light was lazy and subdued—it shimmered as if fresh. At night, sleepless, with the streetlight shining against the faded curtains, the stain looked solid and black, like a gaping tear into a dead realm, throbbing against his grainy eyelids to the beat of its own pulse.

Smith opened his eyes and there it was, frozen against the strengthening daylight. Just a stain, layered in lapping degrees about the edges, proof that its creation had come about gradually over time, until it looked vaguely like Greenland.

He threw aside the blankets with a frustrated grunt, tired of the clock, of trying to will himself back to sleep. The floorboards were cold under his bare feet. They ticked and sighed as he padded over to the window, nudged a careful crack between the curtains, and peered down at the car parked below.

The early morning sky was pale blue, illuminating the street below in subtle shades of gray. Spidery cracks lined the asphalt, and the trees looked heavy and dim, just slumbering shapes without distinction. Already the leaves were beginning to pale and collect in the storm gutters.

Smith looked back at the car.

Dull blue and nondescript, it was nonetheless conspicuous enough to bother him, parked as it was in front of a small brick house that now served as an office for one Murray C. Hefflinger, C.P.A. (so a discreet placard announced). From New Year's through mid-April, the cars came and went from Hefflinger's office like Friday night at the drive-in, disgorging harried-looking individuals burdened with files and bulging shoeboxes. At this time of year, however, business was sluggish, the driveway empty except for the occasional small businessman bringing in his quarterly receipts.

Smith frowned, and the pale light smoothed his worry lines and hardened his unshaven jaw. Though he couldn't see much of the car's interior from this angle, he thought he could perceive a slight shadow on the exposed dashboard, as if someone were seated behind the wheel.

He let the curtain fall back into place and, nervous and edgy from lack of sleep, turned to dress for the day.

The Wheat Bowl Café was bright and noisy. Waitresses in gold and brown uniforms, their hair pulled back into ponytails and anchored with bobby pins, clipped back and forth with hot plates and steaming carafes of coffee. A thin haze of cigarette smoke hung above the light shades, turning the white-fiber acoustical tiles a slow and greasy brown. The vinyl-upholstered booths were sticky from earlier meals, and he avoided touching the cushions with his bare hands.

Smith ordered toast and black coffee for breakfast and listened to the murmur of conversation surrounding him. Most of the customers were retirees, men with gray whiskers who would gather in groups of three or four to sip coffee and while away the morning hours in gossip and quiet conversation. They watched the customers come and go, grinning about whose boys were raising hell and frowning over who was filing for bankruptcy. Lots were cast for the year's pea and lentil crop, and politics (both local and national) were spread out on stained newspapers and torn apart. For the past few days, there had been much speculation about the bad business out at the cemetery.

Grim faces, slowly shaking heads.

Apart from them, a solitary island unto himself, Smith drank his coffee and strained to pick up bits of rumor and innuendo, feeling alarm and relief break over him in alternating waves.

The sheriff suspected...The Sheriff knew nothing...

His waitress set two slices of buttered toast before him, and Smith straightened, reaching for the jam. She filled the empty space in his coffee cup and laid the check facedown on the table.

When she was gone, he looked up and found a pair of eyes regarding him casually from across the room. Almost immediately, contact was broken, but in that single electrifying instant, Smith realized that he was under surveillance. The feeling was strong and intuitive.

His heart began to pound audibly against his chest, and the toast in his mouth turned to a lump, too dry to swallow. He touched a trembling hand to his temple in an attempt to calm himself and reached for his coffee cup.

There was little about the man or his manner to suggest that he was a deputy or a policeman. Slim of build and hunched protectively over his cup, there was a notable absence of the characteristics that usually defined the breed. No crew cut or edgy moustache, no air of authority or arrogance. Rather, he seemed nervous and out of his element. The suit he wore, soft and a bit worn about the edges, spoke of more liberal or solitary pursuits: a high-school history teacher, perhaps, an unambitious clerk, but certainly not a cop.

The confidence he felt in his gut was confirmed as the man raised his cup and glanced over the rim once again— quick, surreptitious, and unobtrusive as hell.

Yes. Just a high school teacher, the look said. Or a harried clerk.

Smith felt an urgent need to get out of the café before his shattered nerves got the better of him, before the strain of appearing sane and unconcerned shook him apart at the ragged joints. He forced himself to finish his toast (normal people didn't bolt out of restaurants mid-meal without some provocation, he reminded himself), but it was difficult without choking. He wet the toast with a last swallow of coffee, dusted his fingerprints lightly on a paper napkin and reached for his wallet.

The long walk to the cash register with the receipt was even worse. He felt as if he'd stepped upon a lit stage, an object of indefatigable interest to his fellow diners. The intervening clutter of tables and chairs was as thick as canebrake, arranged to confuse and trip him up. The wait at the register for a cashier lasted a graceless eternity, one in which every twitch and tremor equated to a sublime confession. And for one awful moment, Smith imagined that the young clerk or high school teacher had left his table and was standing right behind him, close enough to hear him breathing and to scent the sweat standing out on his forehead.

"And how was everything this morning, sir?" a pretty brunette said with a smile as her long, spidery fingers ran up the register keys, totaling his bill.

"Fine, just fine," Smith said, flashing a brief but unconvincing smile.

"That'll be thirty-five cents, please."

He gave her a single bill out of his open wallet, not trusting his fingers to sort exact change from his pocket, then waited for her to count sixty-five cents back into his moist palm.

"You have a good morning now," she said brightly, slamming the till and touching the side of her head lightly, checking that her hair was still in place.

Smith turned to leave. The man at the far table was staring lazily out the front windows, as if contemplating his lesson plan for the day or perhaps wondering if he had time for one last cup before walking back to the courthouse.

Smith ducked out the door. He glanced through the smudged glass facade as he set back toward his apartment.

Inside the café, the man had disappeared from his table.

24

He had to warn Shires; that was a certainty. But it would be worse than reckless to go charging over there when he knew that he was being watched. Smith paced his apartment in nervous agitation, pausing at the window now and again to check on the blue sedan in the street below, studying it through a narrow gap in the curtains. It had moved slightly from its place that morning, but only by a matter of feet. Cigarette smoke, thin and white, wafted occasionally from the driver's side window.

He cursed Shires for not having a telephone, but then again, neither did he.

Effectively paralyzed, caught within the confines of three small rooms, Smith decided—after much indecision and deliberation—that the best course of action would be to do nothing at all. Act as if he hadn't noticed. He was due to meet Shires at The Plowman that evening; hopefully that would be soon enough to avert any disaster. He nodded to himself, unsatisfied, realizing that any sudden change in behavior (and he had to assume that Shires was also under surveillance) might arouse suspicion and force the authorities to move in sooner than they had cause to. And any time he and Shires had might prove very precious now.

Smith sighed and flopped down in a musty armchair to wait out the clock until evening.

25

They worked by lamplight, using a hammer and prybar.

"I still think we're taking a terrible chance," Smith muttered under his breath, reaffirming an opinion he had stated several times since Shires announced his plans to open the crate and resurrect his former mentor. "After all the trouble Davidson caused out at the cemetery, I can't even imagine what *this* one might do!"

Shires blew the dirt from around a nailhead. "If you're worried about the sheriff, you needn't be. If he and his deputies had any evidence that we were even slightly involved in that sad debacle, they'd've come 'round to collect us long ago. And if they *are* watching the two of us—as you suspect—well, there's all the more reason to go ahead with this. Should they come knocking at the door now, search warrant in hand, we've got a corpse on our hands. If we bring him back, we have a visiting guest and a large, empty shipping crate burning piece by piece in the hearth."

The room was rippling with the same choking stench that Smith had first encountered inside the Taylor barn. It was an odor that, unlike most disagreeable smells, proved impossible to grow accustomed to. It offended and brought tears with each and every inhalation.

Shires hooked a nail with the claw of his hammer and pulled. The shaft came away bent in several places. "You know," he said, holding the nail up against the flickering light, "I believe you may be right about that farmer having opened this. Have a look." He tossed his partner the nail.

Smith nodded, not surprised at all, chewing some darkened sentiment like ground glass, too low for Shires to hear. He tossed the nail into a coffee can and picked a tangle of dry straw from one of the pinched seams.

They continued their work in silence. With each nail pulled, the air grew heavier, more oppressive. The stench of John Dunhill's mortal remains became a tangible thing, an element—like wind or rain—to shoulder against and endure. Moving clockwise around the crate, they had it unsealed a short time later. Shires smiled with anticipation and set down his tools. Smith did likewise and then rubbed the circulation back into his hands.

"Well now," Shires whispered across the lid, his eyes bright and restless. "Shall we have a look?" Smith nodded, resigned to his fate, and placed his palms against the rough edges. Together they lifted the lid away.

Dust was all that remained of John Dunhill, a fine, aromatic layer of moldering grit that lifted and swirled in the updraft. They breathed in bits of him and then just as quickly coughed it back out, causing the light in the basement to flicker uncertainly.

"Christ!" Smith said, spitting the deep, gray taste from his tongue. He looked inside, then at Shires. "*Where is he?*"

Shires was gazing down into the crate, only the slightest shade of expression to his face. He might have been thinking of whether to have pot roast or chicken for dinner.

"Shires? What's happened? God...I helped load that thing into the truck...it couldn't have been empty!"

Shires was staring at him strangely now, wide-eyed and unbelieving, as if Smith'd just suggested something ludicrous, that they turn themselves in to the police or burn the house flat in a wild gesture of contrition.

"*What?*" Smith said, uncomprehending. "What is it?"

A sound, liquid and slippery, issued from Shires's open mouth, and in the uneven lamplight, his face began to change. A tremor like splintering bone sounded, and he shook as if gripped by a violent seizure. His pale skin sagged like softened candle wax, and he began to fall apart. Horrified, Smith put his hands to his face and screamed against his rigid palms.

Inside the crate, the ashes were stirring, rising in perfect sympathy to Shires's disintegration, encouraging it. Shires managed to convey an agonizing grimace—lips stretched, teeth blackened—and Smith realized that his partner was laughing.

And that he, Smith, was changing too.

26

He awoke in his chair with a shout.

Footsteps creaked in the hall outside his door—hesitant, as if listening through the panel—and then receded.

The awful intensity of the dream was still upon him, pawing him with ragged feet and licking his face with its long and gritty tongue, as if the objects within the cheap room were slowly but surely losing their solidity. He wondered if this was what it was like to lose one's sanity. Events were spinning out of control, falling to pieces, and there was nothing he could do but stare helplessly as the floor threatened to drop out from under him. The police were moving in the shadows, weaving a strangling web of tripwires about the hateful town.

He had to be careful. Very, very careful.

The feeling abated somewhat as the dream took a step back, fading, and he rose stiffly from the chair, his spine cramped and sore. He put the heels of his hands against the small of his back and stretched until he heard an audible pop.

"Ahhh."

The room seemed unusually dark, and he was surprised to find that most of the day had passed him by. It was nearly five o'clock.

Time enough, he calculated, to immerse himself in a hot bath, shave, and then fry up something for dinner before he met with Shires. Almost as an afterthought, Smith crept to the window and peered down the quiet side street. The blue car, he was surprised to see, had vanished from the curb in front of the accountant's office.

Frowning, he separated the curtains to increase his field of vision, certain it was still somewhere close by, but with the exception of a lone man walking a dog, the street was empty. Smith narrowed his eyes, bringing the man under sharper scrutiny. His pace was slow and leisurely; he appeared to be an elderly man with no particular place to go. The encroaching shadows turned his face an ashen blue beneath the brim of his straw hat, making it depthless and indistinct, though to Smith he looked uncomfortably like a dead man come round to haunt him.

With a shudder, he let the curtain drop.

27

Come seven o'clock, Shires was not at The Plowman.

Glancing nervously about, Smith ordered a glass of beer and took a seat in a dim corner to wait. When the glass was gone, he began to consult his watch with greater unease and frequency. He ordered another beer, and this too disappeared, leaving interconnecting rings of condensation on the surface of the table.

He could *feel* the night coming down beyond the dark walls of the tavern, imbuing the cool air with a sharp sense of expectancy. Partly this was due to Shires (who was very seldom late) and the recent interest of the authorities in his own daily activities, but mostly it was an aching sense of intuition, a black buzz throbbing deep inside his head, warning him that everything was coming to an inescapable head.

He thought of Jonathan Taylor and then pushed the image away as if it were cold and dead.

Swallowing the last of his beer, Smith glanced at his watch, indecisive. It was imperative that he speak to Shires; that meant chancing a trip up the hill, followed or not. He rose from the table and moved cautiously to the door, easing himself slowly into the night as if to test uncertain waters.

He saw Shires's front door standing open and realized something had already gone wrong. The screen hung torn and askew on one twisted hinge, thrown out with such violence that the outer handle had left a deep scar in the clapboard siding.

The loose anxiety inside him finally found a focal point, and Smith's heart began to race, escalating toward panic. It took all of his willpower to continue toward the house, to keep himself from flying away from it as fast as his legs would carry him.

He mounted the weather-cracked steps. There was blood on the doorframe, smeared in a rough arc, and he reached out gingerly to touch it. His fingertips came away wet. Very fresh. Shires, it seemed, had been experimenting on his own, taking a dangerous gamble.

Spurred by the dream, Smith considered the crate in the basement. It was just the sort of temptation Shires would have found irresistible: the resurrection of his old mentor, a moment to hoard jealously to himself, unable to share. Smith stood at the threshold and stared into the house's dim interior, combing the shadows and listening for the slightest tick of movement.

A wind blew down from the hill's fallow crown, whispering through the fallen leaves and dry grass, but the house itself was as quiet as a vault; it was dense and swollen inside, giving back nothing but the echo of his frantic heart.

He called out weakly, winded from his climb, not expecting a reply. When none came, he stepped inside. Six paces into the room, he noticed a thin trail of spilled blood.

Damn it, Daniel! If you're dead, who do you think they'll come looking for?

He advanced toward the kitchen, which was lit by a single bulb beneath a shade of frosted glass. The trickle of blood he'd been following continued through the kitchen, beyond the utility room, and splashed down the stairway into the darkened cellar.

Smith paused, one hand on the wall to steady himself. The cellar was certainly where it would have happened.

He flipped the light switch and nothing happened; the bulb below had either burned out or been broken. Presented with the prospect of descending into darkness, Smith retrieved a flashlight from a shelf in the utility, clicked it on, and proceeded quickly down the wooden steps, not eager to be caught inside if a deputy came around to check on the house. There was a need, however, for him to see the extent of the damage and to assess what, if anything, could be done before it was discovered. Leaving town might prove the most prudent and sensible course of action, but it would be best to know what he was running from, in case he was caught or entertained thoughts of ever coming back.

As always, there was a twinge of excitement and fear as he descended into the unknown, sweeping the light cautiously ahead of him. The atmosphere, foul as it had been since the arrival of the crate, became noticeably cooler, and Smith could almost feel the weight of the earth pressing in against the rough walls. The room itself had an overwhelming quality of unfinished gray, as if it were only meant to be tolerated for brief periods at a time. It came as some surprise, then, that despite the trail of blood, the cellar turned up empty. No bodies, no crate, not even a faded stain or chalk mark on the floor to show it had once been used for something, just the smell and a few last smudges of blood remained, as if hungry ghosts had been licking the concrete floor.

He probed the far corners with the yellow beam, unconvinced his eyes weren't lying, but it was true. Either by chance or by choice, Shires was gone, leaving him cut adrift!

Smith suppressed a bitter laugh. What a fool he'd been to think that Daniel required his curt warnings and observations! Of course he'd seen the net closing and, discovering a hole, made good his escape. All without a word to his faithful confidant.

Smith felt like screaming, like stalking through the house and tearing it to pieces. Instead, his fear got the better of him. He turned and hurried up the cellar steps, through the kitchen and out the front door. The night outside was enormous and still, welcoming him like a lover.

He'd stayed in Colfax too long, Smith decided. He forced himself to slow to a walk as he reached the narrow street, clicking his boot heels. There was really nothing he needed back in his apartment, at least nothing worth risking capture for.

It was better to travel light anyway.

28

Dawn found Sheriff Lonny Cornell standing in a dry lentil field between two low hillocks as a fine brown dust blew over the black shine of his shoes. The highway ran east and west behind him, a flat gray seam. It was almost devoid of traffic at this early hour. Even so, the unexpected novelty of three department cars leaning off the grassy shoulder— lights flashing—was enough to draw a small crowd of onlookers, local farmers mostly. Grizzle-faced men and suntanned boys still rubbing the sleep out of their eyes.

Cornell did not see them. His attention was focused on the soft outline of a man beneath a plastic tarp on the ground. Twice now the chief had seen the body move, drawing its arms slowly in and out and kicking sluggishly at the soil as if to crawl away from the encroaching sunlight.

The man was Daniel Shires, and there was no question that he was dead. His head had been crushed, caved in on both sides as if pressed in a vise.

As his men combed the hillside for possible evidence—be it footprints, tire tracks, or the killing instrument—Cornell stood by the body, sketching out a preliminary report while he waited for the ambulance to arrive. The first time it had moved, the chief had been scratching a pen against his clipboard, convinced it had been his imagination. A trick of the light or the motion of the dust blowing across the fields.

The second time, there was no room for doubt; he was looking right at it. A pale hand, speckled with a dark mixture of dirt and blood, reached out from under the black tarp. The legs, outlined but still covered, kicked briefly as if swimming and then were still.

With a trembling hand, Cornell bent and peeled back a corner of the tarp. The corpse seemed surprised: eyes wide, frozen, almost popping from their bruised sockets. "The nature of its demise," the sheriff murmured unsatisfactorily to himself. Death had come upon the man suddenly, violent and without warning.

He let the plastic drop free and put it down to random nerve impulses, even though Shires had been dead for several hours now, making that explanation a flimsy bit of self-deception.

Still, far stranger things were happening around Colfax as of late.

He turned impatiently toward the highway, wondering where in hell the ambulance was. The tarp wrinkled, and he snapped his head back, as if the body were creeping up behind him, but it was only the wind playing with the corner he'd pulled free, flapping it back and forth over

Shires's misshapen head. Fifty feet away, the small crowd murmured.

Growling, Cornell barked out a name, and one of his deputies turned.

"Get these people on their way! This isn't a sideshow at the county fair!"

"Yes, sir," said Deputy Garrett. With arms outstretched, he walked toward the crowd, now spilling off the narrow shoulder, as if he intended to pick them up like dolls. "All right, folks. You heard the sheriff. Let's move these trucks out of here. Come on now—ambulance needs to get through. Give us room to work."

Grudgingly, with half-voiced groans and protests, the people began to disperse and drift back to their vehicles. One by one, at Garrett's continued insistence, motors turned sluggishly and pulled away.

Cornell bent again to secure the flapping corner and caught the ripening smell of spilled blood. "Lord Almighty..." he whispered, crouching painfully. "What have I done to deserve *this*?"

Black horseflies, slow and nearing the end of their season, lit on Shires's exposed skin, greedy to be about their work. He made a half-hearted attempt to shoo them away and tucked the fold back into place beneath the outstretched arm. He looked around and set a hardened dirt clod on top of it for good measure.

A moment or two later, the ambulance appeared from around an easterly bend. Though the cause of death was strikingly obvious, one of the pages on Cornell's clipboard was an autopsy request. Waiting beneath the courthouse in Whitman County's tiny morgue, Shiro Yahoto would be readying his tools for the anticipated procedure, polishing his scalpels and retractors, lining up his slides and microscopes to receive sections of Shires's dissected tissue.

Perhaps the flesh would move for him too. Perhaps not.

Sheriff Cornell would not be the first to make the suggestion, but he would keep his ears open, poised for the possibility.

Then perchance they would talk, or just bury him.

Quickly and quietly.

PART TWO

Samuel & Caroline: 1959

1

August 2, 1959

Sheriff Jake Garrett dialed the water temperature to cold and stepped under the stinging spray. His breath left him in a loose, shuddering gasp as his sleep-stuck eyelids flew open and his heart, never fully prepared for this, clenched into a knotted fist. He felt his scrotum thicken into leather as his testicles sought the fleeing warmth of his body. He closed his eyes and turned his face into the showerhead, feeling the night's accrual of sweat, now sour and gritty, stubbornly dissolve and slip down the swirling drain.

These showers, which he took two or three times a day, were his only relief from the unrelenting heat. Summer, having hemmed and hawed throughout June and the first two weeks of July, finally decided to get serious, and though the current heat wave was a dry one, it was exceptionally long lived and gave no hint of easing in the foreseeable future. For the third straight week now, temperatures were well above ninety, often creeping past the hundred-degree mark by noon. To Garrett, the heat was a constant press that weighed on him like sandbags and brought a ragged edge to his temper. Those bygone days of June and early July seemed like a blessing now, a lost utopia of gentle rains and mercury balanced in the mid- to upper seventies.

That was something else Garrett had noticed: whenever the season hung at extremes (be it summer or winter), folks began to act like the end of the world was just around the corner, almost visible, like a hazy spiral leaching the color and vibrancy from the world, leaving it sterile and gray. Day after day, the heaviness of the sun could hypnotize you, instilling a poisonous ennui in the bloodstream to the point where you didn't care for anything or anybody. In such a state, you might let your good sense slip and do something you couldn't imagine yourself capable of on better days: something stupid and irrevocable, sudden and violent.

The cold showers helped dampen that feeling some, but not everyone was smart enough to take them. Those who didn't cool down, find some kind of relief, became dangerous and unpredictable. Like sick animals.

And Jake Garrett had to spend his days among them.

2

The day began early, as soon as he walked into the small suite of offices allotted him along the west side of the courthouse. A slip of pink paper was taped to his office door. Polly Stratford's careful, slanted hand informed him what had happened.

While You Were Out:
   Jake,
Jonathan Taylor out on Highway 195 called at 7:17 this morning. Twins Samuel and Caroline missing. Report under your door and Deputy Geotting gone out to farm. Will call you when he has a statement from the Taylors.

Garrett pulled the sheet off the door. *Two missing children*, he reflected darkly, standing before his locked office. That meant a long day in the sun, organizing a search party and beating through the fields, continuing into the sweltering night if the daylight didn't turn them out.

He closed his eyes for a moment and thought of his shower, the cold serenity of the endless spray.

Already the heat had gotten under his clothes. His undershirt was glued to his back, and his shorts were bunched up from the drive into town. With a weary sigh, he unlocked his office using an impressive ring of keys and stepped inside. His shoe slid across a small pile of paperwork—each sheet screaming for his immediate attention—that had been deposited through the bottom crack in the seven or so hours he'd managed to get away. He reached for the light switch and flipped it up. The bulb flashed like lightning overhead, snuffing itself out on the fresh surge of current.

Standing in the gloomy half light (his office had a window, of course, but it looked out at the side of the jail, depressing and gray), the sheriff could feel the inadequate breeze of the central air conditioning against his tacky skin, as warm to the touch as the day outside.

"Polly!" he said, grimacing as his agitation tracked a path in pinpricks up his back. He could hear the brisk *clip-clop* of her heels on the polished floor tiles, winding in from the front lobby.

Her solid silhouette appeared at the end of the darkened hallway, rimmed with white sunlight. "Sheriff?"

"I've got a fried bulb in here. See if you can't round me up a new one."

"All right." She turned to go.

"Oh, Polly?" He tried to sift her expression out of the soft glare but found he couldn't; probably it would have told him to round up his own goddamned bulb. He smiled. "This damn heat. We got any coffee yet?"

"Coming right up, Sheriff."

Thirty minutes later, driving west along 195 toward the Taylor farm, Jake Garrett tried to recall everything he knew or had heard, be it truth or hearsay, about the Taylor family. Aside from their general reclusiveness (which wasn't really so uncommon among his more rural constituents), the most remarkable fact he could readily summon concerned the children themselves: supposedly they were mentally retarded, so profoundly so that they did not attend public school, or any other kind for that matter. This bit of knowledge had come to him by way of Earl Abramson, the postal courier assigned to the Taylors' route.

The two, according to Abramson, were fraternal twins and kept close to one another as twins often did, as if they shared a bond which no one else (aside from other twins) could understand. Usually they were kept inside, out of sight (though physically they looked no different from normal children), except during the hot summer months, when they could be seen wandering about the large yard. Reports of their behavior (this from half a dozen sources) ranged from empty and unresponsive to downright wild. Garrett, knowing how some folks tended to exaggerate, especially when it came to something they did not understand, took these reports with a grain of salt and made up his mind *not* to make up his mind until he'd seen them for himself. More than likely, they would display a wide range of moods and behaviors, which would make them no different in that respect from any other given child.

What Garrett could not guess, however, and was curious to learn, was what the Taylors thought of their children. Were they inclined to be tolerant and loving, as the law and nature dictated they should? Or did their attentions, amplified by disgust or resentment, veer more toward cruelty and abuse?

Since he was the man in charge of solving their disappearance, the knowledge would provide an invaluable framework in shaping the investigation. God knew that some children didn't have to be retarded or even delinquent to suffer.

He told himself to keep an open mind. The Taylors might be reclusive, perhaps even secretive when it came to their brood, but they'd called out for help, and he meant to do his best by them, just as any taxpayer had a right to expect.

Rounding a bend in the road, the house came into view. It was a standard two-story affair, white with green trim and a large red barn beside it. Unlike a great many of the homesteads he'd passed on the way out, there were no rusting hulks of automotive steel or farming implements left to rot out in the yard, no clumps of dead trees ready to fall over in the next strong wind. All in all, Taylor appeared to run a trim and respectable business.

Garrett signaled right and slowed where the gravel drive reached out to meet the highway.

3

Jonathan Taylor, to whom Garrett had spoken by telephone not twenty minutes earlier, was waiting beside the wide, dirt cul-de-sac that formed the terminus of the drive, hands in his pockets, dressed in a long-sleeve flannel shirt and heavy overalls despite the climbing heat of the day. His posture seemed to indicate that he was handling the disappearance of his children with dead-calm indifference.

Garrett stepped out of his cruiser into the solid press of the day. Offering Taylor his hand and a firm shake, he introduced himself in his official capacity and offered a brief word of condolence on the business that had brought him out.

Taylor returned a dry shrug. The story he had to tell was simple enough.

The twins were actually his niece and nephew, though their stay on the farm had always been indefinite, he said, alluding vaguely to some family problem back east. An incapacity of their real parents to properly care for them. Always prone to wandering, Samuel and Caroline had apparently gotten outside during the night while he and his wife were sleeping. Pru had been the first out of bed, and on her way to the kitchen to start breakfast, she'd found the door to the side yard standing wide open. The house had been very quiet then, and the first thing she'd thought of, of course, was the children.

Taylor paused and cast a glance toward the barn. "I guess you've probably heard tell that the two of them aren't much like normal kids. The truth of the matter is that they're retarded, both of them, and have been since birth."

Garrett nodded. "Tell me, Mr. Taylor," he said, squinting against the slant of the sun, "is there any reason you can think of why the children would...well, just up and leave in the middle of the night? It seems to me that most kids that age are scared of the dark."

Taylor shook his head and shuffled his heavy boots in the dirt. "No, but like I said, Samuel and Caroline aren't like normal kids, so you can't put much reason behind anything they do. Once in a while, they'd spark to something...try to get outside or at something shiny that Pru put out of their reach, but on the whole there isn't much sense to be had. Usually they just wander from room to room, making their noises but keeping out of too much trouble. Even trouble takes a certain amount of imagination, I guess."

The sheriff took out a pencil stub and scribbled a quick note to himself. He looked up. "Have they ever tried to get out of the house at night?"

"I suppose so," Taylor said. "Sometimes we'd catch them messing with the doors or the locks after we'd turned in; but you have to understand, Sheriff, that they're always moving about the house. They don't understand that when it gets dark out, you're supposed to lay down and shut your eyes until morning." He shook his head in apparent frustration. "They'd just go and go until they dropped dead asleep wherever they happened to be, and never mind what the clock said. So although you could put them to bed at a decent hour, they'd pop back up just as many times as you cared to say otherwise."

Garrett nodded. "Sounds like they need parents with a great deal of patience."

Taylor glanced back, as if Garrett were implying something, then stared off down the drive. "Well, Pru and I try our best."

Out on the highway, eighty yards distant, a slow convoy of two pickups and a combine rolled by, flashing its orange lights.

"The truth be told, Mr. Taylor, I haven't had much experience dealing with this sort of disability...so what I'd like to do right off is get some idea how well the children function." He rolled his wrist and forearm in an expository manner. "What skills do they possess...do they talk or otherwise communicate? Run or climb? That sort of thing."

"All right," Taylor said, nodding. "I'll tell you what I can."

"Let's start at the top then. Do they talk? Repeat simple words?"

"No," Taylor answered. "About the only sounds that come out of them are these little shrieks and groans...like monkeys who're shut up where they don't want to be. Now don't get me wrong on that, Sheriff. I'm not saying they were penned up or anything; it's just that they were like that by nature."

Garrett scribbled against his notepad. "How did you and your wife communicate with them?"

Taylor wrinkled his sunburned brow as if in thought. "We talk to them...but more like you might talk to a horse or a dog...not really expecting them to understand much more than the tone. Pru has a few hand signals that she uses to get them to do what she wants. But then you can train a dog to do tricks to hand signals."

Garrett took note of the way Taylor kept comparing his children to animals. "Mmm, from what I've heard so far, I gather they get around fairly well on their own...but for the purposes of the immediate search, can they run for any length of time? Climb fences? Jump ditches?"

"No," he said. "I never saw them do any of that."

After a brief, final notation, Garrett snapped his pad shut. "Thank you, Mr. Taylor. That's enough to get started. I have one of my senior deputies forming a search party, and they should start arriving any time. My impression—the case being that they wandered away on their own—is that they can't have gotten too far, so with a little luck, we'll try to have them back to you, safe and sound, before nightfall. I won't trouble your wife just yet, but I think it would be a good idea if the two of you made a *thorough* search of your house once again. Check all the little nooks and crannies you might have missed the first time. You say that when they sleep, they drop wherever they happen to be; keep in mind that may not have been in plain sight or in a place which was otherwise usual for them. Look *behind* things, *underneath* them, anywhere they might have crawled with a little persistence. Check your barn here and all your outbuildings. That way, I can have my men concentrating on the fields and you won't have a lot of strangers tramping about your house." The sheriff paused and turned a slow, pivoting circle in the packed dirt drive, tracing the low, undulating sweep of the surrounding hills with his eyes. "Be a good idea for you or your wife to call up the neighbors," he said over his shoulder. "Let them know what's happening so they can keep an eye out too." He came to a stop facing Taylor again.

"All right," the Taylor said, raising a lazy finger to scratch his neck. All in all, he didn't appear overly anxious to get the search underway, and Garrett had to seriously wonder about that. Perhaps he'd already given the children up as dead—tearlessly, as one might concede a lost cow or sheep to disease or natural predators. Certainly, with the two of them gone, a great burden would be lifted from his shoulders. On the other hand, it was possible—no, make that *probable*—that Jonathan Taylor was one of those flint-faced men who kept a tight rein on his emotions, especially in the presence of other men. Or men of authority, like Garrett.

The sheriff decided to table that debate for another time; it was too hot to stand around in a field arguing with oneself, and at the moment he had more pressing matters to devote his attention to, like finding a couple of lost kids before the shadows all shrank to nothing and the heat *really* became unbearable. He considered what it must be like for them, without shade or water, lost in an ocean of still, dry wheat.

Glancing at the green and white cruiser parked in front of his, Garrett wondered for the first time what his deputy was up to. So far he had yet to see hide or hair of him. Unusual, as Alan Geotting was generally right there to meet him with a preliminary sketched out on his dog-eared notebook, ready to rattle it off at first glance. Garrett frowned, turning back to Taylor.

"I believe that one of my deputies is somewhere hereabouts?" he inquired with a raised eyebrow.

Taylor grunted what seemed like a scornful affirmation. His long, pointed chin took a quick stab toward the farmhouse. "I left him inside, talking to Pru," Taylor said laconically. "I believe she was getting up some coffee. Go on in and help yourself if you like, Sheriff."

"I appreciate the offer, Mr. Taylor, but my search team should be along directly, and I'd like to draw up their assignments as soon as possible." He gazed down the empty stretch of highway with visible impatience. Already, waves of heat were rising off its flat, gray surface, distorting the far shoulder to a shimmering brown laced with weedy greens and golds. "And if you should happen to see Deputy Geotting on your way back in, I'd be grateful if you'd tell him I'm here."

4

Alan Geotting reminded Garrett of a balding and scowling bear, albeit a good-natured one. Had he not joined the Whitman County Sheriff's Department four years ago, it pleased Garrett to imagine that Geotting might have had a fine career as a professional wrestler. At twenty-eight, he was six feet four inches tall and carried upwards of 275 pounds on his squarish frame, managing somehow not to look overweight; just the sort of man to make a lasting impression, particularly when climbing out of a flashing cruiser at 2:10 in the morning along a lonely stretch of starlit interstate. His small ears stuck out like jug handles, and a matting of wiry black hair grew out of the collar and the cuffs of his uniform blouse. The deep, sleepy lines on his face suggested time spent in serious hibernation. This impression, however, was misleading; the man could move like a decent running back when called upon or provoked. Anyone who worked with him for any length of time soon came to realize that Alan Geotting possessed not a shallow or brutish nature but rather a quick and pleasant wit in addition to a fairly sharp intellect. It just took some time to come out.

Garrett had hired him with the late shift—weekends and holidays—in mind, relegating him to handling belligerents and drunks, responding to domestic quarrels and parking lot brawls. But Geotting soon distinguished himself as a thorough and insightful investigator, and Garrett had promoted him accordingly. Regular hours and tolerable duties.

Still, Garrett mused, Alan would have been a terror in black tights and lace-up boots. Perhaps a waxed moustache, with his head shaven clean.

Now Geotting bobbed toward him over the Taylors' spotty yard, squinting from sunlight and perspiration.

Beneath the arms of his olive-green blouse, dark circles were beginning to show; by afternoon they would sag halfway down to his belt.

"Morning, Sheriff," Geotting called out apologetically, as if he had let his boss down for failing to present himself—at attention and with a full briefing standing by— as Garrett's car slowed to a stop at the end of the drive. "I didn't hear you drive up."

With a borrowed mug of black coffee in hand, the deputy searched for his notebook, juggling the hot cup, and Garrett allowed himself a small, bemused smile, as if watching a familiar routine, endearing and well rehearsed. Punchinello, his coffee, and his notebook. Very soon, something both funny and sad would happen unless Garrett intervened.

"Here, Alan, let me hold that for you before you scald yourself," Garrett offered, taking the cup carefully from his hand.

"Thanks, Sheriff," Geotting said with a grin, fumbling against the awkward hindrance of his gun belt. "I know I had it with me inside…" It turned up in his back pocket, creeping up toward his waistband. "Ah-ha."

Geotting flipped to the day's ongoing proceedings, all kept in careful shorthand, and began the report with a recap of Taylor's theory of late-night escape. The sheriff cut him off impatiently, more interested in what Prudence Taylor had to say on the subject. The picture distilled from Garrett's chat with her husband was that *she* did most of the day-to-day wrangling and serious care while *he* looked for ways to stay shy of it. She would know what attracted them (having spent her days keeping those objects out of their reach) and could probably hazard a better guess as to which direction her two birds would fly if suddenly freed.

The deputy flipped ahead three or four pages, found a pause, and began to read:

"'Prudence Taylor present during initial questioning regarding the disappearance of Samuel and Caroline,'" Alan read, "'though unusually subdued. Allowed husband to respond to all questions without comment. Gave only perfunctory replies when addressed directly. Busied herself with small tasks throughout interview. Glanced over at husband in reaction to certain questions—most notably one concerning the adjacent barn—but did not voice thoughts or contradictions. State of both parents flat and unemotional. Mr. Taylor displayed defensive attitude at times; Mrs. Taylor unresponsive and obviously more deeply affected. Observed her staring off blankly much of the time, as if lost. Offered to summon medical aid for her at one point, which Mr. Taylor rejected. She volunteered to make coffee, and Mr. Taylor took the opportunity to excuse himself from the kitchen.'"

Geotting closed his book and tucked it back away. "He just now came back to tell me you were here." Glancing over his shoulder, he added in a voice not much above a whisper: "I've been sitting in there with her the whole time, and I got to tell you, Sheriff, it's kinda creepy."

Garrett narrowed his eyes. "Creepy? In what way?"

The tall deputy chewed his lip and turned a hesitant heel in the dirt. "Well, it's sorta hard to put into words…" Again the backward glance, as if the house might be creaking on its foundations, straining forward to listen. Garrett noticed for the first time that all the second-story windows were shuttered and latched, though there hadn't been a windstorm worth a spit come through in three or four weeks.

"It's all right, Alan; take your time," Garrett said, drifting back.

Geotting's large, round face furrowed at the task, again giving that false impression of a slow intellect, and his hands curled themselves into fists, white with barbs of black hair at the knuckles. Garrett caught the undiluted odor of frustration, itchy and unpleasant, bleeding sharply from Geotting's pores.

"This isn't the first time we've come across something like this," the deputy began, gesturing at the roadway as if it existed only in the past, or were a path to some event which did. "You expect them to be upset...either bawling and out of their minds with grief or screaming at you to get out and start searching, you know?"

The sheriff nodded.

Geotting inched closer, frowning. "*She's* not like that at all. It's almost as if she *knows* she isn't going to get them back!" he said, shaking his head. "I mean, you could tell in the way she sat down after her husband left the room. Everything just drained out of her, all at once, like a balloon that's had all the air let out." He exhaled loudly, his broad shoulders drooping. "I'll tell you something else... If there's anything closer to sitting in a room with a corpse, I sure don't want to know what it is!"

The sheriff looked back to the farmhouse, certain that he could see the oval smudge of Taylor's face watching the two of them from behind one of the downstairs windows. The kitchen, he decided.

"I asked her a couple more questions," Geotting said. "Small talk, really. Nothing too demanding—just to get a response out of her—but all she did was stare down at the table as if it might be kinda nice to be made out of wood instead of flesh and bone. *Seriously.*"

Garrett still had one eye on the window, though the pale spot had faded back some. "Maybe I ought to go in and have a few words with her."

Geotting took a sharp breath. "I don't know, Sheriff. Like I said, the way it stands now...she doesn't think she's ever going to see those kids again, at least not in this world."

Garrett looked up at his deputy with a thoughtful, almost serene, expression. He was about to say something, but then Geotting's dark, brown eyes glanced down the highway, attracted by the appearance of a rag-tag line of cars and pickup trucks. There was a department cruiser at the head. He nodded over Garrett's shoulder and hitched up his belt.

"Here come the men."

5

Jonathan Taylor stood over the kitchen sink, almost touching the window with his long, sunburned nose. He scowled as six or eight vehicles broke from the highway and beat a brown cloud of dust to the end of the driveway. The sheriff and his deputy stood to meet them, no longer casting shadowy looks at the house as if they suspected the twins were inside and that to search anywhere else would be a waste of time. For today, however, they would content themselves with picking through the fields and folds of the surrounding countryside, determined to make a good show of it. It was an election year, after all.

As the dust shifted and settled, Taylor saw upwards of a dozen men gather loosely around the hood of the sheriff's cruiser. Dogs barked excitedly, straining at their leashes to run free over the fields.

A large map was unfolded, and the knot of men closed in around it, drawing up their plans in secret. In pantomime.

Jonathan sighed against the glass and tipped back on his heels. In the dust-worn shadows behind him, his wife pressed her face against her arms and continued her rapid descent into the black belly of the abyss.

He turned toward her, still scowling.

How long had he seen this day coming? *A long time*, he thought. Five years. All the way back to the beginning; even then, that first day after he'd given Smith his cursed crate, the twins had stirred an uneasy mix of emotions in his gut.

A horrible dread and longing, side by side…

Like unnatural twins.

6

Jonathan Taylor recognized very early on that something was profoundly wrong with the twins: a coldness and vacancy that fell far outside his realm of familiarity or experience. Pru accepted them unconditionally and without reserve, with all of their peculiarities intact, but for Jonathan, it didn't come that easily.

The most obvious difference was that they never laughed or cried, nor did they speak or babble nonsense as babies do; indeed, except for the occasional moan or hoarse yell, they were unnervingly quiet.

Secondly, they carried a strange odor that no amount of soap could scrub away. It was a dampish smell: gray as bilge water; unnoticeable at times but at others almost suffocating. When he first held them in his arms, Jonathan thought it seemed to stand out on their breath more than their skin, as if it were coming from *inside*.

Throughout the day, the twins—whom they had christened Samuel and Caroline—would watch them with slack, stony expressions. Their pale faces lingered in the background as Pru set about the day's routine of housework and mothering, and if Jonathan happened to enter the room, their eyes would shift mechanically, attracted by the motion. This sensation unnerved him to the point where he soon found a wealth of ready excuses to be out of the house. Being shut in with those blank stares, which never changed whether they were being rocked, fed, read to, or bathed, was a prospect too awful to endure.

As he explained to Garrett, they wandered about the house both night and day, though this was an allowance that Jonathan never became fully accustomed to. The scrape of a bare foot along the hall carpet or a soft collision with a wall was sufficient to rouse him from slumber, and while it was true that he had never been a particularly sound sleeper, ever since the twins had come along he found his efforts in this essential area steadily eroding, until he came to resemble a man in prolonged combat. He dozed at odd times of the day, wherever he happened to be, with his eyes half-open and his senses tuned to the slightest aberration.

As a boy, Jonathan had once had an exceptionally vivid dream in which noisy, senseless monsters had been turned loose in the pitch-darkened house. What he was able to see of them was vague and inconclusive—large, shaggy things creeping along the dim threshold of his vision—but they made noises as they moved. At times they sounded far away, as if they were quietly tearing apart the kitchen; other times they scraped along the hall and pushed right into his bedroom, leaning over the bed and watching him to make sure he was asleep.

Now the dream seemed premonitory, the monsters smaller but every bit as senseless.

To say that their sleep was irregular was like hinting that war was unpleasant. Sometimes they slept only a matter of thirty minutes or so and would wake fully charged and ready to go again for hours or even days. Conversely, they could fall into a sleep that was deep and unshakable, at times breaking the forty-eight-hour mark. During these days, nothing could be done to rouse them; no sooner would Pru have them on their feet than they'd sink back to the floor, fast asleep and as dead heavy as their forty-five-pound bodies would allow.

The practice of repeatedly putting the twins to bed at what seemed a reasonable hour had long since fallen by the wayside. No sooner would the bedroom door click shut than one or both of them would throw aside their blankets—as if they were meant to be crude restraints—and slip out of bed. Bumping the walls and furnishings in the darkened room, they would eventually happen upon the door handle and, after repeated attempts to get it to turn, release themselves into the silent, moonlit rooms. It became a fierce battle of wills for a period, but in the end, Samuel and Caroline won out. You just couldn't match that kind of single-mindedness, so Jonathan and Pru had to be content with locking the outside doors with security chains (placed up high, out of reach) and letting them be while he and Pru kept their natural hours, or tried to.

All throughout the dead hours, he would listen to their shuffling footfalls, the agitated hiss of their exhalations, the sudden, hair-raising shriek of some madness that drove them so relentlessly.

For the first few weeks after their arrival, Jonathan would wake to find them pacing the close confines of his bedroom or sometimes just standing there in the dark, breathing coarsely through open mouths as they watched the two of them sleep, which unnerved him even more. Once, he started out of a nightmare to find Samuel's vacant black eyes scant inches from his own, and he screamed out in fright, awakening Prudence. "Get them out! Get them the hell out of here!" he roared, causing her to flinch while neither of the twins so much as batted an eye.

The following day, he fixed a lock on the door. Thereafter, they wandered outside his bedroom but never without testing the door to see if he'd forgotten to lock it.

He never did.

7

The sky carried a faint haze, washed out and defeated from the constant bombardment of the sun, and the clouds that formed in that thin ether were wispy and frail, like tufts of bone-colored hair smoothed over a dying man's skull. Against the rolling hills, the trees stood heavy and tired, without the slightest breeze to lift their burden, and cicadas droned happily in the matchstick grass.

Jonathan poured himself another cup of coffee—acidic and bitter from the bottom of the percolator—and watched his driveway with renewed interest as the maps were refolded. The search party was breaking down into smaller pieces, shouldering backpacks and stowing canteens.

Then, alone or in widely spaced pairs, the men took to the fields.

He thought he would eat (it had been hours since his slight and hastily eaten breakfast) and then go out to the barn. The sheriff would want to have a look inside, despite what he'd said about keeping out of their way.

Jonathan rinsed his coffee cup and set it in the basin. He went to the refrigerator and opened the door.

Eating had been a skill that Samuel and Caroline had been able to develop to some degree of proficiency. Although messy eaters, they were able to get down enough calories to sustain themselves. Of course, they'd never been much on chewing, so everything had to be ground down to an unappetizing pap. But over the years they had learned to use spoons to get it from their plates to their laps, then from their laps to their mouths: quite a feat considering Pru had started off spoon-feeding them three meals a day. Gradually they had taken an interest and began to work impatiently with their hands, scooping up the lukewarm mush and literally *pressing* it into the dark cavities of their hungry mouths. As the seasons slowly passed, Pru got them familiar with spoons.

Jonathan had watched this with a mixture of feelings. He was proud of his wife for what she had been able to accomplish yet at the same time regarded the whole undertaking with a sense of abject futility. It just seemed a damned waste of time and effort. They ate every meal, after all, with the same lack of expression they applied to life in general. Oh, they ate all right, but without any preference that he could see, and more than once he'd wondered if those slack, pale faces would even register a change if he served them up plates of lukewarm pig shit instead of mush.

Watching them eat could be downright revolting. Enough to make a man lose his appetite.

In fact, it wasn't long before *everything* about the twins revolted him.

This was not a feeling he felt compelled to share, nor one he was particularly proud of, but deep down in the bedrock of his consciousness, under a pile of loose shale (which occasionally slipped out of place), Jonathan knew there was something wrong with the twins that the term "retarded" didn't even begin to touch. He'd done some reading on the subject in the years since they'd taken the two of them in, and though there were countless classifications, etiologies and syndromes, all conveniently lumped under the general heading of "Mental Retardation," there was a great deal about Samuel and Caroline— physically, behaviorally—which was no nearer the established parameters of "retardation" than it was to being "normal."

For one, they never seemed to age.

This in particular disturbed him, because *everything* in nature aged. Neither of the twins, however, seemed to subscribe to that theory, for they showed no inclination whatsoever to grow out of their shoes or their clothes like other children. By all rights, in the five years he and Pru had been buying them clothes, they should have been going through children's sizes on the average of one or two a year. But they weren't. When it came time to replace some worn-out article, they always, despite trying on larger garments, came out wearing the same sizes they'd gone in with. And as time passed, this fact bothered him more and more.

There was also, despite the temperature or season, a pronounced *coldness* about them. Their bodies seemed to generate very little in the way of surface heat, so that when you happened to pick one up or steer the other to the table, it brought to mind the sensation, repulsive as it was, of handling meat. Naturally, this had been a cause for concern to such new parents and, invariably, a rectal thermometer would be called in for consultation. It always read low, but never alarmingly so. Never below ninety-seven degrees.

And their breath…it was always bad, so bad that nothing—not toothpaste, not mouthwash, not even baking soda—could freshen it. To Jonathan, it smelled like a dead mouse in a pop bottle: something rotting down inside of them.

There were a hundred or more other things, each just as disturbing in its own right, and each just as unheard of or undocumented in the books he studied.

Strangest of all, though, were the sudden and inexplicable episodes of digging.

During certain times of the year, usually the late months of summer but sometimes as early as April, Samuel and Caroline would try to dig holes in everything with their bare hands. These exasperating episodes would last anywhere from two days to a week at a stretch and, as with almost every notion that wormed its way into their heads, the twins could not be distracted from their impulse for neither heaven nor earth. When they were outside, they dug into the lawn and the flowerbeds; when they were inside, they would rake and claw at the carpet or linoleum until their nails cracked and their fingertips bled. Wincing with frustration, either he or Prudence would scream "enough!" and physically restrain them. Usually this meant tying them to chairs or their beds until the urge was gone, and, even restrained, they would clutch and grab at the seats or the bedcovers, in the grip of something too powerful or deeply ingrained to be switched off. Jonathan knew from his reading that humans were said to be born without instincts, just a few basic reflexes, which only made him more uneasy.

Over time, he began to think of the twins as possessed, or at least influenced by something he didn't understand. An urge or purpose, senseless to his eyes, that slipped inside their small bodies for a time and then just as mysteriously went away, leaving the two of them as cold and empty as it had found them. Condemned once again to mindless roaming.

At any rate, he'd never accepted them in his heart as his own or allowed himself to become attached to them. And unlike normal children, he couldn't foresee a time—be it ten, twenty, or even fifty years hence—when they might leave the nest and strike out on their own. Their reluctance to age seemed to confirm this.

And naturally, over the slow course of years, his mind turned to thoughts of ridding himself of them.

The trick, he decided, would be not only in fooling the authorities that their disappearance or demise had been a tragic accident but in turning his wife to this conclusion as well, for as strange and repulsive as they were to him, Pru *loved* little Samuel and Caroline, loved them very dearly in spite of all their confounding behaviors. In fact, she actually seemed to prefer them to normal children. Every passing year she became more attached, more emotionally dependent on the twins, though damned if he could see what they ever gave her in return.

Given their condition, he mused, the chance of an early death by accident, chronic illness, or predisposition was entirely possible, likely even. But that wasn't sure enough nor soon enough to suit Jonathan.

By the summer of 1959, a loose but workable scheme had come to mind.

All that remained was the will to see it through.

8

The initial results of the search were, in a word, disappointing.

The area covered was fairly easygoing since, for the most part, it was treeless; nor were there any briars or thick tangles of underbrush to push and hack through. No drop-offs or ravines, no rivers or streams. What it was, however, was miles and miles of rolling topsoil, hundreds of feet deep in places, arranged in a vast and frozen sea. There were dips and rises, tucks and folds. The searchers trudged up one hillock and down the next, never seeing more than the neighboring rises and a gentle, brown hollow or two from any given vantage. The only constant was the towering blue sky peering down from above. In short, there were a million places to hide without trying at all. The only real landmarks were Steptoe Butte and, far to the northeast, the blue mountains of northern Idaho, which rose off the land like a natural border.

By early afternoon, with the temperature hovering a degree or two above a hundred, two local crop dusters were enlisted in the growing effort, and they began to spiral out from the farm, searching ever-widening sectors by air. Neighboring farms, totaling about a dozen, were contacted by two deputies. The owners were asked to look over their immediate grounds and outbuildings (or extend permission for the deputies to do so) in hopes of uncovering the missing twins.

The radius of the search area was increased by five miles. Still, nothing turned up. Not the slightest sign or indication the children had ever left the farm, which struck

Garrett as decidedly odd. They weren't escaped felons, after all, desperate fugitives doing all they could to eliminate their tracks. They were kids and barely that, just clever enough, he supposed, to put one foot in front of the other to keep themselves from falling.

When he closed his tired eyes and tried to imagine their flight, what invariably came to mind were toy soldiers, the kind you wound up with a key and let roam about the room. The paths they would take would be lazy and incidental, based more on the peculiarities of topography than any real destination. They would be just as likely to turn in circles as to hold a straight bearing. Eventually, though, they had to wind down.

Night fell, and he called in his men, carrying the news to the Taylors like a dead dog wrapped in burlap.

After three days of the same, Garrett was forced to entertain darker scenarios. Two came to mind right away, as if they had been waiting there all along, clamoring for his attention, begging to be let loose and run.

The first was that the twins had been picked up by someone along the highway and effectively removed from the search area, someone who hadn't made it his or her immediate business to notify the proper authorities and therefore could not be presumed to have the twins' best interests in mind.

The second scenario was that they had encountered the Latah Canal, eleven miles north of the farmhouse, and promptly drowned in its swift, brown waters. Despite all warnings, it happened once every two or three years.

Come the fourth day of the search, Garrett called in divers to check the key points along the canal, focusing on the slanted gratings where the wide bed met the roadways or dove briefly underground. He assigned them also to check the numerous outflow junctions, where water was diverted to the fields. Those were the places that bodies usually caught. The effort, however, proved as fruitless as every other strategy considered up to that point. Samuel and Caroline Taylor had, for all practical purposes, slipped silently and mysteriously off the face of the earth.

After a full week of beating the fields with no results, not even the slimmest lead, Garrett began to divert his men back to their regular duties. An APB remained in effect in case they should turn up in some neighboring district, but it was Garrett's personal and unspoken opinion that they had indeed been abducted and were either being held prisoner (for motives he didn't care to think too much about) or were already dead and buried in graves that would never be found.

A third scenario surfaced in idle moments, but he didn't give it much credence. Until, that is, about a week later, when the twins were found by the same man who'd reported them missing.

9

"Where are they, Jonathan?" Jake Garrett inquired after a brief hello. "Will you show me, please?"

"This way, Sheriff," Taylor said, as morose as ever, turning toward the fields behind his house. The sun had set while Garrett was en route to the farm, but the heat was still uncomfortable; the bodies would not be pleasant to be near after such a long stretch of weather, and Garrett wasn't looking forward to looking at their small faces, corrupted by death and the high summer.

Overhead, the brightest stars poked holes in the thin twilight, and the surrounding hillocks—burned into his memory over the past two weeks—settled into a deepening blue, merging slowly together. It fanned a sour spark of defeat in him; this would have been about the time he would have had to halt the search on any given day, and the association hadn't yet had time to fade.

Garrett switched on the large flashlight he had taken from the trunk of his car to better negotiate the furrows and ruts along the way. He had a smaller one tucked inside his belt as well.

"You need a light up there?" he called to Taylor's broad back.

"Nope," Jonathan replied without turning. "I guess I know the way well enough."

They walked up and down gentle folds of stubbled topsoil; the going was slow and difficult on the ankles. After about twenty minutes, Garrett's legs began to stiffen with charley horses, and his breath came with greater effort. They topped a rise and found four elm trees perched upon the cusp of the adjacent hill, little more than silhouettes against the falling night. Taylor came to an abrupt halt. Garrett was almost panting by now as ribbons of sweat ran freely down his forehead, but the jaunt hardly seemed to affect Taylor. He turned in the faint starlight and pointed down into the darkened bowl-shaped declivity.

"They're down there, Sheriff. Straight down to the bottom." The farmer paused, his expression heavily lined in the glow of Garrett's flashlight. "You'll pardon me if I don't go with you. I don't imagine you'll have any trouble finding them."

"Of course," Garrett said with a nod, still finding his breath. "I understand that this is difficult." Actually, he had no idea what the man was feeling, if anything at all.

He left Taylor to wait and started carefully down the slope, sweeping the powerful beam of his light right and left across the dry stubble. He picked up a faint trail to his left and followed it down. As he neared the bottom of the hollow, the first faint tendrils of human decay curled about him, growing hardier and more thorny with each step. The dip, it seemed, formed a perfect inversion in the stock-still weather, keeping this warm bubble of rot down close to its bosom, guarding it jealously like a lover.

Then there they were, caught inside the yellow circle of light: two small figures huddled together in the rough chaff, dark and swollen from the heat.

His first thought, before anything else, was that there was no way his search could have missed them. Then Garrett felt his dinner start to rise as the details became more apparent. Neither he nor Taylor, the truth be known, had been the first to find them. First had been the insects— rabid and hungry in the high summer heat—and then the birds, stealing away all the soft pieces.

He bent over, hands upon his knees, as the light illuminated a tight circle at his feet. Broken stalks and cracked, brown earth. He was not a squeamish man, but there was something in the outlines of those pathetic remains, so lost and lonely, that affected him deeply. Perhaps it was their age and the sad, fragile way the bodies seemed to cling to one another; whatever it was, it totaled more than he could take at the moment. At the same time, he was conscious of Taylor's brooding presence atop the hill behind him and was not particularly eager to put on a display of weakness for the man's silent amusement. Better to turn back to the twins and let the sight wash through him. Swallow it down like raw liquor or bitter medicine.

He crouched and circled about them for a full ten minutes, inhaling their decay and memorizing each new angle, waiting until he felt in control of himself again. Then he snapped off the light and followed the stars back up the hill.

When they returned to the farmhouse, Garrett telephoned the coroner and his own front desk. Within an hour, the fields were crawling again with lights and men.

10

To his frustration and disappointment, the autopsies gave Garrett absolutely nothing he might use to build a case against the Taylors. In both instances, cause of death was attributed to shock and severe dehydration, which had caused a shutdown of the vital organs—all of which dovetailed nicely with their story. Given the extreme heat of the days in question, coupled with the inherent vulnerability of the victims, there wasn't a judge in the world who would rule in his favor against the grieving Taylors, not without solid evidence to the contrary, which he didn't have. He had only a gut feeling or intuition, which would fare no better in a court of law than tea leaves or tarot cards. So, barring any further developments or disclosures, history would record that Samuel and Caroline Taylor, profoundly retarded and incapable of acting in their own best interests, had carelessly wandered out to the fields and died there of sunstroke and dehydration.

Garrett, on the other hand, was left with that first image of the twins in his flashlight beam—a memory that stubbornly resisted time and fading—and the bitter knowledge that Samuel and Caroline had not been lying in that open hollow for two weeks, skillfully evading the most thorough search Whitman County had seen in a good many years. They had been *placed* there, perhaps far into the hunt or, likelier still, after it was over, when the fields had cleared and the excitement had been dimmed by disappointment. Garrett was certain of it.

As a last ditch effort, and allowing for some measure of guilt to come into play, he went back to the Taylor farm several days later and spoke with Prudence Taylor. It was a difficult and uncomfortable interview, conducted over a stale cup of coffee in an ill-lit kitchen which was, by now, showing serious signs of neglect. Dirty dishes sat in precarious mounds in and around the sink, and the scorched smell of cooking grease hung over their heads like a storm cloud, imparting a fatty mist over every surface. Lurking below this, something else was moldering in a dark corner of the pantry or behind the refrigerator—a grim thing he couldn't quite put a name to. A smell like desperation or suicide.

As for Prudence herself, there was an unpleasantness lingering about her as well. She was dressed—covered, really, then cinched tight about the waist—in an old flannel housecoat, frayed and dirty about the edges. It looked as if she and it hadn't parted company in a good many days. Her face was slack and haggard, her brown hair limp and unbrushed. Garrett was sure that she hadn't had a bath (or even a good dunking) in at least a week.

The interview, such that it was, was mercifully brief. The woman spoke in an infectious lethargy, and even then hardly above a whisper. Garrett found himself frequently leaning forward to catch some trailing reply and then, as his hands caught the table—waxy and dead with food grease and fingerprints—sinking back in revulsion. It hardly mattered; Prudence Taylor had completed her transformation into the parrot he had seen emerging two weeks ago. She repeated the same story as her husband, and interestingly enough, in many of the same words and phrases. To Garrett, it was like hearing two slightly different versions of the same well-rehearsed speech, though with her it was even less convincing, if one could imagine that.

With a sigh, the sheriff closed his notebook and let her return to the darkness of her bedroom.

He met Jonathan on the way out, who was none too pleased to see him.

"It seems to me that the sheriff's department ought to have better things to do than go pouring salt in the wounds of a grieving mother."

Garrett apologized for the department's insensitivity and left him standing at the side door.

11

And that, in effect, was the end of the case.

A board of inquiry met and concluded that Samuel and Caroline Taylor had come to their tragic and untimely deaths by misadventure and that, truly, no one was to blame. In Jake Garrett's mind, however, this conclusion was far from satisfactory, and the case remained stubbornly in an angry place at the back of his mind, left to smolder until some new piece of evidence might surface. Perhaps, solely on foot, his search party might have missed the twins in that open hollow, but with two low-flying airplanes, the odds quickly jumped from unlikely to impossible.

So he waited—and waited and waited—for that essential proof to come floating up to him.

And eventually it did come, though much later than he ever had reason to hope. By then, the Taylors were long gone. Jonathan died of a stroke the very next fall, not fifty yards from those four lonely elms where they'd found the twins. Prudence, unable to care for herself, lingered in a Spokane nursing home until 1976, when she expired as well. Garrett attended both of their funerals, though if asked he couldn't have given a satisfactory reason why.

He continued his duties as sheriff of Whitman County, reelected term after term by healthy margins.

And the twins, buried in the Rosalia Cemetery, remained as well.

The farmhouse stood empty and neglected for almost six years until 1966, when it happened to catch the eye of a man named Henry Chambers.

PART THREE

Sparks And Calliope: 1966-71

1

The barn was a large one, two stories and red as barns ought to be. The house itself was white, with a low picket fence of the same dusty shade around the greenhouse and garden. It was picture perfect through the lens of a camera, at a great enough distance to fit both structures into the rectangle of a viewfinder, but up close both house and barn were showing their age. Paint was peeling into the flowerbeds, the concrete steps were cracked and uneven, pipes and fixtures groaned stiffly with rust, and the barn itself was unstable from years of neglect.

For these and other reasons, the house—or the Taylor Place, as it was commonly known—stood empty for six years before Henry and Margaret Chambers bought it in the spring of 1966. The young couple had a newborn daughter, Justine—not even a year old—and the farmhouse, with its tall ceilings and large allotment of land, was just what they'd dreamed of. And the price made it too good to pass up.

For the first year they held their breath and waited for the hidden catch to show itself: something unforeseen like bad drainage or locusts to explain the happy state of their bank account, but nothing of the kind turned up. They existed snugly and comfortably within the house and, four years after taking up residence, added a son to the sum of their good fortune.

Six months after the birth of Henry Jr.—Hank—however, the Chambers' luck took a hard turn for the worse…

Henry Chambers Sr. was alone in the fields when he died. It was late October, three days before Halloween. The winter wheat was in the ground, and a time of lethargy was settling over the farm; there was time to tackle the odd jobs that had been pushed aside throughout the growing season. Calculating that he had a week or two before the weather became unpredictable, Henry decided to pull out a clump of dead elms that sat atop a bothersome wrinkle in his north field. Once the trees were removed, he planned to go over the grade with a disc until it was serviceable for next year's seeding.

The trees, four in all and fully grown, were unceremoniously cut down, sawed into firewood, and then stacked neatly inside the old barn to season. His plan for the stumps was to coax them out of the earth with a length of steel cable attached to the back of the tractor. As he was in the process of doing this, however, easing the noisy treads forward to take up the slack in the cable, Henry was struck by the powerful feeling that he was no longer alone. His eyes and attention had been on the stump and the cable, and, turning in the saddle, he was surprised to find two children (seemingly sprouted from the rough soil) not twenty feet away. Their eyes were fixed on the old, gray stump, as if waiting for it to break loose and roll down the grade.

Henry cut the motor, and the low, undulating hills fell quiet except for the wind and a passing formation of geese overhead, honking south.

"Hello there," he called down, smiling. "Where'd the two of you come from?"

Their eyes, overcast and gray, shifted briefly from the stump. They appeared to be twins, as skittish as cats.

"Do you live around here?" he gently inquired. "Can't say that I've seen either of you. What are your names?" He cocked his head slightly, with interest. "You wouldn't be friends of my little girl, now would you? Justine? She's about your age."

They didn't even blink, and Henry, feeling increasingly uneasy in their presence, felt an itch of irritation at the back of his neck. He forced himself to ignore it as he looked more closely at their pale features: the dirt on their clothes and in crescents under their fingernails, the eyes dark and polished, like coals sunken into the hollows of their skulls.

"You kids shouldn't be out here. Something could happen, and no one would know where you were. Coyotes roam these fields." When this failed to make an impression on them, he sighed. "Go on over by those pulled stumps," he said, pointing. "Once I get this last one done, I'll take you back to the house and we'll figure out who you belong to." He nodded. "Go on now."

The two strays walked slowly but obediently to where Henry had indicated and resumed their watchful positions. Henry shook his head and muttered grimly under his breath as the old John Deere coughed and shuddered. It belched oily plumes of exhaust into the air as the engine roared and the cable grew taut once again.

The caterpillar treads rolled forward, and the cable strained to break the elm's grip on the hillside. Slowly, a dense, black knot rose out of the earth as the last stubborn moorings snapped. Freed, the stump began its sluggish tumble down the grade; its torn and earth-darkened roots cartwheeled through the air in an uneven and unpredictable course. As it gathered momentum, Henry glanced sideways to make sure the children had stayed put. Instead of dark clothes and smudged faces, however, he found only pressing sky and the rolling stubble of his fields. A thread of panic lit through him, and he craned his head about to see where they'd wandered.

Glancing back at the rolling stump, Henry realized, in his distraction, that it was almost on top of him. Leaning forward, he pushed the knobby accelerator up to full, praying he wouldn't run down the children. The tractor jumped, but too late. The stump crashed heavily into the back end, and a thick, black root knocked him effortlessly out of the saddle. He fell, arms outstretched, upon the ratcheting tread, and it pulled him under in a heartbeat, thrashing him to ribbons.

The tractor was found nearly an hour later, moving riderless over the long, rolling fields, dragging a large stump. Three men, all neighbors of the Chambers', followed the tracks back until they came across Henry.

2

Being a cautious man, fully aware of the high rate of accidents on farms, Henry Chambers had invested an almost paranoid amount in insurance premiums so that his wife and children would be taken care of financially. In the aftermath of his death, these had paid off, and there had been no need for Margaret to sell the house or to leave the kids with a sitter in order to pay the bills. Indeed, coupled with the money she got by leasing their fields to neighboring farms, she was able to stay home and raise the children in a way she and Henry both thought fit. It was a terrible struggle at times, but Margaret had always been a practical woman. She learned quickly, dealing in a calm and straightforward manner with each small crisis and catastrophe as it appeared.

Still, the farmhouse was awfully big and empty that first winter without Henry. Hank developed colic two weeks after his father died, and for Margaret, those days wore a faint cast of unreality, as if she were caught inside a paralyzing dream. At the same time that she grieved for her husband, her son's episodes, as crushingly regular as his feedings, would not let her sleep, and though Justine tried to help out with her baby brother, there was only so much Margaret could expect from a four-year-old. Justine needed taking care of herself.

Margaret worried about her daughter (to the extent she was capable within her twilight existence), troubled by the long hours Justine spent alone while she herself napped or forced herself to the kitchen or laundry room, where she worked amongst the sleepy cobwebs, performing the required tasks without thought, without memory, just a slow grinding of will.

Then, in the cold and sluggish month of January, two visitors came to the farm. Justine, then approaching her fifth birthday, answered the knock and let them in. Margaret emerged from the basement that gray afternoon, holding a basket of unfolded sheets under her arm, and followed her daughter's voice into the solarium, which had been converted into a playroom for her.

"Who are you talking to?" Margaret asked with a puzzled smile on her face.

"My new friends," her daughter replied brightly. "Sparks and Calliope. They're from *Idaho*." This last word she said with great seriousness, as if it were a holy land.

Margaret put the basket down and leaned into the solarium. "Where are these new friends of yours?" she asked. "I think I'd like to meet them."

A small wrinkle creased Justine's brow. "They're right here, Mommy," she said with a twist of bewilderment, indicating the empty air beside her. "That's Calliope, petting Franklin"—Franklin being the Chambers' fat, gray tabby—"and the boy by the dolly swing is Sparks, her twin brother."

"I see…" Margaret replied, not seeing at all but deciding to play along. She summoned a smile. "Well, I'm very pleased to meet the both of you."

Justine smiled broadly.

3

Sparks and Calliope settled by gradual shades into the Chambers' household. For the first month or so, they were around—so to speak—only during playtime, in the solarium where Justine kept her toys, in the shady quiet of her bedroom, or out in the yard between the house and the barn. Margaret would hear her daughter talking or laughing to herself, as if they were dolls that Justine brought out of her closet to play with on gloomy afternoons and weekends. During other times of the day—meals, baths, story time, the times Margaret generally devoted to her daughter—their colorful names were never mentioned, as if they existed only within the specific boundaries of playtime. The rest of the time, Justine seemed satisfied with her mother and baby brother for company.

Because her daughter was the only one who could see these new acquaintances, they eventually became a cause of concern, and Margaret made an appointment to discuss them with Karl Wilson, the family doctor.

From a purely psychological standpoint, Wilson explained, the appearance of two invisible playmates was nothing to become overly alarmed about; in fact, given the circumstances, Justine's was almost a textbook case.

"First off," Wilson calmly expounded, counting off the reasons, "you have to look at where you live; the three of you out in that big, rambling farmhouse with nothing but acres of empty hills surrounding you. Take a guess, Margaret: how close is your nearest neighbor? A mile? *Two miles?*"

"About that, I suppose," Margaret said, nodding. "Roy and Elsa Stubbs are the closest; they're a mile or so south of us."

"Yep. Roy and Elsa. They're what...sixty, sixty-five? How about the closest with kids Justine's age?"

Frowning at Wilson's antique medicine cabinet, Margaret thought for a long time and shrugged. "It's hard to say. Maybe the Hamlins. They've got two boys."

"And how close are they?"

"Three, four miles?"

He dismissed them with a wave of his hand. "So what you're saying is that there's really no one available for Justine to play with on a regular basis?"

"No, I guess that's so," Margaret conceded with a sigh.

"All right. Number two—and don't take any offense at what I'm suggesting."

Margaret's frown deepened as she assured him that she would do no such thing. He was perfectly free to speak his mind.

"Fair enough, then. Here it is." He drew a breath. "You, her mother, are now spending a great deal of time taking care of her new baby brother, what some might consider a very demanding job on top of all the other responsibilities you've taken on since Henry passed away. It figures you can't spend the time with her you once did."

"Well, no...of course not." A look of almost wistful regret lit on Margaret's face, a longing and sadness for days that were dead and gone, buried in an oak casket less than a mile from where she sat. She was a different woman from the one Henry left: stronger, to be sure, but also a little harder.

Wilson waited until he had her attention again, until his two points had sunken enough to connect and make an impression. "I'm no psychologist, Margaret, just a humble country doctor, but it seems to me that when you put one and two together, you get a little girl who's just entering a phase of life when she needs to develop friendships, to go out and play with children like herself. Yet she finds no one around to make such ties. She spends a great deal of time by herself." He paused. "Enter two imaginary friends."

There was a logic to his argument, an encouraging attraction, and when Margaret considered his points, she found they led her to the same conclusion. Justine was missing the play and companionship of children her own age, and her imagination, so vivid and unrestrained, had simply filled in the gaps.

"Then you don't think it's a cause for worry?" she asked hopefully.

"No, not at this point," Wilson said. "I imagine these two friends of hers will disappear once Hank gets old enough to be interesting to her, or else when she starts school in the fall. *Real* friends are almost always better than the made-up kind."

"*Almost?*" Margaret found it a very uncomfortable word.

Wilson failed to elaborate, but he assured her once again that everything would be fine and urged her to contact him if she were troubled about any further incidents. "If you still feel uneasy," he added at the door as she was putting on her coat, "I can recommend you to a man in Spokane. A psychologist who specializes in children. He's very good."

She nodded as if to say she'd think it over. The truth, though, was that Wilson himself had gone a long way toward allaying her fears, and she left his office feeling much better about her daughter's imaginary playmates. In fact, she'd already decided to let them be until their need passed and Justine discarded them on her own.

She looked up at the sky as she walked to her car: steel gray, lowering, threatening snow.

Surely by summer…

4

By the final weeks of winter, however, as the weather became increasingly mild, Sparks and Calliope showed no signs of fading. Quite the reverse, in fact: their presence became even more assertive. It was at that time that they made their first appearance at the dinner table, and Justine demanded they be served right alongside her. Margaret humored this request at first, setting out two additional places, complete with cups and silverware, which would go right back into the cupboard once the meal was finished.

"There's no food on Sparks's and Calliope's plates, Mommy," Justine said solemnly after this exercise had been going on—breakfast, lunch and dinner—for nearly a week.

"What are you talking about, honey?" Margaret sighed impatiently. "It's the same food they've been eating all week."

Justine whispered to the two empty chairs beside her. "Sparks and Calliope say that you haven't been giving them any food at all. They were going to say something but didn't want to be rude."

"Uh-huh." Margaret dismissed the subject and returned to spooning mashed squash into Hank's mouth. He pounded his chubby fists on the highchair tray with glee, a bright orange glaze covering his face and hands.

"*Mom-meeee!*" Justine insisted in a whining tone that had begun to get under Margaret's skin lately. "They want some dinner too!"

"Oh, all right!" Margaret said, cursing herself for giving in to such demands; it could only lead to trouble. Putting the jar of baby food out of Hank's reach, she went to the stove and returned with a spoonful of scalloped potatoes. Onto each of the empty plates she dished out a mouse's portion.

"Is that all?" Justine asked, eyes wide.

Margaret sat back down. "If they eat that, they can have more," she said firmly.

The two yellow piles of potatoes did not diminish throughout the meal, and as clean-up time approached,

Margaret told Justine that if her friends were going to eat over so often, then she would be in charge of cleaning up their plates. Much to her surprise, Justine agreed without a word of opposition.

The wasting of food upon empty chairs, however, came to a dramatic halt after two days.

"Where are Sparks's and Calliope's hot dogs?" Justine asked at lunch, astonished. Not only were there no hot dogs on their plates, but there were no places set for them at the table.

Margaret had been readying herself for this. "They're not eating here anymore, Justine. I'm not dishing out perfectly good food just so it can turn cold on their plates," she said.

"But *Mom-meeeee!*" Justine wailed. "That's not fair! You said they could eat here if I cleaned up their dishes!"

"Well, they don't seem to be very interested in what I cook. I doubt they'll even notice."

"Yes they will!" Justine screamed, large tears cutting tracks down her face. Hank, who had been watching with great interest from his highchair, began screaming as well.

Margaret's patience snapped. "I will *not* be spoken to in that tone of voice, young lady!" She whirled Justine around to face her. "I've about had my fill of this nonsense, and I don't want to hear another word about what your little friends want! Is that understood? Because if I do, you'll go to your room with a hot bottom and an empty stomach! Do I make myself clear?"

"But Momma..." Justine cried, her breath coming in hitches.

"No buts, Justine. Eat your lunch if you're hungry, or you can spend the afternoon in your room." Margaret brushed aside a strand of hair that had shaken loose of her ponytail during the outburst.

"I'm not hungry," Justine mumbled into her shirt, bottom lip stuck out.

"Then go to your room," Margaret said, looking for some calm to grab hold of. Hank was still wailing in her other ear, hungry and relentless.

Justine scraped her chair noisily back and sulked off through the dining room.

"And no radio or television!" Margaret called after her.

Later, after the dishes were done and Hank was down for his nap, Margaret paused outside Justine's door, thinking she heard voices, not just that of her daughter but at least one other, childish and sexless. She opened the door and found her daughter alone on her bed, looking through a picture book.

"Justine?" Dappled sunlight fell in boughs across the large canopy bed, making the whole room seem alive.

Her daughter looked up from the book. The anger, though diminished, was still in her eyes.

Margaret hesitated and then smiled. "You can come out now if you want."

The anger melted away.

After she stopped humoring Justine's invisible friends at the table, Margaret found that life on the farm took an unexpected turn, one toward the inexplicable, the unsettling. At first it was no more than portions of food missing from the refrigerator and the pantry.

This was her daughter's doing, quite obviously. Justine was sneaking slices of bread and lunchmeat, fistfuls of crackers and cookies behind her back, feeding her new playmates. Only now—unlike the untouched leftovers she had once scraped into the garbage disposal—there were no stale scraps to be found around the house, which meant that she was either feeding them outside, where the ravens and sparrows would peck apart the evidence, or she was eating them herself.

Understandably, this sort of behavior elicited a stronger, deeper shade of worry in Margaret's attitude toward Sparks and Calliope, and she resolved to keep a closer watch (and tighter inventory) on the kitchen stores. In the meantime, Justine gobbled her meals and after-school snacks as if she were starving. At times she even asked for seconds, which had been unheard of before.

Even more disturbing, Margaret occasionally found herself scowling into the open refrigerator long after Justine and Hank had been put to bed, puzzling over an empty space on the racks where some small item, a wedge of cheese or a carton of whipping cream, had been only hours before. It had disappeared while she was sitting in the living room watching television, directly between the kitchen and her daughter's room. No explanation to turn to in the dark except:

Sparks and Calliope.

"Bull piss," she muttered, shutting the airtight door and taking a watchful seat at the table, as if the old Frigidaire might take a notion to go out for a midnight stroll.

Margaret questioned Justine twice about the missing food, though on both occasions it was clear that her daughter knew no more about it than she did; indeed, Justine would inevitably draw the same impossible conclusion: Sparks and Calliope were hungry.

5

The summer of 1971 came and went.

Sparks and Calliope proved unremitting in their attentions toward Justine and every day kept her occupied about the house or yard. Hot days were spent out on the lawn, either dancing through the sprinklers or quietly hatching plans under the shade of the fire maple. On rainy afternoons, when the wind moved through the maturing fields like ocean waves, the trio gathered in the solarium or braved the musty-scented barn, where they would practice acrobatics in the loose piles of hay. Margaret learned to live with invisible children without trampling her daughter's imagination too badly, though there were times when she was sorely tempted.

Bits of food continued to vanish from the kitchen without explanation, and, for her own peace of mind, Margaret soon stopped looking. Once it was gone, she knew, it was gone for good.

Justine started school in early September, riding the bus each weekday morning to the elementary school in Rosalia and then back again at three. Sparks and Calliope would likely be waiting for her when she returned, though Margaret noticed they weren't *always* around as they had been over the summer. Justine began to make friends with several of her new classmates, and Margaret held her breath, daring to hope.

And the Lord saw fit to answer that prayer. By winter's end, Sparks and Calliope were reduced to memories, nothing but thin ghosts to raise a smile as the years passed on. As Dr. Wilson predicted, Justine made real friends, and her imaginary ones slowly lost their influence over her. Throughout the darker and lonelier days of winter, Margaret kept her ear tuned for signs of them, dreading it like the return of a cancer, but she never heard a peep.

Almost magically, the food stopped creeping out of her cupboards.

Unable to help herself, and after a cautionary period had passed, she ventured to ask Justine about them. On that afternoon, Margaret had found her daughter, now almost six, sprawled on the solarium floor, filling the broad, charcoal lines in one of her coloring books. At the mention of their names, Justine's eyes had momentarily fogged over, as if it were a struggle to recall them.

"Oh," she said at last, after a visible shiver. "They went back to Idaho." Her voice carried a dreamy uncertainty to it, but before Margaret could pin it down, Justine was back at her book, coloring away, as if it were of only passing interest.

Margaret felt like cheering. It was over!

6

By rights, it *should* have been over.

Once children put aside their imaginary friends, they very rarely call them back, and then only under the most stressful or traumatic circumstances.

So it was with Sparks and Calliope. They returned to the Chambers farm (if it could be said they ever truly left) with the demolition of the old barn.

It happened when Justine was fifteen...

PART FOUR

Cold Spots: 1981

1

Faces pressed themselves against the windows of the school bus—a staggered line of ovals between the ages of six and sixteen—eyes wide, mouths open in appreciation of such glorious wreckage. Whispers jumped from seat to seat, wondering at the police presence surrounding the Chambers's barn, the yellow barricade tape, the men in white lab coats, and the ominous black van.

In a state of bewilderment, eleven-year-old Hank and fifteen-year-old Justine stepped off the bus and onto the shoulder of 195. They had been prepared for the barn but not the rest, and the voices of their classmates calling after them went more or less unheard.

"Hey, Chambers, where'd you get the dynamite?"

"What're the cops doing? Hey, Hank, you didn't *kill* anyone, did you?"

"If you're going to jail, can I have your minibike?"

Laughter, a rising cacophony of wonder and speculation, and then the doors swung shut and the bus coughed a black cloud of diesel across the two-lane highway, grinding north toward the remainder of its rounds.

Their mother came out of the house as if she'd been watching for them, calling their names and shepherding them away from the circus sprawled over the south end of the property.

"What's going on?" Hank asked, unable to take his eyes off the scene. "How come the police are here, Mom?"

"Did one of the workers get hurt?" Justine asked, frowning and craning her neck.

Margaret shook her head. "No one's gotten hurt, but the two of you are to stay away from the barn until the sheriff says different. They're investigating something the workers found this morning."

"A body?" Hank asked.

"Gross!" Justine cried. With Dusty's former stall in the old barn, she'd spent more time there than anyone, and it distressed her that this might be true.

"No, it isn't a *body*," Margaret sighed.

"Well *what* then?"

Margaret pointed at the door. "Go on inside and I'll tell you."

They marched up the steps, school bags dangling.

2

"This happened a long time ago," Margaret began. "Years before we bought the house, or before either of you were born."

They were at the kitchen table where Sheriff Garrett had told her the same grim tale just two short hours before. Since then, several vehicles had arrived, and Garrett had gone out to oversee the work. Margaret could see him now squatting beside the hole, the brim of his hat tipped down in concentration. Occasionally, his voice could be heard through the open screen, calling out orders.

In the last two hours, she'd begun to wonder if the farm was cursed. In point of fact, the bad luck hadn't begun with Henry's death but with Jonathan and Prudence Taylor, six or more years before.

The sheriff had asked her how much she wanted to know, cautioning her that the facts were not especially pleasant.

"Everything," Margaret had replied, frowning.

What she was going to tell her children, however, was going to be a highly edited version of that tale, enough to explain the team of men swarming around their barn but not enough to give them nightmares, if that was possible.

"The couple that lived here before us had two children, a boy and a girl, and they weren't...well, they weren't *normal*; they were born mentally retarded," Margaret said gravely. "You understand what I mean?"

"Of course," Justine sighed, indignant, and Hank nodded alongside her, already snacking on one of the tarts she'd made with the leftover pie dough. "We're not babies."

"I know you're not," Margaret said, "but I want you to keep it in mind because they didn't have any sense of what might be harmful or dangerous to them, and sometimes, when their parents were busy, they wandered off." She looked from Hank to Justine. "Most of the time they were found right away, but one day the two of them got out of the house, and when they were found almost a week later, they were dead."

"On *our* farm?" Hank said incredulously, a smear of huckleberry on his lips, as if it were a mystery out of a book. The book's setting, intriguingly, turned out to occupy the same space as the house where he lived, the same house he had been eating and sleeping and playing in his whole life.

Margaret nodded.

3

Justine listened to the tale that the sheriff had told her mother, silently guessing that she was holding something back. There were holes in the tale; the largest, of course, was so obvious that she was afraid to mention it. The sheriff had told her mother that the Taylor children had died while lost among the fields, that the barn had nothing to do with that distant, unhappy event.

Which, of course, was a lie.

She only had to look out the window to see that.

4

Later that night, the twins returned to her in a dream, though in truth Justine thought she might have been awake the whole time. She'd been *trying* to sleep—she did know that—but with all the excitement over the old barn, sleep had been slow in coming.

Lying in bed, Justine suddenly heard her name whispered into the funnel of her left ear, as jolting as an electric shock.

She sat up in bed, clutching the loose blankets to her chest, certain the whisperer was still beside her, but she was too scared to reach out a hand to make contact. There was no moon, and with the exception of a faint halo of starlight above the valance on the south wall, the night was a uniform black. For all she could see, any number of people might have been in the room.

She listened. Her heart throbbed loudly in her temples, quickening as a weight shifted on the floor beyond the foot of the bed. The movement itself sent small ripples through the air, palpable on the receptive dampness of her face.

"Mama? Is that *you*?" she asked, pinned against the headboard, her voice a mere squeak in the dark. "Hank?"

The marrow in her bones told her it was neither.

A voice opened out of thin air, soft and childlike, mere inches away.

"Justine…"

The bedroom smelled suddenly of mildew, of spoiled cheese.

"W-who is that?" she said, clutching her blankets tighter.

"I told you she wouldn't remember!" a boy's voice, almost identical to the girl's, said crossly from the foot of the bed.

"Who's in my room?" Justine shrieked, provoking a flurry of movement in the dark, like scores of bats startled from their roost. Turning to the small nightstand beside the bed, she reached blindly for the lamp. Her fingers glanced off the shade and tipped it away, off the table to the carpet below.

Justine rolled toward the door, panicked, her mind focused on flight. Her blankets, until then her only protection, picked that moment to turn traitor as she tried to toss them aside and get her feet beneath her. Instead, they caught her up, snaring her long legs and sending her tumbling to the floor.

The pink reading lamp she'd knocked over blinked on, and a girl with brown pigtails looked across the bed, smiling. She couldn't have been any older than six or seven. In the far corner, all but hidden in the shadows, a boy stood frozen in the unexpected light. A brother and sister, as alike as twins.

Despite their smiles, Justine felt no more at ease than if the light had revealed a pair of strange men—escaped convicts or burglars dressed in black. They looked oddly out of date as children, slightly out of focus, as if they'd stepped from an old photograph. The eyes were too dark, the skin too pale, and, beneath the smiles, their expressions too somber, too intent for children so young.

They stood still, regarding her. The girl drew a breath as if to speak.

Then the bedroom door flew open, and Justine awoke.

Her mother rushed in like a bird of prey—*no*, she amended, *a vampire*, changed from bat to human form— her long robe open and flowing in rills and billows behind her, swooping down out of the darkness.

"Honey, what is it? I heard you scream." Margaret's sharp eyes darted toward the window and then back to her daughter. "Good Lord! You're white as a sheet!"

Justine looked numbly about the room, her eyes blinking in confusion. She was sitting up in bed, not tangled on the floor; the pink reading lamp was solidly in place on her nightstand, the bulb off as it should have been. The only light was a long, yellow wedge from the open doorway; it lay across the foot of the bed, bright enough for Justine to see that they were alone in the room.

The twins were gone, leaving only faint whispers or impressions behind, names or words overlapping one another.

Sparks, the boy had said with a grin, fading as the hurried footsteps reached her door.

Calliope. The girl's lips were as out of synch with her voice as her brother's, as if she were really saying something else: "Caroline," perhaps. The thought brought a sudden chill.

"Was it a dream?" asked Justine's mother. Wrapped in lavender, she sat beside her daughter on the bed, stroking Justine's hair with her long fingers. "A nightmare?"

The floor creaked, and Hank appeared in the doorway, twelve years old and dressed in striped blue pajamas. His sandy-brown hair (a shade or two lighter than Justine's) was standing up on one side, and his eyes had the shadowed puffiness of sleep. "What's wrong?" he asked, leaning against the doorjamb, knuckling a crust of sand out of his eye.

"Justine had a nightmare," Margaret answered. "Go back to bed."

He yawned and tumbled gladly back into the gloom.

Outside, not too distant, a coyote began to howl. Justine shivered and pulled the covers tightly around her. A sudden premonition, an image of the twins came to her: the two of them crouched under the bed, waiting for her mother to leave.

Margaret regarded her with concern. "Do you want to talk about it?"

Justine shook her head.

Margaret's eyes narrowed to a critical sharpness, as if to cut through her daughter's brow. "It's that story I told you this afternoon, isn't it?"

"I don't know," Justine said with a shrug, embarrassed at having woken everyone in the dead of night. "I don't think so...I can barely remember it now."

"Are you going to be all right?" Her mother touched her forehead again, as if checking for fever, or madness. "Do you want a glass of water? The light left on?"

Justine shook her head.

"All right then." Margaret kissed her on the cheek and rose from the bed. She hesitated in the doorway, belting her robe about her waist. "All that happened a long time ago. It doesn't mean anything anymore."

"I know, Mama," Justine said, frowning.

"See you in the morning. No more bad dreams tonight, okay?"

"Okay."

The door creaked slowly shut.

A chill crept over Justine. She told herself that she was alone but couldn't quite summon the courage to lean down and check underneath the bed.

5

No more dreams that night, but the following days were filled with enough raw fodder to fuel her imagination for weeks to come.

The weather was indecisive, bright and sunny one minute, sprinkling the next. The only constant was the wind, which came steadily out of the west. Within the wreckage of the barn, a large, blue tarpaulin had been stretched over the hole to protect it during the night, but this had been replaced by a bottomless nylon tent when the first rains had become apparent. Inside, the sheriff and his men were digging and chipping away at the soil, sealing away microscopic finds: pieces of stained earth, strands of brownish hair, threads of human misery and abuse reaching back over twenty years, gathered one by one in sleeves of thin plastic and marked with ciphers only a policeman or a court of law could understand.

Sheriff Garrett, with whom Justine had spoken several times, seemed pleased with the progress of the investigation, and the local media began to gather at the end of the driveway, attracted by the tent and the possibility of exhumations.

All in all, their stupid old barn was causing quite a stir.

6

The next night, Justine dreamed that she was four years old again, bursting from the side door and running toward the barn as her father's dying scream, nearly a mile distant, hung in the crisp October air. The sound (or perhaps only its fading memory) caught her ears, and she slowed to an uncertain halt halfway across the dormant, brown lawn.

A bird? she wondered, head cocked to the wind.

Above her, covering the land from horizon to horizon, was a featureless gray blanket through which the sun appeared as a silvery disc, small and without warmth. She found she was able to stare directly at it without the least sting or discomfort.

She lowered her eyes to the contours of the surrounding hills. She dimly heard the faint *chug-chug-chug* of her father's tractor, though it was nowhere in sight. Impatiently, she dismissed the scream as unimportant and turned her attention back to the sky.

Her mother had informed her over breakfast that the radio was predicting a 50 percent chance of snow, the first snow of the season if it came, and early too. Justine was delighted. The only gray spot on her horizon was the problem of recalling where she'd left her sled all the way back in March.

She turned back to the barn, exhaling a white plume of mist.

Over the warm months of summer, the weather-beaten monstrosity had become one of her favorite places. Inside its heavy doors, there were no little brothers wailing, no grown-ups telling her to settle down, just the musty smell of animals and mounds of straw moldering away in the bins. It was there that she could leave the dull sameness of her house and roam anywhere she pleased, anywhere her budding imagination cared to take her. The creaky old structure could become an ancient and lofty castle; an imperial ballroom, infinitely grand; a vast and unexplored cave reaching deep inside the earth; or perhaps an old and dilapidated house, supposedly haunted. And whichever she chose, Justine would take her own place accordingly, losing herself for hours at a time.

This morning, however, she was simply looking for her sled. She walked the remaining distance and slid aside the noisy door. The shadows trapped inside shifted with the new light, and her eyes widened. A soft start whistled between her lips.

She had visitors.

A boy and a girl stood side by side in the cold, gray light. To Justine's eyes, they looked to be a year or two older than herself, though they wore the hard, set expressions she usually associated with adults. She stepped back, wondering where they'd come from and what they had been doing.

"Hello," she said quietly, still holding the edge of the door, putting aside her initial fear and indignation (it was, after all, *her* barn) in hopes that they might play with her. Boredom and loneliness were powerful incentives.

They stared back at her with the disquieting gaze of two wild animals: cunning and unpredictable. *Dangerous,* her mind whispered.

"How did you get in here?" she asked, frowning, no longer sure that these two would make agreeable playmates.

The twins stood in silence, unblinking.

"*Who are you?*" She felt a thread of fear now.

A low growl rose, and the boy's lips parted slightly as a silvery strand of saliva descended from his chin. Justine felt her heart began to hammer, overcome with the dreadful certainty that these weren't really children but wolves, wolves that had changed themselves into children but were still wolves at heart. If she dared turn her back, the thin veneer of humanity would melt away, and she would be left with the beasts within.

No. They weren't fooling her.

The boy started forward on bare feet, and Justine ran screaming from the barn.

The cool air, leaden with the promise of snow, cut deeply into her lungs, and she felt as if she were plowing through dense drifts, plunging foot by foot over the sleepy yard while the twins, having slipped from their disguises, were loping easily behind her, ready to leap. Their black lips curled over long teeth as their pale eyes locked passionately on the kill.

The thirty-five-yard sprint became an ordeal of nightmarish proportions, and as she ran, it felt as if the earth were running with her, for she never seemed any nearer to the house. Hot, vaporous breath licked at her heels, the sound of their panting lusty and strong, playing with her, waiting for her to trip or lag a little slower.

Finally, she slammed into the storm door and yanked it open on the rebound, chancing one quick glance behind her.

The yard was empty except for two lines of footprints in the frost: one traced a leisurely meander to the barn while the other, more urgent and widely spaced, led straight back to her heels.

She collapsed against the doorframe, breathless and confused. She had imagined the whole thing!

Then she saw that the barn door had closed.

Without warning, her father's battered John Deere smashed through it, riderless, rending it to splinters, one of its caterpillar treads splashed with what looked like red paint.

"What's the matter, princess?" her father's voice boomed behind her, crackling like raw currents in the air. "See a ghost?"

And the dream—nightmare—collapsed before she could turn.

7

Out the kitchen window, just over Hank's shoulder, the dark-green tent was still standing amid the ruins of the barn, rippling gently with the morning breeze, empty except for the hole underneath. Stifling a shiver of disquiet, Justine forced herself to look away.

The television was playing its usual Saturday-morning fare, reruns of Tweety and Sylvester, and her mother was standing over the electric skillet, flipping pancakes and gazing absently out at the yard with a touch of brown sleepiness under her eyes.

She's looking at it too, Justine thought, glancing out the window again to see that the tent hadn't walked away on its own. Tatters of yellow tape turned in the breeze like streamers, the bold black warning illegible from this distance.

The sheriff and his men were not due back this morning, but the tent remained to protect the integrity of the crime scene, if indeed there was any left to protect. Justine had her doubts; over the last two days it had likely been the most trod-upon patch of ground in the whole county. Now it seemed all used up, anything of the slightest possible interest broken up and carried away. She had heard Sheriff Garrett tell her mother that the tent would be taken down Monday or Tuesday, barring any further need suggested by the evidence they'd already gathered. She could call back her demolition crew to finish the job and, hopefully, pave over this inconvenient bump that Fate had seen fit to toss their way. The investigation would continue, of course, but away from the field, in the sterile white light of the county forensics lab, which Justine pictured as being in a basement somewhere, encased in tile and thick slabs of concrete.

She sensed a shadow across the breakfast table and looked up to find her mother, fork poised over a serving plate, staring at her as if she'd just asked a question.

"What?" Justine stammered, clearing her throat.

"Pancakes," Margaret repeated. "Do you want one or two?"

"Just one, I guess." She pulled the syrup and butter dish closer. "I'm not very hungry this morning." What she wanted, more than cartoons or breakfast, was to crawl back into bed and pull the covers over her head. After last night's chase (and oh how *real* it still seemed!), she hadn't been able to get back to sleep and instead had watched the day break against her curtains, turning the room from black to blue to yellow, like a fading bruise.

"How did you sleep?" her mother (the clairvoyant) inquired, rolling the hotcake onto her waiting plate as if she were turning back a rug. "Any more nightmares?"

Justine picked up her knife and took a swipe at the butter.

She hesitated, wondering if she should even mention it. It was such a dumb thing to get worked up about, yet it did bother her, these creepy dreams disturbing her sleep just as a hole was uncovered beneath the barn. A very suspicious and evil hole by all accounts. Taken together, the two instilled a strong desire to seek out a photograph of the Taylor twins. Perhaps Sheriff Garrett could help her with that. She wondered: had her bedroom once been theirs?

But how best to answer her mother without begging a trip to the counselor, the one whose card Garrett had left behind? *In case it upsets them*, she'd heard him say in a low ventriloquist's voice, lips barely moving as he nodded toward the tent. Justine had watched her mother fold the card into her pocket as if it never existed.

"I dreamed I was little—about four or five, I guess—and Daddy was still alive," she said, taking a bite out of her pancake. "It was...*strange*." She turned her eyes back to the window and shrugged, as if the details were lost to her now.

Her mother regarded her for a moment, as if weighing the veracity of this, then moved around the table to serve Hank. He laughed as Tweety, under the influence of a Jekyll and Hyde potion, turned into a shaggy monster and snapped up Sylvester in single bite.

"Hank," Margaret said, "turn that down while we're eating, please."

"Okay, Mom." He got up and lowered the volume imperceptibly.

"Lower," Margaret warned, taking a seat herself, reaching for the coffee.

"Ah, Mom!" he protested, indignant in his bare feet and striped pajamas.

"I could turn it off instead?" she suggested, her voice taking on a leaner edge.

"All right," he mumbled, cutting the sound roughly in half and returning to his breakfast like a martyr.

Outside, a robin was singing on the lip of the bird bath. A second joined it, and they began to squabble. After a few contemplative sips from her mug, Margaret turned to her daughter. "What do you have planned today?"

Justine yawned and thought about bed again. "Saddle up Dusty, I suppose. Why?"

"I'm going into town to do some shopping. Groceries mostly, but I was going to stop by the fabric store. Do you want to come along?"

Justine had been working on a new blouse just prior to the big discovery, and Margaret thought it might be a good idea to get her going on it again, to take her mind off the barn. She had been complaining about her selection of buttons anyway; this would give her a chance to improve it.

Justine chewed on the offer over a slice of bacon. Knowing that her mother would keep at her until she agreed, she decided to give in gracefully. "All right. What time are you going?"

"Oh, after lunch. Say one o'clock?"

Hank, aware that he would be roped along regardless, began to moan about having to spend a part of his precious afternoon in the stupid fabric store, which was, in his opinion, the most boringest store in the whole world.

"It's 'boring,'" Margaret corrected. "Not 'boringest.' The most *boring* store in the whole world. And watch your sleeve," she said, pointing. "You're dipping it in your syrup."

He held up his elbow to look.

8

After the breakfast dishes were done, Justine put on a jacket and went out to the stable to groom and saddle Dusty.

Despite clear, deep skies, the air was crisp, and she could see her breath in the morning sunlight. Cooler than she usually liked to ride in, but this morning she wanted to get away from the house and the splintered heaps of the barn, away from her mother's watchful eye (though she meant well) and anything else that would remind her of those two dead children.

The house had always had a way of tapping into her imagination and emotions, ever since she was small, but only recently she had come to sense something darker behind the everyday objects and shadows trapped within the rooms, something watchful and awake. Now Justine felt she always had to be on guard, but she never knew what shape the danger was plotting to take. It left her feeling edgy and nervous.

Of course, it had been exciting at first—like an old ghost movie in which she was cast as the heroine—but after two nights of harrowing nightmares, as real as the morning chill was to her now, the fun had quickly faded. She was tired, afraid of the coming night because she would have to pass another eight hours of darkness alone in her room, with nothing to protect her except the shaky knowledge that none of it was real.

Or was it?

Justine wasn't so certain anymore. There was a spooky sense of déjà vu to the dreams, especially in the faces of the twins, as if all this had happened before... somewhere back in her childhood.

Sparks. Calliope.

Such unusual names, she reflected, sifting loosely through her memories, turning them inside out like a pile of old socks. Surely they weren't real. More like nicknames. Play names.

The association struck a chord in her, and she stopped short of the stable. Her eyes widened as a window opened into the past, a time half-forgotten, when she was no older than she had been last night in her dream. It was dark...

Justine saw the house, gray and large enough to swallow her whole. Infused within its timbers were the slack and sullen faces of the twins, lingering in the half light, watching her play. They looked jealous and hungry, like a pair of cats staring in from the rain.

A hard, immovable knot formed in the hollow of her stomach.

Games in the solarium, laughter in the barn... Blood running down the tines of a rust-colored pitchfork.

She was losing it, coming away with melting fragments, images so tenuous and gray they might have been other dreams, long buried in her subconscious. The window was closing, narrowing to a line where only the most striking vicissitudes were presented, and in these last glimpses she saw her mother sobbing, turning away from her. The force of the memory caused her to recoil, and the connection was lost. When she tried to will it back, it came out false, as a picture composed in her mind that had no basis in reality. But she *had* touched something.

Cold, insistent daylight asserted itself, and a shiver passed through her, as if she had been standing outside for hours. She glanced around at the low, greening hills, at the cars passing on the highway and the stable door right in front of her, waiting to be opened.

She could hear Dusty rustling about inside, snorting softly, anticipating her.

Justine shook her head and paced off the remaining yards, determined to rid herself of such gloomy thoughts. She paused to blow on her palms and then slid the door smoothly open. A semi-pleasant odor drifted out, that of newly fitted lumber, warm straw, and, of course, manure. Dusty lifted his long face over the door of his stall in greeting. He was black against the shadows except for a small, star-shaped mark of pure white above his moist, brown eyes.

"Morning, boy."

She stepped inside and scooped a handful of oats from a burlap bag. She held them out for him and scratched the star as he munched contentedly. "Good horse," she cooed.

He finished off the oats and looked at her expectantly.

"What do you say?" she said, running a hand down his neck. "Wanna go for a ride?"

Dusty whinnied agreeably.

9

Hank went from the kitchen to the living room, hardly missing a beat in the morning flow of cartoons. Bugs and Tweety gave way to the backwoods, hot-rodding adventures of the Trollkins, which Margaret could abide only in small, measured doses. By twenty minutes after nine, she'd had her fill; she walked briskly across the room and snapped the set off.

Under a blanket and still in his pajamas, Hank blinked as if emerging from a deep and pleasant hypnosis.

"Hey! I was watching that!"

"Hey yourself," Margaret said, hands on her hips. "There's no reason to waste your Saturday in front of the television. Get yourself dressed and go play outside. You need the fresh air and exercise."

"I get plenty of fresh air and exercise all week," he moaned, ducking his head under the blanket like a sleepy tortoise. "Saturday morning's for sleeping in!"

"Then you should have stayed in your bedroom."

His face poked out, but just barely, as if testing the air. "If I had a TV in my room, I would."

Margaret uttered a dry laugh. "That'll be the day! I suppose you'll be wanting breakfast served there too!" She snapped her dusting rag at him. "Now get going, mister, before I find you some *real* work to do!"

"All right, all right, I'm going!" he relented, throwing back the blanket.

Once outside, Hank gave the yard a disconsolate look of appraisal and debated how best to pass the time before his mother let him back inside. Being by himself, he could eliminate most of the better options, such as any sort of sports competition or playing army men in the dirt of the garden.

He looked at the lawn from his perch atop the doorstep, still wet and forbidding with the morning's dew.

Finally his eyes lit upon his bike, leaning against the short length of fence shading the back yard. He allowed that it might be fun to practice his wheelies for a while along the driveway. He could try to outdo himself going back and forth, riding as far as he could on his rear tire.

Yeah, that might be okay, he decided, slumping down the stairs.

The bicycle was cold and stiff from being out all night, and the gummy plastic handle-grips felt hard and unyielding in his hands. He put a foot on the pedal, pushed off down the drive and swung his other leg over the long banana seat. He waved to his mother at the window, standing on the pedals to show off his mastery of the craft, flashing her a bright smile to boot.

But she didn't smile back nor return his wave. She was standing very still at the sink, face framed in the window, looking right past him, *through* him. His grin fading, Hank turned to see what she was looking at but saw only the wreckage of the barn, stacked in thorny heaps and piles. And farther on, the tent, wrapped in a long, yellow barricade.

10

Margaret stopped dead at the window, forgetting the damp washcloth in her hand.

Since the day the demolition crew had first begun work on the old barn, she'd gotten in the habit of pausing at the window every now and then to see the changes across the driveway. With the arrival of the sheriff's department (and its various related agencies), the pull she felt to linger there only increased. Even during the lull of the weekend, with not much happening outside, the habit was not so easily put aside. Several times that morning she'd found herself back at the window, gazing through the edgy blur of splintered lumber at the razor focus of the tent, waiting for someone to emerge with an evidence bag in hand. During the past few days, she had waited for something larger than small plastic bags to appear: something roughly the size of a six-year-old, wrapped in shiny black tarpaulin and tied together with bright-yellow barricade tape.

The Taylor twins were buried in Rosalia, she reminded herself, not under her barn. Still, she remained vigilant for anything too horrible or shocking for her children to digest. Too many dark innuendos had already crept out of that hole and into their heads, where they festered at night, and she for one would be glad to see it filled in and forgotten (if that were really possible) come Monday morning.

Now something out there caught her eye again.

She was marginally aware of her son riding past the window on his bicycle, waving his arms in the air, but her eyes were on the tent, watching for the flaps to move again.

A soft heel scraped the floor behind her, and she whirled, letting out a sharp gasp.

With Justine out riding and Hank in the driveway, Margaret knew that no one could have been there, yet the refrigerator door was standing open, spilling a faint yellow light onto the kitchen floor. When she found the courage to open it further, her trembling hand passed through a coldness she couldn't fully blame on the Frigidaire. Furthermore, there seemed to be an empty space on the racks that hadn't been there before; sliced cheese or butter or a tub of strawberry yogurt had vanished.

It evoked a powerful feeling of déjà vu, and a heartbeat later, two names came rising dimly out of the past.

Musical names. Nonsensical.

"Justine," she whispered, suddenly afraid.

11

The slopes Dusty was treading had been left fallow. This was partly because it gave the soil a rest and allowed lost nutrients to be replenished, but mostly it was because Mr. Conkling, who had been leasing the land since Justine's father died, had suffered a stroke last fall and was now enriching his own small plot of soil seven miles away in the Rosalia Cemetery. Mrs. Conkling had since put the farm up for sale and moved in with her daughter and son-in-law in Colfax. As of yet, there had been no takers on the farmhouse, and so it and the fields remained empty.

Though it gave her more space to ride, Justine knew it meant they would have to live with a tighter rein on their finances over the coming year. She felt sorry for poor Alma Conkling too, who used to have her and Hank over for afternoon picnics when her grandchildren came to visit just so they'd have someone new to play with. That was also before Alma fell down the front steps getting the mail one icy morning and broke her leg in two places. Since then, the invitations and the grandchildren came less often. Now, Justine supposed, leaning forward in the saddle to drive Dusty up a long rise, those days were over for good. The thought made her sad, and she allowed herself to soak in its bitterness for a while.

The sky drew nearer and the brown hills fell away, revealing distant farmhouses surrounded by wooly green trees and shrubbery. To the northeast, Steptoe Butte rose above the surrounding countryside. The spiral road servicing its bald summit was cut deep against its muscular flanks, as clear to the naked eye as the bristling crown of relay towers, the tallest of which blinked red to warn away low-flying aircrafts.

She brought the gelding to a gentle halt and unzipped her jacket, thinking it was about time to start back, but it was so peaceful, so silent among the fields, that she was reluctant to give it up. Though their wanderings that morning had been just that, aimless and idle, the course she had followed over the last quarter mile or so was nearly identical to that through which, twenty-two years earlier, Jonathan Taylor had led Jake Garrett to the remains of his two lost children.

Of course, Justine had no way of knowing that, nor did she realize that the vague cluster of shadows lying across the adjacent slope were not cast by passing clouds, but instead by four ragged elms; trees whose stumps her father had been pulling from the soil when the old green tractor had run him over.

Nevertheless, the patch of shade exerted a subtle pull within her and, thinking it a nice spot to rest before turning back, she nudged Dusty down the hill.

12

Hank jerked the handlebars too hard and overshot his balance, slipping off the back of the seat and touching his sneakers to the gravel. The recovery was neatly done, as if he could do it in his sleep, which he probably could.

Walking the bike on the knobby tread of its rear tire, Hank passed the rock he used to measure his best distance and let the bike's front end drop, swinging his leg over the seat and saddling up.

He estimated that no more than thirty minutes had passed since he had been shooed out on the step; too soon to try to sneak past his mother, even though the wheelie popping had lost its subtle charm. He hadn't even come close to breaking his old record either. He just didn't seem to have the touch this morning, he supposed. Too cold, or too early. Until summer vacation hit, bike riding was more or less an afternoon activity, and for good reason too: who wanted to ride a bike wearing a coat?

Best to try to look bored and pitiful, he decided, and then beg to be let inside. Funny: now that he'd been banished, he could think of at least a dozen things to occupy his time other than watching television, all of them inside, where it was comfortable and warm.

He veered across the lawn and leaned his bike against its familiar post, intending to sulk mightily on the steps, when a sudden disturbance behind his back put the thought right out of his mind, like a thread snipped with scissors.

Hank turned and frowned into the slight breeze, unaware of the resemblance the expression lent him to his father, with its subtle lines drawn down in puzzlement.

For a split second he saw the barn, not in its present state of ruin but *whole*, just as it had been a week ago, as if memory had momentarily overlapped the present. The double doors had been shut, but behind them he heard what sounded like pigs, a great many of them, in fact, so close he could hear individual cries swelling out of the greater dissonance of the herd. It was frightening because he knew full well they'd never kept pigs, much less a whole herd of them inside the barn.

When he blinked, the barn disappeared, or rather it fell to its present state, but the squealing of the pigs remained, rising, as if they sensed a predator circling the low hills behind the house. A coyote or a wolf.

After a moment's indecision, Hank moved toward the wreckage, deciding that he'd better have a look. As he started off, however, the sound changed. It shifted and dissolved like an image he was trying to keep perfect and still inside his memory, and while it never completely faded, it was whittled down to two or three disgruntled oinks, at times sounding patently false, as if a few of his friends were playing a joke on him. He crossed the rough clearing at the end of the drive and waded carefully into the area roped off by the sheriff's department, realizing that he was standing in an oblong of morning shade where the barn should have been.

A helpless chill passed through him as the pigs continued to snort and chortle, as if laughing at him. The sounds came from a short distance ahead, twenty or thirty feet, and to his left—roughly the spot where the evidence tent stood covering the hole.

Hank hesitated. He stared at the tent, at the bright glow of sunlight passing through it, and saw a shadow stir within. It was a slim shape resembling a child's head and shoulders in silhouette, but when it moved again, he saw pointed ears and a flattened snout.

Snooorfff-snooorrf-snuff.

An imitation of a pig sniffing at the side of the tent, pressing the nylon panel briefly out of shape. A very good imitation, but an imitation nonetheless.

A second silhouette appeared, thinner and more indistinct, but laughing like a cartoon. It said his name, and all the hair stood up on the back of his neck.

"Hank!"

He jumped, his heart suddenly beating, as if he had woken from an unexpected dream. He turned and saw his mother standing on the step above the narrow strip of lawn. The screen door was open, and she had a dishtowel in hand.

"What were you doing there?" she demanded. Her tone was a strange mixture of contradictory emotions he didn't quite know what to make of.

"Just looking," he said, deciding not to gamble on a half truth or outright lie with his mother in an uncertain state. "I thought I heard something."

"You know you're not supposed to cross that yellow tape!" she said. Then her demeanor suddenly changed, as if she too were scared. Shading her eyes against the sun, she asked, "What was it you heard?"

"Pigs."

"*Pigs?*" He might as well have said Martians. "What would *pigs* be doing in our yard?"

He shrugged. "I didn't see any."

Behind his back, a soft snort or giggle spilled out of the tent and was quickly smothered. Margaret sighed as if to say *of course not* and looked toward the fields behind the house. "You haven't seen Justine, have you?"

He frowned. "No."

Another sigh. Unreadable.

"Can I come in now?" he asked, looking duly repentant for watching cartoons in his pajamas while fresh air was wasting outside.

"What?" She was distracted again, looking out over the demolished barn. "Oh." There was a long pause while she seemed to consider the request "I suppose so. No TV, though."

"Yes," he said with a grin. As he squeezed past her on the steps, she muttered something grimly to the effect that, when she was his age, she'd never been at a loss for finding things to do away from the television.

And it was on his lips to shoot back: *Yeah, but I'll bet you didn't live out in the middle of nowhere. I'll bet you had friends to play with.* But he didn't. It would only hurt her, and he'd probably end up back outside, cursing himself. It wasn't really her fault that they lived where they did.

He held the screen for her, thinking she'd be right behind him. The door hung unaccepted, however, and when he turned he saw her gazing out at the fields.

"Mom? You coming in?"

"In a minute, honey," she said from far away.

13

"Come on! What's the matter with you?"

Dusty balked, absolutely refused to move a step nearer, even when Justine slipped out of the saddle and tried to lead him by the bridle. She gave the reins a tight jerk, which might have worked on an unruly dog, but failed to move the four-year-old gelding. He was resolute, immovable as stone.

"Fine, then," she huffed, releasing the reins, letting them swing down to stir the ground. "Stand there like a big dummy! I'll be sitting up here in the shade!" With a flip of her ponytail, Justine turned her back on the animal and made a show of marching up the grade, knowing eventually he would follow. And if shame didn't work, she had an apple in her pocket.

Dusty reared his head and whinnied. His long legs stamped the weedy dirt.

"I'm not interested in your excuses," Justine replied without turning.

He evinced further protests, crying out again skittishly as if a snake were near, which made Justine pause long enough to look amongst the ruts.

"Well, come here then, you stupid horse!" she called back, a little concerned now. She'd never seen Dusty like this and wasn't sure what it meant. "Come up here!" she said, clapping her hands sharply in the crisp morning air.

He stamped and stammered and blew steam out his wide nostrils.

But he would not move any further up the slope.

Justine decided to ignore him, at least until something tangible appeared. It wasn't a good idea to let your animals start pushing you around, telling you what they would or would not do. He could wait right where he was until she was good and ready to leave. *So there.*

She reached the top a minute later—much to her horse's continued disapproval—and it was only then that the first tentacles of real fear began to coil about her, gripping harder as they gained their small and bloodless holds.

She noticed that the hillcrest was covered in a strange black frost; what she'd first taken to be a cloud shadow now looked like a blight or mold that had worked its way into the stubble, causing it to turn brittle beneath the soles of her riding boots. It rose in powdery plumes with each step, imparting a bitter chill that clung to her despite the rising warmth of the sun. She breathed it into her lungs and started to gag as a frightening paralysis set in, penetrating all the way to the marrow. Her movements became stiff and infirm; worse still, there seemed to be a presence lurking on the hillside, incorporeal as a ghost. It *enjoyed* playing with her, reaching inside and touching her heart with a cold finger.

You don't really belong here, do you?

She gasped as frigid air forced its way down her throat, suffocating her. Black clots gathered at the periphery of her vision, running like drops of rain on a dirty windshield. The ground tipped beneath her feet, and as she struggled for balance, she saw two thin shadows circling her own, fleeting shapes rushing and snapping at her like wolves. They were feral, laughing, like spirits out of an old Indian carving. She saw her own shadow, foreshortened but clearly defined in the midmorning sun, yet the two others were lengthened, falling back down the hill in the opposite direction as if it were late afternoon wherever they were.

And trees.

The black and poisonous blight was shaped like a copse of trees, with four trunks clearly supporting the greater mass and rooted uphill to where she stood, as if they too were ghosts. Things that were no longer there.

Justine swooned and dropped to her knees; a numbing cold enveloped her as if she were tumbling into the grave. She felt as if pieces were being taken from her, ripped away by invisible jaws and swallowed whole, one right after the other. She struggled to stay upright and then wondered why she bothered. Above her, four elms shimmered into existence like an oasis in the middle of the desert. She found that if she concentrated on one spot, she could see through it, like smoked glass. Wispy clouds, little more than a high-altitude haze, were strung out like a veil across the mesosphere.

Justine's arms and legs were tingling. She let herself go limp and began to roll down the hill toward her whinnying horse.

It felt as if she had never lost consciousness but had browned out instead.

The hillside was tumbling beneath her. The soil and sky traded places with such rapidity that they melted together in a streaking blur, and the sun spiked her eyes once every revolution. Jaw clenched, eyes wide open, she did her best to hold on to consciousness, feeling every bump and furrow that rose to meet her, relishing its jarring impact as pieces of the bitter freeze around her were thrown off into the sunlight. Left to die upon the warm soil or to slink back to the eddying mass atop the hill.

Still, some part of the day (surely only a sliver) was misplaced or missing, because now Dusty was gently nudging her face with his muzzle, tickling her nape with his soft, warm breath. But she couldn't recall ever coming out of the spin.

She sat up too quickly; the world lurched half a beat behind. Her breath came in shallow rasps, and she kicked at the dirt to get to her feet. The reedy sensation of urgency, however, of enveloping danger, was evaporating away like mist. It was like a dream from which she'd struggled to awake.

Clutching the reassuring solidity of Dusty's forequarter, Justine scanned the hillside behind her. She wouldn't have recognized it, couldn't have picked it out of a dozen others. It was as plain as an overturned bowl: no scrim of blackened frost, no stand of elms settled comfortably beneath the crest, no ghosts stamping their tiny feet in frustration.

There was only the wide, ragged arc of her fall to show she'd ever been there.

And a memory of dying, rapidly decaying in the morning sun.

14

Her mother seemed anxious when she returned home.

"You've got dirt on yourself," she remarked as Justine emerged from the stable. Dusty had been fed, watered and brushed down for the afternoon.

Justine stopped and looked down at herself. "Where?"

"All down your backside," Margaret said, stepping behind her and pointing. "Lord, girl! What have you been doing, taking a dust bath with that lunkhead horse? *Look at this!* You're *covered* with it!" She shook her head, patting the back of Justine's denim jacket. "And in your hair too!" she sighed.

Slapping the seat of her jeans, Justine tried to recall what she'd done to get so dirty. Had she even gotten off Dusty during the ride? It seemed that she had, just before coming back, but it was funny that she couldn't remember it, at least not in any detail. The rest of the morning, by contrast, was as clear as glass.

God, she really *was* covered with dust! *Fallen* off the horse was more like it, then drug along in the stirrup for awhile. Maybe she'd fallen on her head? She did have a slight headache, but it was far down inside, not on the surface where an injury would crop up in a tender lump. Just the same, she did a quick exploration of her head.

"What are you doing?"

"Nothing." She pulled her hand away as if she'd found a wasp, tangled and buzzing. "You said I had dirt in my hair."

"Well, you're not going to get it out *that* way. Honestly, Justine! Get inside and hop in the shower. Lunch will be ready in fifteen minutes. I'm not taking you into town looking like *this!*"

They started toward the house, raising clouds of thin, brown dust out of Justine's clothes.

"Take off your boots on the step," her mother said, pulling open the door. "They're probably full as well."

And they were too. Justine couldn't figure it out; she always got some dirt in her boots while riding, but this was ridiculous! Having emptied them, she picked them up and went inside, pausing by the kitchen arch to look in at her mother. There was a pan of soup simmering on the stovetop and slices of bread laid out on the counter. She must have left them there before going outside.

"Mom?"

Margaret was washing her hands at the sink. The sunlight shone bright on her face as she gazed out the window. Justine was surprised as she came over the last ridge and saw her mother standing amid the wreckage of the barn. She recalled an electric-blue bolt of adrenaline jabbing her at the time, as if something terrible had happened.

"Mom? What were you doing out by the police tent?"

"Oh, nothing," Margaret said, shrugging. "Just snooping." She cast a level glance at Justine and then reached for a towel. "Better hurry up. Lunch is almost ready."

Hesitantly, as if there were something more she wanted to say, Justine pushed off toward the bathroom. It was strange: the day was already five hours underway, but she felt as though she were just waking up.

15

After a quiet lunch, the three of them piled into the Chambers's secondhand Citation. Conversation was at a lull as Margaret started the car and turned it sluggishly around. They all stared out different windows, wrapped inside their own thoughts. Even Hank hadn't complained as expected; in fact, he looked almost eager to be getting away for a few hours, to a sewing shop or any other place. All in all, quite a turnabout from this morning's groans and protests.

Margaret was distracted; her eyes not especially focused on the potholes in the drive nor the approaching ribbon of highway. She was thinking about the open door of her refrigerator and what she had seen inside the police tent just before Justine had come riding down from the fields.

It hadn't been particularly repellent or alarming; it was only a mouse, after all. Small and brown and lying on its side in the gray shadow of the pit. Not at all unusual to see on a farm, but this...this was somehow different. Had she found it anywhere else—in the greenhouse, down in the basement, even in the pantry—it wouldn't have shaken her so badly. But *there*, where those children had died, it seemed like a bad omen, the continued stirrings of an ill wind, though she'd never considered herself the least bit superstitious.

Until then, ghosts (malevolent or otherwise) had simply been a nonentity, existing only within the strict confines of cheap novels and second-rate movies. No one except crackpots believed they actually existed, and Margaret Chambers had never considered herself a crackpot.

But now...

Her foot touched lightly on the brake to halt the car at the edge of the highway—a move performed so often that she could have done it in her sleep. It was the sudden jerk on the back of the bench seat, however, that caused her to finally shake off her trance and take notice of the dark car parked along the shoulder of the roadway. Hank had pulled himself up against the back of the seat to get a better view, and she could feel his warm breath on her neck, whistling down her collar.

It was a hundred feet or more east of the driveway, but even so, it was clear that there was someone seated behind the wheel, head turned to study their house, or perhaps the shattered wreck of the barn.

"Who's that?" Justine said, squinting against the glare of sunlight off the hood.

"I don't know, honey," Margaret said with a frown, nervously tapping the vinyl padding of the wheel with her short fingernails. Cars or pickups parked along the highway were nothing new these past few days, compliments of the local paper, but something about this car struck her as ominous.

"Maybe it's the FBI!" Hank said, excitement coloring his voice.

Justine craned her head around with obvious disdain. "What do you know about the FBI?"

"I know they drive cars like *that!*" he shot back heatedly.

Margaret had to admit he was right. The car was a dark sedan, late model, nondescript, and clean to a fault. As unobtrusive as a suit and tie in the city, but out here in the sticks, it was conspicuously out of place. Country people, as a rule, didn't bother to keep their cars glossed to a showroom shine; it was a losing battle. So *who* was this joker?

She thought about it. Everyone in tarnation had developed a burning interest in their property just lately, as the scores of muddy footprints around the barn could attest...why not the FBI?

Because the FBI would come knocking at the door like everyone else. She and the children weren't criminals, after all; they weren't likely to bolt if a strange man in a dark suit and conservative tie turned up on their step. Or meet him with a gun.

She closed her eyes and exhaled.

This is stupid. A hole gets unearthed beneath the barn—sinister yes, but twenty years old—and you start imagining the worst possibility behind every little bump and irregularity that comes your way: things you'd otherwise shrug off and forget, if you happened to take notice of them at all.

The man was likely a lost motorist feeling confused by the eerie sameness of the narrow roads. Probably he had pulled over to get his bearings after missing the turnoff (which was more of a veer, actually) to Spokane a few miles back. It happened a lot: people streaking through at seventy or eighty miles per hour, wanting to put down miles so they wouldn't be caught after dark in this godforsaken country. Undoubtedly there was a state map spread out on his lap, and what he was trying to make out across the road was the mile-post marker and not her house.

That was all.

Margaret sensed a restlessness building in her children, and she made a decision. Taking her foot off the brake, she made a slow right turn onto the highway and accelerated toward town, keeping her eyes close to the rearview mirror.

Any sort of confrontation with the kids in the car would be a mistake; she'd end up looking foolish and overwrought if it turned out to be nothing, vulnerable and alone if it was trouble. The best course to take, she reasoned, was to proceed to Rosalia as if she hadn't noticed the car, telephone Sheriff Garrett from the pay phone in front of the grocers, and let him send a man to sort things out. If it turned out to be an innocent mistake, the driver would be grateful for the timely assistance; if not, an armed deputy with a radio car would be much better equipped to deal with any surprises than a thirty-seven-year-old widow with two gaping children.

And Rosalia was only six miles away. Six *minutes* if she kept it up to sixty, which she thought she could manage without causing a panic.

It was nothing anyway. She was sure it was nothing.

16

After a slightly embarrassed call to the sheriff, Margaret allowed herself the luxury of forgetting about the dark sedan. Jake Garrett hadn't been angry or condescending about her suspicions, though very likely a good portion of his attitude could be traced to the sealed crime site standing on her unprotected property, which was perfectly visible from the highway. Still, it was enough that his appreciation sounded genuine as he assured her that it would be no trouble at all to send a man out.

So she hung up the phone, walked across the street to the fabric store, and started her shopping, secure in the knowledge that the matter was being looked into. That she needn't worry about it anymore.

And eventually, some fifteen or twenty minutes later, she did just that.

17

It was something of a shock then, two hours later, to find the mystery car parked not across the highway where they'd left it but lodged squarely in front of the house. The tall figure of a man leaned casually against the driver's-side door, smoking a cigarette as he watched their approach.

Justine had her stockinged feet up on the dash, nose buried deep inside a fashion magazine. Hank was likewise occupied, having spent his time at the Rosalia Public Library while Margaret and Justine were browsing the fabric store. He'd emerged with two intermediate adventure novels, both having to do with skin diving, sharks, and lost treasure. Margaret hadn't heard a peep from him since they'd gotten into the car, only the occasional rustle of time-worn pages.

When she hesitated, however, they both paused long enough to peel an eye from their respective pages and glance through the front and then side windows.

"Hey," Hank exclaimed, "that's the car that was parked across the road when we left!" He nudged his sister over the seatback. "I told you it was the FBI!"

"Knock it off, you little grub!" Justine growled, folding her legs off the dash as she straightened in her seat and peered past her mother through the driver's-side window.

"Quiet, *both* of you!" Margaret said, turning off the highway and into the drive before someone came around the bend and rear-ended them. As soon as she was off the road, however, she tramped down on the brake and brought them all to an abrupt halt. A thin cloud of dust rose from the undercarriage, drifting slowly up the ruts instead of the car. A faint breeze pried at the crack in her window, and the loneliness of her circumstances occurred to her once again, as stark as the brown slope of the hills against the empty sky.

A strange man was blocking her driveway, and while she couldn't see him clearly yet, something inside told her not to trust him, not to get too close.

"How come we're just sitting here?" Hank asked. Justine quietly told him to shut up, and Margaret glanced sharply across the seat, wondering if her daughter felt it too. The expression resting lightly on her face was curious and mildly expectant, no more, as if she were on the sidelines of a marathon, waiting for the runners to appear.

Margaret shifted her gaze back to the man. Dropping his cigarette and grinding it beneath his heel, he turned to face them, slipping his hands into his pockets.

"Mom?" Justine asked, wriggling her feet into her fallen shoes. "What are you going to do?"

Margaret swallowed, hoping her voice wouldn't sound splintered when it came out, afraid. The smile she tried on felt hideous, not at all reassuring; she caught her own eye in the rearview mirror and looked away.

"Well, honey, I guess we'd better find out what he wants, don't you think?"

Justine shifted on the seat but didn't offer any reply. Her jaw moved slowly back and forth, grinding the enamel off her teeth. It was an unconscious habit that appeared in times of nervousness and tension.

All right, thought Margaret. *I guess that's clear enough.*

Margaret took her foot off the brake, and the car moved gently forward.

"You two stay in the car," she instructed, veering left to avoid a long rut. "And lock your doors. Right now."

18

Jake Garrett was beginning to feel uneasy.

Hell, *beginning* was stretching it a bit; truthfully, the first sour rumblings in that direction had slithered down the telephone line over an hour and a half ago when Margaret Chambers informed him that there was a strange car parked on the side of the road by her farm. The man behind the wheel looked as if he was interested...

In what?

His crime site? That patch was picked clean, no more than a hole in the ground and, at this late date, not a particularly interesting one at that. Come morning he was ready to pull up stakes around it anyway. Of course, this guy had no way of knowing that. Maybe he thought, with all the barricade tape wound around it, that there might be a body or a skeleton tucked inside.

Some people were like that: slavering ghouls, and sometimes they drove BMWs.

Or maybe it was the farmhouse itself. Isolated by the surrounding hills, it might look like a tempting target for burglarizing, though any professional thief worth his salt would have driven right past. Certainly he would not have been so obvious in his scrutiny or so glaringly out of his element. As a rule, farmhouses did not make the most attractive or profitable targets for experienced burglars. Money had a way of running right back into the land in the form of irrigation improvements, better seed, or a new tractor. Any purchases over and above that became bulky to move and impossible to liquidate, such as new living room furniture, a dependable washer and dryer, a television that didn't turn everything a pale and sickly shade of green.

These were the things that were important to farm families, not diamond necklaces or Rolex watches. Christ, where would they wear them? Grange meetings and sewing circles? Or just out to till the south forty?

Nope. About the best a thief could hope for would be a nice set of silver, or maybe a few pieces of highly breakable crystal on display in the china hutch.

And every farmhouse had a gun too. That had to weigh heavily into any equation.

Garrett set the novel he'd been trying to read facedown on the coffee table. He stared out his living room window into the deceptive light of day. He'd spent the morning out in the yard, raking away the dead, brown grass and last autumn's missed leaves, getting it spruced up for spring. At noon he'd eaten lunch, satisfied with the work he'd accomplished, enough to allow himself the luxury of an hour or two of idle reading, providing nothing demanded his immediate attention when he checked in down at the station.

That had been when Margaret Chambers' call had come in, and he'd sent Troy Stebbins in a squad car to check it out, expecting the desk to call back within the hour, reporting the car gone. No apparent trouble, just someone who'd missed the turnoff.

Ninety minutes had crawled by since then, and his stomach had grown tight and upset, turbulent with the leftover chili he'd shoveled down over saltines. He found himself munching Tums like chalk-flavored candies, though a fat lot of good they were doing him.

It was *that* house. Always and forever the Taylor house. Everything about it made him edgy, irritable, as if it were his own private grain of sand, always worrying at the lining of his stomach, churning up bitter juices.

He looked at the jacket of the novel—darkening from red to maroon as his eyes adjusted from the bright sunlight—and sighed. *Damn.* He unrolled the foil from the last of his Tums.

Sunday was supposed to be his day off.

19

She rolled down her window less than four inches, enough to speak through but not an easy space to shoot an arm inside if that was what he had in mind.

"Can I help you?" she called out the crack as the sunlight, now in the west, struck her upturned face, bringing out all the worry lines. Her voice sounded strained to her, and she could feel her heart beating higher and faster in her chest.

The stranger smiled and moved nearer. He was a handsome man, with dark hair and brown eyes. His moustache reminded her of a sleepy caterpillar, and a large, oval-shaped mole sat high on his left cheek. To Margaret he looked like a young teacher, not much older than thirty-five, or an old student: someone who spent a great deal of time with books. The clothes he wore were somber, almost plain, as if he didn't spend much thought or money on them: solid, subdued colors over a white dress shirt, no tie. She might have been strongly attracted to him were she not scared to death, and she could feel Justine leaning toward her in the seat to keep his face in view.

Like mother, like daughter.

"I hope so," he answered, hands loosely in his pockets, consciously non-threatening. "Are you Margaret Chambers?" He had a trace of an accent: Australian or British Isles, charming when he spoke her name.

"Yes, I am." Incredibly, she found herself returning his smile. "Should I know you?"

"No, not unless you believe in time as a fourth dimension, that we've already lived out our lives and this particular moment is just one plane of your total existence, forever repeating." He shrugged, still grinning disarmingly. "In that case, yes, I suppose you should know me."

Her smile faltered as she scrutinized this odd supposition through the crack above the window.

"If not, my name is John Dunhill, and you've never laid eyes upon me until today."

"Yes," she affirmed. "You've been watching my house."

"Guilty." He raised the palms of his hands in defense. "But if I might explain, I was about to pull in earlier and introduce myself when you drove off, and if the sheriff's deputy who appeared shortly afterward is any indication, I'm afraid I gave you a bit of a scare, for which I sincerely apologize." He bent down and nodded to each of her children. "Hello. Hello."

Justine murmured something shyly, warily, and Hank pressed closer to the window, making Margaret tense in her seat.

"I told them you were probably FBI," Hank said cheerfully. His excitement, his youthful eagerness, was a palpable current flowing up and over the seat. "You are, aren't you?"

John Dunhill threw his head back and laughed, apparently quite pleased with the suggestion. Margaret herself had dropped the possibility as soon as she'd seen his clothes.

"No. I'm sorry to disappoint you, young man, but I'm not. Nor the CIA or the IRS. So you can relax. I'm actually sort of a freelancer." His hands, smooth and white, slipped back into his pockets.

This information, far from relaxing, told Margaret nothing. At this point, she would have preferred an agent of the FBI or CIA. Even the IRS. So far, this man had yet to offer her any form of identification. Her expression hardened. "What exactly is it you freelance in, Mr. Dunhill? And why are you so interested in our house?"

The stranger shifted his weight backward, though he looked far from taken aback or off balance by the direct manner of her questioning. He glanced at the highway to mark the loud passing of an unmarked freight truck, and when his eyes returned, they were earnest and clear. His wide smile had shallowed to simple amicability, light and conversational.

"Mrs. Chambers, I'm going to be very direct with you; in my line of work I find that's often the best. I investigate certain disturbances or phenomena some might call psychic or supernatural, though I prefer the term 'paranormal' as it more accurately reflects my own biases, its root being more *scientific*, you see. I investigate cases that fall beyond the established sphere or jurisdiction of ordinary police proceedings. In other words, I'm something of a ghost hunter, though that colorful title is also somewhat misleading."

"I see." Margaret's expression remained neutral, though her hand tightened visibly on the wheel. Hank, on the other hand, could not have been more thrilled. An exclamation of pure awe rose from the back seat, expressing impatience to be out of the car.

"Furthermore," Dunhill continued, raising a cautionary hand, "let me also establish right up front that I am in no way sanctioned by or otherwise affiliated with any branch of law enforcement. I work on my own, publishing my findings in the form of journal articles and full-length manuscripts, available"—he grinned—"at your better booksellers. I don't charge any fee for my work, and I won't release a word of what I've written without your full consent. I can work with pseudonyms, for your convenience, but I prefer to remain as factual as possible. Now, there are sever—"

"Whoa, *whoa!*" Margaret cut in, motioning with her arms and shaking her head. "Look, Mr. *Daniels*, is it?"

"Dunhill, madam. John Dunhill."

"Fine. I'm sorry to interrupt your little spiel here, but did I miss something? Where on earth did you get the idea we were in any way in need of your...services?"

He pressed a halting finger to his lower lip, as if this were a question he'd wanted to avoid, at least until he got past the door. "This is difficult," he said, "but as I was driving by—this was just prior to your leaving, incidentally—I saw something that caused me to double back and pull the car over. I get these flashes from time to time, you see, and what I happened to see were two young children there amongst your, ah, *debris*."

He was pointing at the old barn. Margaret didn't even have to turn to see. The fact that he'd said 'children' sent slow creepers along the back of her scalp. She thought of the open refrigerator, the missing food...all the odd things that had been happening around the house since they'd started work on the old barn. And hadn't she seen something herself—maybe even *two* somethings— prowling out there among the piles of rotting hay and splintered wood? Always out of the corner of her eye: vague shadows slipping over the scattered hillside, crazy shadows that seemed to wave like animals. Or children.

Two names she refused to acknowledge.

Still, he wasn't telling her anything he couldn't have gleaned from the local papers. Her barn had made copy several days running, and the two Taylor children were always prominently mentioned. How easy for him, fresh from breakfast in Colfax or Rosalia, to drive out here, playing upon their fears to hatch some scheme.

No. She wasn't letting him in, not unless he became a lot more convincing.

"I'm sorry, Mister Dunhill, but I'm afraid you've made a mistake. Now if you don't mind, I'm going to have to ask you to leave."

"*Mom!*" Hank protested, all but climbing over the seat to get between them, to keep her from sending Dunhill away.

"Hank," Margaret warned, her voice crisp and clear, gleaming with a tangible edge. "Sit back and be quiet. This doesn't concern you. If you have something to say, we'll discuss it later."

"But *Mom*—"

"*Hank!*" she barked, the sound virtually exploding inside the car.

He slumped back, dejected, and Margaret saw Justine reach a hand back to comfort him. The both of them probably wondered, half in shock, what was happening to their mother.

John Dunhill was watching her through the crack with a look of puzzlement laced with yards and yards of tepid understanding, as if his had always been a difficult calling.

"All right, Mrs. Chambers," he said, looking at the barn, the highway, and back through the crack. "But please believe me, it was never my intention to frighten you or your family, nor to touch upon a subject you're not yet ready to come to terms with. I only meant to point it out to you as a favor and offer my help in any way possible. You see, it's somewhat rare, and stumbling across it in the open here...well, I'm afraid I let my excitement get the better of me, for which I deeply apologize." He bent down again to take in her children. His eyes, brown and compassionate, jumped back and forth between them. "I'm not a bad man, just a little tired and homesick. You see, I have a son too. He just turned five last week, and being on the road and all, I missed his birthday."

Margaret raised a trembling hand to her temple and squeezed her eyes shut. Oh, this was a mistake! Rolling down the window and allowing him to play his charm flute...his tone so soothing, so hypnotic. Having adeptly divined that she wasn't going to open her door, he'd shifted his stance in a heartbeat and had gone to work on Hank and Justine, reasoning, from Hank's outburst, that he had indeed struck something that might be coaxed to the surface, bleeding and raw if necessary.

"...eating mostly out of greasy diners," his easy, loquacious voice hummed in her ear, persistent as a gnat. "So you're not seeing me at my best."

She turned to face him, letting the anger in her eyes burn clearly through. "Mr. Dunhill. I've asked you once to leave my property. I won't ask again."

He stopped talking at once, as if slapped, his mouth standing open in a loose "O" of surprise. The wind soughed through the crack, and he blinked.

"If you're not back in your car and driving away in two minutes, I'm going to call the sheriff." She paused for emphasis, her lips pressed to a thin, white line. "You may have noticed a cordoned crime scene standing over there"—she tipped her head toward the wreckage—"which I'm certain will hasten his arrival."

The stranger closed his mouth and glanced at the wreckage, and when he opened it again, the same song came pouring out, wheedling and honey sweet.

"Please, Mrs. Chambers. I'm not trying to upset you *or* your children." He looked at her, his eyes more penetrating, more direct now. She almost expected him to start pawing the side of the car like a dog that wants to be taken for a ride. "I don't need to frighten anyone to find work because in nine out of ten instances the lodger already knows what I've told him is true, or at least suspects it might be, if he could simply put aside his skepticism long enough to consider it! My driving away isn't going to change anything! The bumps and thumps, the missing items, the cold spots and flashes, the nightmares in the dead hours…none of these are going to disappear willingly!" He thrust an accusing finger toward the rippling nylon of the police tent, proof irrefutable. "That hole in the ground leaves no doubt! Is it an *ordinary* hole, Margaret? No different than any you or I might dig with a pick and shovel? When you stand next to it, gazing down, don't you *feel* anything?"

Margaret regarded him flatly, without emotion. As he paused for her to answer, she pointedly checked her watch, counting down the seconds until she put the gearshift in reverse and made good her threat.

Dunhill sighed and scratched the back of his neck in open irritation. His eyes traced the ribbon of the highway once again, as if he were watching for something: perhaps a whole truckload of "paranormal" investigators to help him take the property by storm, all in the name of pseudoscience.

Or a single police car.

"You've let loose a force you don't understand!" he screamed through the crack, filling the interior with his frustration. His hands were balled up into fists, white knuckled and demanding.

That cut it with Margaret. No one stood over her in her own driveway, shouting and raving like a madman, trapping her and her children in her car. She stamped down on the clutch and wrestled the gearshift into reverse, swearing heatedly under her breath. The car shuddered as she floored the accelerator, coughing as it backed away with a high whine. Dunhill jumped back to keep his foot from being run over, and she whipped the wheel around, pointing the car toward the roadway.

She fought for first gear and sent them jerking forward.

Justine let out a high squeak and scratched for a handhold on the door's inner molding. Her other hand pushed at the dash, keeping it at arm's length as they buckled over ruts and potholes. Hank was bouncing in the rearview mirror, his face pale and unhappy. Beyond him, John Dunhill was waving his arms in resignation and cutting quickly toward his car.

He was shouting something at her.

"Crazy bastard!" Margaret growled, baring her teeth in the mirror.

The nearest telephone was half a mile away—on Bert and Alma Clemenson's kitchen counter—and she took the most direct route available to reach it, not pausing once along the way.

20

The deputy assigned to the dispatch desk was Angelo Ramirez.

He was a man of average height and weight, with dark hair, dark eyes and the blackest, bushiest moustache the department would allow. His eyebrows, likewise, were thick and black (thinning only slightly as they dipped toward the bridge of his nose), so that when you first saw him, up until the moment he spoke, you were never quite sure what mood he was in or what was running through his mind, all of which did wonders for his luck in the occasional department poker game. It was the moustache, mostly; it grew down, shadowing his lip, so that he appeared to carry around a perpetual scowl to anyone more than three feet away. Jake Garrett, however, generally found him to be both calm and good natured in temperament.

As the sheriff pushed through the glass door fronting the station, however, Ramirez looked neither calm nor good natured. Today his moustache failed him, and his face betrayed an air of anxiety and frustration that Garrett could read from across the room. Angelo had the phone pinched between his ear and shoulder, so intent upon his call and the nonsensical notes and doodles on the legal pad in front of him that he failed to notice his supervisor's arrival.

It turned the lump in Garrett's stomach colder. He reached a finger inside his shirt pocket for the familiar roll of antacids and came up empty: nothing but lint and foil. With a grimace of irritation, he remembered he'd ground the last one to paste before he'd left home. A mental note was made to check his desk for a spare.

"¡Maldita sea!" Ramirez swore, grumbling heated expletives in Spanish as he slammed down the receiver. "¡Mierda!" He was lifting the heavy, gray microphone from its stand to send out a message on the police band when the lobby grew noticeably darker, as if the sky had taken a bite out of the sun. He glanced up, and his eyes tripped over Garrett. It was the sheriff's day off and he hadn't bothered to change into his uniform before driving down. It was like seeing Santa Claus without his red coat and cap.

"I've been trying to reach you!" Ramirez said, surprised.

"What's up, Angelo?" Garrett could hear the fatigue in his own voice.

"It's Stebbins," the deputy replied, straightening himself in his seat to regain some of his lost composure. "I can't raise him on the radio, and he was supposed to check in…"—he consulted his watch, a chrome-plated wristband with a face as large as a silver dollar—"Christ, over half an hour ago!"

"Did he report back about that suspicious car parked out by the Chambers's place?" Garrett asked, frowning.

Ramirez shook his head, and the lobby grew darker still.

"Are you telling me that no one's heard from him since?"

Angelo nodded, all traces of surprise and agitation smoothed away, pulled back under the mat of his moustache. "I called Bishop fifteen minutes ago, asking him to cruise by and check it out." He shook his head. "Nothing so far, but I was just about to try again." He showed the sheriff the microphone in his hand as irrefutable proof.

The sheriff made an absent gesture of approval, telling his deputy to go ahead. His eyes, red from the season and lack of sleep, considered the lacquered countertop; the darkening pits and scars in the finish struck him as somehow prophetic. With a sigh, Garrett realized he'd be driving out to the Chambers farm again, no matter what Bishop had to say. He'd never sleep tonight if he didn't.

Before either of them could get far, however, the telephone rang. Two rings separated by a short silence, indicating an outside line. For a brief instant, their eyes met over the scuffed black of the receiver. Curious but hesitant.

Angelo lifted it from its cradle before it could ring again and answered:

"Sheriff's Department. Deputy Ramirez speaking."

His dark eyes turned thoughtful and then blinked, revealing nothing. "Yes, ma'am," he replied when a brief pause broke the insistent buzzing in his ear. He looked up at Garrett. "He's standing right here if you'd like to talk to him, ma'am. Just a moment."

He held out the open line.

"For you, Sheriff," he said. "It's Margaret Chambers."

Ten minutes later, Garrett was behind the wheel of his cruiser, chewing on a fresh roll of Tums and listening to the radio spit out bits of coded static in Angelo's crisp, calm voice. He was moving quickly out of town, bound for the Chambers' place after a short detour to the Clemenson farm, where Margaret Chambers had placed her call and insisted on meeting him.

She wasn't setting foot on her property, she'd said, until he sent another man (or better yet, came himself) to check the house and outbuildings. No way was she taking her kids back there with that lunatic still around. And while they were on the subject, whatever happened to the first man he'd sent? How come he hadn't run this Dunhill character away?

Garrett had replied sympathetically to her concerns, though he didn't go into any detail over the phone as to why his deputy hadn't shooed the man away, partly because he didn't want to frighten her any more than she already was, but mostly because he'd yet to receive a satisfactory answer himself. He simply assured Margaret that he would be looking into the matter personally and was on his way out to meet her. Under no circumstances was she to go back to the house on her own.

As fields of wheat unfolded about him, rolling past and then folding once again, Garrett marked the position of the sun over the westerly hills. The afternoon was dying, he noted with concern, casting lengthening shadows over the highway and collecting in deepening pools amongst the fields.

He urged the speedometer up to seventy-five.

The radio squawked, and he heard the voice of Craig Bishop, who was already circling the farm. Bishop's tone was tight and clipped, as if he were holding his breath, and what it told him was that, after a preliminary drive-by, there were no lingering signs of any strangers nor of Deputy Stebbins.

Garrett picked up his mic and ordered him to stay in radio contact, to remain in his cruiser and investigate any secondary or access roads in the immediate vicinity of the Chambers farm; he would join him there after a brief stop at the Clemenson's, and together they would conduct a search of the house and grounds. Garrett was aware that he was being overly cautious, but until he found out what happened to Stebbins, he wasn't taking any unnecessary chances with his deputies.

Bishop confirmed the order, and the radio fell silent again.

Before he'd left the station, he asked Angelo to initiate a background check on Jonathan Dunhill for outstanding warrants or prior offenses, but the way his luck was holding lately, he was already certain that the name was an alias, made up on the spur of the moment. Another ghost for him to follow.

He ground his teeth in frustration, thinking of Stebbins.

Damn it, Troy, where are you?

This should have resolved itself by now, either with Dunhill complacently on his way or already brought into the station for questioning, explaining his sudden interest in the Chambers place. Even in a worst-case scenario— ending, perhaps, with Stebbins dead by the side of the road after the sudden appearance of a gun—it should have resolved itself, and that made Garrett very uneasy; in the absence of a solution, he was left with a number of more unpredictable possibilities.

A hostage situation, perhaps. Or a loose psychotic.

And either way, he was hurrying toward a time bomb, without the slightest notion of where it was or how to defuse it.

He noticed he'd let the speedometer slip back down to sixty.

"Supposed to be my day off," he complained again, pushing back down on the pedal.

21

In the dusty twilight of an abandoned barn a mile and a half northwest of the Chambers's farm, the man who'd introduced himself through a narrow window crack as John Dunhill took off his jacket and laid it across the front quarter panel of Deputy Stebbins's cruiser.

Above him he could hear a faint stirring in the dry rafters, a hollow whistling through the holes in the roof. Other than that, the world was blessedly quiet—stark and windswept—as if it too were stiffening toward the grave.

As perspiration gathered in layers beneath his arms, he rolled the left sleeve of his shirt past the elbow, searched for a vein, and slowly pressed the tip of a hypodermic needle beneath the skin. The barrel was filled to its midpoint, fifty cc's, with a clear solution he'd extracted from a large vial kept in a black leather bag, much like a doctor's satchel in appearance. He kept his needles and syringes there too, along with an oral thermometer, a stethoscope, and a secondhand sphygmomanometer. The glass vial itself was labeled "ADRENALINE," though that was not what it contained. It was an elusive mixture: odorless and colorless, much like water but thicker and more viscous.

With his thumb, he depressed the plunger into the nose of the syringe and grimaced as the potent substance lit through his veins. He shuddered instinctively, and a tight, animal grunt broke from his lips.

He leaned against the side of the cruiser, moaning as life and vitality melted back into his limbs. He took a deep breath and shakily exhaled.

In the pocket of his jacket was a pen and a small spiral notepad; once the initial tremors subsided, he dug them out and set them on the hood of the car. He took the thermometer out of his black bag, shook the mercury down, and jabbed it under his tongue. After consulting his watch, he recorded the date and time on the first available line.

His temperature had risen to 95.2 degrees.

His pulse was thirty-five beats per minute and his respirations eight.

His blood pressure was seventy-six over thirty-two.

With a sigh, he closed the pad and tucked it away. The vital signs were a great improvement over the original serum, but they were still too low, hovering just below the threshold of acceptability. What he needed was a stronger distillation, one with a greater longevity in the bloodstream. Two shots a day were leaving his arms like a junkie's, so scarred with needle marks that he had to wear long-sleeved shirts all the time, even on the hottest of days.

His hand slid from the cruiser, and he staggered toward the BMW as a bolt of white pain tore through his midsection like shrapnel. He screamed, startling a small colony of bats from the crossbeams, and keeled over sideways, losing his breath as he struck the barren dirt with a heavy thud.

A soft rustling came from the trunk of the BMW, then a knocking, dull and without cadence, as if something were calling to be let out.

Curled up on the ground, his skin leaking fire, John Dunhill shivered and waited for the terrible spasms to pass, laughing all the while from the abysmal depths of his insanity.

22

The reagent turned out to be a marvelous preservative. If his own flesh and bone wasn't proof, he found that out five weeks earlier.

Smeared with dirt and hunkered over a ragged hole in a cemetery in eastern Washington, Dunhill had been amazed at the lack of decomposition in Daniel Shires's broken face and restful hands. It was there, to be sure, reaching out from between the fingers and spreading down from the hairline, but after twenty-some years in the ground, sleeping through the ever-changing seasons, he had no right to expect much more than dust and parchment hanging in leathery tatters off the bone.

Shires had been buried in a pauper's grave, a simple pine box, without sentiment or ceremony, but his body felt solid and whole, his limbs stiff but firm.

Dunhill chuckled softly to himself. He knew from reading his former colleague's journal that Shires had succumbed to the same indulgence that he himself had been guilty of. Indeed, that was what had drawn him back to Whitman County after all these years: the hope that his partner might somehow be revived, brought back to some semblance of his former self. The reagent, quite obviously, was imbued with a kind of half-life, like uranium, that remained active within the host tissue long after death. He needed only to look into a mirror for proof of that.

He looked thoughtfully at the withered face. The truth be told, the last twenty years had been lonely ones, two decades spent as the solitary traveler, forever the outsider out of necessity for his work. It would be pleasant to have someone to talk to again, an old friend who knew his history. A companion in whom he could confine.

Perhaps there was a small current of consciousness alive within Shires as well, lethargic and introverted after all these years. Dreaming or insane.

Very soon he would find out.

Raw, pungent dirt trickled into the grave; it clung to the dead man's hair and eyebrows, smudged his cheek and dribbled between his colorless lips. One eye lolled half-open, glazed and cracked as if caught by a milky freeze. Dunhill focused the flashlight upon it, and a darkened pupil appeared beneath the narrowed slit, fathoms deep. He separated the lazy lid with two fingers and held it open, gazing down as if into the mouth of a well, wondering if there was still water at the bottom or just a worthless residue of dampness.

"Hello, Daniel," he had whispered, wiggling the light back and forth, as if Shires were merely sleeping. "Are you in there?"

Nothing glimmered. If Shires had life within him, it had guttered too far down for him to reply. "No matter," Dunhill murmured, unperturbed. He set the flashlight aside and climbed from the grave. One end of the cheap coffin collapsed with a sigh beneath his weight, disintegrating as a fine powder danced in the strong, white beam. His faithful black bag lay in the grass nearby. Inside it were the tools he would need to raise poor Shires out of his torpor: the needle and syringe, the sluggish bottle of "adrenaline."

Satchel in hand, he lowered himself back into the uncertain excavation and straddled the corpse. Bending, he grasped it by the lapels, grunting with effort as he tipped the reluctant body into a sitting position, wedging it against a corner of its splintered box. The back of Shires's jacket was streaked with mildew, and, with an expression of distaste, Dunhill scooped up a loose handful of dirt and rubbed his hands briskly together, as if that were preferable to fungus.

The body began to weaken and slide back into its coffin, as if Shires knew what his old partner had in mind and preferred the grave to that rekindled existence.

"None of that, none of that," Dunhill muttered, grasping Shires by the jacket again and pulling him back.

Overhead, the stars shone down, icily indifferent, as he opened his bag.

"Now then..." He punched the needle through the rubber stopper, and the syringe drank deeply of the reagent. "We'll start you off with one hundred cc's and see if that doesn't warm your old bones."

The solution had to be injected directly into the base of the brain, into the primordial stem, so Dunhill bent Shires forward with a gassy groan and tugged at his dampened collar to get a look at the back of his neck. The skin beneath was dark and spotty, with flora cropping up in colonies like bread mold.

He held up the syringe and bled the air until the needle tip threw off silvery drops of moonlight.

Grimacing, Dunhill inserted the needle into the soft hollow beneath the skull, his thumb poised upon the plunger. It occurred to him that he should be writing this down, step by step, in case some complication arose. *Never trust to memory.* How often had he lectured Shires on that very point? *Write it down! Learn from your errors! Only halfwits and fools make the same mistakes twice!*

With the loaded syringe still sticking out of Shires's neck, Dunhill patted down his pockets for his notepad, and the small scrap of pencil pushed through the middle of its spiral binding. The pencil flew in hurried loops and dashes, describing his efforts thus far in his own specialized form of shorthand. On the last line, he consulted his watch, noted the time, nodded with apparent satisfaction, and then tucked the notepad away.

Shires hadn't moved and offered no complaint when Dunhill pushed a glutinous bubble of reagent into the atrophied tissue of his brain stem. He withdrew the needle and cast it aside, tipping the tired corpse back into its corner and glancing again at his wristwatch, impatient for something to happen.

Neither the warmth of the flashlight nor the coldness of the moon were much good at picking up subtle changes in color and skin tone, but after five minutes, Dunhill thought he saw some improvement. True, with a crushed skull, Shires was never going to look natural or even passable in the real world, but there was a definite firming beneath the surface as the muscles responded. His dead colleague flushed, as if in the shuddering grip of a fever; his eyes rose higher within their sockets, assuming a healthier clarity, and the bruised eyelids drew slowly back.

With a ragged scream, Daniel Shires awoke from the dead.

Reanimation occurred in just under eight minutes, Dunhill noted with an oily smile, hushing his companion with a soiled palm slapped over his hard, dry mouth.

23

Despite the improvements he'd made over the years, the serum never fully brought Shires out of the grave, even after repeated doses. Perhaps it had to do with the bone fragments still lodged within his brain, slicing up capillaries or blocking critical synapses. Or perhaps Shires had developed a new breed of madness, forever past the point of reclamation; yet if that were the case, why hadn't *he* developed it as well? He had been just as dead as his one-time friend and collaborator, though admittedly not as long, dreaming the same lonely dreams.

Maybe it varied by time or by individual…

Or by the desire to come back.

Still, he wasn't giving up on Shires. Not yet.

24

As the dosage and potency increased, so did the time it took for the burning and tremors to expire. Gradually, however, as the bats settled back to sleep and the minute hand of his watch counted off another quarter hour, John Dunhill found he could stand once again. He paced the derelict barn until the spasms subsided and his legs felt like steel. Only then did he retrieve his bag and approach the trunk of the BMW.

He paused, listening to the soft, padded knock, like an animal bumping about in the enclosed darkness, looking for a way out. He shook a ring of keys out of his pocket, inserted one into the trunk lock and let the lid lift upon its counterbalance.

Daniel Shires writhed in the sudden wash of filtered daylight, thumping his head blindly against the right tire well. A foul glaze of spittle foamed down his chin and his eyes. His face was haunted and dark, rolled upward in an agitated grimace.

Dunhill smiled. "Hungry, Daniel?"

Ridiculous, of course. All of Shires's internal organs had been cut away and removed during the autopsy twenty years past; the telltale "Y" stitched up his abdomen and across his chest was adequate proof of this. Perhaps the organs had been replaced by the medical examiner after they were weighed and examined, but if so, they were an unconnected mass, dysfunctional filler for the empty cavity to be sewn shut against.

Still, Shires gnashed his broken teeth until a bright thread of scarlet slipped over his cheek, as if he were, indeed, feeling pangs of hunger. He thrashed against the confines of the trunk, like a squat worm enclosed from the neck down in a rough sack of stained, blue canvas. Once it had been a laundry duffel, bought for under five dollars at Fonk's Variety as they were passing through Colfax, complete with drawstring; now it was all the clothing that Shires was ever going to need.

For the sake of convenience and available trunk room, Dunhill had amputated Shires's arms and legs, reasoning that he was never going to need them again, looking and acting as he did. This man who had once been his closest friend and confidant was now his most unwilling subject.

"How about an injection instead?" he teased, searching through his black bag for the hypo he'd marked for Shires. "An apéritif of serum in the back of your rotten head, and then we'll see about dinner."

He found the plastic syringe, capped it with a fresh needle, and drew out the same dosage he'd just administered to himself.

"Hold still, old man," he murmured, leaning in the open trunk with an outstretched hand. "This is liable to sting a bit."

These days, with the lack of progress or cooperation Shires was exhibiting, Dunhill wasn't so particular about where he gave the injection, so, channeling the day's frustration at the Chambers's house, he simply jabbed the needle indiscriminately through the filthy blue bag and slammed the plunger down, delivering all fifty cc's in the space between heartbeats.

That done, he stepped back, extracted his pencil and notepad, licked the dull point, and recorded the now-familiar screams and seizures which characterized the solution's rapid progress through Shires' abbreviated system.

Baring his teeth and hissing poisonous flecks of saliva, Shires bucked and thrashed and succeeded in reopening the ugly amputation wound on his right shoulder, the one that never seemed to heal. As the reagent bit deeper, he rolled limply on his side, curling up as best he could and riding it out, whimpering softly to himself as if he were going to die, which, at this late date, was the only avenue that was blocked to him. Even if the injections were immediately discontinued, Dunhill conservatively estimated, poor Daniel now had enough reagent soaked into his tissues to keep him preserved (and minimally functioning) halfway through the next century. The same held true for himself, of course, but he wasn't much like Shires. He might put that time to good use, whereas Shires would only find fulfillment and acceptance in a circus sideshow, side by side with the pickled fetuses and three-headed calves.

The two of them had become like vampires; only fire could wholly destroy them now, or acid. Even if their bodies were hacked to pieces, the pieces would continue to live, wriggling about like bits of earthworm. He'd learned that from Shires when he'd sawn off his arms and legs. The amputated limbs never accepted the fact they'd been detached, even as he pitched them into their shallow grave, where they still wiggled and clawed for all he knew.

He removed his gaze from the trunk, satisfied that no new developments would sprout from the wretched torso this day. Actually, he had only one last hope for Shires, and Margaret Chambers had effectively blocked that opportunity today. That didn't particularly worry him; there was still the night, the next day, and then the following night if necessary. She would come around or simply cease to matter, one way or the other.

Take Deputy Stebbins, for instance. *He* had been a problem with his gun and his badge and his olive-green uniform, bullying and prodding him along the side of the highway. Then he had ceased to matter. Speaking of which…

He picked up his bag and limped over to the silent cruiser. The keys were still dangling from the ignition. Dunhill leaned inside, pulled them free, and, bouncing them against his palm, moved to the trunk. It took him a moment to find the right one on the plentiful ring, but when he did, it slid smoothly into the lock, and the lid popped neatly open. Really, it was marvelous how well American law-enforcement officers kept their cars. He himself took exceptional care of the BMW (presented to him as a sort of gift by a man who, sadly, could no longer enjoy it), but then again it was a pleasure to care for.

He looked down at the deputy and sighed. The man still looked surprised. Dead over three hours and still he couldn't fathom it. *How could this have happened?* his wide eyes seemed to plead, though presently directed at the left tail-light assembly. *How in the world could this possibly be?*

"Blame it on the rampant availability of handguns in your country," Dunhill said, setting his black bag inside the cramped splay of the man's legs. "And the complete lack of conscience it takes to use them so effectively."

In fact, there was very little blood, no more than what spilled from a broken nose. Death had come quickly, mercifully, meeting him on the shoulder of Highway 195 like a runaway cement truck. He'd been dead before he hit the ground, and what stray splatters had fallen to the weathered asphalt Dunhill was able to rinse away with a thermos of the deputy's own coffee.

For the first time, Dunhill noticed the wide gold band around the man's left ring finger. It was the only thing that still looked unchanged and alive.

A notion occurred to him, and he looked at his bag.

A smile spread slowly across his face.

"Let's see what we can do about getting you home, shall we?" he said soberly, with all the charm and inflection of a doctor on television. "Your wife, she must be terribly worried."

Out came the needle.

Rubbing his hands briskly together, he bent into the trunk a second time and picked up the fallen deputy. The body felt cool beneath the dried blood and starch of his uniform, and Dunhill wrestled it into the front seat of his BMW. With some difficulty, owing to the rigidity that had settled into the deputy's arms and legs, Dunhill was able to buckle him into an upright position behind the steering wheel, using both the waist and shoulder restraints.

The outer door to the barn rattled open, as stiff as Deputy Stebbins, and after a long pause to see that no one was about, Dunhill strode quickly back to the waiting BMW to administer the injection. Time and hard experience had shown that, whatever refinements he made to the serum, the subject's initial reaction could never be predicted. Some awoke like madmen, roaring and raging like tigers, while others came slowly to, as if awaking from a satisfying nap. Between these two extremes lurked every other shade imaginable.

He recalled one bull-necked brute back in London, a reasonably fresh cadaver laid out naked on the table, who'd grown a club-like erection moments after the injection: the first obvious stirrings of life. Upon regaining his remaining faculties, he'd leapt up and tried to become amorous with a number of nonreciprocal objects: a bundle of his own soiled clothing, a stained porcelain sink, the torn and helpless remains of an earlier experiment, even poor Shires himself, who'd had a bad moment or two in the thug's needful grasp before Dunhill was able to intervene with a well-placed scalpel.

You never could tell. Even though he had the deputy buckled securely behind the wheel, there was a distinct possibility that the one bit of knowledge he'd bring back from the great beyond was the quickest way to unfasten a seatbelt.

Dunhill reached through the driver's open window, crooked his arm around the steering wheel, and twisted the ignition key. The faithful BMW coughed quietly and then settled into an even purr, smooth and content despite the absence of a foot against the accelerator. John Dunhill decided he was going to miss the car: its style, luxury, dependability, not to mention its generous trunk space. He would have to look into getting another once things settled down, but at present it couldn't be helped. After his run-in with Margaret Chambers, the authorities would be on the lookout for it. For the present, however, why, he could drive the cruiser right up to the Chambers' back door without alarming anyone.

The thought made him smile.

He spied Stebbins' six-cornered hat resting in the wedge between the dashboard and the windshield, reached in to return it to its owner, then decided to keep it for himself. With the night falling, it would make his silhouette behind the wheel that much more convincing. He tried it on for size and found it a trifle small (not surprisingly) but not enough to toss back.

"Guess I can't blame you for the head you were born with, can I?" he said, coughing on the noxious taste of exhaust filling the barn. The bats didn't like it either; he could hear them squeaking and flapping about the rafters.

From the trunk of the idling BMW, Shires thumped his head and moaned.

"Right," Dunhill murmured to himself, as if reminded that time was growing short. "Let's get on with it, shall we, Daniel?"

He opened the trunk of the cruiser and transferred his meager belongings (along with an unwilling and highly vocal Shires) from the BMW and then, panting, slammed both lids shut.

Before climbing behind the wheel of the cruiser, Dunhill tipped his too-small cap to the nodding deputy, brought up the needle and, holding Stebbins firmly by the hair, injected all the syringe would hold into the stem of the man's brain.

"Cheers, old man."

He switched on the BMW's headlamps and pushed down the door lock before turning to the waiting cruiser.

"Daniel!" he called, hammering the trunk with his fist in passing, black bag in hand. "We're off again! Best sink your teeth into that spare; we've a bumpy ride ahead of us!"

He opened the door and slid behind the wheel. A Smith and Wesson .357 lay on the seat beside him. It was fully loaded, as was the shotgun in its passenger-side mount. He twisted the ignition, revved the engine a few times, and threw the transmission into drive.

The sun was just setting below the hilltops. The sky ran from pink to faded blue. Above him, the bats were flying, escaping into the cool evening air.

As Dunhill drove the cruiser out under the gathering stars, the pale oval of Troy Stebbins's face bobbed up in the windshield of the BMW. His spidery hands gripped the steering wheel.

25

John Dunhill had first read of the Chambers's farm earlier that week, over a breakfast of bacon and eggs at the Wheat Bowl Cafe.

Come to find out, however, that wasn't exactly true. He'd first read of the farm under a different name, in his old partner's journal. Back then, the residence had belonged to a Jonathan Taylor, and, if he were to go back a step further, Dunhill himself had spent several days nailed within a crate inside the Taylor barn.

The very barn that seemed to be making such a splash in the local papers.

He read on, intrigued by the story, by the way it dovetailed with the secrets buried in the last few pages of Shires's journal, giving him a measure of insight that no one, not even the sheriff, possessed.

The paper ran three photographs alongside the article: a large image of the demolished barn, complete with sheriff's deputies and barricade tape, and two small photographs of Samuel and Caroline Taylor, who'd disappeared in the summer of 1959, only to be found dead of dehydration and exposure.

The two smaller renderings were obviously snapshots, black-and-white portraits cropped out of a larger scene, distorted by time and the imprecise matrix of newsprint. You had to close one eye and squint with the other to bring them into focus, and even then they looked awkward and indifferent, as if they'd languished in a press file for twenty-two years.

The next day, the Whitman County Gazette ran a photograph of the barn as it stood in 1961 and an election-year photograph of Jake Garrett. The article focused on the Taylor case, updating subscribers on the fate of the property and all the key players involved, and concluded with Garrett's refusal to comment about it.

John Dunhill cast his mind back decades to when he'd first found himself in that unlikely corner of the world. He didn't remember his resurrection, nor much of anything, for several weeks after, but one of the first things he did recall was a sense of regret at the death of his former colleague. There was no guilt or sorrow associated with the event, even though Dunhill guessed that Shires's death had come at his own hands; he'd seen enough resurrections to know that subjects were rarely in a calm or rational state of mind when they came up off the table.

He *had* had the reflex or presence of mind to take Shires's battered medical bag (which had contained the journal, a few basic medical instruments, spare syringes and an ampoule of the reagent). Inexplicably, he'd also emerged from his post-death fog carting about an odd-looking contraption that turned out to be a mechanical fish counter (useless outside of a hatchery) and a rusted alarm clock (useless, period). These later items fell by the wayside as his intellect and rationality returned, but he poured over Shires's journal for months afterward, taking a special interest in the small refinements that Shires had made to the original serum.

During those early years after his reawakening, bits and pieces of his former life came back to him without warning, attacking him like seizures, ambushing him wherever he happened to be, until only a few gray pieces remained. The two most notable, and frustrating, were his death and his rebirth, and by this late date Dunhill guessed that, despite his best efforts, they would stubbornly remain gray.

Nevertheless, this was not his first return to the county of his rebirth.

He'd come back once before. He had not bothered with Shires that time; the solitary life, as he knew, held its undeniable charms. His chief focus at the time, rather, had been to find the man whose name appeared again and again within the pages of Shires's diary: a new partner taken into his confidence (God help him) by the name of Smith.

Dunhill didn't know what he'd do if or when he found Smith, but the question turned out to be moot because, by all he could discern, the mysterious Smith had long ago parted ways with Whitman County. Either that or he was no longer experimenting.

John Dunhill had a nose for such things.

By luck and a little persistence, he *was* able to find the Taylor farm, though by that time the twins were long dead. Curious, he took a trip out there anyway, but he quickly learned that the farm belonged to someone else. He knocked on the door and spoke to a young and amicable man by the name of Henry Chambers, who was able to put his mind at ease about the Taylors. Jonathan had been dead for six or seven years, and his wife had moved away shortly afterward, Chambers regretfully informed Dunhill, who had come posing as an old family friend visiting from California.

End of the trail, Dunhill had thought, driving away, though the name "Smith" still bothered him. It caught his attention whenever he heard it in conversation, like a sliver under his skin.

Now this, years later: a hole in the ground, kept secret even from the property's owner, threatening to shed light on a twenty-two-year-old mystery. It coincided oddly with his second return to Whitman County, though John Dunhill did not believe in coincidences.

He folded the paper on the table and picked up the bill for his breakfast, frowning. By the time he left the cafe, he'd decided to drive out to the old farm again.

If only to satisfy his own curiosity.

26

At the same time, Dunhill was at something of a crossroads as to what to do with Shires.

Five weeks had passed since he'd dug Shires out of the ground, hoping that there might be something left of his old partner. This notion was by no means a new one. In fact, the idea had been flitting about his head for five years or more, but it wasn't until he'd reached Huehuetla, Mexico, that the compulsion to revisit the Palouse country of eastern Washington solidified into something more substantial than idle thought.

Aware that his own rebirth had taken a matter of weeks, Dunhill had been willing to wait; yet in those intervening weeks, keeping watch over Shires quickly became a twenty-four-hour-a-day job. Shires's appearance had improved somewhat, but there was no mistaking him for anything other than a living corpse. His flesh was like rotting leather, his eyes were sunken and cloudy, and an odor like concentrated mildew clung to his emaciated frame. There was no intellect or rationality left, only an overwhelming will to run away from Dunhill or crawl back into the ground.

Two weeks earlier, Shires had actually made it across the two acres of open field that stood between their rented house (a dilapidated farmhouse that had been on the market for eight years) and the old highway. He'd been shuffling west along the weedy shoulder when Dunhill finally caught up with him. Fortunately, it had been late in the evening, and no one had seen him.

Or, at least, Dunhill prayed that no one had.

In a fit of pique, he'd taken a rusty saw to Shires's arms and legs, removing all four in the space of a half hour, allowing Dunhill the first night of uninterrupted sleep he'd had in weeks.

But the burden of carting an agitated torso about, moving it from the cellar of the house to the trunk of his car, not to mention sharing his injections, was beginning to wear on Dunhill. The one thing that kept him from disposing of Shires completely was the nagging suspicion that his old friend was more cognizant and self-aware than he was letting on.

True, the man was nothing remotely like his former self, but neither was he quite the mindless thing that Dunhill had first supposed. There was an awareness there, deep down below the surface, that bobbed up from time to time, especially in moments when Shires thought he wasn't watching.

The strange torso reminded Dunhill of an octopus a fellow student had kept in a lab aquarium back in Oxford. During the day, the octopus kept to the bottom of its tank, but at night, after everyone had gone, it would crawl out of the aquarium and manipulate objects within the lab, even hauling some of them back to the tank. It left telltale trails of water about, but everyone believed it a prank until a camera equipped with an automated timer was left pointed at the creature overnight.

Shires was like that octopus. Even in his abbreviated state, it was clear that the man had a secret, perhaps something brought back from behind the veil.

This intrigued John Dunhill.

The trouble was that he hadn't yet discovered the proper tool or leverage to force it out into the open.

The trip to the Chambers's farm changed all that.

Two days earlier, as the late afternoon sun was leaning toward the horizon, they'd cruised slowly, leisurely past the Chambers' farm; Dunhill sat behind the wheel as Shires rolled about the trunk. Dunhill was well able to see the remains of the old barn where it had once stood facing the farmhouse. What surprised him, however, were the two small figures standing within the wreckage, both gazing back at him, their heads tracking the car as it slowed and then drove past.

Samuel and Carolyn Taylor, he thought, astonished, as a slow chill crept up his spine. The dead twins whose faces had graced the first newspaper article.

There came a sudden noise from the trunk. It was fearful, agitated, as if Shires felt it too: the simple recognition of the dead by another of their kind.

His thoughts whirling, Dunhill found a gravel crossroad on which to turn around. He sat in his car, smoking a cigarette, and decided to take something of a chance. He waited until the highway was clear and then hurried behind the car, opened the trunk, and moved Shires to the front passenger's seat, propping him in place as best as he could. From several yards away, with the setting sun casting long, purple shadows, Shires looked like an infirm old man sleeping against the window.

Behind the wheel again, he drove back to the Chambers' farm.

As soon as the twins came into view, Shires began to moan and squirm in his seat, clicking his teeth loudly together to express his displeasure. Dunhill hesitated, glanced into the rearview mirror, and then turned into the Chambers' driveway. He brought the car to a halt, not venturing too far into the property in case someone happened to be watching from inside the house, just enough to make it look as if he'd taken a wrong turn and was thinking about turning back.

Motionless as lions, the twins stared, their eyes like coins facing the westering sun.

Slowly, without taking a step, they drifted toward the car.

Shires began to panic. Between the gnashing clicks of his teeth, a hoarse wail rose from his throat, and he beat his head against the window, marking the glass with an oily excretion that was tainted with a rusty smear of blood. His groans broke into stuttered dots and dashes, as if his scabrous mouth was trying to form syllables. As the twins came within a hundred feet of the car, he settled on one: a hissing sputter that to Dunhill's ear sounded as if Shires was trying to pronounce the name "Smith."

"What, Daniel?" Dunhill grasped Shires by the head and turned his face away from the window. "What is it you're trying to tell me?"

But Shires didn't want to be turned from the window. His eyes, as wide and expressive as Dunhill had seen them in these past five weeks, rolled sideways, keeping the twins in sight.

At the same time, Dunhill sensed a movement to his left.

A woman was standing on the steps of the farmhouse, looking at him. The frown on her face suggested that chasing away sightseers had become a burdensome chore these past few days.

Dunhill released Shires and shifted the car into reverse. A truck towing a trailer of potassium nitrate rumbled past his rearview mirror, its horn blaring. Dunhill swore and stomped on the brake.

He looked left, right, left again and then shot backwards onto the highway, tipping Shires roughly against the dash.

Accelerating east toward Colfax, Dunhill glanced into his side mirror and saw the pale oval of the woman's face, watching to make sure sure he went all the way around the bend.

Shires thrashed and complained, trying to right himself, and Dunhill pushed him off the seat, out of the sight of passing cars.

As the next mile marker slipped past, Dunhill started to laugh.

Over the next two days, John Dunhill thought long and hard about how he might approach the woman, whose name he learned was Margaret Chambers. Her amicable young husband, he also learned, had died tragically some years back.

Did she know about the twins? Did her children?

And, more importantly, what might Shires tell him about the mysterious Mr. Smith if forced to pay another visit to the farm? A longer, more intimate visit.

Dunhill decided to find out.

27

By the time Garrett and Bishop met up in the Chambers's kitchen, full darkness had dropped over the house like a magician's cloak, velvet black and lined with stars. The shapes of the surrounding hills, the stable, the barn, and the highway that wound past them all faded into obscurity, so that when they gazed out through the window glass, all they could see were their own scowling reflections, ghostly and blurred from the double panes.

They'd searched for over an hour about the farmhouse and its outbuildings, beating the bushes, frightening the horse, kicking up the ghosts of long-gone chickens and peering cautiously through the piles of wreckage, reasoning that a man might easily hollow out a niche and wait out the daylight. Inside the cordoned tent, they found Margaret's dead mouse and, lifting it by the tail, Garrett briefly considered popping it into a sealed evidence bag. He threw it into the long grass instead, reasoning the case didn't need any new wrinkles or surprises. It was, after all, only a mouse, not a thing, he felt certain, that would come back to haunt him.

As it began to get dark, they moved inside.

Garrett took the cellar, and Bishop started on the main floor. They looked under beds and poked through closets, wriggled into crawlspaces and crisscrossed their flashlights through the large and neglected space of the attic. Behind chairs and draperies, in cupboards and boxes, anywhere a man might reasonably find a place to hide. The whole thing might have been routine, nothing but motions performed to ease the worries of a frightened family, but lurking behind each closed door was the shadow of a missing deputy, so they took the task seriously, wondering if they might find a corpse instead. One of their own.

Garrett had a bad moment when his own shadow, thrown harshly from the light of a naked bulb, peeked out at him from behind the furnace. For Bishop, a pulsing dread came with the confrontation of the bedroom closets, as if something were lying in wait for him, a sharp knife in hand.

When they met in the kitchen, however, having left a blazing trail of light to show where they'd been, Garrett was convinced that the house was safe. He would have bet on it. As he reached for the telephone, it occurred to him that he was doing just that: wagering the lives of a woman and her two children. The thought caused a chill, and he felt vulnerable standing with his back to the window as the silent vastness of the night looked in.

He took a breath, told Bishop to draw the drapes over the large window facing the breakfast table, and dialed the number of the Clemenson farm. Alma Clemenson came on the line after only one ring, as if she'd been poised with the phone in her lap for the past hour and a half. "Is everything all right?" she asked. Garrett asked her to please put Margaret on, and, reluctantly, Alma relinquished the receiver, satisfied she would get the story secondhand.

There was a brief pause. Cloth rustled over muddled voices as Alma smothered the mouthpiece with her breast. Garrett heard the sound of a magpie chatting in the foreground, then Margaret's husky voice. "Hello? Sheriff?"

What he had to report took less than thirty seconds: the house and surrounding grounds had been given the fine-tooth treatment, and everything had come up clean. She could bring the kids home, and he would be glad to wait until she got there.

He hung up the phone after she thanked him and turned to Bishop, who was pretending to study the pictures on the refrigerator. The wiry-framed deputy met his gaze, dark eyebrows raised. "Well, Chief, what now?"

Scratching his unshaven cheek, Garrett thought it over and sent him out into the night to continue looking for their missing deputy. He told Bishop to put in a call to Ramirez at the station. Higher authorities would need to be notified in order to widen and intensify the search; he himself would make those calls, but Ramirez would need to get the ball rolling locally.

"Check," Bishop confirmed, already moving toward the door.

Garrett watched out the window over the sink, frowning through his own reflection as Bishop got into his waiting cruiser and drove slowly away, red taillights flickering.

PART FIVE

Deaths: 1981

1

The first thought that crossed Jake Garrett's mind when he saw the headlights turn off the highway was that Margaret Chambers must have cut a new land speed record driving over from the Clemenson's. Bishop's taillights had just disappeared around the bend.

He rose from the kitchen table and went out the side door to meet her. His shadow slithered down the cement steps and stretched itself across the worn patch of lawn.

Well, hell, that's not her car, he realized, hands stuffed into his pants pockets, leaching warmth out of his goose-bumped thighs. It was, quite obviously, a department car: green and white and boxy, just like his own. Bishop must have forgotten something here at the house; either that or he'd picked up some new information on Stebbins or this Dunhill character, knowing he'd still be in the kitchen and not in his car, where he could relay it by radio. Garrett figured it must be the latter; Dave Bishop was not a man apt to lose anything or be forgetful.

Hands still in his pockets, Garrett moved to meet him at the end of the driveway.

The cruiser's horn tapped impatiently as it slowed to a stop, and the driver's-side window, reflecting the bright porch light, began to roll down, letting in the night.

"What is it?" Garrett asked, pigeon stepping the last few yards over shadowed ruts. "Has someth—"

Cold realization slammed into his breast, leaving his thick and stupid tongue wrapped halfway around the question. Several important revelations struck him at once.

The first was that this was not Bishop's assigned car. It was Troy Stebbins's.

Another was that he could not see the driver clearly despite the fact that he was almost on top of him. He could see only a vague silhouette in a six-cornered hat; whoever was behind the wheel had dimmed the dashboard lights down to nothing. Also, the sun visor had been flipped down.

The worst and most sickening realization of all came as he fumbled his hands out of his pockets and noticed that the familiar weight of his service revolver was gone from his right hip. He was defenseless. There was a shotgun in the cab of his cruiser, but it wasn't likely to do him much good, being locked and on the other side of Stebbins's car.

If the man inside the car meant him harm, there was nothing he could do now to prevent it. He could turn and run and take one in the back; he could dive down out of the driver's line of sight behind the car (in which case the man could simply throw the gear selector into reverse and tramp down on the accelerator); or he could stand right where he was and hope to God that it was Stebbins behind the wheel after all.

These thoughts, helpless and frail, whirled through his mind like autumn leaves as the window continued its slow descent. As the last sliver disappeared into the door's hollow panel, Garrett realized that his options had narrowed inexplicably to one. He stared into the car's dark interior with the blank fixation of an animal frozen on the highway's center stripe, fascinated by the inevitability of his own death. His body was a stone, heavy and tired, his legs weak with old age and fear, his stomach (true to form) in bitter turmoil.

A contradictory odor wafted out the open window: corrupt yet strangely antiseptic. It reminded Garrett of a hospital corridor, on the quiet wing where they kept the terminal cases. It meant death to him as well; he could see that now, quite clearly.

Both thought and odor vanished on the breeze. Shadows, glossy and spidery, shifted inside the car, knitting themselves together. Glassy eyes, yellow teeth, and the steely muzzle of a loaded revolver all gazed out at him.

Then an undeniable force, a brick wrapped in thunder and dropped from the top of a grain elevator, slammed into his chest, and his feet left the ground. He tumbled backward, gasping, into darkness.

2

John Dunhill stepped from the car's interior through a lace of acrid gunsmoke, his ears ringing with the sharp concussion of firing a powerful gun within an enclosed area. It created the most annoying hum: a glass-bottle moan like the wind combing a deserted stretch of beach. It made everything else sound lifeless and flat.

Which fairly well described the condition of the man at his feet. Middle aged, overweight, the man was still struggling to hold onto his life, though any child could see it was a lost cause. Best done with and forgotten. Stupid of him to come trotting out to the car like that, though Dunhill supposed he knew that by now. Funny, though: with the second cruiser in the drive, he'd been expecting *cops*, two at least. This bloody geezer looked too old to be much more than a nuisance, and he—

"Oh Christ," Dunhill swore aloud. He crawled back inside the stolen cruiser and opened the glove compartment. A slim, weatherproof flashlight fell out into his hand, exactly what he wanted. He backed out into the night, thumbed the oversized switch and stabbed the strong, white beam into the dying man's face.

"Ah, bloody hell."

The man wasn't in uniform, but Dunhill recognized him all the same. His photograph had been prominent in the papers just lately, right alongside those miserable black-and-white snapshots of the Taylor twins. There was no mistaking him.

"Hello, Sheriff," he sighed, slowly shaking his head. "Did Margaret Chambers tell you I was annoying her? Or are you still looking for your lost deputy?" He glanced briefly over his shoulder at the unseen highway. "I imagine he'll be along directly. I left him my car, you see."

Garrett began to bubble at the mouth and cough blood, speckling Dunhill's trouser legs and the side of his car. Then, with a last rattling exhalation, he grew still.

Dunhill prodded his ribs with the tip of his shoe, as one might an animal.

3

The farmhouse was lit like a brilliant jewel against the fold of the surrounding hillside, sparkling against the wide curve of the windshield and then drifting slowly through the side windows as the car drew closer. Margaret took her foot off the accelerator and coasted the last hundred yards, applying the brake only as she signaled her intent to turn north off the highway.

She breathed a tired sigh of relief. In the wide splash of the porch light, two green-and-white cars were clearly visible, both belonging to the sheriff's department, side by side between the house and the barn.

Justine and Hank had grown quiet in their seats, peering at the uncommon brightness of their house, watching as it grew larger and then loomed over them like something out of a pulp novel as the car halted beside it. When Margaret turned off the engine, no one made an immediate move to get out; instead, they sat in the car and stared out the windows with mistrust.

Astonishing, Margaret realized, how quickly the weeds of doubt and suspicion could take root, feelings of violation and betrayal. Houses were supposed to protect and shelter, to instill within their owners a sensation of safety, of warmth and security. Yet, somehow, over the past week this house had fallen asleep on the job, and something had gotten inside. Something cold and malicious.

They might not feel it right away with the lights blazing and the police gathered around, but alone, once the lights were turned out, it would slink out to find them, unhappy and dissatisfied.

Margaret paused to study the windows. The curtains were drawn in the kitchen, which struck her as odd, but if brightness counted for warmth, they would all be suffocating within ten minutes.

"Mom?"

She wondered what Henry would have made of all this, had he still been with them.

Just lately she found herself thinking of him often. She was assailed, really, by random thoughts and images streaking like meteors across the blackened firmament of her fears. The clear and pale-washed blue of his eyes. The way he held his fork at the table, upside down so the tines curved down toward his plate. The strong, sharp smell of his sweat mixed with the dust of the fields as he rode in from a long day's work. The touching and oddly compulsive habit he had of rubbing his feet together under the bed sheets, as if slowly trying to spark a fire.

She brooded over the strange way he'd died, crushed beneath the unforgiving weight of the tractor, his body broken and bleeding, pushed down as if being forced upon the soil. But then, considering the hole beneath the barn, that wouldn't have been the first time it had tasted blood.

How many deaths did it take to make a haunting? How long until the soil bit back?

Justine touched her shoulder. "Mom?"

A helpless shiver jumped up her neck, like a cricket.

"What, honey?" She turned to her daughter and saw the houselights reflected in Justine's eyes. Behind them was a gnawing, rat-toothed apprehension.

"Do we...do we *have* to go inside?" She hesitated, opening her mouth and closing it again without finding the right way to explain, or even where to begin. She'd meant to utter some warning, something about trees or pitch-black bedrooms, about dreams that were both real and unreal, but the words turned into a lump on her tongue, all tangled and melted together, ridiculous if spoken aloud. Hank leaned forward in the back seat, further distracting her, and she made blunt fists out of her frustration. "I mean, couldn't we at least wait until morning, when it's light?"

To her surprise, Hank nodded in agreement. "Yeah, Mom. What if that crazy guy comes back?"

Margaret craned her neck and saw the same look in her son's eyes, though now it didn't coil and threaten to jump out at her. It touched off an anger instead.

She ground her jaw, picturing Dunhill. *How long until they feel safe again in their own house, you bastard? In their own yard? How long until I feel safe?*

Until he was caught, behind bars? That might never happen, and even if it did, how long would he stay there? The world was filled with men like Dunhill—you read about them every day in the newspaper—and the three of them were pretty much on their own out here. No use kidding them about that.

"I think we'd better go inside and talk to the sheriff," she said, twisting the keys out of the ignition, wondering in the back of her mind why he hadn't come out to meet them. "Then we can talk about where we're going to sleep tonight."

4

The lights were all on, but no one was home.

"Hello? Sheriff Garrett?"

Hank and Justine were right behind her, breathing on her neck as they paused in the short stretch of hall outside the kitchen. The sound her voice threw back from the living room was unmistakable: intuitive but nonetheless certain.

The house was empty.

There was no one milling about the kitchen, drinking scorched coffee or seated in the dining room, writing up reports in ballpoint on her antique tabletop. There was no one in the bathroom, urinating into the toilet or drying his hands on her clean towels. No one shuffling about the bedrooms.

Something's gone wrong, a small, frightened voice (nothing like her own, but more and more familiar these last few days) whispered in her ear, turning the soft, pink lining of her stomach to frost. It seemed impossible, but in the time it had taken her to pack the kids into the car and drive over (which couldn't have been more than ten minutes), the sheriff and his deputy had vanished.

The coat closet stood immediately to her right, mute and ominous. On the white plaster wall beyond it hung a framed piece of needlepoint (threaded by Margaret herself, once upon a time in front of the television with her drowsing husband by her side) spelling out the Lord's Prayer in faded strands of green and gold. Another, farther down the hall, depicted an old, red hand pump outside a leaning, brown barn.

The archway to the kitchen was two steps away, but she was suddenly afraid to look inside for fear that she was wrong, that someone *was* inside and waiting, crouched just out of sight.

She stood in the entryway, frozen with indecision. The compressor inside the refrigerator clicked on, and that somehow made it worse. What that soft droning might conceal from her ears might easily kill them all.

The night, cold and certain, pressed at their backs with a renewed sense of urgency, and a whiff of something like rust or old pipes slipped through the screen, chilling her.

"Mom?" Justine said. "What's wrong? Where's Sheriff Garrett? Wasn't he suppos—"

Margaret turned and shushed her with a quick finger to her lips. *Yes*, she nodded, *he was. Now quiet.*

Justine shrank against her brother, and, over her shoulder, Margaret glimpsed the silent shapes of the two cruisers, brooding side by side in her driveway; they looked strangely impotent, as if they were nothing more than ghosts or cardboard cutouts.

Hank, who'd left in only a worn sweatshirt and jeans, began to shiver.

Water was dripping slowly into the kitchen sink.

Plunk...plunk...

"Come on," she said hoarsely, marshaling them on since they couldn't very well perch in the doorway all night. Grouped together, they shambled forward enough to close the door.

Plunk...

Before she even looked through the arch, Margaret should have known the loose drip wasn't in the sink. It didn't leak anymore, not since last summer when the new countertops went in. She'd had the old fixtures and the basin replaced as well, which cheerfully took the place of the chipped and rust-spotted ones she'd inherited from the previous owners. She should have known, but the sound of dripping water had never been unusual in the house, and when the three of them spilled from the hall to the kitchen, the sight of Sheriff Garrett sitting at ease in their breakfast nook took them all by surprise. His head was thrown back, as if contemplating the ceiling or caught in mid-stretch. His arms dangled loosely at his sides, and underneath the table, his long legs were splayed in a tangle. What really caught

Margaret's eye, however, was the small puddle forming beneath his padded vinyl chair.

Plunk...

Not that it was especially large or dramatic, no more than would melt off a tall pair of snow boots after shoveling the walkways, but this wasn't snow or water. It was blood. And a second, harder look into the sheriff's slack face brought home the jarring realization that he wasn't stretching or relaxing. He was dead.

Directly behind her, Justine, hands pressed to her chalk-white face, began to scream. It was an eerie, unnerving sound.

Hank just looked stunned. His eyes and mouth hung open as if someone had dropped a fifty-pound sack of grain on him. Margaret feared that soon he would start making that noise too and that it would then spread to her, paralyzing them all with its easy venom. She realized that she had to get them out of there.

With a force of will, she dismissed the sheriff for the time being; he could offer them no protection, and it was clear he was beyond her own meager help. She clapped her hands sharply, painfully together and barked out her daughter's name in her most commanding tone, thankfully cutting the horrid wailing from the air as effectively as a scissor snip. Justine blinked, still very much shaken but *there* at least, open to direction. Her eyes switched from Garrett to her mother.

"Listen to me," Margaret instructed, doing her best to keep her voice calm and level. "Take your brother, *right now*, and go back into the hall and wait for me. I'm going to call for help, and then we're all going to walk out to the car together. Do you understand?"

Justine's attention had wandered back to the breakfast nook. Tears were forming in her lashes, ready to spill over. Margaret raised a hand and slapped her daughter, hard. "Justine!" she shouted. "Move!"

Reeling, Justine touched a hand to the angry imprint glowing against her pale cheek. Her lower lip quivered, ready to blubber, but the message got through. Voicing a cracked affirmation, she turned from the awful finality of the sheriff's glassy stare and, taking her younger brother by the arm, shepherded him back toward the hall.

Margaret turned and took a breath. The telephone waited on the counter. She picked up the receiver, but the line was dead.

Plunk...

Margaret felt herself swaying, teetering on the brink of a dangerous panic. She looked at Garrett as if for direction, for a sign; his face was uncomfortably direct from this angle.

She set the phone down and yanked open the drawer where she kept her good knives, grasping the first one that presented itself: not the largest in the set, but large enough, and agile in her hand. Its blade gleamed wickedly beneath the overhead fluorescents. She decided she could use it if she really had to.

The storm door banged shut as she was pushing the drawer closed, and she jumped, gasping. The knife jumped too and took a piece of her skin: a small, pointed jab at the base of her thumb that drew a dark bead of blood.

Hank and Justine started to howl as John Dunhill walked them forcefully back into the kitchen, his hand clamped tightly about each of their necks.

He was all white teeth and smiles, like a wolf in a corduroy jacket.

5

Sweat rolled out of his dampened hair, and his cheeks were flushed with the excitement of the kill. Eyes wide and unpredictable, twitching everywhere at once, John Dunhill looked like a junkie near the end of his ride. There was blood on his shirt, blood on his hands, blood smeared in a horizontal stripe across the sheen of his forehead, as if he'd marked himself for God and the world to see.

Margaret uttered a crow's ragged caw when she caught sight of him. Stepping nimbly into the kitchen, Dunhill shoved Hank and Justine roughly to the floor. There was a black revolver tucked into the waistband of his trousers, gleaming like a satiated leach, and he jerked it out to cover her movements as soon as the children were clear. Margaret still had the knife in her hand, though in truth she'd forgotten it was there.

"Drop it," Dunhill panted as the steely barrel bobbed in the charged air between them. Hank and Justine were crawling frantically across the floor, like two unarmed pawns who'd suddenly found themselves far behind enemy lines, on a collision course for Margaret's legs.

"I said *drop* the fucking knife!" he roared, dusky lips curling back into his droopy moustache, forming a cruel snarl. The gun dipped abruptly to the floor; he cocked the hammer and brought it back to bear on her, ready to fill the kitchen with flash, black powder, and still more blood.

The knife clattered to the floor, inches from her son's blind reach.

"Now move. All three of you." He made a quick motion with the gun. "Over against the wall."

"Please," Margaret sobbed. "Please don't shoot my children!"

Dunhill laughed, a tight, pressurized sound that pushed through the cracks of his teeth like oxygen escaping into the vacuum of space. "Mrs. Chambers," he said, shaking his head on its crazy axis. "You misunderstand me! I've not come to harm anyone! And if you and your darling *children* would kindly oblige me, we'll have no further need of these guns and knives. You have my word on that, dear lady." Leather soles tapped lightly on the linoleum as he moved closer, arm still outstretched. "Now come on, up against the wall there, behind the table. That's it."

Margaret felt as if she were caught in a dream. Only in dreams did the comfortable surroundings of home became so hostile and alien, leg muscles degenerated to jelly, incapable of support much less escape, guns and butcher knives became as common as cups and spoons around the kitchen table, you were forced to tread through a puddle of blood and stare into a dead man's eyes while his killer decided what to do with you and your family.

It seemed inevitable that he was lining them up to be shot, as mobsters or Nazi soldiers did in the movies. Given time, he might even hit upon the idea of taking them outside so they could dig their own graves before he dispensed with the bullets. She saw all of this, felt it happening, and yet was powerless to prevent it. It was all she could do to hold onto the frail thread of survival, to live from one tentative breath to the next. As Justine and Hank clutched painfully at her arms, Margaret shuffled forward to take her place along the wall.

"Please…" she pleaded, though the word came out stillborn. "Just tell me what you want."

"Very good," Dunhill said and nodded, allowing a shifty wink. "I *do* like your spirit of cooperation, Mrs. Chambers. May I call you Margaret? It might turn out to be a very long night."

She nodded mechanically, open to anything short of rape to keep him happy, to get them safely through the night.

Dunhill slipped across the textured face of the refrigerator, rustling pages of Hank's artwork and brightly colored school bulletins in passing. He bobbed down and picked up the knife with quick, birdlike grace, and the heavy eye of the revolver was on them again before Margaret even registered the fact. He laid the blade on the counter.

"I hope you'll pardon me for this rather indelicate invasion of your house," he said, turning his head as he began banging drawers open and shut, searching, "but since you wouldn't allow me to stay this afternoon—on what would have been, I'm quite sure, more agreeable terms— you've forced my hand to more, ah, drastic measures. *Aha!*" He was peering with one eye into the drawer she'd just shut after extracting the knife. It was where she kept all her kitchen knives, sharpened and ready for use.

"Gorgeous set you have, Margaret dear. The cutlery, I mean. Were they a wedding gift?"

She nodded numbly as he reached in and gathered them out, piling them with a noisy clatter upon the counter.

"There's nothing quite like precision German steel for cutting and slicing. I used to procure my own surgical instruments from a German manufacturer. I forget the name just now...but it was a small firm, just outside of Leverkusen. Beautiful work they did, highly specialized. Did you know I used to be a doctor?"

This bit of knowledge seemed preposterous to Margaret, utterly at odds with the picture she'd already formed of him.

"I was a brain specialist," he continued, musing over the cutlery, offering the clarification as if reading her mind. "A rather good one too. I could have worked at any clinic in the world, but in the end it was the promise and potential of research, of advancing the field beyond its present grasp, that lured me away. To test the limits of the brain's physiology..." He'd let the gun drift in his reverie and, waking, brought it back up, concluding with an enigmatic smile. "But all that was ages ago. Dust now."

Margaret shivered and wrapped her arms around her children.

With the inclusion of four steak knives, the pile on the counter numbered an even dozen. One by one, Dunhill began to drop them behind the refrigerator, grimacing as they clattered down the Freon coils and came to rest amongst the hidden grit and dust bunnies.

"They should keep well back there," he said with a satisfied nod. "And when all of this is over, one of the sheriff's obliging deputies will no doubt help you retrieve them. No harm done."

He tucked the revolver away and rubbed his hands briskly together. "Now then. There's someone I'd like you to meet."

6

He marched them in a line through the arch and back out the side door. They shivered in the night breeze while he trotted ahead to try his keys in the trunk of the nearest cruiser. The lid sprang open like a giant metal jaw, poised to bite him in half as he leaned inside. Margaret willed it to do just that, leaving a bloody stump in the driveway she could run over on her way out. When this didn't happen, she used the time to glance about the doorstep, looking for something she might use as a weapon, while his attention was caught inside the bowels of the police car.

Unfortunately, he'd left them in the middle of the yard, with only the damp grass underfoot and nothing within reach. Any movement would surely draw his attention and the unwelcome return of the gun. Hunched together as they were, a mere ten yards away, he'd have no trouble shooting them down. Best, she decided, to appease him. Now that the edge had been shorn from his desperation, let him get comfortable while she waited for her chance.

Dunhill straightened from the trunk, and she snapped her gaze back to neutral.

"Come on," he called, beckoning them over. "It'll take the three of you to hoist him out and carry him inside."

Justine turned a frightened and questioning eye to her mother, and Margaret nodded. "Just do as he says," she whispered, urging them forward. "We'll be all right."

"He's going to shoot us, isn't he?" Hank murmured, the syllables tumbling out hoarsely as he shuffled forward. The distance between his steps was rapidly decreasing, as if he were walking into a powerful magnetic field, though one that repulsed instead of attracted. Margaret felt its influence too.

"Not if we keep doing what he says," she said, squeezing his shoulder. "I think he just wants to scare us is all."

"But he shot Sheriff Garrett," Hank pointed out, and something in his voice told Margaret that he was never going to be the same boy she'd shooed off the couch that morning, even if he survived the night without a scratch. None of them would. She promised herself she would hurt Dunhill for that if she got the chance. Hurt him so that *he* would never be the same either.

"Come along, hurry up!" Dunhill growled, putting his hand on the grip of the gun. "Plan your little conspiracies on your own good time, not out here on mine. Any car that turns up that drive while we're outside is going to find three dead bodies when it gets to the end, you hear? Now *move!*"

Margaret flashed him a look that was pure loathing but kept her mouth shut and did as she was told. As they moved nearer, Dunhill stepped away from the bumper.

"Easy, Daniel," he said in a warning tone, as one might speak to an animal or a child. "I've brought some friends to help move you inside, so lie still and don't give them any grief." He nodded to Margaret. "The light blue duffel, if you please, and be careful; it's liable to wriggle and squirm about. Try not to drop it."

As they approached the open trunk, their preconceptions of what lay inside varied enormously. Hank pictured a leathery monstrosity, all bound limbs and snapping jaws. Margaret was sure it was a boy, no more than four or five, kidnapped and beaten from his travels with Dunhill. Justine (closest of all to the truth) sensed a dead thing, or some pitiable creature very nearly so. What they found, however, was uncertain. A large, canvas bag to be sure, filthy with layers of dried stains and so sharply nauseating that all three of them coughed and staggered back, as if hitting a wall.

And it was *alive.* Moving and scratching beneath its roughened shroud, making noises of distress and dissatisfaction.

"What in God's name *is* this?" Margaret said, her voice numb, pitched scarcely above a whisper. Despite this, the thing in the trunk heard her. A large and rounded mass, too big to be the head of a child, rose from one end of the duffel and strained its lumpy features against the clotted fabric. There came a sniffing sound, as if it were scenting them, then a long, shuddering moan, thick with phlegm or saliva.

Hank and Justine recoiled a step, their eyes wide and shocked, glassy in the cold starlight.

"Never mind what it is," Dunhill snapped, his face an angry shadow, jaundiced in the glow of the trunk light. "Just pick it up and carry it inside! *Now!*" He reached out and shoved Justine forward, propelling her over the lip of the trunk. She screamed and threw herself back, stumbling, as if the bag were filled with rattlesnakes, coiled and ready to strike.

Dunhill stepped forward and cuffed her, which brought Margaret forward with a sharp and anguished cry. The gun was out of Dunhill's waistband in a heartbeat, wavering excitedly between the three of them. In that instant Margaret was given another scalding glimpse of the monster, the snarling wolf beneath the veneer of pale skin. She would do well, she told herself, to keep that face in mind, no matter how calmly or eloquently the words tumbled from between its gleaming white teeth.

"You'll do as you're told, girl," the wolf panted, "or so help me God I'll fill little brother here so full of lead it'll take the *both* of you to lift him off the ground!"

Tears ran freely down Justine's face as Margaret stooped to help her to her feet. Hank seemed frozen in place, hypnotized by the deadly eye of the gun.

"Come on, honey," she said, turning her gently toward the trunk. "You take that end." She pointed to the bottom of the duffel, where she supposed the thing's legs and feet would be. "Hank, you take the middle, and we'll lift on the count of three. Just pretend it's a fifty pound bag of manure."

"And you wouldn't be far wrong, at that," Dunhill snorted contemptuously.

Together, the three of them reached into the trunk and took the duffel in an uneasy embrace, legs up against the bumper, backs bent, groping the filthy bag for purchase. Margaret found what felt like shoulders and suppressed a shudder.

"Ready?" she asked softly, looking first at Hank and then Justine.

Solemnly, they nodded back, the unabashed horror of the burden well apparent in their eyes.

"All right. One…two…*three.*"

Daniel Shires was borne out of the trunk and carried screaming into the blinding light of the house.

7

"Take him to the tub," Dunhill said, holding the storm door open. "May as well bathe him straight away and give our noses a rest." The revolver was still in his hand, though no longer threatening. Its blue-black muzzle pointed down at her flowerbed, at the tulip bulbs slumbering beneath the newly spread layer of peat moss.

Hemmed by the narrow confines of the hall, the bag (to which Dunhill kept referring as "Daniel" or "Shires") became much more awkward to manage. It jerked, twisted, and thrashed wildly about, scraping and knocking them against the walls. A piece of Margaret's dusty needlework was upset, and, surprisingly, it was Dunhill who bent to retrieve it, returning the frame carefully to its nail.

"Here, here, Daniel!" he bellowed after them, cursing. "Give it a rest, you nasty old stump! They're taking you to the bath is all! Sweeten you up a bit, if that's at all possible."

The sound of his voice served only to aggravate the sack, and by the time they reached the hard left turn leading to the bath, it was bashing its head blindly (or perhaps intuitively) against the house's right angles. Fresh blossoms of gore spread against the canvas. Justine stumbled over a small pile of dirty laundry that Margaret had collected from the bathroom that morning and uttered a hiccough of pure terror, mindful of the warning she'd been delivered outside. Margaret and Hank, fearful of dropping the burden and rekindling Dunhill's wrath, struggled to redistribute the thrashing weight of the load while she regained her balance.

All the while, the thing inside the duffel was bleating and moaning like a deformed goat, doing its best to upend itself and fall.

"Christ to God Almighty!" Dunhill murmured. Margaret tasted fear like rusty steel on the surface of her tongue. "Hold it," he said. "Stop right there."

The gun, which had been nuzzling his crotch since the porch door, came out again, and Margaret froze, the stress and unpredictability of the situation cutting deep arroyos in the bedrock of her emotions. Dimly, she recognized the probability that she would snap like an old twig if this monster executed her daughter before her eyes.

And then God help Hank.

Dunhill stepped forward—impatient, aggressive—and Margaret tensed for the blow. He gritted his teeth, reversed the revolver, and lashed out in a quick downward arc that ended at the bag's midsection.

A winded noise, almost comical in its surprise, blew through the head of the sack. Margaret, who was holding that end by what she supposed were its shoulders, felt its passing on the inside of her wrist: warm and moist, like some noxious gas forced out of the ground.

"*Stop messing about, I said!*" the wolf screamed, his lips ruddy, flecks of foamy madness caught in the underside of his moustache. He stepped forward and delivered another jarring blow. "Stop it right now or we'll fill the tub and dunk you in as you are now, like a sack of bloody laundry! You hear me, Daniel? Would you like to drown in your little bag?"

The thing abated in its convulsions; it shivered rather than shook, sobbing quietly within the confines of its loose prison.

"I thought not." Dunhill nodded to himself, winded from his outburst but apparently satisfied. He holstered the gun in his waistband and shifted his gaze to Margaret. "Carry on. Into the tub with him." He paused, licking his lips casually, and his eyes sharpened on her, as if he expected a fight. "You'll be the one to bathe him, dear."

A stone flipped over in Margaret's stomach, the underside damp with white fungus and silverfish. The revulsion must have shown in her face because Dunhill smiled.

"Yes," he said, clearly enjoying himself, "I believe I'd feel that way myself. But don't worry; he can't harm you, not unless you get careless around his mouth, that is."

"Don't you think it's time you told me what you want?" she said flatly, returning his gaze. "You didn't drive all the way out here and murder the sheriff just so I could give your little pet here a bath."

"No?" Dunhill said, raising a black eyebrow. "Didn't I?"

Margaret shook her head, frowning.

"Ah, well, true enough," he conceded, allowing the smile to creep back, wanton and mischievous. "But we have all night to discuss that, and if we're lucky, my plans won't concern you; *any* of you...ah, except Daniel here. So you see how expendable you are? An empty, peaceful house would suit my purpose splendidly, but since you're here, the three of you, and I can't let you go..."—he touched the protruding end of the gun—"*cooperation* is the key, the essence of your collective parts in this impromptu little drama."

"Fine," Margaret exhaled. "If you don't need us, then why can't the children wait in their rooms? There's no sense in putting them through—"

"Ah-ah," Dunhill said, cutting her off with a brusque wave of his hand. "I'm beginning to lose patience. Into the bathroom, please. I don't intend to stand here debating while the clock ticks away. Remember: *cooperation*."

A muffled snarl of protest cut through the duffel as they lurched forward again, shambling the last few yards to the bathroom. Margaret, in the lead, paused at the threshold to elbow the light switch and caught a quick glimpse of herself in the mirror. The day seemed to have aged her terribly. The weight of a decade hung on her head and shoulders, stooping them, pressing down lines which hadn't been there that morning, drawing out her complexion until it seemed a morbid study of paleness and waxy shadows. It was not a sight she felt like lingering over.

Justine, now in the center, edged through the door and then Hank, looking withdrawn beneath his unruly bangs, like a young soul sold into slavery. She renewed her promise to hurt Dunhill if given the chance, to pull the trigger of his gun where it sat in the crotch of his trousers and watch him sink, wide eyed, to the floor.

"What the hell are you waiting for?" he shouted, voice booming off the tiles as he leaned through the doorway. "Set him down in the tub!" He flashed Margaret a look meant to wither, yet it just struck her as tiresome. "If you three aren't the most *useless* clods! Do I have to tell you *everything*? Whip you like senseless cattle?"

Hank flinched as they lowered Shires into the wide porcelain basin, as if prodded by a hot wire. He looked up abruptly, spooked, his eyes round and black.

"Gently now, *gently*!" Dunhill cried, suddenly worrying over a bag he had pistol whipped and threatened to drown.

They placed the indignant package carefully on what they supposed was its back, letting it slide off their aching forearms and onto the cold, hard surface. Sighs of relief were expressed over creaking joints as they straightened and stepped awkwardly from the tub, letting Shires fuss and wriggle in his cloth like a litter of newborn kittens.

Margaret reached a hand toward Justine and received an unhappy nod for her concern. Hank, however, looked beyond the reach of a reassuring touch, incapable of a nod. Instead, he stood numbly like a draft animal awaiting its next command. He had hunkered down, preparing himself for the worst, no doubt thanks to Dunhill's threat of shooting him outside if Justine didn't stop screaming.

Over my dead body, Margret thought.

She shepherded him into a corner (forgetting Dunhill for the moment, who was busy clucking over Shires anyway) and knelt down in front of him, looking imploringly into his eyes.

"Hank?" she said softly, combing back a lock of blond hair from his brow. The skin was cool underneath.

Nothing in response, or perhaps only a faint twitch in the awful slackness of his jaw.

"Sweetie? Can you hear me?" A single tear, long and bitter, ran down her cheek, and she struggled not to give in to it. Not in front of him.

"Leave the boy alone, Margaret," Dunhill said as he pushed up from the wide lip of the bathtub and dusted flecks of grit from the palms of his hands. "There'll be no secrets behind my back." He adjusted his gaze to include Justine.

Margaret rose slowly, defiantly, and snaked a protective arm around her son's shoulders, pressing the other against his chest. "You're the one who's done this to him." This was spoken with tight, clipped assurance, convincingly and without the need to raise her voice. The accusation was heavy enough without it.

Dunhill laughed lightly. "My dear," he pointed out, "I haven't even touched him."

"Not hardly, you haven't" she returned, wanting to spit in his loathsome face, working her tongue to do just that—damn the consequences. Hank interrupted, murmuring quietly into the fabric of her blouse.

"The pigs, Mama." He turned up his face and looked deeply into her troubled eyes. "Do you hear them, too?"

"What, honey?" She stroked his head, hoping her touch would soothe him. The word "Mama" was going back a few years for him; he'd started calling her "Mom" shortly after his seventh birthday, after Justine started teasing him about it. That told her something about his regression, though it was nothing she could take comfort in.

"The pigs." He shuddered, peeking out fearfully at Dunhill and then burying his face in her breast.

"*Pigs?*" Margaret realized he might be speaking from somewhere else, somewhere safe.

Justine was starting to slip away from her too. Without an immediate task to occupy her hands and mind, her eyes had settled on the empty threshold with an expression of shock and horror, as if the pause had given her a chance to catch up with what was happening, starting with the dead lawman out at the kitchen table.

An unexpected shiver touched the back of Margaret's neck, bringing a chill as if a sudden draft had entered the room, turning her skin to gooseflesh. Actually, it was more of a cold patch, drifting in without the accompaniment of a breeze.

Hank clutched at her more desperately, moaning as if from the depths of a dream.

The thing in the bathtub grew quiet and still.

Dunhill's eyes grew narrow and wary. He looked hard at Justine, who startled them all with a small gasp or choking sound in the back of her throat, her attention unquestioningly focused on the doorway.

The strange chill withdrew just as suddenly as it had come, as if an open door or window had been discovered and firmly shut.

"What the devil are you gawking at?" Dunhill snarled at Justine. He glanced into the hallway again, as if expecting to catch someone there: the police, perhaps, having located their missing sheriff. It remained empty, however, save for their overlapping shadows.

Muttering a few heated expletives under his breath, Dunhill shook his head and returned to the task of releasing Shires from his sack. The simple square knot he'd tied to secure the heavy duffel had shrunk into an unyielding stone, the threads of nylon cord fused together in a stiff mass. Usually he went at such hard cases with his teeth, biting and loosening the threads; instead he gestured impatiently to Margaret.

"You've got long nails, haven't you? See what you can do with this." He stepped aside to allow her room, blocking the door with his body.

Margaret gently detached herself from Hank's clinging embrace (he'd grown quiet again as the cold retreated) and knelt on the mat beside the tub. In truth, she kept her own nails trimmed back to the nubs, but at this point it seemed useless to protest, so instead she picked up the limp end of the duffel and went to work at the knot with more dexterity than Dunhill had the patience to muster.

He watched approvingly over her shoulder as the knot began to crack and then soften. "Actually," Dunhill mused, stroking the rough stubble under his jaw, "there's no need for the rest of us to stand about, taking up much-needed space and getting in the way. Why don't I take the children out to the sitting room where we can get better acquainted, while you finish up in here?"

Margaret clenched the line in her fist and looked up at him, angry and silent.

"Really, all you need to do is dump him out and give him a good scrubbing. Plenty of suds and hot water should do the trick. I'm sure you have something, a nightshirt or a bed sheet you can wrap him in once you're done."

"And *then* what?" Margaret asked, moving her hand defiantly from her hip to brush away a stray lock of hair.

"We *wait*, dear," he replied coolly, resting his hand on the butt of the gun. "We sit and wait until I say different. All right?"

8

Alone in the bathroom with the disturbing Mr. Shires, Margaret went at the stubborn knot again, this time with a sharply pointed pair of beautician's scissors she kept in the sink drawer for trimming her bangs when they started to tickle her lashes. Dunhill, in his eagerness to excuse himself from any further effort on Shires's behalf, had been more concerned in herding out the children and had neglected to check the room for such things that might be used against him. Margaret intended to keep the pair handy now, in case they should, well, come in handy.

On her knees beside the tub, making short work of the knotted cord with the fine carbon steel, Margaret braced herself to face whatever horror was certain to come slithering out. She opened the puckered mouth of the duffle with both hands and rolled it cautiously back.

An abrupt gasp came out of the bathroom and bounced around the living room walls: not quite a scream, but certainly more than a moan or a choked exhalation. Justine and Hank, huddled together on the far end of the sofa—as far away from Dunhill as they could manage—looked toward the archway leading to the hall with renewed expressions of terror and concern.

Seated in an adjacent recliner, a slow grin spread over John Dunhill's pleasant features.

Margaret thought she'd prepared herself for deformities, for a lack of arms and legs at least; that much she'd been able to guess simply by carrying it from the car to the tub. She had also been holding out hope that these defects were congenital, smooth and untattered, and not the mutilations of a madman's whim.

Not so. The hasty stitch marks, the obvious cauterization and subsequent scarring: this was the handiwork of Dunhill, the doctor who had now fallen to pointless sadism and butchery.

And that wasn't the worst.

The thing had the clammy pallor of a corpse: gray with a toneless layer of stringy muscle stretched beneath the translucent surface of its skin. Sores flowered along the bony edges and in other places, between cadaverous ribs and the taut cords of its clavicles. The tissue had torn or broken down to an alarming degree. The crowning horror, however, was the head itself, for it looked to have been badly crushed at some time in the distant past and then reset (if such a thing could be done) with the greatest indifference. The hollows along the temples were traumatized and uneven, the gray-brown hair over the sickening pate grew in withered clumps, and its mouth—which worked itself in a constant chewing motion—was cracked and bloody from chronic dehydration. The teeth inside were little more than shards, broken and at odds with one another.

The eyes, however—oh, Lord, the eyes!

They were cloudy and senseless as she pulled back the hem of the bag, but when they caught on her they *changed*, and what Margaret saw in them threatened to tip her over the brink. Caught below the cloudy surface of its own insanity, a visible intelligence still lurked inside: a presence of mind that knew all too well what it had become. It gazed up into the shocked oval of her face, reading her thoughts, her repulsion obvious, as if printed there in block capitals.

It weighed her expression and then pleaded for release. Not just out of the filthy duffel or out of John Dunhill's cruel reach, but out of existence. Wholly and completely. Erased and buried like its other missing parts.

Overwhelmed, appalled and sympathetic toward its wretched condition, Margaret forgot for a moment about her own predicament. She picked up the long scissors from the bath mat and looked down at the unfortunate Shires as if he were a badly wounded bird she'd happened upon while walking across the fields, one that would never survive.

Moaning softly, he fixed his eyes hungrily on the gleaming blades, offering her the flesh of his unprotected neck.

The reality of her situation returned to her. Dunhill would surely take exacting measures for such impulsive actions. Releasing her last breath, hardly aware that she'd been holding it, Margaret lowered the scissors back to the floor, tucking them out of sight beneath the thick pile of the bathmat where Dunhill wouldn't see them if he happened to look in.

Shires held her eyes with his own, his body still and attentive now. Margaret wasn't sure he understood, or if, in fact, she'd read his intentions correctly, but the line seemed to be open between them. In spite of the awful stench rising up to meet her, she leaned closer, afraid that Dunhill might be lurking in the hallway, listening.

"I'm *sorry*," she said in a trembling voice, one that had been rubbed raw with emotion. "He has my babies…"

With a sigh, Shires relaxed his long neck and took his eyes from her. His mouth began to work unhappily again, and he became restless on the cold floor of the tub.

Easing back, Margaret straightened herself for the work ahead, wanting to get back to her children. "I'm going to give you a bath now," she explained, shielding his head from the spigot. "I…I'll try not to hurt you."

She opened the taps slowly, dialing the temperature to as warm as she thought he could take it, then added generous amounts of Mr. Bubble and her own expensive bath salts to cut down the odor. As for the washcloth and towel, she searched out a pair of old ones because once she was done she wouldn't think of using them on a dog, much less her own skin.

The water level had risen halfway up Shires's emaciated trunk by the time Margaret returned from the linen closet, and she hurried to shut it off, letting the bathroom fall once more into silence.

Dunhill's voice drifted lazily from the living room, distant and amiable, trying to draw Hank and Justine into conversation.

Kneeling, she looked down at the head atop the battered torso, trying to divine its thoughts. It appeared calm and contemplative, staring through the paint and plaster ceiling with an expression she couldn't begin to fathom. She put the attempt aside; it was enough that the water hadn't thrown him into a panic.

She picked up the soap and washcloth and began to work.

The bubbles that gathered around him, once sparkling white, began to take on a pinkish tinge, and Margaret frowned; somewhere, he was bleeding.

She tried a lighter touch and prayed to God he wouldn't fall apart before she was through.

9

Dunhill saw himself reflected as a monster in the children's eyes. There was a time when this might have bothered him, but not tonight. With the blood on his hands, soaked into the fabric of his clothes, he rather relished the part. Oftentimes he felt like a monster, not quite whole, as if something crucial had withered away between his death and resurrection: his conscience, perhaps. But then again, he'd never been a saint.

He rose from his chair and walked to the window, looking as far left as the glass would allow. He couldn't see the barn, not from this side of the house, but it felt as if the twins were out there, watching.

He tapped gently on the pane. "Come out, come out, wherever you are," he whispered, fogging the glass.

The day wasn't going as planned. He'd expected to see Samuel and Caroline Taylor just where he'd left them, standing amidst the ruins of the barn, as if they were toys he'd left out in the yard: sad, sulky, but more or less intact. When that hadn't been the case, he'd pulled the BMW to the shoulder of the highway, focusing his gaze on the dark-green ripple of the tent. It felt empty and deserted to him, as if the ghosts had all fled; the silence from the trunk seemed to confirm this unhappy suspicion.

He had taken a breath and reached for his cigarettes, trying to decide what to do next. At the same moment, Margaret Chambers emerged from the side door of the house in a light jacket and scarf, her two children in tow. She hadn't spotted him yet, making straight for her car instead, as if the three of them intended to drive into town and do a little shopping, though the boy seemed to be dragging his feet.

Margaret opened the door to the Chevrolet Citation, uttered something sharply to her son, and the three of them piled into the dusty and tired-looking car.

Dunhill forgot about his cigarette, watching as the car backed up, turned itself around, and then jounced its way toward the highway. Margaret caught sight of him at the end of the drive and braked abruptly to a halt.

Dunhill turned his face away, looking off into the fields and then down, as if he were consulting directions or a map.

The Citation remained where it was, undecided for almost a minute, and then turned right. Rosalia was only a few miles away, and if she intended to notify the sheriff, that was the place she'd most likely do it.

Better wait and see, Dunhill thought. If he turned onto her property, he could be rousted for trespassing. The shoulder of the highway, on the other hand, was fair game, and he kept a Kodak Instamatic in the glove compartment; it was a convenient excuse for being caught in graveyards or along lonely stretches of road. After all, there was no law against taking snapshots.

And if the camera didn't do the trick, there was always the .38 revolver tucked under the seat. A desperate step if things went badly.

Dunhill rolled down the window and lit a cigarette, settling back to wait.

Less than ten minutes later, a deputy pulled up neatly to his back bumper.

Margaret, it seemed, had made excellent time to Rosalia.

Dunhill touched the camera on the seat beside him and stubbed out his cigarette. He smiled out the window as Deputy Troy Stebbins approached the driver's side of the BMW and asked for his license.

The smile faded as Shires bumped loudly against the wall of the trunk. After that, the situation had rapidly disintegrated.

On the shoulder of Highway 195, a tipping point had been reached, a place from which he could no longer retreat with any safety or certainty. From then on, John Dunhill stopped thinking about the consequences. He pressed forward until something blocked his way, then either ran over the obstacle or, if it proved too large, worked his way determinedly around it.

The dead deputy in the trunk of the cruiser was one such obstacle. He simply couldn't leave the car parked in front of the Chambers' place, nor did he have much time to dispose of it.

He cast his eyes about, frowning, and then happened to recall an abandoned barn he'd passed a mile or so back, one of dozens, or hundreds, that dotted this corner of the state, just one hard wind or heavy snowfall from collapse.

He pulled the BMW into the Chambers' driveway, parked in front of the house, and then trotted back to the roadway. Once behind the wheel of the deputy's cruiser, he started the engine.

Thirty minutes later, he was back on the farm with the place to himself.

Even then, the twins did not appear.

He stomped through the wreckage, shouting at the rusty nails and splintered lumber. He crouched inside the tent and spit curses into the open ground, trying to provoke a reaction.

Yet, no reaction came; the wind whispered about him, but that was all.

As a last-ditch effort, he carried Shires to the tent like a bag of dirty laundry and deposited him inside the hole, a measure that must have surely struck the dead as offensive, if not sacrilegious, yet even Shires appeared unperturbed.

Something, quite obviously, was missing, and John Dunhill had a pretty fair idea of what it might be.

From his researches into the occult, when he and Daniel were attempting to coax not only life into bodies but *spirit*, Dunhill knew that ghosts generally attached themselves to people or places. Until now, he'd assumed that the Taylor twins were clinging to the barn itself or the hole hidden beneath it. As time passed, however, he abandoned that notion, favoring one of the family members instead.

But which one? he wondered, turning his attention from the night outside (and thoughts of the day) to the reflection of the two children seated behind him on the sofa. *Hank or Justine? Or Margaret, for that matter?* Had she not lost a husband here, which by itself would have the potential to stir up a haunting or prolong an existing one? He knew that spirits were more likely to attach themselves to women or girls than men. Some so-called authorities blamed this on the acuteness and complexity of female emotions, while other suggested it had more to do with the tissue and blood expelled within the monthly menstrual cycle, especially amongst adolescent girls.

Whatever the cause, it had put Justine at the top of Dunhill's list. Until, that is, Hank had started babbling about pigs in the bathroom, as if from deep inside a trance.

Dunhill turned from the window and frowned.

It made for a sticky situation because, without that certain knowledge, it severely limited what he could do with his gun. He could wave it around and threaten to his heart's content, but when it came to pulling the trigger, he chanced breaking the thread that could finally bring Smith within his reach.

Dunhill ground his teeth together at the very thought of the man running about, somewhere out there, with *his* formula, doing God knew what.

"*No*," he whispered, shaking his head. That could not be borne, not while Daniel held the key. He would either deliver it tonight, on command, or else go back into a hole in the ground, this time without the benefit of a cheap pine box.

Dunhill strode back to the easy chair and made himself take a seat, smiling at Justine despite the restlessness he felt.

One thing he did know: Daniel was agitated once again, and had been ever since the Chambers family returned from town. Dunhill took that as a sign that the twins were near, perhaps just below the threshold of perception.

Glancing at the door leading to the bathroom, he felt the shadows of both Stebbins and the sheriff at his back, nagging reminders that, despite his immortality, time was running short. He ruminated on this for an unpleasant moment and decided that if the hour wore on without any tangible results, he might try his hand with the knives, just to see what it provoked.

Five more minutes, he thought to himself, waiting for the tub to drain.

10

John Dunhill was perched like a spider in the overstuffed recliner Justine's mother usually sat in to do her reading or mending as they watched television in the evening. Tonight the TV remained off, and the night outside pressed softly, inquisitively against the windowpanes. To Justine, it felt as if the house had fallen to the bottom of a deep and sterile lake, one whose inky waters would eventually break through the glass and engulf them all.

The hollow ring of water filling the bathtub had squeaked off some minutes ago, leaving only soft and intermittent splashes as the thing they'd carried inside was made presentable. Occasionally Justine could hear it moan or chide, which only made her imaginings worse, because the sound wasn't exactly human.

She stole a look at Dunhill, so smug and relaxed in her mother's chair, and wondered what sort of thing he might keep in a filthy blue duffel. Carrying it into the house, her arms felt as if she were embracing a ribcage, all curved bones and spasms, or perhaps a large and rabid badger, a dark curiosity he'd found one night along the side of the highway. It must have been *horrible*, she thought, biting her lip, to have made her mother cry out as she had.

As these thoughts flew through her head, she turned to find Dunhill looking back at her.

"Scared, little dove?" he asked, showing a thin crescent of a smile.

She nodded stiffly. Actually, she was terrified.

"You're a smart girl." He uncrossed his legs and leaned forward. "Sometimes that's for the best because it keeps you *alive*. Take now, for instance: it's keeping you from doing all the stupid things that are flashing through your pretty little head. It keeps you in line. You understand?"

Again she nodded, not trusting her voice to answer.

"Fear," he elaborated, leaning back, "is one of the world's great motivators. Right now it has your mum washing up something she wouldn't bring herself to pick off the road with a ten-foot shovel. It has you two sitting there on the davenport like perfect lambs when what you'd really like to do is run screaming from the house." He laughed softly. "I've struck a nerve there, eh? Good! You needn't hide it, pretend it isn't there. I can see it in your eyes...the dread that I might take this revolver and put it to work."

Quiet tears began to fall down Justine's cheeks as the killer took the gun from his lap and pointed the oily barrel at her face. She squeezed her eyes shut and wished him away, casting him as far as her imagination would allow.

"Very good," Dunhill concluded, letting the weapon relax once again. "Keep that in mind and I won't *have* to."

Hank stirred uncomfortably against her side, and she heard him murmur something in the same blurry tone as when she roused him from a sound sleep.

"It also means," Dunhill said, sharpening his voice, "that if I were to go look in on your mother, I'd have every reason to believe the two of you would still be here when I returned, just as you are now. Because if you weren't...if one or both of you were missing...well, please believe me when I say that would leave me no choice but to walk back to the bathroom and shoot your poor mother in the head." He looked intently between the two of them, letting the full import of the threat take hold. "It would be," he added gravely, "as if you yourselves had pulled the trigger."

They stared back at him as if he were Satan himself. A fiend in borrowed flesh.

Slowly, he rose from the chair, the gun at his side. He smiled and strode toward the hallway. The ashen horror stamped on their faces was answer enough.

11

Hank had been silent beside Justine for so long she'd almost forgotten he was there. Her own mind was racing, searching for a way around John Dunhill and his gun. There was no doubt in her mind that he would use it if provoked. In fact, it was probably just a matter of time until he found a reason to shoot them anyway. They were nothing more than loose threads now, threads he'd have to snip before making his escape. What more did he have to fear, really? He'd already murdered Sheriff Garrett.

So it caught her by surprise when her brother twitched and grasped her arm, his grip urgent, painful, and when Justine tried to free herself, he only pulled her closer.

"*Hank!*" she cried, trying to keep her voice down. "What are you doing? Let go of my arm! *Ow!* You're *hurting* me!"

"Do you hear them, Justine?" he asked, speaking in a voice that she hardly recognized. It was dry and husky, produced without moving his lips. His eyes, conversely, were straining from their sockets.

"Hear *who*?" She squirmed, wresting her arm back. If he meant Dunhill and their mother, then yes, she could hear their voices, though not the actual words. The bathroom tiles had a way of throwing sounds out the door like billiard balls; where they ended up depended on their various angles of deflection. But Hank wasn't looking that way. He was looking toward the kitchen.

"The pigs," he hissed, his face gone alarmingly pale.

"Pigs?" She wrinkled her nose. "Hank? What are you talking about? I don't hear anyth—"

A sudden cold reached out from him, wrapping her tight.

And then she saw them.

The Taylor twins stood side by side beneath the wide arch leading to the dining room, watching Justine and Hank with the quiet intensity of two unblinking sparrows. Their eyes were round and black, as if it were always night where they were and the irises had lost the ability to contract. The clothes they wore were simple and without pretense to period or style, cut whole and unskillfully sewn out of coarse, durable fabrics.

As haunting as they were in their dreams, they didn't look like ghosts, at least not in the lurid way Justine was accustomed to imagining such things. They didn't shimmer or glow, for one thing, nor could she see through them, like images from a projector.

What did set them apart was much more disturbing and sublime.

Mostly it was in the eyes, in the queer way they didn't glimmer or throw back the light but instead took it all inside, greedily, warming up to it as if from a sealed hole in the ground, a place that was unvaryingly cold and dark. Justine could feel it in the chill they carried with them, caught in the loose folds of their clothes and between the waxy layers of skin. They had an aura of quietness that did not come from living beings.

They were like shadows, reflections, the rare result of light striking a faint and lingering dampness, creating the antithesis of a rainbow. Looking at them, Justine found that if she tipped her head just so and listened closely, they almost seemed to call to her. Their voices caused something within her to respond, to vibrate and pull toward the surface, like bits of shrapnel under the influence of a powerful magnet. It caused old scars to open up inside her and bleed.

Justine, they whispered, smiling their strange and enigmatic smiles. Their plump lips never moved, and their dark eyes consumed the light. As silent and unmoving as two transparencies held against the blue screen of her subconscious.

Justine.

It was a sad, oddly familiar song, far off in the distance. As she heard it, she felt as if she was running through dimly remembered fields of her own lost childhood.

Without taking a step, they came closer, out of the archway and across the carpet to where Justine and Hank had pressed themselves against the back of the couch. All in an instant, as if they'd folded the space between.

The hum became a sudden roar, the rush of white water down a spillway, and a penetrating cold washed over her, bitter and darkly jealous. Trembling, Justine felt a stark fear that had been absent for years, one that pierced her skin and punched through the other side like a needle through one of her mother's swatches. She realized too late that she'd opened herself up to them, only to discover that they'd lied.

Their smiles weren't for her. They weren't even smiles.

They were skulls, dead and grinning. Covered with grave rot and mold.

She felt herself falling into blackness and opened her mouth to scream.

12

Dunhill tried to sneak up on her, but Margaret had kept an ear cocked toward the living room, listening to what was happening to her children. She'd nearly finished with the washcloth and was ready to pull the plug when she noticed the change. Conversation (or Dunhill's attempts at it) in the other room had dropped off to an uncomfortable silence, which meant that he had either given up the pretext or left the room altogether.

Straightening, letting the bathwater settle, she found her suspicions confirmed by the slight but familiar squeak of the loose board in front of the linen closet. She glanced down at the bathmat as adrenaline stabbed through her heart. The bulge made by the scissors was visible to her eye, but hopefully it was not too obvious. She wondered if she'd ever get the chance to use them.

Reaching in to drain the tub, Margaret heard a weight settle against the molding. The light in the room was subtly dimmed, enough for her to guess that if she turned, he would be looking down at her, arms crossed upon his chest, his expression a mixture of amusement and arrogance. And of course the gun would be there too, displayed for her benefit.

"How's he coming along? Not giving you too much trouble, I hope?" Dunhill took a step nearer. "I thought I'd better come check on the two of you. We haven't heard much since you gave us that first little jump. I wanted to make certain you hadn't fainted dead away at the sight of him."

As the water gurgled slowly away, Dunhill looked over her shoulder and shook his head. "Horrid looking, isn't he?" Though his voice was pitched low to express a wellspring of pity, Margaret also detected a sickening note of pleasure, as if he were proud of his creation and enjoyed the horror and repulsion it brought out in others.

Without looking up, Margaret agreed. "He's a monster," she said. "But not the worst here by far."

"Unkind, Margaret" he protested, mocking her with a wide grin.

The last of the water was sucked loudly down the drain, and Shires was left shivering as patches of soap bubbles slid down his trunk. He would now need a thorough rinsing, but as Margaret reached for the tap, his eyes fastened on Dunhill, and he began to gnash his teeth in agitation.

She turned to regard the man standing behind her; his face was a complicated mire of lines and shadows. "He doesn't seem to like you much, doctor." She placed a contemptuous accent on the title and then, with half a smile, said, "Whatever else you've done to him, at least you saw fit to leave his judgment intact."

Dunhill shifted his weight back a step, and the light from the overhead bulb fell upon her like the glow of a full moon. Despondently, she saw that she'd called back the wolf. His fist lashed out and came down hard against her right temple, knocking her roughly over.

"You don't know me," he softly chastened, rubbing the reddened skin of his knuckles. "You've no right, no right in the world to call me a monster. You have no idea of the circumstances which have led me here, to *this!*" His gaze, wild and penetrating, shifted to Shires. "And as for Daniel here, whom you seem to fancy an innocent, what do you know of *his* history? Precious little, I'd say if you think him deserving of your pity. If I were to tell you even *half* of it, you might see him in a clearer light, without the blinding halo of his deformities. You might even find him deserving of his fate."

Tears in her eyes, Margaret touched the side of her head and felt a sharp thread of pain race away toward the center of her skull, booming there like silent thunder. Dark stars briefly lit the walls and ceiling as she straightened herself, conscious again of the steely shape of the scissors beside her. They seemed to be straining through the bathmat, itching for her palm.

Dunhill looked at her and sighed wearily.

"Get on with it," he said, pinching the bridge of his nose as if to ward off a headache. He blinked twice, clearing his vision. "This business is wearing me down. I want the both of you out front in the sitting room in five minutes. No more dragging your heels or messing about."

"I haven't been *messing about*," she said, steadying herself with a hand on the edge of the tub. Dunhill was gazing once again at the discontented stump, as if he too were surprised at how far he had declined. Margaret took the opportunity to uncover the scissors with her free hand, blocking them with her body.

Do it now while he's away from the kids and distracted, getting tired.

She wavered, wondering if she could really take him by surprise, wound him badly enough to get the gun and then—

From the front room came a scream and the decision was made for her.

"*Justine!*" Hank cried.

Dunhill turned toward the open door, and, in a heartbeat, Margaret was upon him. The long, pointed blades of the scissors flashed once in the overhead light, throwing a bright, ephemeral arc against the wall.

Dunhill threw his head back and screamed, filling the small room to overflowing with outrage and pain. His arms flew up, fingers scrabbling at the shocking spread of blood just below his left scapula. She'd missed the ribs and the blades, all five inches of them, punched through to the soft core of him, leaving the round handles flush and trembling against the back of his shirt.

He shrieked insensibly. "You *bitch!*"

She darted forward once again, attempting to hook the revolver out of the front of his trousers. Dunhill's hands raked down on her forearms in a rage, causing her to lose her grip. The sighting notch at the end of the barrel caught briefly on his waistband, and before either of them could reclaim it, the gun clattered loudly to the floor.

Again she took him by surprise, for as he bent to snatch it up, Margaret charged and hit him low, connecting solidly with his injured shoulder. He virtually flew out the open door and crashed into the opposing wall. While he was down, she scooped up the gun and had the drop on him.

For a moment, their eyes met in silence. There were no pleas for mercy on his part, no bouts of indecision on hers. Without another word, she took aim and pulled the trigger.

In the small, tile-covered room, the sound of the heavy-caliber gunshot was deafening. She shot him once, driving a bullet through his chest and pinning him securely to the angled junction of the wall and the floor with a dark red spray of blood.

As Dunhill let out a last, rattling sigh, his eyes looked up and found hers once again, incredulous. Margaret backed slowly away, colliding with the cool plaster of the wall, her arms and legs beginning to shake. And inside the tub, Shires grew quiet, listening warily to the ringing silence, wondering, perhaps, what it held for him.

13

Her back against the wall, Margaret crouched and waited until she was sure he was dead, watching for a sign—be it shallow respirations or a faint muscle spasm—that might indicate he was only playing possum until she got within reach. In leaving the bathroom, she would have to step over him, and she worried about him reaching up and grasping her ankle in passing—like a jarring scene in some horror movie.

The revolver hung limply in her hand, barrel pointed at the floor. The smell of blood and spent powder was still sharp in her nostrils. There was a hum too. It was growing hollow and distant now, but she suspected it might never fade completely. She imagined it haunting her bedroom late at night like a ghost, quietly calling.

John Dunhill died with his eyes open, staring intently at the vacant spot where she had once stood. Minutes had passed now, and he had yet to twitch an eyelid.

He must be dead, she decided, closing her eyes with grim relief.

Shires, on the other hand, was still very much alive and apparently none too happy about it either. He was banging the back of his head against the porcelain in an attempt to do himself in or else attract her attention. She did glance down at him as she rose from the wall, long enough to read his eyes and decide she wasn't ready to deal with him just yet. What concerned her most (now that she'd pronounced Dunhill dead) was the silence screaming at her from the living room.

"Justine?" she called, loud enough for them to hear from almost anywhere in the house. "Hank?"

Why weren't they answering? What had happened out there? Why in the world had Justine shrieked like that when Dunhill had been in the bathroom with *her*?

Margaret needed to know; she needed to feel them safe and whole in her arms before she could even think about what to do next. Her first step down that path, however, was blocked by a man she could not convince herself was one-hundred-percent dead. It was a feeling she had, strong and irrational, that held her trapped long after she should have fled.

"You're *dead*, you piece of trash!" she asserted, bolstering herself to walk across the floor and step over his outstretched hand.

Dunhill lay where he was, quietly bleeding. Margaret stepped back to the place where she'd shot him and found his eyes again.

"You're dead," she whispered, inching forward, shivering. A stealthy motion caught the corner of her eye, and she turned to find her own reflection in the mirror. There was blood on the sleeve of her blouse from when she'd stabbed him with the scissors, just three or four tear-shaped drops, but red and shocking in the harsh light. Her face was ashen, drained, and she purposefully avoided meeting her own eyes for fear of what she might see lurking inside.

In the tub, Shires quit pounding his head and uttered a low, despondent moan.

"All right," she said to herself, taking a deep breath and letting it seep slowly away. "Here we go." Ignoring Shires, she held the gun stiffly out before her, training its eye resolutely on John Dunhill's slippery midsection, and forced herself over the narrow threshold.

She made her escape without incident and, chancing a glance back, almost wept with relief.

If Dunhill had a spark of life left in his body, he chose not to show it.

Margaret gasped as she rounded the corner into the living room. Waiting for her, sprawled on the floor near the couch, was a prominent page out of every mother's book of nightmares: her daughter's back was arched in spasm, and her eyes had rolled back inside her skull until only the whites were visible. Her complexion was deathly pale.

"Oh my God! Justine!"

Hank sat curled at the end of the couch, staring down at her with the stone rigidity of a statue. He held his knees up tight against his chin and rocked himself on the cushion in short, compulsive jerks, mouthing some tuneless chant under the dry rasp of his breath. As Margaret flew across the room to where Justine lay, his eyes caught her movement, and he wakened at the sight of her.

"Mama!" he cried, unknotting himself, his thin legs springing free. Still, he couldn't quite stand, and so he crawled to her.

Margaret hugged him quickly, fiercely. She kissed his face and told him that the monster was dead, that they were safe now. Then she turned her attention to Justine.

It was a seizure. Justine had had them once before when she was a year old, when three days of high fever and diarrhea had left her weak and dehydrated. It had been a shock to witness then, and it was no less so now that her daughter was grown. The sickening sense of helplessness returned, along with the knowledge that there was nothing she could do to stop or even soften the tremors.

They'll pass all right, echoed the amiable voice of the now-deceased Dr. Wilson. *About the best thing you can do is keep her on her side so she doesn't choke. Make her as comfortable as you can and talk to her; let her know you're there. Think of how frightened you are,* he advised, adopting a more serious tone, *and try to imagine how* she *must feel.*

Hank shifted his gaze doubtfully to his sister, frowning with a finely knit brow and pale, trembling lips. She was on her side now, with Margaret's hand firmly on her shoulder, keeping her from rolling on her back again, but she was still shaking, arms and legs tapping at the soft mat of the carpet, banging out a senseless rhythm.

Margaret ran a hand across Justine's forehead, smoothing her hair out of her face and wincing at the clamminess of the perspiration there. Five or six minutes must have passed since she'd heard the sound of her daughter's scream from the bathroom. So much had happened in that short space of time that it seemed much longer, but really it couldn't have been much more, and if her past episodes were any indication, Justine ought to have been on the downward side of it now. Yet the tremors seemed to be holding steady.

"*Come on*, Justine," Margaret urged, stroking the moist heat of her brow. "Come on back to us, baby."

Shivering, Justine stared past her at something in the far distance. Something that held her attention and would not let go.

PART SIX

Justine: An Interlude - 1971

1

The mouse was small, brown and terrified. It had been lured into an old milk pail by a piece of smelly cheese it now chose to ignore.

A long piece of fishing line was tied to the handle of the pail, rising sharply over one of the heavy beams into the barn loft. The other end was clutched in Calliope's hand. When the mouse crept inside to get the bait, she'd given it a hard tug, pulling the pail upright and hoisting it into the dusty air, trapping the poor rodent. Carefully, she lowered the pail back to the floor.

The three of them—Sparks, Calliope and Justine—scrambled down the fixed wooden rungs to the floor to claim their prize, moving quickly for fear the mouse might jump out of the trap before they could slap the rusted screen down on top of it.

Justine was the first one down; she could hear tiny claws scratching at the galvanized steel, clambering up from the bottom and falling sideways, unable to find purchase on the pail's inner wall—though this didn't discourage it from trying again and again.

Poor old mouse.

Justine already felt sorry for it and would have let it go if not for her two playmates, who had thought up the idea after seeing it scurrying about the bales of hay. She picked up the frame holding the torn piece of screen and watched it jump again, its tiny, brown body throbbing with panicked respirations.

"Hurry, Justine!" Sparks scolded, giving her a pinch. "It's going to get away!"

She put the screen across the broad mouth of the pail, jerking her hand away with a frightened yelp as the mouse leapt toward it. Sparks laughed, and his sister, the last down from the loft, pushed between them to get a closer look at their captive. She squealed with elfish delight, tapping a dark fingernail against the screen to make it scurry around the bottom of the pail. Sparks leaned closer too, their heads almost touching, as the mouse cowered inside and soiled itself in the extremity of its terror. This brought raucous screams of approval from the twins. They cheered and pointed and made room for Justine to come closer and see.

Unable to resist them for fear of scorn, Justine inched forward and took an obligatory peek. "Uh-huh," she said, feeling a bit dizzy inside.

"What shall we do with him?" Calliope said, grinning.

"Oh, let him go," Justine suggested, knowing her vote would be defeated.

The twins looked up, regarding her with doubt, as if the hour they'd just spent in the loft not making a sound (and they were good at that when they wanted to be) were all for nothing.

"Mice aren't good on farms, Justine," Calliope explained, her eyes narrowed and sharp.

"Yeah, Justine," Sparks said, his teeth small and pointed. "Don't you know *anything*?"

Justine kicked at the dirt with the toe of her shoe. Right now, all she wanted was for the two of them to go away, to stop these cruel games they'd taken to lately.

"Look here," Calliope said, rising off her knee. She squared her slim shoulders and waited for Justine's full attention. "You *know* we can't turn it loose, don't you?"

Justine looked through the barn's open doors at the house. Out of the corner of her eye, she saw Sparks reach inside the pail and extract a patch of gray on the end of his finger. He sniffed at it cautiously and then put the finger into his mouth.

"Justine." Calliope's hands were on her bony hips, waiting for a reply.

"I guess so," Justine said in a voice that was small and dry.

"You *guess* so?" Calliope shook her head and glanced down at her brother, who was back inside the pail, licking his lips. "I just told you mice were no good for farms, didn't I? *No good at all.* They scare the animals and chew holes in the seed bags. They're dirty and disgusting, and they spread icky germs all over. *Look at me, Justine.*" Her grin was ferocious. "They build their nests in the straw…and they bite."

Lightning quick, Calliope tipped the pail and snatched up the mouse.

"See?"

The mouse was in her small, mean fist. Its tail flicked like a little, brown whip down her wrist, and its tiny head protruded from the tight circle of her thumb and forefinger. When she had scooped it up, the mouse had made a noise like a bird, shrill and argumentative, and then it clamped its teeth down on the first flap of skin that presented itself. It bit down and, when Calliope refused to release it, bit down again, black eyes wild and panicked.

Calliope seemed oblivious to the pain, or else it was something she thrived on, for the smile on her face never faltered. Sparks cast the pail aside and stood, taking an interest in the mouse's struggles. As she increased the pressure within her fist, the mouse squealed, and blood, shocking and red in the muted daylight, began to drip down Calliope's pale arm.

Laughter echoed in the rafters. "Pinch its head off, Callie," Sparks urged, getting right up close, his breath fermented and foul.

"No!" Justine cried, unable to take the sound of its screams another second. "*Stop it*, Calliope!"

"All right, Justine." Calliope shrugged and aimed a sly wink at her brother. In her loosened grip, the mouse lay stiffly panting, exhausted and defeated. Its small, dazed eyes focused on its own death. Calliope looked around the barn's shadowy interior and passed judgment.

"There," she said to her twin, pointing. "That pitchfork."

A cold horror crept up Justine's spine. The pitchfork stood, prongs down, near the ladder to the hayloft. What Calliope had in mind was monstrous.

Sparks capered nimbly over the weathered floorboards, eager to retrieve it. Of the two of them, Justine had learned that Calliope was capable of the worst. She took the time to plan her deeds, and here was the result.

"Turn it over," she said, "so the points curve up."

The dulled and slightly rusted tines were proffered for her inspection: five in all, twelve inches long, wickedly thin, and spaced three inches apart. Calliope reached out with her free hand and tested one with the tip of her finger.

Justine turned away, not wanting any part of what was certain to be a very grisly dispatch for the unfortunate mouse, though she knew full well her participation would become compulsory, as a witness at the very least. This would not be the first time they had insisted. It was their way of breaking her down, of trampling her innocence into the ground.

"Justine." Calliope's voice was prying at her, no longer that of a child. It had a way of slipping through her defenses. "Watch this."

"No!" Justine shouted, mustering an uncharacteristic show of defiance. She clamped her hands over her ears and squeezed her eyes so tightly shut that fireflies danced across her reddened lids. Tears leaked out, the essence of all her fears, burning as they ran down her cheeks.

A hand fell on her shoulder, and she screamed to be left alone. Please, *please* just go away and leave her alone!

No, Justine.

Even through the pressure of her flattened hands, the insistent voice got through, as if it were actually inside her head and had been all along.

Turn around and I'll let it go.

"No you won't!" Justine cried, choking on the words. "You're just saying that to trick me!"

The hand at her back hesitated and then dropped away. It left a ghostly imprint behind: a penetrating cold that caused her skin to pucker and crawl. It was always like that when one of them touched or brushed against her. Always cold.

The tiny hairs on the back of her neck began to tingle, detecting a gentle swirling or displacement of the air, as if they were circling about her, predatory like sharks. She held her eyes and ears firmly shut until the sense of movement faded completely away, then kept up the effort until she was sure they had given up, gone to find other, more willing playmates or to carry out their petty cruelties in private. When she dared think about it, Justine imagined they came from a hole somewhere, one as deep and black as a well, for they were always dirty and pale and smelled of stagnant water.

Cautiously, she parted two fingers and cracked a single eyelid.

A high-pitched scream leapt from wall to wall like a crazed bat.

The points of the rusty pitchfork floated before her, held less than three feet from her shocked face. Calliope had the mouse poised over one of the long, curved tines, and she brought it triumphantly down, skewering its small body from tail to head. The shaft pierced through the top of its skull with a wet, gristly sound, ejecting a thin spray of blood and brain matter over Calliope's hair and cheeks.

They hadn't gone. They were simply playing a game with her, standing still in that strange way they had and playing possum, waiting for her to lower her guard so they could take her by surprise.

Justine watched in horror as the mouse paddled its paws lazily at the air, dreaming of escape even as its blood ran slow and red down the underside of the prong. She stumbled away, dropping to her knees halfway to the door and vomiting into the sweet summer hay.

Laughing behind her, the twins began to feed.

A full week passed before she spoke to them again, but they became so contrite, so ardent in their apologies that eventually they had bullied her into forgiveness. Killing the poor mouse that way, it had been *wrong,* they admitted, now without the faintest hint of a smile. They could see that now, and it would never, *ever* happen again.

So Justine let them back into her room, and, for a while, they were as good as gold.

Time, however, proved a better judge of character. The respite was merely a lull; each day of quiet increased the pressure, building toward the next release.

"What are you doing, honey?"

Justine looked up from the carpeted floor of the solarium, surrounded by what looked like three mismatched sets of pinochle cards. An alcove of glass and sunlight, the solarium had become her playroom, a place where she could close the French doors yet still be within sight as Margaret cleaned the house or attended to Hank.

"Playing cards," Justine answered matter-of-factly.

"So I see," Margaret said, a smile trying to grow on her tired face. Hank had kept her up most of the night screaming as the first of his lower teeth tried (and ultimately failed) to break through the gum. Now it was a little after two in the afternoon, and as he'd finally drifted off to sleep, she was ready to lie down too. "What game are you playing?"

"Oh, it's called Bloody Bones," she said in her light, childish voice.

Margaret, leaning on the jamb of the door, felt her smile turn leaden and gray. "Bloody Bones," she slowly repeated. "Where in the world did you ever learn such a game?"

Justine flipped up a king of spades and said: "Sparks and Calliope are teaching me. They know lots of games."

Now the smile wasn't just wilting; it was dead, exchanged for an icy frown at the mention of those abhorrent names. Margaret hesitated. She decided she was too tired to open that particular box and let it pass.

"I'm going to lay down for a little bit while Hank's sleeping," she said, waiting until she had Justine's attention again. "I want you to keep these doors open so you can hear him if he starts to cry. Okay?"

"Okay, Mama." She flipped another card. The queen of diamonds.

"I put his little, blue teething ring in the refrigerator, in the butter compartment in the door. If he wakes up, go ahead and give it to him and see if that quiets him down."

Ten of clubs.

"Justine? Are you listening to me?"

"Uh-huh."

Margaret sighed. "All right. If that doesn't suit him, come and wake me up. I'm going to close my bedroom door, so I might not hear him. There are some brownies on a plate for you in the kitchen, and a glass of milk in the fridge. That should hold you until dinnertime."

Justine looked up. "What about Sparks and Calliope?"

Margaret raised an eyebrow. "What about them?"

"What do thcy gct to cat?"

Tapping her fingernail against the white paint, Margaret counted silently to ten. "I guess you'll have to share."

"Your mother doesn't like us," Calliope said sourly.

Half an hour had passed with lackadaisical indifference. The card game was over—Sparks had taken all the bones—and the house brooded about them in atypical quiet. The sun had climbed over the peaked roof and now had a direct view of the solarium; it spread a slow and comfortable warmth over the room that soon had Justine feeling sleepy. The twins, as usual, seemed unaffected. In her lap, Calliope was paging through a book on insects while Sparks, bored with the two of them, had climbed on the bench seat to watch cars whisper past on the highway.

Justine yawned.

"I think she's *mean*," Calliope added, her jaw working from side to side as she glared through the French doors, grinding dull sparks between bone and enamel.

"She's just tired is all," Justine responded, turning her eyes with feigned interest to a crack in the white plaster ceiling, not allowing herself to be goaded into a fight, which was what Calliope was fishing for. That or else a nod of unqualified agreement.

"No, that's not what I mean," Calliope said, eyes flashing yellow with a brief kiss of sunlight. "It's not just today, you know…it's *every* day! She never says hello, never smiles, never even looks at us. You'd think we weren't here at all!"

"Not here at all," Sparks echoed from his roost. He raised a finger and traced the progress of a passing grocery truck on the glass, pushing it along until it disappeared between hills, moving off toward Rosalia to restock the town's dusty shelves. As the sunlight waned, he hopped down and grinned.

"Let's go look at the baby!"

"No, you'll wake him!" Justine snapped, too late. From the bedroom came the startled sound of Hank waking up, which (for him) was always an unpleasant surprise. At fifteen months, he seemed to prefer the unconscious warmth of his dreams, rudimentary though they must have been, to the cold touch of reality. Justine, watching him sleep, often imagined his dreams to consist primarily of raw shapes and colors, or of tones ebbing and flowing into one another like jet planes crossing high overhead.

Calliope turned to her brother, and a secret look—one that Justine caught out of the corner of her eye—passed between them, akin to a nod or handshake. It was something they'd drawn up between themselves, which could only mean trouble.

"You'd better go check on him," Calliope said, a mischievous smile playing about her dark lips.

Justine rose tentatively to her knees. Her blue eyes shifted suspiciously between the two of them; she knew she ought to hurry before Hank woke her mother, but she was afraid to let the twins out of her sight for fear of what they might do. The mouse incident hadn't faded *that* far out of memory.

"Come on, Justine," Calliope cheerfully urged, hopping up from the floor. "We'll help you."

This suggestion brought with it another alarm, far greater than the first: it was the baby they wanted to get close to—and had all along. Small and pink, warm and helpless in his crib. A sudden, horrifying vision of the two of them in the nursery, alone and unchecked, presented itself with terrible clarity. Justine shut her eyes against it, wishing it away. In the meantime, Hank was finding his true voice, working himself into a disconsolate lather.

"Hurry up, Justine!" Calliope barked, hands bossily on her hips. "He'll wake up your mother!"

They ran out into the wide living room, intent on being helpful.

"*Wait!*" Justine called after them. The edge of her apprehension roughened her voice, scraping the tender sides of her throat as it rose. "I have to get his teething ring out of the refrigerator! Don't go in there without me!"

They laughed and ducked through the hallway arch, fading like ghosts into the cobweb-colored gloom, not heeding a word she said.

"Stop it!" Justine screamed shrilly, imagining too clearly the sight of her baby brother sliding down the tines of a pitchfork, his blood running deep red on the nursery carpet, the twins parading him about the house like a victory banner—all because of her. Because she was the one who'd let them inside.

"Don't you go in there!" She was sobbing now, and the light and shadow of the living room melted together within the salt of her tears. She stumbled after them, wiping her eyes with a bare forearm.

A door creaked open in the hallway, bringing with it a dim glow of late-afternoon sunlight. Her mother emerged from her bedroom in cotton panties and a long, white shirt dampened with spots of breast milk. Her eyes were swollen and red from dreams interrupted and narrowed at her daughter in a mixture of anger and confusion.

"Justine! What are you yelling for?"

From the nursery, Hank's cries became more insistent.

Margaret glanced toward his closed door. "I asked you to look after him while I was sleeping," she said heatedly.

"I *was*, Mama!" Justine howled, tears falling freely down her plum-colored face. "I was...I was going to get...his...his..."

"All right now, settle down," Margaret said, softening her voice, realizing just how upset her daughter had become. "Tell me what happened."

"I was going to get his teething ring!" Justine said in a wet burst of emotion. "But...but...but..."

"Easy, Justine." Margaret combed her daughter's hair gently back.

"*They* went in there, Mama!" she bawled, her voice a raw, wet terror. "I...I tried, but I couldn't stop them! They...*they're going to hurt the baby!*"

"Who's going to hurt your brother?" Margaret asked, kneeling down to establish eye contact, taking Justine firmly by the shoulders. "Honey, there's no one here but you and me."

"Sp...Sp...Sparks..."

"And Calliope," Margaret finished, shaking her head. "Oh Justine," she said quietly, with sadness and resignation.

"Mama, they're in there!" Justine shouted, pointing insistently at the closed door.

"All right, *all right*. Just stop right there, young lady!" Margaret took a breath, her skin dancing with irritation. "*Look* at yourself! All wound up into a panic, blubbering, and for *what? Nothing*, that's what." She reached out and took her daughter by the arm, pulling her into the hallway and toward the nursery. "I'm going to show you something, Justine, and I hope to God it sinks in this time because...because, frankly, I'm at the end of my rope with these so-called friends of yours."

"Mama!" Justine protested, twisting in her grip. "You're hurting my arm!"

"Then quit dragging your feet," Margaret snapped, opening the door and pushing Justine into the room ahead of her. "Go on. I want you to see what you're making such a fuss about." Hank's crying, which had leveled off a little since he'd awakened, spiked upward again at the sound of the creaking door. Below that, Justine could hear other voices, laughing together now over some wicked joke, making loud animal noises.

"*Well?*" Margaret demanded, taking in the space of the nursery with an expansive wave of her hand. "I don't see anyone. Show me where they are."

Justine kept her eyes on the carpet, unable to look up.

"Come on, introduce me to your friends."

"Mama..." Justine sobbed, her small body shaking with emotion. She clutched at the hem of her mother's

261

nightshirt, and Margaret felt her resolution weaken. She knelt and hugged her daughter as tears gathered in her own tired eyes.

"I...I...I didn't..." Justine stammered. She coughed wetly over her shoulder, trying fiercely to heave out some last burning declaration. "I didn't mean to wake you up!" she bawled.

"It's all right, honey," Margaret whispered, kissing her cheek and smoothing back her hair. "Shhhh, I know you didn't. I'm sorry I yelled at you." She leaned back on her heel far enough to look into her daughter's eyes. "You know what? I think we're *both* tired. Having a little baby like Hank around is a lot of work, and that's okay because we need to keep busy, but sometimes...well, it doesn't seem like we get much of a break anymore for fun things, does it?"

Justine nodded solemnly, her face damp and swollen.

"I know that, sweetheart, *really* I do. Since Daddy died, it's been rough on *all* of us, and I don't know how I'd have gotten along without your help. It's just that...well, sometimes I forget that you're still a little girl who needs to laugh and play and have fun just as much as you need hugs and kisses and a mama and a daddy."

A large, salty tear rolled down Justine's cheek, and Margaret rubbed it away with her thumb. She forced herself to smile. "Maybe what we need is to get away from this big old house for a day, huh? What do you say? Just the two of us, like old times?"

Slowly, Justine returned the smile, nodding in agreement.

"Mrs. Clemenson has told me again and again how happy she'd be to watch Hank for us. I think it's about time we took her up on that offer. We could take the car to Spokane and do some shopping and have dinner in a sit-down restaurant, and maybe even see a movie? How does that sound?"

"Uh-huh," Justine said with a nod, which was all she could manage as her sobs died away in fits and hitches. Colors of happiness mixed with warm relief washed over her, and then she stepped forward and hugged her mother fiercely.

"My goodness, girl!" Margaret cried, surprised by the strength of her own emotions. "Just look at us! The baby's screaming to be changed and here we are bawling our eyes out! If your father were here, he'd shake his head in wonder!" She laughed out loud and ran the edge of her hand across her cheeks.

Justine chanced a look over her mother's shoulder.

They were there, of course: the two of them swinging and climbing like filthy monkeys all over the bars of Hank's crib, leering and screeching down at the red-faced infant.

Calliope whooped loudly, drumming her feet on the headboard. Sparks, hanging over the top rail by his armpits and kicking at the air in an attempt to hoist himself inside, was making noises like a stuck hog.

"Oink oink, smelly piggy!" he squealed, glancing wickedly at Justine. He snorted through his flattened nose. "*Suuu-eeeee*, little pig!" He reached down and tickled Hank's upturned feet.

Oblivious to the unseen threat behind her back, Margaret patted Justine gently and pulled back. "Come on, honey," she said, rising with a tired groan. "Help your mama get him changed and dressed, and then we'll see if he's hungry."

"Okay." She looked up at the twins' unwholesome faces as her mother took a tissue from the box on the dresser and blew her nose.

"This hoglet's going to be *mine*, Justine," Sparks asserted with a throaty growl, like a tiger rolling in the blood of its kill. "You for Calliope and this little one for *me*."

She stared silently at him as his eyes glittered back like twin suns, dead and collapsed on themselves, pulling all they could reach inside. Justine realized that she had been wrong in assuming that Calliope was the stronger of the two. They were twins and, by definition, equals. Sparks had simply been biding his time, waiting for Justine's brother to fatten on her mother's milk.

She made a resolution in the clarity of that moment, a decision to rid the house of them so they would never cause harm to her baby brother.

Her mother still had her back turned as she rustled through the closet and drawers for a fresh set of clothes and a diaper. Justine crossed the nursery in a straight, angry line and, one by one, caught hold of Sparks's dangling feet.

"Hey!" He glared down at her, furious.

She pulled him off the wooden rail with a jerk.

He hit the carpeting headfirst, landing with a thud that shook the old floorboards underneath.

Margaret turned from the bureau, holding a pair of red corduroy rompers. She looked worriedly at the crib. "What was *that?*"

"What was what?" Justine asked, looking around.

Margaret smiled and shook her head dismissively. "Nothing, I guess."

Knowing that she could never hope to banish them simply by asking them to leave, Justine spent the next few days in serious contemplation of the matter and, in doing so, realized there was a great deal she didn't know about the twins, beginning with where they came from each morning and disappeared to each night. Was it some neighboring house, a place much like her own home? If so, they never mentioned it or invited her over to play.

Did they have a mother and father? Someone who took care of them while they were away? Someone who dropped them off in a car and then picked them up before it got dark? And if so, why hadn't she ever seen them? Surely they didn't live all on their own, like wild animals.

Did they?

And most puzzling of all: why was it that her own mother couldn't seem to see or hear them? Why did she get angry and tell her to quit making things up when they were right there in plain sight?

Justine wasn't at all certain, and the questions themselves frightened her so badly at times—especially as she lay in bed, imagining their faces in the gray shadow land between drowsiness and dreams—that she wasn't sure she wanted to know the answers. But neither did she want them near her any longer, or around Hank, so she resolved to find out what she could, starting with where they spent their night hours.

She had noticed of late that they had a way of disappearing as the day drew to a close, a habit to which she had never given much thought before. It was a manner of fading away, unobtrusive as mist dispersing in the morning sunlight, to the periphery of her vision and then, at a moment's distraction, slipping away without a sound. There one minute, chattering and playing, and then gone as the hills turned blue outside the windows of the solarium.

It was at that time of day that she would have to pay close attention, feigning interest in whatever was at hand, and then follow wherever they led.

The next afternoon, as the sun sank and the solarium turned warm and sleepy beneath its slanted rays, Justine fought the natural inclination to become listless and drowse, waiting instead for any change or hint that the twins were leaning toward their departure. She and Calliope were playing paper dolls, and Sparks, contemptuous of such stuff, busied himself with a box of dulled crayons and one of her old coloring books.

It was because of this heightened awareness that she was able to pick up on the subtle changes as their time drew near. The evening shadows joined hands, creeping eastward, and a natural lull fell over the day. Lunch was a distant memory, and energy was at an ebb. Justine found her mind retreating toward more introspective activities. It was little wonder she'd never noticed the oddity of something so welcome as peace and solitude after a long day of their incessant demands. It was simply an unquestioned relief to be shed of them.

Sparks stretched and closed the dog-eared coloring book, and although Justine kept her eyes on the carefully folded tabs of the doll she was dressing, she perceived, out of the corner of her eye, that he was studying her. A moment or two later, he rose to his feet like a cat and stole soundlessly out of vision.

She looked at the lingering rim of the sun, half-devoured by the rustling fields, and in that second, Calliope padded away too.

Panicked, Justine leapt up just in time to see their motley shadows dissolve beneath the archway that led to the side door. A muffled and metallic click told of their intentions to escape outside, and she heard the hinges of the door pull back with a gentle groan of resignation.

Running after them in her bare feet, Justine crossed the living room with a dread certainty that, once they were out of sight, she would lose them, that they would slip away into the darkening ether of twilight, gone until the sun came round again, and then she would have to pass another day in gnawing anticipation.

This, it turned out, was not quite true, for as she threw open the side door, dispensing with any pretense of stealth, she caught a fading glimpse of one of them melting inside the haggard mouth of the barn. She gave quick chase, but as she passed inside the wide, listless door, the gloominess of the space inside conspired to hide them, and they would not respond to her repeated calls. Her voice, however, did startle several bats from their roosts in the high rafters, and as they screeched and swooped down to escape through the open door, Justine fled back to the bright safety of the house in terrified defeat.

Her mood was sullen the following day. The twins showed up after breakfast as usual as if nothing had happened. Her eyes had been on the door of the barn as she gulped her orange juice and shoveled down cold cereal, but it was just afterward, while she was brushing her teeth, that they decided to come in.

All morning, despite their best efforts to draw her out, she remained aloof and uncommunicative, and it wasn't until lunch that a new idea occurred to her. She began to open up to them again. It wouldn't do, after all, for them to grow suspicious as the afternoon hours started to dwindle.

They played outside for most of the day, setting up a sun-bleached croquet set on the front lawn and hammering the wooden balls back and forth through the rusty wickets, but as the sun descended and the sky got pale and hazy, Justine maneuvered them back inside the house. She knew, from the previous day's observations, around what time they would start their disappearing act, and this time she meant to beat them at their own game. When it came time for them to go, it would be *she* who was nowhere to be found, and rather than try to chase them down once again, she would wait for them to come to her.

The time came as they were playing a modified game of Monopoly, one that Parker Brothers would never have imagined or approved. Justine rolled the dice (or stones, as they were known in this game) and banged her marker around the board.

"Ah-ha!" Sparks shouted, rubbing his dirty hands together. "That's *my* yellow square! Give me half your money or I'll burn one of your houses down!"

Justine yawned. She stood up and stretched. "I'm tired of this dumb game. How about a snack?"

The twins pricked their ears and nodded enthusiastically; they were never ones to turn down offers of food, especially meat and dairy products, as Justine well knew.

"There's some carrots," she offered slyly, enjoying the look of disappointment that hardened upon their features. "Or slices of cheese."

"Oh, *cheese*, please!" Calliope begged, pawing hungrily at Justine's pant leg. A strand of saliva descended to her lap, and she raised an arm to wipe it away, too late.

Sparks was on his feet, cheering as if they'd never eaten such riches. "Cheese! Yaaay!"

"Okay, okay! You two stay here, and I'll go sneak some." Justine grinned, giving them a conspiratorial wink over her shoulder. She started toward the kitchen as if she were really going to pull one over on her mother, swiping cheese with dinner less than an hour away.

She left them simmering happily behind her back. The word "cheese" stretched out into long, blissful whispers as they huddled together and watched her cross the room. She kept up the act, tip-toeing, though she had no intention of bringing them back anything so unlikely as a heaping plateful of individually wrapped slices. As long as they thought she might, however, they would probably stay put. All she needed was a few minutes, two or three at most.

Her mother was at the sink, peeling potatoes, and Justine paused only long enough to say "hi" on her way to the side door. Once there, she turned the knob with the greatest of care, using her two small hands to smother the sound of the latch as best she could so that it wouldn't reach back to the solarium.

Out on the concrete step, she used the same caution in closing the door, expecting the whole time to see their furious faces scowling out at her, but their greed evidently convinced them of the virtue of patience, for they never appeared.

As she turned from the house, she found that her heart was racing, her limbs weightless enough to fly.

Here I go...

She streaked across the lawn toward the barn, angling for the flat, brown wedge of its musty interior. The distance seemed impossibly long, and not until she was safely inside did she dare look back, her breath coming hot and quick.

There was a face at the kitchen window, enough to give her a start until she realized it belonged to her mother, still skinning potatoes for dinner.

Justine sighed with relief and, resting her hands on her scabby knees, took a moment to watch the house and let her breath catch up with her. Right about now, the twins would be wondering where she was, why it was taking her so long. And with an eye toward the window, they would notice that the sun was about to set on the day.

Justine allowed herself a thin smile and left the vantage of the door, turning to look for a good place to hide. Above her, the loft stretched across the entire front of the barn. It would have been perfect; she could burrow into the straw and keep watch over everything from there. But if the twins were sleeping here, it was also the place *they* would most likely go. She would be trapped.

There were the stalls, empty now, but they were way in the back, and she wouldn't be able to see over the high sides without the likelihood of being spotted herself. There was a neglected woodpile, old and partially collapsed. Justine generally avoided it because it was a favorite haunt of spiders. Her mother also left it alone, preferring oil heat to the mess and bother of the fireplace. The pile had thrown out a few tentative sprouts over the years, but these too had died, leaving the bark to peel off like a scab layer. The soft wood underneath created an inviting home for the small, leggy things that spiders liked to eat.

Hurry...hurry!

Stacks of heavy seed bags, fertilizers. A tool bench covered with straw dust and faded oil spots. A stool that always creaked as if it wanted to fall apart and thereby end its miserable existence.

Through the doorway, she thought she heard a shudder in the wind like the porch door ratcheting on its hydraulic arm. In a panic, she ran to the shadowy kneehole beneath the workbench, dragging the rickety stool in close to take what little cover it offered.

Squatting, she steadied herself on the tips of her fingers, almost touching the bottom of the bench with her head. It made for an uncomfortable position, but she found she was able to see almost everything.

She waited as the smell of old wood and sawdust rose slowly, wrapping her in its arms. Another smell, darker and more elusive, lay beneath this corner of the barn, ripe with unpleasant associations. It was what wafted out of the black crawlspace in the basement, out of the old shed and inside the shut-up chicken coop: dark places where the sun never reached. The odor of abandonment and decay.

She tried to hold her breath and then breathe only through her mouth, but that only seemed to bring it out as a patina on the surface of her tongue. Then she heard voices approaching, cunning and low, and promptly forgot all about the smell.

The heavy door sighed, and suddenly they were there: two squat and grayish figures lit by a blue rim of twilight. Justine watched, terrified, as they crept in from the newly formed night, shuffling their feet through dust and loose strands of hay like two very old dwarves. Whatever had been the subject of their whisperings as they approached the barn now appeared to be settled, for their path was as silent as it was straight. They glided past her (close enough to spit on, had her mouth not been so dry), halting at a shadowy place along the back wall, a niche between the woodpile and a penned area where they had once kept sheep. Neither here nor there as far as the barn was concerned.

Sparks knelt down as a long-legged spider tip-toed across the back of Justine's hand. This would normally be worth an ear-shattering shriek, but today it got only a hurried shake and a fast death under the toe of her shoe. A muffled, almost furtive squeak brought her back to the twins, who were pulling loose boards from the floor, exposing a narrow, slit-like egress through which they lowered themselves. Sparks went first and then Calliope, who paused on her haunches to cast one last look about the thickening gloom.

At that moment, Justine thought she had given herself away. She was certain that Calliope had spied her under the bench, but the moment passed. The girl's eyes moved on, lighting briefly on the loft and the open door before a curt swing of her legs and a shrug of her shoulders dropped her beneath the floor.

Plump hands, pale and uncomfortably rat-like, emerged to probe for the loosened boards, dragging them neatly into place with an ease that could only come with practice and long familiarity.

The ground exhaled a final sigh, and then the barn grew as still and silent as an empty house.

Justine counted slowly to one hundred before she dared quit the safety of her hiding place. Twilight was almost gone, and her withdrawal was a stiff one; she pushed the stool out of the way, wincing at the creaks and wobbly stutters its legs made against the floor. At every sound, she expected the twins to leap out at her like trapdoor spiders, dragging her down to feast on her prying eyes before dispensing with the rest of her, but their hole must have been deeper than she thought. Nothing save the same level quiet emerged, as if she were alone in the barn and always had been, even when she'd thought otherwise.

When the noise failed to raise any notice, Justine grew bold enough to delay her retreat a moment longer. Warily, as if approaching a live explosive, she crept toward the back of the barn to within four or five yards of where they'd gone underground, where she thought she might reasonably hear them even through the dust and loose boards.

What she heard, however, was only the urgent beat of her own heart. Not even a whisper emerged from the hidden hole, which was odd. Surely two such boisterous and quarrelsome beasts couldn't shut themselves in such close quarters without picking a fight. It went against their nature: to peck, argue, and tease whenever possible.

She took a step closer, certain now that they were playing some awful trick on her, that not only had they seen her crouched beneath the workbench but that they'd watched from the windows and had known what she'd had in mind even before she did.

After all, what kind of children slept in the ground?

A chill crept up her spine at the thought of their pale faces, like two dolls she'd put in an old shoebox and buried, pretending they were dead.

There was a flashlight on a hook just inside the barn door; her mother had had the electricity to the barn shut off since they no longer kept livestock. Its white beam was as powerful as a car's headlamp. What if she were to take it down, kick the loose boards aside, and shine it down on them? Wouldn't *that* go a long way toward fixing them? Not only would it spoil their surprise, but for once she would be getting the better of them.

She swayed on the brink of doing just that, looking back and forth between the door and the covered hole, measuring her need to rid herself of them against the likelihood of being caught and dragged down. She turned the toe of her shoe against the grit underfoot. There was also, she reflected somewhat pointedly, the very real chance that it wasn't a joke but something far more terrible. Suddenly exposing them down there might be like flipping over a particularly nasty piece of wood, expecting to find worms for fishing but getting black widows instead. It was something she'd rather not see or even think about, so perhaps the flashlight with its overly bright beam would best be left alone.

Still, she had to do something, because as sure as the sun would rise the next morning, they would be back to haunt her, as they would every morning after that until they bled her dry with their insatiable needs or caused some unspeakable accident.

You for Calliope and this little one for me.

She felt paralyzed as her thoughts raced helplessly with her heart. The floor under her tipped as if she were poised at a crucial moment in time. A window had opened before her that might never open again, and she had to decide whether to climb through or shut it for good.

She was only six years old.

If she could only keep them down in their hole! Away from life and sunlight and away from her family. But what could possibly appease them? What would they willingly accept in trade?

She frowned. *Nothing...willingly.*

But then again, why did she feel she had to have their stamp of approval on anything? Their fate, she realized, need not be voluntary.

She set her teeth against her lower lip and considered the situation well.

Can I do it?

There were a hammer and nails sitting right on the workbench, a little rusty for disuse but perfectly suitable for the purpose she had in mind. And it wouldn't take long to fix two loosened boards.

A distant, familiar creak slipped through the door behind her, and she jumped. A scream perched on her lips, ready to tear through the roof.

"Justeeen!" her mother called from the house.

Justine cast one last apprehensive glance at the gloomy spot where the twins had concealed themselves. Still not a whisper nor a peep. It was as if she'd imagined them.

The screen door banged shut. "Justeeeeeeeeen!" Her mother's voice was moving out over the hills, getting stronger.

"Coming, Mama!" she answered, appearing at the slit of the barn door.

"Young lady, you scared me half to death!" Margaret said as Justine trotted across the driveway. Under the full moon, she looked unnervingly like a smallish ghost emerging from the listing mouth of the barn. "What in heaven's name are you doing out there in the dark?"

"Just playing," Justine replied, giving Margaret an unexpected hug. They turned toward the house, walking through the yellow spill of the porch light. Justine could smell dinner waiting on the table, ready to be served.

"Didn't you notice that it was getting a little hard to see?" Margaret said jokingly, nudging her daughter.

"Mmm, I guess so," Justine murmured absently, as if it really hadn't struck her in the least.

At the step, as she held the door, Margaret couldn't resist a look back at the barn. She frowned. Inside, it would have been like pitch.

"Must have been something pretty absorbing if you couldn't tell the difference between night and day," she prodded, hoping for a little more illumination.

Justine paused and turned slowly in the doorway. Her face was strangely pale. It took Margaret a little aback, so curious was her expression.

"Mama?"

"What is it, honey?" A black thread stretched taut in Margaret's belly, worrying her.

"What if someone did something that was wrong to keep something else…something *really bad* from happening?"

Margaret felt the familiar droop of facial muscles that meant Sparks and Calliope were hovering near. She let the screen door close behind her and put a cautious hand on her daughter's shoulder. "I don't understand, Justine. Do you mean something that was against the law? That they would have to go to jail?"

There was a catch in Justine's expression, as if she were digesting some new concern.

"No," she said at last, apparently discarding the wrinkle. "I mean would God still love me?"

She lay rigid in her bed, gazing into the warm splash of her nightlight. She saw not the loose stacks of books and shadowy playthings that huddled around its weak glow but an inky slit in a rough wooden floor. A thing she knew she'd have to fix before morning.

Without the nightlight, her bedroom would have been a solid curtain of black, relieved only by the moon as it made its descent against the back of her curtains. That light, however, was almost worse than the darkness. Wan and silvery, it was all too easy to imagine things shambling about outside her window, throwing weird, mossy shadows against the glass.

Usually she was asleep before it was that late, but tonight she was waiting, listening to the earthy groans and creakings of the house as it settled into its own kind of slumber. She had been listening for a long while, passing time as hushed voices from the television chatted to her mother. After the voices were silenced, she listened to the sound of footsteps, the deep shudder of the plumbing as her mother got ready for bed, and the click of the bedroom door falling into place, like a gentle period putting a final end to the day.

That click had been a long time ago, Justine thought after a while. Surely her mother must be asleep by now.

Justine threw back the covers. She was already dressed, and her shoes waited where she'd placed them at the foot of the bed. At the door, she paused again to listen, afraid that the sound of her footsteps might have been picked up in another part of the house, but nothing answered. Everything was just as it had been before: quiet, settling.

During the long hours of her waiting, it occurred to Justine that the twins might be more easily placated if she took something to offer them, some small toys or trinkets that would help pass the time. A soft doll to hold or a ball to play with, maybe some food so they wouldn't starve. Something to soften the blow and the uneasy rumblings of her own budding conscience.

Justine slipped silently out of her room and tip-toed to the solarium, where she searched among her things for one or two favorites. She visited the kitchen next, collecting cookies and candy bars, stuffing her pockets with cheese-flavored crackers. All bits and pieces that she knew the twins would like.

The hardest part was actually getting outside without bringing her mother along too. Ever since Hank was born, her mother had become a very light sleeper, rising almost telepathically at the slightest stirring from the nursery. So she took it slow, passing through the side door as a statue might, moving with the unseen patience of a thief. The screen door was notoriously creaky, and getting past it was far from easy. Five minutes after unlocking the inner door, though, there she stood, shivering in the dark of the yard with the moon shining brightly overhead. The barn itself was now blacker than the surrounding night, and it waited with its mouth open for her. A sleeping giant, old and gone to seed.

Quickly, she crossed the driveway and, pulling the flashlight down from its hook, began the task she'd been steeling herself for. The light was in good working order, and the dusty beam it threw was able to probe the rafters without losing any of its intensity. She walked to the neglected workbench with her usual step, no longer attempting to muffle the sound of her footsteps. She reasoned that even her mother's heightened senses couldn't penetrate both the house and the barn. Here she set the light down, focusing its beam on the back wall, just above the loosened boards. She approached the cache with a dreadful lump in the back of her throat and emptied her pockets of the various offerings she'd brought from the house.

Her only hesitation came in lifting one of the boards high enough to sweep the trinkets down inside. If they were waiting for her, then that would be the moment the trap (or joke, however you chose to look at it) would be sprung. She trembled as she felt for the edge, imagining their grubby hands breaching the narrow gap, seizing her painfully by the wrist, and pulling her down.

No one would ever know what had become of her.

The thought almost crippled her. It almost sent her stumbling away from their reach, but a stronger part of her rose just then and took control of her weak-willed limbs, prepared for anything that might come. Like a distant, unwilling spectator, she watched as her own fingers pried up one of the splintery planks and pushed the meager bribes down into the hole.

What she saw in that fleeting moment beyond the crack was simply a section of the floor's cross support: a cobwebbed and anemic length of two-by-four into which the upper boards would have been fixed. That and a moldering gloom that readily consumed the snacks and toys and gave her nothing in return. It was a soundless space that might have spiraled down for miles like a cave, or perhaps it extended only a few feet. She couldn't tell; she was content not to see their slack faces staring back at her.

The board dropped back neatly into place, and Justine exhaled with a gasp, unaware that she'd been holding her breath. She scrambled to her feet, retreating to the relative safety of the workbench. There she stood, with the flashlight aimed directly at the hole, quietly panting as she listened for signs of life or wakefulness down below.

Would they be sleeping? Would her gifts attract their immediate interest?

Were they even there?

More and more she wondered. Why should they be? It must be after midnight now. The barn had stood empty for hours, and they wouldn't have any reason to believe that she'd be returning before dawn.

Justine frowned. Her careful planning was in danger of falling apart under the logic of this new consideration. Once out of sight, the twins had the tendency to take on the weight of ghosts, of conversations held within dreams.

To be on the safe side, however, it wouldn't hurt to pound in some nails.

She found the coffee can where her father kept his stray nails and spilled a handful across the surface of the bench. They seemed to come in all shapes and sizes: large-headed and small, rusted and galvanized, even slightly bent, as if pulled from some broken-down pallet and patiently waiting to be used again. She sorted through them carefully with her small fingers, picking out four of the largest. The rest she scooped back into the can. The hammer, a standard carpenter's model with a claw, lay in a dented toolbox alongside an assortment of wrenches and screwdrivers. It felt large and awkward in her hand, but she thought she could reasonably make it drive four flat-headed nails.

Justine carried them back to the secret hole, kneeled down, and lined up the nails so that she wouldn't lose any of them. That done, she turned her attention and the head of the flashlight to the loose floorboards. She blew away the straw dust to look for the holes where the missing nails had originally sat.

Less than ten minutes later, she was done. The new nails were wider than the empty holes, so the fit was a firm one.

Maybe they *had* gone. Maybe they had slunk away while she was eating dinner or lying in her bed. It felt like false optimism, too good to even hope for.

She sat listening on the floor by the back wall for another fifteen minutes until she began to feel sleepy, cradling the hammer in her lap.

Sparks and Calliope did not resurface the following morning.

After breakfast, Justine went out to the barn and stared down at the loose boards, where the four new nailheads now winked back. She got down on her hands and knees and pressed an ear to the floor, but she might as well have been listening to wood. Nothing moved so far as she could tell, and if the twins really were trapped down there, they didn't seem to mind.

She quit the barn and played inside the house until lunch, but afterward she felt compelled to go out and listen again, in case they'd changed their minds.

For a week she kept vigil over the mended hole, but never once did they shuffle or scratch or call out to her. Never once was there any indication they were even there.

Eventually, she made up her mind that they weren't and allowed herself to forget about them.

PART SEVEN

Reanimations: 1981

1

Angelo Ramirez stroked his thick, black moustache with indecision, vacillating over what to do next as the earpiece buzzed distantly in his ear. The line to the Chambers' place was still busy. It had been for the past twenty minutes, and the sheriff was overdue checking in. Likewise, there had been no response when he'd tried to hail him in his cruiser.

With a deputy already missing, Angelo had a bad feeling brewing in the pit of his stomach. The find at the Chambers' barn had been getting a lot of attention, not only in police circles but in the regional newspapers as well. It was developing quite a history, and places like that tended to attract the wrong sort, not only the usual knots of curiosity seekers but also oddballs who felt or imagined some sort of twisted kinship or pull toward sites of tragedy or murder.

This Dunhill character Mrs. Chambers reported might be one. Stebbins had been sent to check on him, and the hills had swallowed Stebbins without a trace. And according to Bishop, the sheriff had been alone out there on the Chambers's farm after he'd left.

Across the lobby, night pressed against the glass doors, obscuring all but the occasional sweep of headlights as cars turned from Last Street onto Grand.

Angelo cut off the busy signal and tried the sheriff at his home one last time, receiving the same unanswered ring.

Shaking his head, he turned to the radio and put out a call to Bishop.

2

Troy Stebbins sat behind the wheel of a strange car in a dark and abandoned barn a little ways off the main highway. He felt strange—dazed and detached, as if lost within the frayed wrappings of a dream.

The last thing he could recall with absolute certainty was the gravel-speckled shoulder of Highway 195. It had been mid-afternoon, and he was standing in the sunlight directly across from the Chambers' farm, leaning down to talk to the driver of a dark-blue sedan: this very BMW if memory served correctly. He also recalled a dark-haired, soft-featured man of about thirty-five with a moustache and a mole, smiling up at him. Then...

Now the sun was all but gone, reduced to a faint, blue glimmer along the edge of the world, and he felt terribly hungover, as if the lid of his skull had been peeled back and stuffed with rusty pins and damp cotton wadding. *A concussion*, he told himself sagely, without the least bit of trouble believing it. What was a bit harder to accept was the trickling hole he'd just discovered in his belly, looking for all the world like an entry wound from a high caliber handgun, fired at extremely close range.

A slow bolt of panic shot through him then, though it too was far away and vague, as if he'd made up his mind that he really *was* dreaming and that therefore it was nothing to get overly concerned about.

The smell of blood was real enough, and beneath the sickly, yellow glow of the dome light, so were the powder burns that speckled his uniform blouse. If it were a dream, he thought, frowning, it wasn't missing many details. Either he was the luckiest man on earth or heaven was shaping up to be a real disappointment.

He started to laugh and coughed up a thick wad of blood instead. The rusty pins clawed at the inside of his skull with renewed agitation. Dimly, he wondered how long he'd been sitting here and looked at his wristwatch. The crystal had cracked. It read 1:53, and the second hand, bent down toward the face, was twitching in a vain attempt to bully its way past the minute.

A quiet moment or two passed unrecorded, and he lit upon a half-formed notion of getting himself to a hospital. His wounds needed to be looked at and properly dressed, though at the moment he had no idea where the nearest hospital might be.

He leaned forward, peering tentatively out the top of the windshield. Shafts of bright, silver moonlight were stabbing holes in the roof overhead. It was a barn, quite obviously an abandoned one.

One of about a thousand in the county.

The thing to do was to climb out and have a look around; maybe, he thought doubtfully, he'd even recognize the place.

He felt along the door panel for a latch and, one by one, set his spindly legs outside the car. Swearing breathlessly, he struggled to pull himself out of the seat, clumsy and weak from loss of blood. Once standing, wedged in the V of the open door, he felt a fresh trickle down his leg, and there was a slippery shifting of weight within his abdomen. The barn faded in and out, and, next thing he knew, he was lying flat on his back in the dirt as moonlight shone down in his eye.

Now isn't that a funny thing...

A deep longing settled upon him like a warm blanket, draining the tension from his aching muscles and turning his tired bones to lead. More than anything in the world, he wanted to stay right where he'd fallen; simply close his eyes and let the ragweed cover him. Even the thought of spiders crawling out of the woodwork to wrap him in a silken cocoon seemed more desirable than the task of getting to his feet again.

The moonbeam shifted slowly from one eye to the other, and the faces of his wife and son appeared before him, apprehensive and sad; this became his only torment. He couldn't stand the thought of leaving them behind, and, comfortable though the ground might be, he knew he couldn't abandon them. He had to get back in the car and drive home.

He scrabbled with his arms and legs, raising a thin cloud of dust, yet even as he was rising to his feet, the soil was calling him back.

Once he got home he would rest, he thought dreamily as he dropped back into the driver's seat. Or else he would try to find a way to take them with him.

Nodding, satisfied, he shut the door and reached for the ignition.

3

Margaret stayed by her daughter's side until it was clear that the seizure had passed. By her reckoning, it had lasted six minutes, and even now, resting on the floor with a pillow under her head and an afghan tucked over her shoulder, Justine remained sluggish and unresponsive. Hank, on the other hand, seemed to be shedding his own protective layer as she repeatedly assured him that Dunhill was dead. She showed him the gun the madman had threatened them with and, as an afterthought, told him to stay out of the bathroom and hallway. Hank nodded as if this were not a problem, as if he had no intention of ever using that bathroom again.

"Are you going to be all right if I go call the police?" she asked, worried about the continued wariness he was showing toward his sister, as if she weren't really sleeping but lying in wait. "The phone's dead, so I'll have to go outside and try from one of the cruisers."

He nodded again, looking scared but determined to be brave. Margaret watched him shoot another glance at Justine and opened her mouth to ask what was wrong; she hesitated, deciding to wait until she got back. She didn't want to delay her call any longer than she had to; Justine needed an ambulance. For the moment, it was enough that he was responding to her questions.

"I'll be right back," she said, rising on legs that were weak from exhaustion. "Keep a close eye on Justine. If she starts to seizure again, make sure she doesn't roll on her back."

He stared back at her and swallowed. In the bathroom, Shires was moaning and thrashing about again.

"Hank, did you hear me?" she barked, her voice rising sharply.

"Uh-huh."

She lingered a moment longer, wondering whether she could trust him to act. What choice did she have, really? Help had to be summoned. There were two dead men in her house, one of them the sheriff, and a third in the bathtub that would do anything to join them. God! She still couldn't believe what was happening!

"I'll be back as soon as I can," she promised, deciding he would at least run to the side door and call her back if anything happened. She turned toward the dining room. Through the lighted arch, she could see a portion of the sheriff's pant leg and his right shoe, relaxed and at rest. He looked as if he might have been waiting on a phone call or a cup of coffee. It made her think of all the times he'd sat there over the past week, keeping her abreast of the investigation, offering quiet words of assurance that their lives would soon be back to normal. The past would close as it was meant to, and the truth would become a matter of record. Once he'd even surprised her by inquiring if she'd ever thought of selling the place and moving closer to town.

"Whatever for?" Margaret had asked. It was, after all, only a hole in the ground, a point of contention where two children she'd never known may or may not have died. She wasn't frightened by the prospect of ghosts. She liked to think she was more practical than that. She'd survived her husband's death in the field just over the back rise; compared to that, the niche beneath the barn was hardly a ripple.

"Well, I hadn't meant it in that way, exactly," Garrett had returned, his expression mild and bemused in the late morning light. "More along the lines that the place might have *outgrown* you, so to speak...especially since you're not working the fields anymore." There was a note in his voice, unspoken but there to take or ignore as she pleased, that reminded her that she was a woman alone with two children, with the nearest neighbor more than a shout away in case there was trouble, and this was a scant few days before John Dunhill had come along to show them how bad trouble could be.

Now Garrett was dead, and she was still alive. Being a man, and a trained lawman at that, hadn't made him bulletproof. In the end, it was circumstance that had played the most influential hand, dealing her a secret ace (and the desperation or presence of mind to play it) at the same time it had dealt him out for good. Some things you couldn't predict, and who was to say it couldn't have happened closer to town?

Walking through the arch, she made up her mind not to look at him out of simple respect.

Drip.

At once, her eyes turned helplessly; Garrett's head was still thrown back at the ceiling.

Something brittle splintered inside her.

Her lips pressed tight as the kitchen blurred into nonsense. She felt a paralyzing burn at the back of her throat. The first sobs were soundless and racked her body in spasms, brute and forceful enough to smash through her emotional beachhead. It left her helpless and blind, groping for the cold support of the countertop.

A large nest of mixing bowls glanced off her elbow and fell to the floor with a crash.

~

Hank looked worriedly at the light pouring through the archway and listened to his mother cry. It was not a sound he was used to or, by any means, comfortable with. Heard late at night through closed doors, it was a sound he associated with great calamities and the end of the world, but tonight was the first time this supposition held true.

From his perch on the couch, he peered over his knees at Justine. A thin line of drool had run out the side of her mouth and down her cheek, but otherwise she looked okay, as if she had fallen asleep in front of the television.

The sound of the pigs had gone away too, though he wasn't sure if that was good or bad.

The crash of something being thrown, rattled, or shaken leapt out at him from the kitchen, and he winced, shifting position. His eyes settled thoughtfully on the dark slant of the sheriff's exposed pant leg, and he slowly relaxed their focus.

Would the two of them have to carry Justine out to the car and drive her to the hospital themselves? Leaving was fine; he was all for that, but it also meant that they would have to come back, and Hank didn't want to come back, at least not at night. He frowned and wondered if they would have to bring the sheriff, Dunhill, and Shires along too; he didn't think they would have enough room in the car for all those people, not with Justine stretched out on the back seat.

His stare continued to relax and deepen. The brown shadows of the dining room merged seamlessly together, and the lighted archway, already fuzzy and distant, split hesitantly in two and drifted apart. From far away, a sound he paired with a flopping blue sack moaned insistently.

Out in the kitchen, his mother had stopped crying.

4

Deputy Ramirez turned in his padded chair and regarded the face of his dispatcher's radio with a frank mixture of curiosity and disapproval. The disapproval was more reflex than reaction; by law, private citizens were not allowed use of the police and emergency bands, so his initial impulse was to warn the prankster to leave or face possible charges. Since the voice was female, he knew it wasn't one of theirs; with the exception of a few clerical positions, there were no women on the force. Yet at the same time, it was vaguely familiar, harried sounding, perhaps, but familiar all the same. It aroused his curiosity enough to put the usual lecture on hold.

"This is Deputy Ramirez of the Whitman County Sheriff's Department," he announced. "Please identify yourself. Over."

Amid a crackle of static, the woman's voice seemed to sigh with relief. "This is Margaret Chambers. I live out on Highway 195…about six miles from Rosalia. My telephone line's been cut, and I…I didn't know how else to get ahold of you."

Angelo straightened in his chair at the mention of her name. At the same time, a dark stone sank into his belly. His thumb activated the microphone, though he scarcely felt it. "Mrs. Chambers, I've been trying to reach you too, or rather the sheriff. Is he there with you? Over."

There was a long pause, and, readjusting himself in his chair, he opened his mouth to repeat the question just as her reply came back, wrapped in a choking little sob that caused the hair to stand up on the back of his neck.

"He's *dead*. John Dunhill was here, and he…he shot the sheriff dead."

Shocked, Angelo waited impatiently for her to release the mic switch and then spoke quickly, urgently: "All right,

Mrs. Chambers, I've already got a man on the way. He should be there in about two minutes, so just hold tight. I'm going to send an ambulance out for the sheriff, just in case. Is anyone else out there in need of medical assistance? Over."

"Yes, my daughter Justine. She, she's had some kind of seizure." She hesitated and then in a smaller voice added: "Dunhill's dead too. I shot him."

Jesucristo.

Angelo stared numbly at the speaker grill.

"Please send help, Deputy. I've got to go now…my son and daughter are still inside the house."

"All right, Mrs. Chambers. I understand. Just one more thing: are you and your family still in immediate danger? Over."

He scowled at the cold, gray face of the console, waiting for her voice to break through the static.

"Mrs. Chambers, I repeat: *are you in any immediate danger?* Please reply. Over."

Ten seconds passed, then twenty. She was no longer in the car.

"Damn," he swore softly as frustration crawled up and down his back like ants.

5

Margaret was halfway across the moonlit yard when she heard a shrill sound from inside the house, propelling her on with greater haste. It was Hank, she realized. He was shouting for her in a panicked voice that cut through to the bone.

Justine! Oh, please God, no!

Putting her hand on the door handle, she sensed something terrible unfolding out of the night. Glancing past the eaves, she saw a large owl with its wings spread silently against the moonlight.

As she flung open the door, she thought that this was somehow a sign, an omen or portent of what was to come, though she was too distracted to decipher it. She ran down the hall without so much as a nod at Garrett, failing to notice, in her hurry, the occasional smear of blood along the walls and in the carpet under her feet. A partial handprint stained the wall near the linen closet like a broken starfish, and near the baseboard was an elongated crescent.

Hank was as white as paste, backed up against the corner of the couch and still shouting. Justine, who Margaret was expecting to find in mid-seizure, was lying just as she'd left her, right down to the lock of hair that had fallen across her right eye.

Confusion caused her to falter.

What is happening? she thought. Justine was okay, or at least she wasn't any worse. Yet Hank kept right on screaming as if the house were burning down around them and he was the only one who could smell smoke. *What…?*

She started uncertainly across the room, eyebrows pinched and frowning.

"Mom!" Hank shouted, stabbing a finger toward the darkened alcove of the dining room. "Look out!"

Margaret turned her head toward the dining room, and there was John Dunhill, silhouetted against the kitchen arch; the lamp from the living room barely touched his face. He was leaning over the far end of the table, and his chest and midsection were a great red stain.

"Hello, Margaret," he said with a grimace. "Thought you'd gotten rid of me, eh?"

His left sleeve was rolled up past the elbow, and he seemed to be holding it there with his right hand. Before him, on the table, was a black bag or satchel she hadn't noticed before, its mouth open wide. Beside it, a small jar stood glistening and upright.

"What are you doing?" she demanded shrilly, staggered by his resurrection. Then her eyes sharpened, and she saw the syringe in his right hand. He found a vein with two probing fingers and jabbed the needle into it. Awkwardly, his thumb rose to work the plunger, searching for its end and then ramming it home.

"Why, you're nothing but a goddamned junkie!" Margaret said, her voice trembling, her fear turning to disgust. "That's why you're not practicing anymore!"

"Not quite, dearie," Dunhill said through gritted teeth. A dark wave of blood seeped down his shirtfront as he leaned forward and dropped the syringe into the satchel's hungry mouth. With trembling hands, he replaced the vial too. He did this with much greater care, which told her that it contained something very precious to him.

"You should know I've called the police," she said defiantly, one hand on her hip. "They're on their way right now."

"Then we don't have much time, do we?" he said, pressing a firm hand to his midsection and slowly straightening himself. "And so much left to do."

The drug was working quickly, she saw with alarm. When she'd first caught sight of him, he looked like a man tottering on the rim of life, so debilitated that, despite the shock of seeing him standing, she hadn't considered him much of a threat. It looked as if one good blow would finish him off; now, however, as he started around the table, she wasn't so certain. Step by step, he was recovering himself, assuming his former menace.

"That's far enough!" Margaret warned, taking a step back. He no longer had the gun to point and threaten with, but neither did she; before she'd gone out to use the car radio, she'd placed it out of Hank's reach atop the refrigerator. It was still there (at least she prayed to God it was), and so long as they kept out of the kitchen, there it would stay. The police, she reminded herself, were probably turning up the drive now.

She cast a quick glance out the south window toward the highway but saw only her own frightened ghost staring back.

"Not quite as punctual as you'd hoped, are they?" Dunhill said, pausing at the near end of the table. "Your trust is misplaced, Margaret. You've done quite well on your own tonight, haven't you?"

"Don't you come a step closer!" she said, eyes moving rapidly around the room, searching for something heavy and wieldy enough to use as a weapon. She glanced past Justine at the brassy gleam of the tool stand beside the fireplace. Retreating quickly across the room, she drew the iron poker from the stand, upsetting the small shovel and broom with a clatter. Gripping the tool in both hands, she recovered her steps and took a stand in front of her children.

Dunhill coughed violently. So far he hadn't found the strength to step away from the table.

"Now," she said to him with a savage smile, "you take one more step and, and—"

"*What*, dove?" he said with a grin, resplendently gruesome with fresh blood on his teeth. "You'll *what*? Kill me?" He laughed aloud, coughing out a fine crimson spray. "Perhaps it hasn't had time to sink in yet, but you've already accomplished that. Look where it's gotten you."

"I, I don't know what you're talking about," Margaret stammered with uncertainty in her voice and in her eyes, "and neither do you. You're no different from a common junkie. Worse, in fact, because as a doctor you ought to know better."

"You stupid, stuttering *cow!*" He glared at her in furious silence and then slapped his palm loudly against the table. "Clean the chaff out of your ears and *listen* to me!

Listen!" His voice dropped to a whisper. "I *am* dead! Do you understand that plain enough? Am I getting through to you? The solution in the vial—which you just saw me administer—is *not* morphine, as you seem to think, nor opium, laudanum, or any of the derivatives thereof, but a serum of my own creation. A practical reanimating agent which, injected into dead tissue, reawakens it!"

Margaret allowed herself a thin, humorless smile, having listened patiently to his measured outburst, flinching only once as his hand hit the table.

Dunhill smiled too, mildly and without teeth. "I take it you don't believe me?"

"That you have the power to raise yourself from the dead?" She shook her head. "No. The only thing I believe at this moment is I should have put a bullet in your head."

"Ah-ah!" he said, raising a finger. "Not only myself, but anyone I choose."

"That thing in the bathtub, for instance?" she said skeptically. "Shires?"

"An excellent example," he said. "You washed him with your own bare hands! Tell me, Margaret, did his flesh feel the same as your own? Or was it harder and cooler than you expected? Didn't you sense something fundamentally *different* about him?"

"What I sensed and what I saw," she answered hotly, "was a man pushed to the limits of another man's cruelty! And if you really believe otherwise, *Doctor*, then all I can say is that you're insane!"

He sighed, slowly shaking his head. "I'll not stand here arguing fact with you. If, as you claim, the police are practically at the door, I would suggest a demonstration is in order."

Margaret tensed. "You stay right where you are." She brought the poker to the ready.

He smiled slyly, and she saw within that smile the terrible knowledge that a yard-long poker was a very different animal than a high-caliber revolver. A gun could command obedience and respect from across a room, but a poker could not. To use it, she would have to get right up close to him, close enough for him to catch it and take it away if her swing was predictable or lacking in strength. Attack was a different thing as well, and Dunhill seemed to understand that she didn't have the confidence to use the poker, except in a purely defensive manner. If, for example, he threatened her or her children.

Using the dining room chairs for support, John Dunhill turned and creaked back to where he'd left his satchel and pulled it close to him.

"I have a few spare syringes," he said, stirring a hand inside its leathery mouth as the muffled tinkle of glass and surgical steel escaped. "Including one I've been using on Daniel. Still, I hate to waste a sterile one..." —He threw a calculated glance toward the kitchen—"and I don't think the sheriff will mind sharing needles." His fevered eyes searched hers. "What do you say, Margaret? Shall I bring him back?"

A part of her suddenly believed him, believed without a doubt that she *had* killed him and that somehow he'd come back, that he now meant to try the same trick on the sheriff and that it would work just as he claimed. Why else waste his few remaining minutes? Because he *knew* the police were on their way, and if the sheriff was no longer dead when his deputies arrived, well, they certainly couldn't call it murder.

Dunhill found his syringe and picked up the large, colorless vial.

"No!" Margaret took a step forward, the poker trembling in her hands. "I won't let you do it!"

"Try to stop me then, angel." Dunhill said, looking at her flatly. "Come on and try."

Dismissing her as if she were a child, he turned the vial upside down and pushed the needle through the soft rubber cap, drawing a full barrel of the drug down into the syringe.

"No?" He stepped away from the table, seemingly fully recovered, and ducked nimbly through the archway.

Margaret lowered the poker and let it relax until the dull, black point touched the carpet, leaving a smudge of gray ash on the fibers. She looked over her shoulder at Hank, who was gazing past her toward the kitchen. "Mind your sister!" she said, wondering what this experience was doing to him inside. What was it doing to *all* of them? If Dunhill's horror came true and the sheriff really did awaken, how could they go on as if nothing had happened? Dead was dead, and once you died, there was no coming back. But what if that boundary softened to something negotiable and gray? If word got out, *what would become of the world?*

She shuddered at the thought, at the countless crawling nightmares the possibility hatched, too terrible to even comprehend.

Still, she might spare her son that glimpse, with a little luck.

In the kitchen, Dunhill was trying to tip Garrett out of his chair. Margaret turned her back on him and, sliding the poker out of sight beneath the sofa, motioned Hank over to help her move Justine. He responded quickly, which lightened her worries some.

"Get her legs," she whispered, down on her knees so she could get a good grip beneath her daughter's arms. She tossed the pillow and afghan aside. "We'll take her into my room. Careful now!"

As Hank took hold of his sister's ankles, there was a jarring crash, like a large tree being felled. The sheriff's chair overturned with a hollow clatter, and they heard Dunhill swear sharply to himself.

"Ready?" Margaret hissed.

"Yes." His voice was quick and dry. He was scared to death.

She counted quickly to three, and together they lifted Justine off the floor, bearing her quickly away like two medics carting a wounded soldier off the battlefield. Dunhill and the sheriff disappeared from sight as the dining room partition intervened, and they entered the welcome gloom of the hallway.

As they navigated around the corners of the house, Margaret changed her mind suddenly. Although the bedroom, with its large bed, was the natural choice for Justine, it would offer little in the way of protection since there was no lock on the door. Only the bathroom had one, but Shires was still in there.

"Hold it," she instructed her son, readjusting her grip. Over the tacky spread of blood on the carpet, she vacillated between the two rooms. "Let's take her into the bathroom," she decided. "Your end first."

Once inside, they laid her on the cold floor. Shires, who had quieted down in the interim, began his thrashing and gnashing anew. Margaret snatched up the towel she had brought in earlier and threw it on top of him as Hank got his first eyeful.

"Don't look at it!" she said, reaching in front of him for the edge of the shower curtain. She jerked it across the tub, obscuring Shires further from view.

"All right, listen to me, honey." Hank was still staring at the dark blur behind the curtain; she took his chin gently in her hand and turned his eyes back to hers. "Are you listening?"

He nodded, though Shires was calling him back.

"I left the gun in the kitchen, on top of the refrigerator." She peeked over her shoulder at the open door, at Dunhill's voice, low and conspiratorial in the kitchen, as if he and the sheriff were planning an escape.

"He's busy now, so I don't think he'll notice, but I want to get to it before he does. Okay?"

A look of sheer terror gripped Hank's face. "No!" he screamed, clutching at the hem of her blouse. "I don't want you to leave! You said the police were coming!"

"They *are*, baby, but if he gets trapped inside the house, there's no telling what he'll do. If he has a gun, he might kill more policemen. Or *us*." She took a breath. "If I can get the gun back, there's nothing more he *can* do."

Hank appeared to give this grave consideration, creasing his brow as he weighed the possibilities and repercussions. That he was against it was clear, and his consent was only granted with one inflexible provision:

"You're coming right back, aren't you? After you get the gun, you'll come right back."

She touched his cheek and ran her fingers lightly through his hair. "Of course I will," she promised, and then her face became dark and serious. "But if something *does* go wrong—it won't, but just in case—I want you to lock the door and don't open it again until the police are here. There'll be a lot of them, so you'll know." Her troubled gaze dropped to the floor. She knelt and, with his help, positioned Justine on her side. The discarded bathmat was folded into a thick pad and tucked under her head as a pillow. Satisfied that she'd done as best she could to comfort her, Margaret bent and kissed her once on the temple. She whispered something loving into her unconscious ear and then, gripping the tub and the basin, pulled herself wearily to her feet.

"You need to take care of her while I'm gone." A stinging tear was gathering in the corner of her eye, and Margaret wiped it away before it could fall and cause him further worry.

"I will," Hank quietly promised, his lips strained and white.

Shires vented another blast of rage and indignation, sounding eerily like a mad dog.

"And don't pay any attention to him," she said, nodding once to indicate the shower curtain. "He can't get out, and he can't hurt you if you leave him alone. Okay?"

Hank nodded unhappily, not certain of anything.

Margaret found a smile, one that felt forced and artificial but that hopefully lent him a small measure of comfort. She held out her arms to him. "All right then, here I go. Give me a kiss for luck."

He stepped forward and hugged her fiercely, still not willing to let her go.

6

Troy Stebbins was lost.

The night sky filled the BMW's gently curving windshield as he rounded yet another featureless bend in the roadway. The stars reminded him of tall ships and mariners, but for the life of him, Stebbins could make no sense of the guiding constellations. It was as if he had been transported to another planet half a galaxy away, where none of the old stars held true or were recognizable in their altered positions. The Big Dipper lost its cohesiveness and had fallen apart; Orion sprouted tentacles and a long, curved beak; Cassiopeia was dead, and in her place rose a black and lifeless void.

Worse still were the road signs; each one was an illegible jumble of nonsense, like strange insects pinned to bright rectangles of sheet metal. The glowing instrumentation under the dashboard was likewise indecipherable. Stebbins had heard of head injuries that played such havoc with the mind: areas of pressure or swelling affecting key points of logic and perception.

Perhaps he ought to get someone to assist him when the next town or farmhouse came into view. He could have them put through a call to his wife too, just so she wouldn't worry.

A wink of colored light caught his eye in the rearview mirror. A bright line of headlights, topped with blue and red emergency beacons, pouring like hornets around the last bend.

"Well, now," he murmured, taking his foot off the gas and veering onto what little shoulder the highway offered. They sped by in a continuous blur, seven or eight cars in all, leaving the night to close back upon on their agitated wake, taillights flickering as the next bend approached.

Something stirred inside Deputy Stebbins, something as solid and black as bedrock.

He punched the accelerator and leapt after them.

7

Margaret crept like a spider along the hallway. The floorboards creaked under her weight as Dunhill cursed and coaxed his unwilling subject back to life. *Crazy bastard*, she thought bitterly, wondering what she would do if Garrett were waiting for her around the next corner, or if Dunhill had happened upon the gun after all.

The side door would be right there, hers for the taking, and there was a chance she might circle around to the bathroom window, but that would leave Hank and Justine at Dunhill's mercy while she stood out in the back yard. True, he still had a bullet hole through the center of him, but she was no longer taking it for granted that that would be any sort of debilitation.

The best thing to do would be to keep her promise to Hank and get back to the bathroom as quickly as possible. She might even get them out of the house easier that way, provided Dunhill gave them enough time. And the police *had* to be on their way.

She was close enough now to see some of the kitchen through a slice of doorway: the cupboard where she kept her plates and bowls, a section of countertop lined with matching canisters, the left side of the sink, and, above that, a depthless piece of sky hovering over the highway across the darkened fields. It was the window glass itself, however, that caught her interest, giving her pause. In it flickered a dim reflection of the breakfast table and the dining room arch. John Dunhill was crouched on the floor, and the top of his head was also in view. It was tilted slightly to the left, as if he were listening.

A low chuckle arose, bubbling with stale blood. "I can hear you, Margaret," he called, though in the wrong direction, through the dining room. Even so, her scalp prickled at the confidence in his voice, the animal cunning. Suddenly, she was certain he'd found the gun.

The refrigerator was just around the corner, close enough to touch if she could reach through walls, yet she was afraid to step in for fear he would shoot her.

And then bring her back with his filthy needle.

No, she resolved, she wouldn't even consider that. It was impossible, and he was deranged, incapable of holding his own life together.

His back was still turned. All she had to do was step in and step out.

Presto.

"Easy now," Dunhill softly cautioned, and something gurgled beneath the sound of his voice. There was a choking gasp and then the rigid shudder of a shoe heel across the linoleum.

Oh my God!

Margaret felt an icy weight against her chest, a terror so complete and overwhelming that she thought it might crush her to bits. She would become a figure etched in glass, cracked through to a milky haze, fragile enough to shatter at the slightest touch.

Her heart pounded sharply, forcing her to take another breath. The slice of kitchen, real and reflected, trembled before her eyes, and a sudden darkness began eating away at the light. Margaret realized that she was in danger of breakdown, of collapse, and the only way to fight it was to move. But that meant inching around the corner to face what the reflection wouldn't show her, and she wasn't sure she had the courage for that.

Her frozen limbs began to tingle and gently fall asleep while, outside the window, the moon came out of hiding. The glass became transparent, more a window again and less of a mirror.

Soft, yellow light was breaking across the fields, picking out shadowy clumps of debris from the barn. It was enough to distract her for a few vital seconds from what was happening in the kitchen, time enough for the paralysis that held her to safely dissipate. Her vision cleared, two yellow headlights bounced into view, and she realized that what she was seeing was an approaching car.

A solitary police car.

Everything changed. The fear that had been building boiled effortlessly away, and in its place rose a scorching rage. She was furious at the sheriff's department for this contemptibly meager response and at herself for putting her trust and her children's lives into someone else's hands— and for leaving the goddamned gun on top of the refrigerator! *My God!* she fumed, *I reported the sheriff murdered!* Didn't Garrett rate a little higher than this? She'd known dead cows to attract more attention! It just didn't make sense; there *had* to be more men on the way.

But in the meantime, this lone, unsuspecting deputy was walking into a death trap; if Dunhill had found the gun, he was as good as dead. Unless, of course, she could get to it first.

Silently, bitterly, she cursed the idiot whose lack of judgment had put her in this position. Didn't she have her hands full already just keeping herself and her children alive? Did they really expect her to cover their asses as well?

She clenched her fists as the cruiser rolled slowly out of view, leaving a fading red glow in its wake. She could hear the low-pitched rumble of its engine now and wondered how much longer Dunhill could fail to notice. Perhaps he already had and was waiting for the man to draw closer; playing dead, she well knew, was a role he could portray quite convincingly.

Brake lights brightened the weedy drive. Very soon now, the deputy was going to climb out of his car and slam the door. That sound, as well as a rap on the door, would cut through the kitchen, which gave her only a few seconds to act. Either the gun would be there, or it wouldn't. Her responsibility was with her children; besides, she had to assume the deputy would have a gun of his own and be trained to use it.

Margaret took a deep breath as her fingertips searched for calm and serenity along the cool surface of the wall. Softly, she exhaled.

One.

Outside, the motor in the muscular cruiser growled once and then sputtered out. The bubble surrounding the house fell into an untimely silence.

Two.

The kitchen floor creaked gently with a palpable shudder, and then a fit of coughing erupted. In the window reflection, John Dunhill's ghostly head dropped out of view, and in its absence, Margaret imagined she could hear *two* sets of respirations.

Three.

Justine opened her eyes.

They had changed from blue to muddy brown as she gazed up into the surprised face of a baby who had now become a boy. He bent closer, frowning as the overhead light struck his sandy hair and cast an image like a tarnished halo. He looked like an angel passing judgment.

"Justine? Is that you?" Hank looked doubtful.

She pushed herself up into a sitting position, bringing her legs awkwardly around. The lighting was bright, her mouth dry, and as she ran her tongue over her lips to moisten them, she tasted the salty residue of the day's exertion and fears. Her arms felt weak, trembling beneath her weight.

"You'd better lay down until Mom gets back," Hank nervously suggested, reaching out to hold her back.

Justine uttered a low, feral grunt and slapped his hand away.

"Hey!" he cried, recoiling, shock falling from his wide, brown eyes. Justine turned her head slowly, as if it were an unfamiliar weight, and surveyed the small, pink bathroom. A smile settled on her face, and her lips peeled back. An unformed sound issued toward Hank's horrified face.

He found his sister's intent, steady gaze disturbing. There was a cruelty or hunger to her eyes that he had never seen before, like a spider gazing upon a fly.

"Justine?"

With alarm, he watched her muscles flex beneath the skin as if she were preparing to spring at him.

Hank shouted at the locked door, his voice hoarse and cracked. The sound filled the small room to overflowing, disturbing the ambiguous shape caught within the drawn shower curtain. Shires, quiet since Justine awoke (as if sensible of some new danger) began to beat his softened head against the bottom of the tub.

Justine froze. Her head swiveled toward the hazy curtain, which was decorated with pink blossoms and falling petals. Hank saw surprise form in unfamiliar lines on his sister's face, a sudden realization that they weren't alone in the room.

She reached for the curtain. Hank shut his eyes and screamed for his mother, but there was no mistaking the bounce and tear of the curtain separating from its overhead rings.

Then everything got strangely quiet.

Margaret stepped into the kitchen, registering the presence of two figures on the far side of her kitchen: one splayed out on his back and the other crouched down beside it. She passed them over, however, without further notice or study in her haste to reach up and sweep the top of the refrigerator. Her fingers probed the dusty back corners, coming up empty before she had a chance to stand on tiptoes and see what she already knew. She was too late; the gun was gone.

Laughter bubbled out of Dunhill's mouth as he turned on one heel and showed her the revolver, cupped like an ace in the crease of his right hand.

"Looking for something, dear?" he said, eyes sparkling as he took casual aim at her. Behind him, the body of the sheriff was laboring to breathe, and small tremors were evident in the hands as well. Synapses were misfiring along corrupted nerve endings, causing the extremities to jitter and dance. Surprisingly, witnessing this did not cause Margaret to fall apart or freeze up. Instead, she tried to picture the deputy in the driveway, who now seemed to be her best and only hope.

"Please," she said. She put every ounce of despondency she could manage into her voice, hoping to stall Dunhill until the inevitable knock. "Don't do this! You don't have to do this!"

At the sound of her voice, Garrett opened his murky eyes. He raised his head to look at her, but this went unnoticed by Dunhill, whose attention had narrowed to the sights of his gun.

In the bathroom, Hank screamed for his mother, and Shires began his tiresome knock.

Dunhill sighed, slowly shaking his head. "Margaret, it pains me to say this, but I've no more use for you." He put on his bloody, lop-sided grin and cocked the hammer of the revolver. "You say the police are on their way, but I say they're past due. I'm afraid I'm going to have to call your bluff."

His smile faded as he extended his gun arm and concentrated on her face.

"But don't think me unmerciful. I'm going to give you a last gift right here and now, just between the two of us. Your precious babies won't have to watch you die. I promise you that." He paused, amused by some new thought. "Perhaps they won't even have to know…"

Hank screamed again, more frantically this time, and a distant part of her wondered what had happened to the deputy. She'd never even heard his car door slam shut.

"Please!" she pleaded, overwhelmed by a torrent of emotion. Anger, fear, helplessness, and frustration crawled over her like waves of static electricity. "I'm begging you!"

"Good-bye," Dunhill said, clenching his teeth to keep the gun from wavering. She closed her eyes against the coming bullet, waiting for the bang that would carry her away.

One second lumbered by, long and elastic, then two. She was afraid to open her eyes for fear he was playing with her, waiting for her to look before he delivered the killing blow, wanting to see the terror in her soul.

An odd sound came to her: brittle yet muffled, wet. Then she heard a thud as something heavy struck the floor.

Margaret opened her eyes, and a piercing scream flew from her throat.

John Dunhill was twitching facedown on the floor with the trigger guard still curled around his index finger. His skull had been crushed, cracked open against the linoleum like an overripe melon. Behind him, Jake Garrett was sitting up and hissing as if his head were full of snakes. His large hands were covered in a gory burst of scarlet. He looked at Margaret, and his lips moved thickly, lethargically, as if he had been given a large dose of Novocain. It seemed to her that some of the murkiness and confusion had cleared from his eyes, leaving him in horror, in agony. His teeth clicked together, reminding her of Shires, and his eyes dropped to Dunhill, still squirming on the floor.

Dark blood and saliva dripped from Garrett's chin as he reached out for Dunhill, gathering him closer, biting and squeezing as if, despite the gun, his teeth and hands were his only weapons.

Margaret backed slowly through the archway into the hall. Another scream erupted in the bathroom, and she turned and ran.

Margaret Chambers disappeared, and Garrett had the odd satisfaction of finding himself alone with the man who had shot and killed him. Smiling, he leaned forward to pry the gun out of Dunhill's cramped hand, which fought for the weapon like an alligator, not knowing what it fought for, and winced as a sharp pain tore through his midsection. He ignored it long enough to secure the gun and then hooked a clumsy finger into his shirt pocket, fishing out a familiar roll of Tums.

Peeling back the tight-fitting tin foil proved a task beyond his dexterity, so he bit off an end and, after chewing it to a dry paste, swallowed. He soon began to feel better and, resting the service revolver in his lap, watched with dull interest as his assassin crawled slowly under the Chambers' kitchen table, entangling himself in a forest of chrome-plated legs.

Garrett found this mildly amusing, though in a dim sort of way. His mind was not right, he knew, but he understood enough of what was happening to feel confident in his decisions. His own resurrection was not clear, since he knew that he was dead, but since Dunhill seemed reluctant to die as well, he let it pass.

Perhaps he could help them both.

Garrett picked up the revolver. It was long and heavy, with a six-inch barrel and a handgrip made of burnished walnut. He pointed it at John Dunhill's head and was about to pull the trigger when a worrisome thought crossed his mind. Half-formed and inconclusive, it concerned itself with the issue of bullets and the importance of not wasting them. Not when he had unfinished business.

Frowning, Garrett glanced about the immediate area, looking for a viable truncheon. Interestingly enough, there were an empty syringe and an ampoule containing a small amount of clear fluid discarded casually beside him on the floor. But these things were meaningless to him, and nothing he found within reach was half as effective as what he already had in hand.

He hefted the revolver, feeling its satisfactory weight, and tried to think. It was difficult to concentrate, and Garrett pressed his free hand against his forehead in an effort to keep his mind from wandering. After a long moment, a thought occurred to him, tugged like a long, white tapeworm out of the folds of his brain. He felt a painless pressure, ending with an image, a solution to his flaring concern.

Reversing the gun, holding it like a hammer by its long, steely barrel, Garrett tapped the butt solidly against the open flat of his palm. Grinning, he pushed aside weightless chairs, grasped Dunhill by the scalp, and pulled him out into the merciless light.

The steel-framed handgrip came whistling down with enough force to drive tent stakes into hardened clay. A sound like teeth biting into a firm apple issued out of Dunhill's skull at the first blow, and as the bludgeon continued its work, the apple went soft and rotten. Garrett didn't pause, however, until the limbs stopped moving and the head became a blurry mass of pulp and splintered bone.

He crawled back around the table, leaving Dunhill to haunt a dusty corner near the window, all sticky and red. Still, one of the hands opened and closed, as if searching about for something to grip. Garrett watched it for a while and then decided it would expire soon enough on its own. Like a fish in a boat.

His hands felt itchy and restless, and when he looked down he saw the gun's matted grip had eased back into his palm, like an unconscious desire.

He looked longingly down its barrel, wondering if it would still fire. He raised his arm and eased the barrel into his own throat, the bitter taste of lubricant and gunmetal resting heavily on his tongue.

Trembling, Garrett closed his eyes and tried to recall the words of a simple prayer.

Gently, still searching, he squeezed the trigger.

8

Justine peered at the thing inside the tub. Despite its broken and cadaverous face and its much-abused body, there was an awful familiarity struggling to be dredged from its lopsided features, a nagging reminder carried over from a time when memory had no point of reference, no language with which to record.

Only fractured images. Like this face.

Justine bent closer, her expression growing rigid.

"You..." she hissed with undying hatred, her eyes dilating to a murderous black, wide enough for the equally transfixed Shires to look beyond the girl and recognize the accusing finger of his own past. He could see the two dead things that he and Smith had dug up out of an Idaho graveyard and given to Jonathan and Prudence Taylor to raise as children, a pair of tormentors harboring more ill will and hatred toward him than John Dunhill. Vehemently trying to escape the shallow well of the tub, Shires began to scream.

Justine reached down to pinch Shires nostrils. Leaning inside the tub, she covered his mouth with her own and, with a sharp series of convulsions, expelled her old friends into Shires.

The door shuddered open, and Margaret gasped as she caught sight of her daughter. Bent over the bathtub, Justine's lips were pressed over Shires's sore-covered maw in a desperate kiss, pinning his chest and shoulders to the porcelain with her forearm. He was screaming into her open mouth, and Justine was shaking with another seizure. Horrified, Margaret watched as the tremors passed into Shires, who fought and strained but, without benefit of arms or legs, had little chance escape.

Margaret shrieked and called out her daughter's name as Hank tried to slip past her to the open door. The look on his face suggested a stark area between dreaming and trauma, as if he might keep running until his heart or his sanity gave up on him.

"Go!" she ordered him, her voice distorted and haggard. "Out into the hall, and wait there for me!" The words bounced against his upturned face. She watched him disappear and then turned back to the bathtub.

Margaret had no conscious thought other than to separate her daughter from Dunhill's monstrosity. She meant to grab Justine by the shoulder, but when her hand grasped her hair instead, Justine's head lolled back like a broken doll's, her mouth yawning, bloody with pleasure.

"Oh my God! Justine!"

Margaret was never quite certain what she saw just then.

A nebulous substance, vaporous yet *alive*, was dripping out of the corners of her daughter's mouth, crystallizing rapidly into a gray and fungal-looking growth, speckling her lips and the point of her chin. Shires's tongue was black with the stuff; he was trying vainly to spit it back into Justine's face.

A gunshot exploded from the kitchen. Margaret gasped and recoiled from the tub, still clutching her daughter's hair. Justine's eyes widened, and she began to choke as some obstruction, birthing in visible contractions, slowly forced its way out of her throat.

Margaret leaned against the vanity and cradled Justine tightly in her arms, feeling the shudders and spasms pass through her like loose jolts of electricity pulled out of the charged air. One thing she did know: if this was a seizure, she had never seen its kind before. Discharging its energy through frail conduits of muscle and bone, it was liable to tear Justine apart before it ran its course.

Justine started to cough thickly, as if she had aspirated honey.

"They're coming back," a voice whispered, and Margaret looked up. Hank had returned to the doorway, frightened by the gunshot. He was clutching the jamb, staring down helplessly at Justine. A helpless shudder passed through him.

Margaret frowned and tipped her head to listen, thinking he meant Dunhill, but all she could hear were Shires's incessant squeals, horrendous against the porcelain and bare tile. She shook her head. "*Who*, honey? *Who's com*—"

Justine convulsed and vomited. A thick, gray matter spilled out onto the floor near Margaret's hip, half-digested and with the consistency of raw eggs.

Hank put his fists to his mouth and screamed. Margaret felt the foundations of reality shifting beneath her once again, as if the house were standing upon a psychic fault line, one given to strange rumblings now and then. Perhaps Hank had the right idea in keeping to the doorway.

The puddle of bile began to stir on its own, and the faces of two dead children stared balefully up at her from the floor, half-formed and monstrous.

Old, hateful names reawakened in her mind.

Sparks. Calliope.

A low moan scraped Margaret's throat as the awful truth struck home. These...these *things* had once been Justine's playmates! Her most constant and devoted companions!

"Oh my God," she whispered as the faces lost cohesion and sank back into the puddle, mingling like tiny embryos in a spilled sac of amniotic fluid. A strong compulsion arose in Margaret to hammer the heel of her fist against the slippery, gray nuclei, but it passed with a shudder as thin streams of the stuff, in defiance of gravity, began to climb the side of the tub. Leaving behind the extraneous contents of Justine's stomach like a single, sloppy footprint, the silvery threads slithered over the porcelain rim and, quick as a wink, disappeared over the other side.

Shires's vocalizations took on a choked and panicked quality as the tendrils stole between his lips and up his nostrils. His throat bobbed, and a long, gargling scream opened like a tear through his middle. The sound rose in a raw and terrifying crescendo and then, quite suddenly, stopped.

Shires settled back to the bottom of the tub and grew quiet and still, almost tranquil. Margaret drew slowly back, and his eyes—thoughtful, with purpose and malice—followed her.

The irises had changed from blue to brown, and a hideous grin slowly spread across his face. It wasn't too difficult for Margaret to imagine two new faces staring up at her.

A flower burst open against Shires's emaciated chest, directly over his heart, spreading its dark-red petals beneath the skin. A second followed, rippling down the right side of his abdomen, long and agonizing.

The twins were tearing him apart from the inside out, forcing Shires to hold on to his rigid grin even as blood began to bubble between his clenched and broken teeth, spilling down his neck and into the open drain. In counterpoint, a long, glimmering tear carved a fresh channel down the shunted slope of the opposite cheek. It pricked at Margaret's conscience, reminding her of her broken promise.

She became aware of a dull and distant hammering, as of heavy fists against her side door, rattling the windows and loosening the hinges. Loud, excited voices were shouting to be let inside.

The police, she thought to herself, her eyes still locked with Shires's. *More than just the one now. Well, it's about time.*

Without pausing to reconsider, she rose to her feet and hoisted herself upon the broad lip of the bathtub, grasping the showerhead pipe with one hand for balance. The dark eyes followed her, and the grin, she saw with satisfaction, slipped a notch.

Good.

"Mom?" Hank said behind her, his voice soft and uncertain.

She looked down over her shoulder. "Turn your head, Hank. It's all for the best. I think you know that by now."

He opened his mouth to object. He swallowed instead and said simply, "I, I think the police are here."

"I know they are, baby," she replied. "That's why I need to hurry. Now turn around and close your eyes. Put your fingers in your ears and try to think of something good."

He shuffled his feet obediently to face the bloodstain in the hall. Squeezing his eyes tight, Hank pictured the ocean: gentle waves over a golden stretch of sand on a fine summer's day. The breeze was in his hair, and seagulls were sailing like kites overhead. Far out to sea, a ship was sailing slowly northward.

Margaret jumped, focusing all 130 of her pounds into her heels. They connected squarely with Shires's badly mended skull, and he broke apart like a moldy jack-o'-lantern.

9

The sound of gunfire, a single high-caliber shot, impelled Bishop to advance upon the Chambers' house even as the sound of his backup came rolling between the low hills. The tall, white house was bathed in moonlight, so it seemed to shimmer between the darker borders of lawn and sky. Every window spilled light, a glow so warm and yellow it looked inviting, yet Bishop had the feeling that nothing but nightmares lay crouched inside, all of them tragic and splashed with blood.

He drew his gun and crept across the narrow yard toward the door, now hearing screams from inside. A flimsy screen door stood in the way, though he wasted no time knocking on it to be let inside. Passing through the squeak of its weathered hinges, he immediately tried the brassy, inner knob.

It was locked.

He swore, exhaling the sour taste of his own fear. Another scream rattled his nerves, this one long and continuous, like the sound of a man being skinned alive.

Bishop made a fist and, shouting to be let in, beat it against the heavy face of the door. In its grain he felt a dense solidity, a capacity in its bolts and hinges to withstand the likes of him for as long as it pleased. He thought of his revolver, of the necessity of shooting his way past the stubborn lock. He had seen it done dozens of times in movies (always with one well-placed shot), but it was a trick he had never found a use for in real life.

Until now.

Inside, the terrible cries reached a bursting pitch and then abruptly stopped, as if cut whole from the solid air.

Bishop called out Garrett's name, certain the voice belonged to the sheriff, but when no reply came forth, nothing but a dreadful silence, he stepped back and assumed a firing stance at the edge of the step.

Gritting his teeth, he squeezed the trigger, and a muzzle flash lit the doorway. Splinters of wood rained over the welcome mat as a section of the decorative molding dissolved, but when he went forward to test the lock, he found it as resolute as ever.

"Shit!"

A flashing line of emergency vehicles turned into the driveway behind him as he stepped back once again and fired two more bullets into the lock. This time his aim proved better, and the door shuddered open, revealing a slice of dull yellow light.

He kicked it open, revolver outstretched, and saw two figures burst through an arch down the right side of a dimly lit hallway. His finger tensed in surprise and then relaxed as he recognized Margaret Chambers, accompanied by her son. They looked as if they'd been through a war.

Margaret cried as she caught sight of him. "My daughter!" She pointed back through the arch, her voice rough and anguished. "Please, *hurry!* She's in the bathroom!"

Nodding, Bishop moved forward, winding cautiously around two blind corners to a small, pink-tiled room he would visit many times thereafter in his sleep. There would be other rooms, other horrors, but that first room and what lay waiting in the tub, dead but somehow still squirming, always came as a shock.

Night after bloody night.

Margaret waited until the deputy was out of sight and, bending to whisper a word of caution to her son, stepped quickly into the scarlet abyss that had once upon a time been her kitchen. The sheer scale of the violence took her breathlessly aback.

There was blood *everywhere*: in a skin over the floor, splashed in clots against the cabinets, running in drips down the appliances. And somewhere—probably under the refrigerator, she supposed—it was *burning*, sending up a nauseating cloud that tasted like scorched pennies on the tip of her tongue.

Pieces of flesh, severed and torn, shattered at the bone and crushed beyond recognition, crawled about like dying fish. Dead but still moving, twisting over and over upon themselves like raw nerves.

She let her eyes wander among them, taking in each new horror until—

There! Just beyond the front table leg, she saw what she'd come for, hiding like a glass spider with poison glistening inside its hollow belly. Without hesitation, she crossed the room to it.

The sheriff was lying near, though she tried not to look at him.

With a hand on the tabletop to keep herself from slipping, Margaret bent and plucked up the tightly capped ampoule, which had somehow survived the slaughter intact; the syringe, she was happy to see, had not been so fortunate and lay in sharp pieces near the heel of Garrett's shoe.

Lazy sirens were warbling up the drive, filling the night with a banshee cry, and through the sink window she saw red lights churning, drawing to an agitated halt behind the three silent cruisers.

Time was fleeting, but she thought there was enough. It had taken all her will to leave Justine lying on the cold floor of the bathroom, unconscious and in a heap, but one last thread remained before she would allow herself the luxury of catching her breath, something perhaps more important than her daughter's life.

Clutching the ampoule tightly in her fist, Margaret moved across the kitchen to the sink (no longer concerned with the blood) and dashed the bottle into the open maw of the garbage disposal. She heard it shatter, but just to be certain, she flipped open the tap and hit the wall switch.

With satisfaction, she listened to the sound of glass being ground into sand and then sluiced down the drain. She let it go until the blades caught and choked on the steel rim of the rubbery cap, stalling with an angry whine that filled her nostrils with the sharp scent of ozone.

She flipped the disposal back off and, glancing distractedly through the ghost in the window, picked up the soap and began to scrub her hands.

10

There was a great measure of comfort to be had in the swift, practiced way in which the machinery took over.

Justine was being attended to before the last of the sirens died away, and although she was still unconscious, her vital signs were strong and steady, stable enough to be transferred onto a gurney and loaded into the first ambulance. Margaret and Hank rode with her, leaving the pale-faced deputies and paramedics to poke and puzzle through the well-lit chambers of her house, sorting through the flesh and drawing what conclusions they could from the wreckage.

Let them, Margaret thought with exhausted resignation. She was finished with the house. Period. If she set foot inside it again, it would only be to remove the practicalities and whatever good memories were left to be salvaged. The rest could burn to the ground for all she cared and probably should.

She thought uneasily of the silver tendrils leaking out of Shires's ruined skull, slipping silently down the bathtub drain.

What about Sparks and Calliope? Was that the end for them, too?

She didn't know, and that, more than anything else, was why she wouldn't chance another night in the house.

There would be more questions; of that she had no doubt. Someone in uniform would apologetically interpose himself between her and Justine in a muted hospital room and ask for help in stringing together the ill-fitting pieces.

Perhaps it would be the same tall, imposing deputy who'd pulled her gently aside while Justine was being strapped atop the padded stretcher, the one with the tattered notebook and the dark-ringed look of insomnia about the eyes. Geotting had been his name. He'd been brief with her, his questions precise, and not once did he allow the chaos of their surroundings to get between them.

"I won't keep you but a minute, Mrs. Chambers. I know you want to get back to your daughter, but I'd like to ask you a few questions while everything's still fresh in your mind."

"Yes, all right. Just so long as I can leave with her," Margaret had replied, and they'd moved off to a less trafficked corner of the living room, near the solarium. The deputy cleared his throat and clicked open a ball-point pen, which he held above a pocket notepad that looked as if it had been rescued from a dog fight.

"Could you give me the names of everyone who was here tonight prior to Deputy Bishop's arrival?"

"Well, let's see...there was myself, my daughter Justine, my son Hank...Sheriff Garrett, John Dunhill— *Doctor* John Dunhill, he said—and that thing in the bathtub. He called it Shires. Daniel, I think."

"And to the best of your knowledge, no one else was on the premises? Either inside the house or any of the outbuildings?"

A visage of two ghosts on the bathroom floor flashed across her mind's eye, and she'd decided that was a box best left unopened. "To my knowledge, no."

"Were you a witness to any of the killings here tonight?"

Margaret hesitated; this was not as clear cut as it seemed because, according to Dunhill, Shires was already dead. Garrett *certainly* had been, and Dunhill himself probably was too. Things were apt to get very tangled if she didn't pick a line and stick to it from here on out.

"The two in the kitchen, no. The one in the bathtub..." She screwed her face into an expression of extreme distaste. "He was already dead."

The deputy checked his notebook for the name. "That would be Daniel Shires?"

"Yes."

"Would you describe what happened?"

Again she hesitated. "Yes, but first can I ask you a question, just for my own peace of mind?"

He lowered the pen and notebook. "Of course."

Her gaze shifted briefly across the room, at the men in rubber gloves and white plastic smocks. They were busy at work. No one seemed to be paying the slightest attention to their hushed conversation.

"After you're through with them, what will happen to the bodies?"

The deputy raised an eyebrow. "Well, after the autopsies, they'll be released to their respective families for burial."

Margaret frowned. "What if they have no families to speak of?"

Something akin to suspicion darkened the deputy's features. "I'm not sure I understand what you mean, Mrs. Chambers. Do you know something about these men you'd like to tell me?"

She bit her lip. "No…it's just that I don't think they're from around here. I was curious as to what would happen to them if no one claimed the bodies."

"Oh." The deputy studied her for a moment in silence. "I can assure you, Mrs. Chambers, that every effort will be made to locate a next of kin."

"But if you don't?" she prodded.

"The county will take care of them."

"I see. You'll bury them, you mean."

"Not exactly. Policy dictates cremation if a next of kin can't be found. It's less expensive."

Margaret relaxed, satisfied. "Good," she said.

11

Deputy Troy Stebbins moved contentedly amongst the bustle of his colleagues, wandering from room to room in the large and rambling farmhouse without any real sense of purpose or direction, feeling nothing but a gauzy satisfaction in being a part of the group. In the *rightness* of his belonging.

"Jesus, Stebbins! Is that *you*?" a voice boomed behind him.

He had been standing in a cramped doorway, gazing over a technician's shoulder at a large splash of blood in an otherwise empty bathtub. There seemed to be, in fact, a great excess of blood about the many rooms of the house, which in turn found its way onto the clothes and protective garments of the investigating officers, turning the whole scene into something out of a slaughterhouse nightmare.

Stebbins turned toward the voice and found a face to match its familiarity.

"Well, son-of-a-bitch, it *is* you!" a fiery-haired deputy swore in open amazement. "God damn! Don't you know that half the force has been looking for you since this afternoo—"

The man's face fell in open shock. The bright-eyed enthusiasm was suddenly dry on his lips as a new expression took over. The change was almost comical.

"Holy crow!" the deputy cried. "Look at yourself! You've been *shot*!"

Half a dozen men in the immediate vicinity stopped what they were doing and turned to look. The tight hallway became suddenly quiet, and Stebbins looked down at himself with something like real surprise.

"I *was* shot," he told the staring faces calmly, parting the front of his jacket with his fingers and smoothing the black eye of the bullet hole.

The damned thing was that he really *had* let it slip his mind in the general confusion of the roadway!

A slow drip of new blood, the color of overripe cherries, saturated what was left of his shirt front and made a patter of dime-sized droplets on the carpeting.

The next thing Stebbins knew, he was lying on his back in the rear of a fast-moving ambulance, the siren blaring out in all directions as a very young-looking paramedic took his blood pressure with an electric cuff. The medic frowned and shook his close-cropped head at the readout, heatedly discarding the device for an old-fashioned stethoscope and sphygmomanometer.

Stebbins found it hard to breathe despite the oxygen feed that had been taped to his nostril, and as he raised his head to take stock of his condition, he found that a wide pressure bandage had taken the place of his jacket and shirt.

"You'll want to lie as still as you can," the acne-dotted medic advised, easing Troy's head back down against the gurney.

"My wife," Stebbins said, looking foggily into the young man's eyes. "I need to call her."

"We'll be at the hospital in ten minutes," the paramedic told him slowly, in a tone usually reserved for the demented or very elderly. "She's probably already there."

12

"Physically, aside from some minor irritation and swelling in her throat, she's fine," Dr. Freeman said, looking at Margaret Chambers over his clipboard. "We did an EEG and it shows only *slightly* elevated activity within the brain, but I think it *is* likely she had a major seizure, or possibly several small ones within the past 24 hours...she is, however, responding well to treatment."

Margaret nodded. "So we can go in and see her?"

Freeman sighed. As a doctor, he wanted his patient to have uninterrupted rest. But how could he argue that point to a distraught mother, especially one with bloodstains on her clothes. He nodded. "Yes. Just try not to upset her," he cautioned. "She's mildly sedated, and I'd like her to rest."

"I'm her *mother,*" Margaret said then frowned, as if glimpsing a shadow in Freeman's eye. "Is there something you're not telling me?"

"No… of course not," Freeman said, seeing no need to add to her burden at present. There would be time to talk about the emotional scarring later, once the bodies were buried and the bedrock of normality reasserted itself. He wasn't altogether sure what *had* happened at the isolated farmhouse on 195—a dead sheriff was likely just the tip of the iceberg—but he'd heard enough from the paramedics to guess that the town would be talking about it for quite some time. He hoped the three of them would be strong enough to see it through.

Margaret was either convinced by his answer or just too impatient to see her daughter because she turned and headed down the corridor, her son in tow. Freeman watched as she paused outside Room 17 and whispered something to the boy. He protested briefly, digging in his heels, then gave in to her, their shadows struggling silently on the far side of the hall.

Then the shadows retreated and the door clicked shut.

Hank was reluctant to approach the bed, preferring to hover near the door, as if Justine were contagious. Margaret tried to nudge him closer, but he seemed on the verge of bolting, so she let him be. He'd been through enough in one evening and was still on his feet. Lord knew they *all* had.

She turned her attention to Justine, who was gazing up from the bed as if from the bottom of a deep well. Just staring as if her own mother were a stranger. *The sedative,* Margaret thought, touching a hand to her daughter's cheek. The skin there felt cool and dry; *No fever, thank God.* She felt Justine's forehead and ran fingers through her hair, convincing herself (by all the little gauges a mother possessed) that her daughter would be well.

"Mama?" Justine blinked, as if waking from a dream. "Did you see them?"

"See *who,* sweetheart?" Margaret said, the shadow of her head tilting slightly against the pillow. "Do you mean the doctor?"

Justine put on the puzzled expression of a child: light brown freckles wrinkling, her finely-knit brows drawing together.

"No, the *twins,*" she said. "Sparks and Calliope."

Hank uttered a sound as if he were choking on a splinter of bone. "She doesn't believe in them," he croaked, his voice all but gone.

"Quiet," Margaret said firmly, not certain *what* she believed anymore. She took a deep breath and put on a smile. "The doctor says you can—" Margaret erupted into tears. "The doctor says you're going to be just fine."

Go home tomorrow, was what she was going to say, but that wasn't true, was it? The house they had left—the house they'd spent the past fifteen years in—was no longer their home. Margaret tried to imagine living there again and couldn't; the thought seemed preposterous, obscene. She could no more raise her children there than in a drafty slaughterhouse. Every time she filled the tub she would see Shires staring back at her, Sheriff Garrett would forever haunt the breakfast nook, and every creak and whisper would remind her of John Dunhill...grinning from the shadows like a wolf.

A shiver passed through her and she wiped her tears away. Margaret didn't know where they would wind up after tonight, but she knew the one place they absolutely *would not,* and that was as far as her tired mind allowed her to reach. But it was enough.

Justine, however, seemed to have other plans. Wild, unimaginable notions...

"We have to go *outside*, Mama," she said, clutching at Margaret's sleeve as if unaware she was in a hospital bed.

"*To the barn*... We have to make sure the boards are nailed down *tight*. We have to make sure they *never* get out again!"

"The barn is *gone,* Justine," Margaret assured her. "It's *torn down,* baby. Don't you remember?"

Justine grew suddenly still. She turned her head, as if listening to something outside the window. Margaret looked up and saw only her own ghastly reflection. "Yes, I...I do remember." A shiver seemed to pass through Justine. "But they're still there," she said solemnly, dark eyes staring back at her mother. "Waiting, I suppose..."

There was a pause, like an intake of breath, then Justine let go of her defenses, collapsing into tears.

"He said... he said he'd shoot Hank if I didn't do as I was told!" Justine bawled, quite clearly back in the present. She reached blindly for her mother, her anguish a near-palpable rip through the center of the room.

"Shhhh..." Margaret whispered, cradling her daughter's head against her breast, smoothing her hair back and rocking her as best she could. "That man's gone now. He won't ever bother us again."

"No!" Justine lifted her head and shook it emphatically. "Don't you see? He's a part of that place now, just like *they* are. He won't *ever* go away!"

"Well that's *fine,* honey," Margaret replied, as if this were the best of all possible solutions. "Let them have it, because we're not going back."

Justine wiped at her tears, looking sharply at her mother, wondering (Margaret guessed) if she could possibly be serious. Would they really just abandon the place?

Just wait and see. Margaret nodded, resolved in her decision.

Hank looked doubtful. "Where will we live?"

"Well... I'm really not sure. A place in town might be nice, don't you think?" She raised an eyebrow and smiled wearily. "At least for now." Another notion came into her head. "Or maybe we'll take some time off and go visit Aunt Marylou."

"In Florida?" Justine looked stunned but happy, as if the possibility of sunlight and hope really *did* exist, somewhere out there...

She squeezed her mother's hand softly and, with a content smile on her face, relaxed back into her medicated sleep.

13

In another room, just down the hospital corridor, six strange days passed.

Somehow, the flesh around the bullet wound knit itself back together, though no one could account for the amazing rapidity of his recovery. His own family practitioner shrugged his shoulders and dismissed it as the combined result of good physical conditioning, proper rest and nutrition, and a finely focused, positive mental attitude. This pronouncement, though, did not deter him from ordering a battery of specialized tests and examinations that would have put NASA to shame. Deputy Stebbins became familiar with every doctor in residence. They dropped in on him daily, in white-coated clusters or in pairs, asking permission to peel back his johnnies and gawk in wonder at the progress he was making.

On the downside, there were some disquieting anomalies present in several of the tests. Also, his guts flared and itched as if someone had opened him and packed him full of fiberglass insulation. By the end of the week, however, as his room grew heady with flowers, these inconsistencies too had ironed themselves out.

His requests to leave became more forceful and frequent until, on the sixth day, his doctors relented. They had to admit they weren't doing anything to speed his recovery, at least nothing that he couldn't get at home. Whatever was mending his wounds, they had no part in it.

Seven days after being shot dead along the side of Highway 195, Deputy Troy Stebbins stepped out into the April sunshine to pick up his life where he'd left it.

Starting with his wife and family.

EPILOGUE

East Texas

The crumbling motel stood on the outskirts of town, alone and dejected, on the shoulder of a narrow highway running east to nowhere in particular. By daylight, it looked dark and abandoned, but as night fell its weathered sign sputtered slowly to life, burning the words VACANCY in baby-blue neon and WEEKLY RATES in cotton-candy pink. Over these, REST EASY MOTEL was painted in cloudlike letters of white.

For Smith, it was just the latest in a long line of many cheap and dilapidated inns, but the Rest Easy was somehow a little more depressing with its gaudy furnishings, its lingering dampness, and the odd, rust-colored stain spread out against the ceiling over his bed. It was shaped like Greenland, this stain, and sometimes, in the early-morning hours when his mind was idle, he imagined it was blood, stolen from him in slow droplets while he was asleep.

Tonight, however, with an empty whiskey bottle on the nightstand and a typewritten letter crumpled on the spread, Smith's mind was anything but idle. The letter had come to him in the morning's mail, tucked innocuously between a grocery store circular and a form offer to lend him an outrageous amount of money at an equally outrageous rate of interest. The return address, he had noted with a sharp twinge of dread, was a community clinic he had recently visited to have some tests run that he could not afford to have done anywhere else.

He'd torn open the envelope right there in the motel's dingy little office. The results of said tests, they were very sorry to inform him, were positive. The cancer was both inoperable and advanced.

He'd felt the room start to sway around him, as if he were slipping into a dream.

The letter went on to suggest, though the prognosis was dim, that he return as soon as possible so that he might receive whatever small treatment they could arrange to provide.

Smith laughed out loud. The manager stared at him over the cluttered countertop while a portable television shouted an advertisement for static-free dryer sheets. The voice-over was so bright and ecstatic it seemed obscene.

"You got a problem there, guy? Why don't you take it outside, huh?"

He'd gone willingly enough but was back in his room within the hour, a bottle of whiskey and a brown paper sack in hand. The blue logo stamped on the sack told of a visit to the drugstore.

He closed the curtains, sat down on his bed, opened the bottle and poured himself a drink.

Slowly, the day faded into night.

It wasn't that he had so much to live for, he reflected, surveying the room through the bottom of the glass, but like most people, Smith was afraid to die.

Perhaps that was why he'd never forgotten the formula. He'd been carrying it in the back of his mind, hidden away from God and himself, since those long-dead days in the Palouse, swearing with each dawning day he'd never use it.

That had been an easy promise to keep until now; the reagent had never been intended for the living. Only the dead.

Smith looked at the crumpled letter on the nightstand and then let his eyes wander back to the dim light falling through the bathroom door. The brown and blue sack was right where he'd left it, on the chipped counter next to the sink. In it was a box of insulin syringes and about twenty dollars worth of chemicals. Simple stuff, really.

The lines deepened on his face.

What did he have to lose but his soul?

He rose heavily from the sagging mattress and staggered toward the sickly wedge of light, laughing at his folly.

After all, what man cares for his soul when he's doomed to live forever?

ABOUT THE AUTHOR

Michael James McFarland was born in the eastern Washington Palouse country where *Fallow Ground* is set. He has since married his high school sweetheart, fathered two exceptional children, and currently lives in central Washington state. By day, he works in a sprawling brick building that was erected in the late 1940s as a tuberculosis hospital. Many of his coworkers claim to have experienced ghosts and disturbances within its rooms and corridors.

He has been writing for over twenty-five years, and his short fiction has appeared in a variety of formats. Among these, *"The Hypnotist"* was selected for an Honorable Mention in *The Year's Best Fantasy & Horror* (15th Annual Collection), *'The Duel'* & *'Mira'* were produced by Pseudopod as audio podcasts, and *'Deadline'* & *'The Yellow Wind'* have appeared in print anthologies. With the rise of digital publishing, he has self published two well-received novels, *Wormwood* and *Blood on the Tracks* and a novella, *Duplex*.

www.ingramcontent.com/pod-product-compliance
Lightning Source LLC
Chambersburg PA
CBHW030408180626
46812CB00005B/1972